Greetings from

INSANE CITY

# Also by Dave Barry

## NONFICTION

*I'll Mature When I'm Dead*

*Dave Barry's History of the Millennium (So Far)*

*Dave Barry's Money Secrets*

*Boogers Are My Beat*

*Dave Barry Hits Below the Beltway*

*Dave Barry Is Not Taking This Sitting Down*

*Dave Barry Turns 50*

*Dave Barry Is from Mars and Venus*

*Dave Barry's Book of Bad Songs*

*Dave Barry in Cyberspace*

*Dave Barry's Complete Guide to Guys*

*Dave Barry Is NOT Making This Up*

*Dave Barry Does Japan*

*Dave Barry's Only Travel Guide You'll Ever Need*

*Dave Barry Talks Back*

*Dave Barry Turns 40*

*Dave Barry Slept Here*

*Dave Barry's Greatest Hits*

*Dave Barry's Homes and Other Black Holes*

*Dave Barry's Guide to Marriage and/or Sex*

*Dave Barry's Bad Habits*

*Claw Your Way to the Top*

*Stay Fit and Healthy Until You're Dead*

*Babies and Other Hazards of Sex*

*The Taming of the Screw*

# Dave Barry

G. P. Putnam's Sons
*New York*

Greetings From

# INSANE CITY

HOTEL

PUTNAM

G. P. PUTNAM'S SONS
*Publishers Since 1838*
Published by the Penguin Group
Penguin Group (USA) Inc., 375 Hudson Street, New York, New York 10014, USA •
Penguin Group (Canada), 90 Eglinton Avenue East, Suite 700, Toronto, Ontario M4P 2Y3,
Canada (a division of Pearson Penguin Canada Inc.) • Penguin Books Ltd,
80 Strand, London WC2R 0RL, England • Penguin Ireland, 25 St Stephen's Green,
Dublin 2, Ireland (a division of Penguin Books Ltd) • Penguin Group (Australia),
707 Collins Street, Melbourne, Victoria 3008, Australia (a division of Pearson
Australia Group Pty Ltd) • Penguin Books India Pvt Ltd, 11 Community Centre,
Panchsheel Park, New Delhi–110 017, India • Penguin Group (NZ), 67 Apollo Drive,
Rosedale, Auckland 0632, New Zealand (a division of Pearson New Zealand Ltd) •
Penguin Books, Rosebank Office Park, 181 Jan Smuts Avenue, Parktown North 2193,
South Africa • Penguin China, B7 Jaiming Center, 27 East Third Ring Road North,
Chaoyang District, Beijing 100020, China

Penguin Books Ltd, Registered Offices: 80 Strand, London WC2R 0RL, England

Library of Congress Cataloging-in-Publication Data

Barry, Dave.
Insane city / Dave Barry.
p.      cm.
ISBN 978-0-399-15868-1
I. Title.
PS3552.A74146I57      2013                    2012028009
813'.54—dc23

1  3  5  7  9  10  8  6  4  2

*Book design by Lovedog Studio*

Fic.

ALWAYS LEARNING                                                        PEARSON

For Michelle, who's perfect

# 1

Two days before his wedding, Seth was in a cab with his best man, Marty, who was advising him on the responsibilities of the groom.

"Your job," Marty said, "is to get hammered."

"I've seen the movies," said Seth. "It never ends well."

"It's a *tradition*," said Marty. "The groom, about to give up his old lifestyle forever, spends one last night partying with his buddies, laughing with them, crying with them . . ."

"Throwing up on them," said Seth.

"Not on the best man," advised Marty. "That's the function of the lower-ranking groomsmen."

The cab was approaching the American Airlines terminal at Reagan Airport.

"One thing," said Seth. "No stripper."

"Seriously?"

"If a stripper shows up, I will run. I will run like the wind."

"Strippers are traditional," said Marty.

"Strippers are *hookers*. Remember the one we got for Kevin?"

Marty made a face. "OK, I'll admit hygiene was not her . . ."

"She was *disgusting*, Marty. She personally controlled two-thirds of the world supply of stank. I'd rather get a lap dance from Charles Barkley."

"You want us to get Charles? Because I hear he's pretty responsive to fan requests."

"*No stripper*, that's what I want."

They were pulling up to the curb.

"I got this," said Marty, paying the cabbie, which was unlike him. "You go inside."

"I gotta get my suitcase."

"I'll get it. You're the *groom*, man. Let people cater to you."

Seth frowned. It was also unlike Marty to cater. Marty was, by nature, a cateree. Feeling a twinge of suspicion, Seth put a hand on Marty's shoulder, leaned in eye to eye. "Marty," he said, "swear to me on your mother that there will be no stripper."

"Absolutely. I swear on my mother, may she rest in peace."

"Your mother's still alive."

"Unfortunately, yes. Now go find the rest of the Groom Posse."

The rest of the Groom Posse consisted of Kevin (he of the stanky stripper) and Big Steve. The four of them—Seth, Marty, Kevin and Big Steve—had been close friends since they met as roommates at the University of Delaware, where they had distinguished themselves by amassing the largest vertical stack of used pizza delivery boxes in the school's history, and quite possibly in the annals of higher education. After graduating they had pursued different career paths, but they remained close friends, connected by the bond of college, as well as the bond of being unsuccessful at everything they had tried since.

Seth spotted the hulking mass that was Big Steve by a boarding pass machine, his finger hovering uncertainly over the touch screen, his face scrunched into a frown, looking like a man about to enter the code that would launch a nuclear strike against Pyongyang, as opposed to a man confirming his selection of an aisle seat. Big Steve was a man who always . . . wanted . . . to . . . make . . . absolutely . . . sure . . . of . . . *everything*. Standing behind him in a movie concession line was a nightmare. He could take five full minutes to choose a beverage, before moving on to the far more difficult issue of what *size* beverage. Not to mention the popcorn decision, which more than once had made him miss the beginning of a feature film.

Pacing around Big Steve like a small, jittery asteroid orbiting a planet was Kevin, who, as always, was on his cell phone, lying to somebody about something. As Seth drew near, he gathered that in this case the person being lied to was Kevin's wife.

". . . feeling a little sick, to be honest," Kevin was saying, shaking his head at Seth to indicate that he was in fact feeling fine. "No, I'm still going. It means a lot to Seth. I'll just take it easy, skip the partying." Here Kevin grabbed his crotch to indicate that he did not intend to skip the partying. "I know, baby, I know . . . I am soooo sorry you can't come . . . Right. You too. Bye." Kevin pocketed his phone, then, with a swift and fluid motion, reached past Big Steve's still-hovering finger and stabbed the boarding pass machine's screen.

"Hey!" said Big Steve. "What the hell!"

Ignoring him, Kevin turned back to Seth. "You ready? Everything good in WeddingLand?"

"I guess," said Seth. "There was an issue with the centerpieces."

"What issue?"

"I'm still not sure. Couple days ago, Tina calls me up, she's crying like she found out she has cancer, I mean *sobbing*, and I go, what's wrong, and she says something about the centerpieces, and I go, hey, the important thing is we love each other, and we're getting married."

"You stupid shit," said Kevin.

"I know. She goes, 'I can't *believe* you sometimes,' and hangs up."

Kevin nodded. "We had these wedding favors, little custom-scented soaps that said 'Love and happiness always, Karen and Kevin,' but two hours before the wedding Karen discovers they spelled *happiness* with a *y*."

"Oh man."

"Yeah. Talk about a wedding *totally* ruined."

"So what happened?"

"Her mom and her aunt opened up all the soaps, we're talking a hundred forty-five soaps, and used razors to change the *y*'s to *i*'s."

"No."

"Yes. You look at the soap from our wedding, you'll notice that the *i* is leaning, and has no dot."

"No offense, but I never looked at the soap from your wedding."

"Of course not. Nobody did. Nobody gives a shit about wedding favors. But Karen and her mom and her aunt still talk about it, how they saved the day with their razors."

Marty appeared, towing his and Seth's suitcases.

"Ready, men?" he said.

Big Steve was frowning at his boarding pass.

"Row twenty-six," he said. "That's pretty far back, isn't it?"

"We're all in twenty-six," said Seth.

"Maybe we should try to move closer to the front," said Big Steve.

"Good idea," said Kevin. "Get to Miami a little sooner."

"Maybe we should go through security and find a bar," said Seth.

"You're the groom," said Marty.

They took the escalator to the lower concourse and got into the TSA line. Kevin went first, followed by Big Steve and Marty. After they went through the screening they all turned to watch Seth. This was the first indication he had that something was up. The second was when the TSA agent, a large African-American woman whose name tag read R. WILLIAMS, pointed at his suitcase and said, "Is this your bag?"

"Yes," said Seth.

"I need to search it," she said, picking it up off the baggage carousel.

"OK," said Seth, following Agent Williams and his bag. He heard a snorking sound from the direction of the Groom Posse. Agent Williams hefted the bag onto a table, then put on a pair of blue latex gloves. She opened the bag and, after a few moments of rooting around, pulled out and held up a pinkish, soft rubber object about the size of a football with a dangling electrical cord.

"What is *that*?" said Seth.

"I was going to ask you that," said Agent Williams.

"That's not mine," said Seth.

"This is your bag, right?"

"Yes, but that thing is not mine."

"But it was in your bag."

"But it's not mine."

"I understand that, sir, but it was in your bag."

"But it's *not mine*."

Another agent came over, a thin, prematurely balding man whose tag said W. PITTOWSKI.

"Is there a problem?" he said.

Agent Williams showed him the pink thing. "This was in his bag, but he says it's not his."

"It's not!" said Seth.

Agent Pittowski was peering at the object. "That's a male sex aid," he said.

"A what?" said Agent Williams.

"Artificial vagina," said Agent Pittowski.

Agent Williams dropped the thing. It bounced off the table and rolled, jiggling, across the floor, trailing its cord, like a badly deformed pig having a seizure. Some travelers stopped to look at it.

"I'm sorry," said Agent Williams. "But I ain't touching that."

"That is *not mine*," said Seth. The onlookers' eyes went from the pink thing to Seth, then back to the thing.

"Excuse me," said Marty, stepping forward.

"Who are you?" said Agent Pittowski.

Marty pointed at Seth. "I'm this man's attorney."

"No he's not," said Seth. "He's not even an attorney."

"Well, not *technically*," said Marty. "Not in the sense of practicing law or passing the bar exam. But I do have a hundred and seventeen thousand in tuition debt from a third-tier law school, and by God that should count for *something*."

"He doesn't need a lawyer," said Agent Pittowski. "He needs to pick up his vagina and move along."

"It's not my vagina!" said Seth. The onlooker crowd was growing.

"Do you have any proof that it's his vagina?" said Marty.

"Shut up, Marty," said Seth.

"Sir," Agent Pittowski said to Seth, "if you don't pick it up and move along right now, I'm going to have to detain you."

"He's getting married this weekend," said Marty.

"That is not my problem," said Agent Pittowski.

"It's *somebody's* problem," said Agent Williams, looking at the thing on the floor.

Seth, with a glare at Marty, grabbed his suitcase, picked up the vagina and stalked out of the security area. He went to an overflowing trash can and put the vagina on top of the pile, then turned to face the approaching Groom Posse, festooned with idiotic grins.

"Not funny," he said.

"Yes! Funny!" said Kevin. He held up his phone. "And soon to be on YouTube."

"I'll kill you," said Seth. "Seriously, I will."

"Totally worth it," said Kevin.

A briefcase-carrying, suit-wearing man in his fifties approached the trash can. Looking neither left nor right, he opened his briefcase, put the vagina inside, closed the briefcase and walked briskly away.

"I'm guessing Secretary of Commerce," said Kevin.

"Well, he's got himself a nice little unit there," said Marty. "The Fleshmatic Orgo-Tron, top of the line, with heat *and* pump action. Hardly used."

"Wait," said Seth. "You *used* it?"

"Hardly."

"Jesus," said Seth, watching the suited man's back as he disappeared down the concourse.

Kevin said, "The bar is this way."

# 2

The man was telling Laurette to get up, but she was too weak from vomiting; she could not stand, especially not on the wet and slippery deck of the boat, pitching in the turbulent waters of the Gulf Stream.

"GET UP! GET UP!" shouted the man. The crew were Dominicans, and Laurette had trouble understanding their crude, heavily accented Creole. The man grabbed Laurette's arm and yanked her to her feet so roughly that for a moment she thought she would drop the baby. The thought flashed through her mind: *Maybe it would be best. Maybe we should all die right now in the angry water.* For the hundredth time since she had boarded this wretched boat, she wished she had never listened to her sister in Miami, never trusted these men, never left Port-au-Prince with her babies.

Stephane, her little man, had risen with her and was holding on to her dress. "What's happening, Mama?" he said.

"It's all right," she said. The man was pulling her to the back of the boat. She almost fell, struggling to hold on to the baby and keep Stephane close. "What are you doing?" she said to the man.

"You are getting off here."

Laurette looked around, seeing only water in every direction.

"No!" she said, her voice rising. "We are nowhere!"

"We are close to Miami."

"Where is it?" Laurette waved at the horizon. "Where is Miami?"

The man gestured vaguely. "Just over there. But we can't go closer."

"NO!" shouted Laurette. "You said you would take me to my sister! To the meeting place! You promised this!"

"I'm sorry," said the man. "This is not possible."

"How will I find my sister? How?"

The man didn't answer. They had reached the back of the boat. The other men were pulling a rope attached to the tiny beat-up rowboat they had been towing since they left Haiti. Several inches of water sloshed around the bottom of the boat.

"No!" said Laurette. She tried to yank her arm free.

The man tightened his grip. Laurette cried out in pain.

"The current will take you right to Miami," the man said. "You will be there in an hour."

"Please, no," said Laurette. "We will go back with you to Haiti."

"No," said the man, dragging her toward the little boat. "You must get off here."

"NO!" screamed Laurette. "NO, PLEASE!"

The man ignored her. He and the others grabbed Laurette and Stephane and lifted them roughly over the side, into the little boat. It was pitching violently; Laurette fell awkwardly, bumping the baby's head against the side. The baby was screaming now. Stephane was crying. Laurette pulled them both to her. She looked up at the men.

"Please," she said. "They are babies. Please."

The men looked away. The motor rumbled, and the big boat churned away. In a few minutes, it was a tiny dark shape in the distance. Then it was gone.

The little ship pitched up and down in the rough water.

"Mama," said Stephane. "What's going to happen to us?"

Laurette meant to lie to her son, tell him they would be all right. But all that came out, before she could choke it off, was a wail.

# 3

The airport bar was full of people sitting alone and staring at screens. Seth had a Grande Margarita; Kevin and Marty each had two. Big Steve had none, having been unable to decide between the Grande and the Supremo. The Supremo featured Patrón tequila, but it also cost two dollars more and Big Steve wasn't sure it would be worth it. In an effort to decide, he had asked the bartender a series of increasingly specific ingredient-related questions, but this line of inquiry came to an abrupt halt when the bartender, who was busy, asked Big Steve if he planned to drink the margarita or use it as an enema.

The flight, miraculously, was on time. Kevin, taking charge, maneuvered the Groom Posse so they got into the boarding line directly behind two attractive women, one blonde and one brunette.

"You ladies headed for Miami?" he said.

The women looked at each other, then at Kevin.

"No," said the brunette. "We just like being in line."

"Good one!" said Kevin, sticking out his hand. "I'm Kevin."

Neither woman stuck out her hand.

"Kevin's married," said Seth.

"She's a lucky woman," said the blonde.

"Who's not going to Miami, as it happens," said Kevin. "No, it's just us four guys, looking for a good time. How about you ladies?"

"No," said the brunette.

"No what?" said Kevin.

"Just generally no," said the brunette.

"My name is Marty," said Marty. "By the way, I'm not married."

"We're lesbians," said the blonde.

"Fine with me," said Marty.

"Are you really?" said Kevin.

"No," said the blonde. "But keep this up and we will be."

"I apologize for my friends," said Seth.

"I bet you do," said the brunette.

They boarded the plane, found their seats. Seth, as groom, got the window; he was next to Kevin, who was still lobbing unsuccessful pickup lines forward, like grenades, across three rows of increasingly annoyed passengers at the blonde and the brunette, seated in row 22. They did not respond, but Kevin persisted until the flight attendant *shush*ed him for the safety briefing.

"Kevin," said Seth, "let me ask you something."

"What?" said Kevin.

"What about Karen?"

"Karen?"

"Your wife. Who you're married to. Karen."

"What about her?"

"Do you love her?"

"Of course I love her. She's my wife."

"So how can you do this?"

"Do what?"

"Try to screw every woman you meet."

"Not *every* woman. Ninety-two percent."

"But . . . I mean, how would Karen feel?"

"Karen doesn't know."

"What if she found out?"

"I'd say it was a terrible mistake and I was very sorry and would never do it again."

"And would you mean that?"

"Absolutely not."

"So being married means nothing to you?"

"No, it means I have a person that I love very much and want to raise a family with."

"And cheat on."

"Wait, so you think it'll be different with you and Tina?"

"Yes."

"So you're saying if one of those two very hot women sitting up there, let's say the blonde, if that woman said she wanted to get naked with you, no strings attached, just crazy animal sex that Tina would never find out about, you'd turn her down? You'd say, 'No thanks, hot blonde with breasts like honeydews, keep your nakedness to yourself, because I'm in a committed relationship'? Is that what you're saying?"

"That's what I'm saying, yes."

"You're full of shit."

"No I'm not," said Seth, and he genuinely believed he wasn't, although he knew in his heart that if the question had been about the brunette, he might have been.

They drank more on the flight, even Big Steve, who was aided by the fact that there were only two brands of beer available, which meant he was able to make a selection in under five minutes. After two vodka-and-cranberrys, Kevin made one last valiant effort to storm the blonde-brunette beachhead, walking up and handing them a note he'd written on an airsickness bag. He stood waiting as they read it.

The blonde looked up.

"Seriously?" she said, loud enough that several rows' worth of passengers tuned in to the conversation.

"From the heart," said Kevin.

"No, I mean, seriously, you don't know the difference between *y-o-u-r* and *y-o-u*-apostrophe-*r-e*?"

"It's a rough draft," said Kevin.

"Also," said the brunette, tossing the bag back to Kevin, "there's no *e* in *horny*."

Kevin returned to his seat next to Seth. "Bitches," he said.

"I know!" said Seth. "If women don't want crude propositions written by illiterates on barf bags, what *do* they want?"

In two hours they were over the vast green muckscape of the Everglades, banking toward the skinny strip of hyperdevelopment where several million South Floridians live close together in nothing remotely approaching harmony. They landed, taxied, parked at the gate. Seth and his Groom Posse joined the line of exiting passengers and shuffled unsteadily out of the plane. In the Jetway they were enveloped by the sweetish aroma of tropical decay that welcomes visitors to Miami the way Mickey Mouse welcomes them to Orlando.

"What's that smell?" said Marty.

"Miami," said Seth.

"What, the whole city has mildew?"

"Basically."

Seth's phone rang the instant he turned it on. He looked at the screen: Tina. He saw she'd also left six text messages. This was not good. There had been a time when many of Tina's messages were playful, flirtatious, romantic, even sexual; but in the past few months the vast majority concerned the ongoing and infinitely complex crisis that was the seating chart for the reception.

"Hello?" he said.

"Are you in Miami?" said Tina.

"Yes. We just la—"

"Come to Baggage Claim *right now*."

"You're still in the airport?" Tina had flown in on an earlier flight with her bridal party; she was supposed to be at the hotel by now.

"I got delayed," she said. "By this *stupid dog*."

"A dog?"

"Seth, it alerted on my dress!"

"It what?"

"They're saying I have to . . . Wait a minute. Don't touch that! You're going to ruin it!"

"Tina, what . . ."

"Just get down here, OK?"

"OK, but what's happening? Which Baggage Claim? Hello?"

Tina was gone.

"What was that about?" said Marty.

"I don't know. Tina said a dog did something on her dress."

"Like, *peed* on it?"

"I don't know. I have to go to Baggage Claim."

He heard her from twenty-five yards away. Tina had a strong, confident voice. It was the reason Seth had met her in the first place, on the grounds of the Washington Monument. He'd heard this woman's voice talking through a bullhorn and he'd wondered if the owner of the voice was hot and it turned out she was. She was leading a protest either for or against something, Seth could not remember which. He had stuck around and managed to meet her afterward. She had believed then, and still did believe, that he was there for the protest. He had never told her that he was merely passing through on his way home from playing Ultimate Frisbee.

Tina was a fast-rising, plugged-in lawyer in a D.C. firm that specialized in social causes and getting on television. She cared passionately about disadvantaged people, all of them. She was intelligent and beautiful and had a killer body. Men wanted and pursued her; it was a source of widespread bafflement that Seth had managed to win her hand. Seth himself did not understand it. He knew he was fairly good-looking; he'd been told that by enough women. But Tina had plenty other attractive men after her and many of them possessed desirable qualities that he did not.

Employability, for example. Upon graduating from college, Seth had discovered that he was fundamentally unequipped to do anything that anybody was willing to pay serious money for. His degree was in marketing, and he'd earned a solid B average, but the harsh truth was, he had never actually marketed anything, and neither had any of the professors who had taught him what he knew about marketing.

After college he'd gone to Washington, telling himself that there were many good reasons for him to look for work there aside from the obvious and pathetic truth, which was that he could live with his parents. This led to two years of unemployment and humiliating underemployment, including a stint handing out flyers at a mall for a twenty percent discount at a teeth-whitening booth.

It was during this stint that he found himself handing a flyer to

Jennifer Claremont, whom he had dated for two years in high school. She went on to graduate *summa cum laude* from the University of Michigan and was midway through Stanford medical school. By the time Seth had realized who she was, she had the flyer in hand. He quickly assured her that her teeth did not need whitening and in fact looked great. This was followed by a hideously awkward pause-filled conversation during which they avoided any discussion of what Seth was doing and agreed, at least four times, that it was really great to see each other. When they finally managed to break apart, they walked briskly in opposite directions, neither looking back. Seth proceeded directly to a trash can, into which he dumped all of his flyers. He then drove straight home from the mall, went to his room and played Grand Theft Auto 3 (Where Lunatics Prosper) for seven straight hours.

He finally found permanent work, of sorts, at a large beltway public-relations firm, where he was assigned to the Social Media Mobilization Team, which sounded a lot more impressive than what the team members called themselves, namely, tweet whores. Seth's job was to try to generate buzz for clients by posting Facebook updates and sending out enthusiastic tweets under various Twitter screen names. He had tweeted enthusiastically about a wide range of products, including forklifts, energy bars, and douche. He was paid a salary in the low thirties, augmented by incentive bonuses based on total followers, retweets, etc. In a typical week, Seth's bonus was around $20, which was why, when he met Tina, he was still living with his parents.

Tina, who came from money—buckets of it—had her own place in Georgetown. She was dating an attorney who looked like Jude Law, had argued before the Supreme Court and had been named one of Washington's most eligible bachelors by two different glossy magazines. And yet when Seth asked Tina that day near the monument— she glowing radiantly from bullhorning on behalf of or against something, he sweating from Ultimate Frisbee—if she'd like to meet for coffee sometime, she'd said, yes, as long as it wasn't a Starbucks. Seth didn't know then—he still didn't really know—*why* it couldn't be a Starbucks. This, he would learn, was one of many principled stands

Tina took as a consumer. It seemed to Seth that at least half of the products in any given supermarket offended her.

They met at a coffee shop specializing in coffee that did not take advantage of the disadvantaged. She asked him what he did and he told her he was in marketing. Via skillful lawyerly probing, she quickly determined what he actually *did*, then whipped out her iPhone and started looking up his tweets.

"Wow," she said, reading the screen.

"So," said Seth. "What kind of law do you . . ."

"'WomanFresh,'" she read. "'Because you never know when some-body unexpected will drop in.'" She looked up at Seth and said, "Drop in?"

"Hey," said Seth, "that got retweeted."

She stared at him for several long seconds, during which he was sure she was about to walk out of his life forever.

Instead, she started laughing. She had a deep, hearty laugh, very unladylike. She insisted on reading all of his WomanFresh tweets. Each one struck her as more hilarious than the one before, to the point where it took her nearly thirty seconds to gasp out, "When you need to feel confident down there."

"Confident?" she said. *"Down there?"*

"What," said Seth. "You don't call it that?"

She couldn't answer; she was weeping, fighting for breath, waving her arm in a *Stop it, you're killing me* motion.

He decided, right then, that he was in love with her.

They went out again. Then again and again. He sent her flowers. She formally broke up with Jude Lawyer. He started attempting to become informed about current events other than sports. She followed him on Twitter. On their fifth date, she invited him to spend the night. At a critical physical moment he made a joke about dropping in, which gave her such a case of the giggles that he thought he'd blown his opportunity. But it turned out he had not.

Two months later, he moved in with her, having concluded that the embarrassment of being provided for by his girlfriend was more bearable than the embarrassment of living with his mom and dad. She got to know his friends and found them to be amusing but not of long-term interest. He got to know her friends and found they ranged from serious to deadly serious, with tendencies toward assholery. For their part, they found Seth to be unimpressive. As did Tina's parents, who viewed Seth as unworthy to house-sit their pets, let alone marry their daughter.

Seth basically agreed with their assessment of him. One night at a restaurant Tina got into a lengthy, passionate argument with her law-yer friends about the Commerce Clause. Seth went to the men's room and hastily, in a stall, took out his iPhone and read the Wikipedia article about the Commerce Clause, but he still didn't see why it was a big deal. He spent the evening sitting silent among the brains, feeling like an entirely different organ, or an unusually large hemorrhoid.

When they got home that night, he asked Tina why she wanted to be with him.

"Because I love you," she said.

"But *why*?"

"You make me laugh."

"So does Danny DeVito."

"Yes, but he's taken."

He tried many times, but never really got a better answer than that. For whatever reason, Tina was attracted to him, and for whatever other reason, she was not interested in explaining specifically why. Eventu-ally he gave up trying to figure it out. His feeling was, if this beautiful, smart woman wanted to be with him, why ask why? And so, after a year of cohabitation, he had asked her to marry him, and to the poorly concealed dismay of her friends and parents, she had said yes.

In their first few happy, innocent hours as an engaged couple, they talked of a small, informal wedding, just immediate family and close friends. When Seth told Kevin about this, Kevin snorted beer out his nose.

"What," said Seth.

"Really?" said Kevin. "Small and informal?"

"Yes," said Seth. "That's what we want."

"That's what *you* want."

"Tina wants it, too."

"Tina *says* she wants it. She might even *believe* she wants it. But that's not what you're going to have. Not once her mom starts reminding her about all the second cousins whose children's weddings her mom got invited to. Not once Tina starts reading the bride magazines. And *definitely* not once she meets with the wedding planner."

"We're not having a wedding planner."

"If you don't have a wedding planner," Kevin said, "I will get on my knees and personally blow you at a major intersection during rush hour. Because, trust me, you *will* have a wedding planner. You're already caught in the force field of the wedding industry Death Star, my friend. It has you in the tractor beam and it's sucking you in. There's no escape. You will also have a floral installation artist."

"You mean a florist?"

"No, I mean a floral installation artist."

"What the hell is that?"

Kevin snorted again.

Seth now knew what a floral installation artist was: It was a florist, only way more expensive. He and Tina had one whose name, as the payee on checks, was Warren Kramsden, but who went professionally by Raul—no last name, just "Raul." They also had a wedding planner, whose legal name was now Blaze Gear, it having been legally changed from Gretchen Wentworth. Blaze had two assistants, Traci and Tracee.

Under the relentless guidance of these professionals, Seth and Tina's small informal wedding for close friends and family underwent wedding bloat, mutating into a large formal affair that would be attended by many people neither of them knew. Seth objected at first, but he backed down when he realized that Kevin had been right: Tina *wanted* a big wedding.

"Just go along," advised Kevin. "Here's how you look at it. Tina has a disease. Bride's Disease. They all get it. There's no cure, except having a wedding. Until she has one, she's going to be basically insane. She's going to demand that you give a shit about silver patterns. Just hang in there until the wedding and then it'll all go away and she'll be basically normal again, except for sometimes making people watch the video."

Seth took Kevin's advice: He went along. Over the past year, he'd spent countless hours looking with a frown of attempted interest at place settings and cakes and calligraphy samples (they finally settled on Bickham Copperplate, with swash capitals). He did his best to stay connected with what he thought of as Real Tina, who was trapped inside Bride Tina; he saw glimpses of her, and sometimes even got Real Tina to laugh at Bride Tina. But she hadn't laughed much in recent months, and now that the wedding was at hand, she hardly laughed at all.

She was definitely not laughing now. Seth couldn't yet see her, as he trotted toward the baggage carousel: a crowd of onlookers was blocking his view. But he definitely could hear her. She was using her bullhorn voice.

"ARE YOU FAMILIAR WITH THE FOURTH AMENDMENT?" she was asking somebody, evidently rhetorically. "CAN YOU MORONS EVEN *COUNT* TO FOUR?"

Seth, trailing his carry-on suitcase and leaving the Groom Posse behind, started running toward his bride.

# 4

Laurette knew now that she and her children were going to die.

The men had lied to her; the current was not taking the little boat to Miami. She saw nothing in any direction but the dark, tossing Atlantic. The little boat was taking on water; it was over her ankles now. From time to time she tried to splash it out with her hands, but it was difficult to do this while holding the baby and with Stephane clinging to her.

The baby had finally stopped crying, too exhausted now even to whimper. Stephane was trying to be brave, but his eyes shone with fear. Laurette hoped he could not see her own terror. She dared not meet his eyes when he asked her, over and over, when it would end, when they would reach land. Soon, she told him, over and over. Soon.

She prayed that, when death came to them, it would be swift.

# 5

Seth pushed his way through the crowd of onlookers and found a standoff at the baggage carousel. On one side stood Tina, in jeans and a scoop-necked white T-shirt, looking angry but, as always, spectacular. On the other side were two uniformed U.S. Customs officials, one of whom held a leash attached to a German shepherd. On the floor between the two sides was Tina's $950 Tumi suitcase, which was open, revealing Tina's wedding dress. This apparently was of great interest to the dog, whose sleek black snout was zeroed in on the suitcase at a range of about two inches. Watching from several feet away was Tina's younger sister and maid of honor, Meghan, who would be considered beautiful if she weren't always being held to the standard of Tina, a comparison that lowered Meghan's status to merely very pretty.

"Hey, babe," said Seth, reaching Tina's side. "What's going on?"

Tina looked at him for a second, registering his presence, then turned her attention back to the dog.

"If that animal drools on my dress, I will sue for damages," Tina said. "That is my wedding dress, and I am getting married Saturday. I am getting married *in that dress*. Do you understand?"

"We understand that, ma'am," said the Customs agent holding the leash, a stocky, balding, worried-looking man named Vincent Peppers. "You made that very clear. Several times."

"Six times," said the other Customs agent, a dark-haired, muscular man named Roberto Alvarez.

"But like I told you, ma'am," continued Agent Peppers, "when we get an indication from the dog, we have to investigate it. And Sienna alerted on your luggage."

"Sienna?" said Tina.

"Sienna is the dog," said Peppers. "It's a color. Like the crayon. Burnt sien—"

"I *know* it's a color," snapped Tina.

"Well, not everybody does," said Peppers. "So what we're going to do is, we're going to take out the dress and . . ."

"You're *not* going to touch the dress," said Tina. "I am *getting married* in that dress."

"Seven," said Agent Alvarez.

"It's hemp," said Seth.

"What?" said Peppers.

"The dress," said Seth. "It's made from hemp."

Tina wanted a green wedding and had insisted on using, wherever possible, sustainable fibers. The floral installations featured organic, locally grown flowers, herbs and grasses; the wedding rings were made from recycled gold. The band and the DJ had pledged to offset their electricity use with renewable energy certificates. And to compensate for all the air travel, a company in Guatemala was theoretically planting a shitload of trees.

"Who're you?" said Alvarez.

"Her fiancé," said Seth.

Alvarez emitted a snort. Seth gave him a look, got one back.

"It doesn't look like hemp," said Agent Peppers. "It's white."

"It's *ivory*," said Tina. "That's a color. Like sienna."

"You don't need to patronize me, ma'am," said Agent Peppers.

"Is there a problem here?" said Marty, arriving on the scene.

"Go away, Marty," said Seth.

"Who're you?" said Alvarez.

"I'm this woman's attorney," said Marty.

"No, he's not," said Seth and Tina simultaneously.

"Overruled," said Marty. "Now, Officers, we can either do this the easy way or we can do it the . . . Hey!" Propelled by a shove from Seth, Marty stumbled back to Kevin and Big Steve.

Seth turned back to Peppers. "Here's the thing," he said. "Hemp and marijuana are related, right? So maybe your dog smells the hemp and he thinks it's marijuana, so he . . ."

"She," said Peppers. "Sienna's a female."

"A bitch," said Alvarez, looking at Tina.

"An overly aggressive animal with a small brain," said Tina, looking back. "And no ability to think for itself."

"Oh, Sienna's pretty smart," said Peppers.

"I'm not talking about the dog," said Tina.

"My point," Seth said hastily, "is that Sienna here has probably just picked up on the similarity between the hemp fibers and marijuana."

"Maybe so," said Agent Peppers. "But we still have to examine the suitcase."

"You will not touch that suitcase," said Tina.

"I'm afraid we have to, ma'am," said Peppers.

"No you don't," said Tina, stepping in front of the suitcase.

"Ma'am," said Peppers, "if you don't let us examine your suitcase, I'm going to have to bring the police into this."

"Go right ahead," said Tina.

Seth said, "Um, Tina, maybe that's not a great idea."

She spun toward him, eyes blazing, and snapped, "Don't you *dare* take their side."

"I'm not taking their side. I'm just saying if he calls the police . . ."

"Let him," said Tina. She added quietly, "I already called my father."

"Oh," said Seth. Tina's father was the only person Seth knew who owned two personal helicopters.

As if on cue, Peppers's phone rang. He removed it from its belt holster and said, "Hello? Yes, it is. That's right. And who . . . Oh. *Oh.* Yes, sir." He listened for about a minute, said "Yes, sir" a few more times, then reholstered the phone. His face was now the color of Hawaiian Punch.

"OK," he said to Tina. "You can go."

"*What?*" said Alvarez. "Who was that?"

"I'll tell you later."

"Wait a minute," said Alvarez. "She can't just *go.*"

Tina smiled sweetly at Alvarez.

"Yes, she can," said Peppers. "Come on, Sienna." He led the dog away. Alvarez stayed a few more seconds, looking at the suitcase. Then he looked at Seth and said, "I bet you'll look beautiful in the dress."

"Something for you to fantasize about," said Seth.

Alvarez started to say something, then turned and walked away.

"Asshole," said Tina, crouching to zip up the suitcase.

Seth said, "I can't believe the dog reacted to the dress."

Tina looked up. "It wasn't the dress," she said.

"It wasn't?"

"It was Meghan's pot. It's under the dress."

"Jesus, Tina," said Seth, looking at Meghan, who smiled sheepishly. "What the hell?"

"She had it in her purse, but she got all paranoid that TSA would find it so she asked me to put it in my suitcase."

"And you *did?*"

"She's my sister, Seth. And I didn't think there'd be drug dogs here."

"It's *Miami*, Tina. There's drug dogs in the *preschools.*"

Tina stood. "Well, it doesn't matter now, does it?"

"I guess not," said Seth. "Thanks to your father."

She looked at him for a second, then said, "It's a stupid law, OK?"

"OK," said Seth. In the distance he could see Alvarez looking back at him.

The Groom Posse had drifted up; Kevin, Marty and Big Steve exchanged hugs with Tina and Meghan.

"So," said Tina. "You boys have big plans for Seth tonight?"

"Big plans," said Marty.

"Huge plans," said Kevin.

"No stripper," said Seth.

"*What?*" said Kevin.

"No stripper," repeated Seth.

"Then what's the point of even getting married?" said Kevin.

"If we're not getting the stripper," said Big Steve, "I want my forty dollars back."

"Wow," said Meghan. "Forty whole *dollars*?"

"Apiece," said Marty.

"Oh, forty *apiece*," said Meghan. "So this will be, like, the Mercedes-Benz of strippers."

"Marty," said Seth, "you swore on your mother there would be no stripper."

"Yes, but I hate my mother," said Marty.

"He has you there," said Kevin.

"OK!" said Tina. "Sounds like you boys have important matters to discuss. We've got a car waiting outside and lots to do at the hotel, and then we've got dinner with my parents. I'll see you later, OK?"

"Tina," said Seth. "I'm not going to let them . . . I mean, it's not gonna be . . ."

She stopped him with a hand on his arm. "Just have fun with your friends and don't get any diseases," she said. "And be ready for the rehearsal dinner tomorrow night, OK?"

"OK," said Seth. She kissed him and left with her sister.

"She's really not threatened, is she?" said Kevin.

"If you looked like that," said Marty, "would *you* be threatened?"

"If I looked like that," said Kevin, "I would spend all day standing naked in front of a mirror."

"Hey," said Seth.

"OK, but I would."

"Let's get the bags, grab a taxi to the hotel, start the party," said Marty.

"Maybe there's a shuttle to the hotel," said Big Steve.

"Good point," said Kevin. "Why don't you look into that, weigh the pros and cons, text us your findings in the next day or so. We'll be at the hotel."

"I *do not want a stripper*," said Seth.

"Absolutely not!" said Marty.

They collected their bags and hailed a taxi van driven by a man in a bulging Rastafarian hat who radiated pot fumes and whose radio was playing a song that apparently consisted of a single extremely low note played over and over at the volume of artillery fire.

"WE'RE GOING TO THE RITZ-CARLTON ON KEY BIS-CAYNE!" shouted Seth.

The driver turned and looked at Seth, frowning.

"DO YOU KNOW WHERE THAT IS?" shouted Seth.

"WHAT IS?" shouted the driver.

"THE RITZ-CARLTON HOTEL!" shouted Seth.

"COCONUT GROVE?" shouted the driver.

"NO, THE RITZ-CARLTON, ON KEY BISCAYNE!" shouted Seth.

"RITZ-CARLTON HOTEL?" shouted the driver.

"YES, ON KEY BISCAYNE!" shouted Seth. "DO YOU THINK YOU COULD TURN THE MUSIC DOWN?"

The driver, not turning the music down, put the cab in gear and began driving.

"Friendly chap," said Kevin.

"WHAT?" said Seth.

"Never mind," said Kevin.

Since conversation was impossible, they all whipped out phones, put their heads down and commenced thumbing. After twenty minutes, the taxi pulled to a stop. A doorman opened the van door and said, "Welcome to the Ritz-Carlton."

They got out, unloaded their bags. Marty paid the driver, who pulled out of the hotel driveway, his taxi still throbbing. Seth looked around.

"Wait a minute," he said. "Where are we?"

"The Ritz-Carlton," said Kevin, pointing to a sign that said RITZ-CARLTON.

"It looks wrong," said Seth. He turned to the doorman and said, "Is this Key Biscayne?"

"No," said the doorman. "Coconut Grove."

"Shit," said Seth.

"We should've taken the shuttle," said Big Steve.

"Can you get us a cab?" Seth asked the doorman.

"OK," said the doorman. He stuck two fingers into his mouth and emitted a shrill whistle. From around the corner came the sound of booming bass. The same taxi rolled into the driveway, Rasta dude at the wheel.

"I don't believe this," said Kevin. "Is this guy the entire Miami taxi fleet?"

"Can we get another taxi?" Seth asked the doorman.

The doorman whistled again, then again. No taxi appeared.

"Not too many taxis around right now," he said.

Reluctantly, they got back into the taxi. The driver gave no indication that he recognized them.

"WE WANT YOU TO TAKE US TO KEY BISCAYNE!" shouted Kevin. "OK? KEY BISCAYNE!"

Without answering, the driver put the taxi in gear. He drove to Bayshore Drive and turned right.

"NO!" said Seth, waving his arms. "I THINK IT'S THE OTHER WAY!" He pointed toward the back of the cab. "I THINK WE NEED TO GO THAT WAY! TO KEY BISCAYNE!"

"I KNOW KEY BISCAYNE!" said the driver. "YOU KEEP TELLING ME KEY BISCAYNE KEY BISCAYNE KEY BISCAYNE! I KNOW THIS!"

Seth fell back against the seat. "Fine," he said.

"I'll handle this," said Marty. "You're the groom. Just relax, OK?"

"OK," said Seth.

"DRIVER!" said Marty.

"I KNOW," said the driver, "KEY BISCAYNE!"

Seth, who was developing a headache, closed his eyes and tried to relax. After about fifteen minutes, he felt the taxi slow. He opened his eyes. They were inching along in heavy traffic next to a row of hotels.

"This is Ocean Drive," he said.

"I know!" said Marty. "Nice, huh?"

"Marty, Ocean Drive on *Miami Beach*."

"Is that on the way to Key Biscayne?" said Marty.

"No!" said Seth. He shouted to the driver, "WE WANT TO GO TO KEY BISCAYNE!"

"I KNOW! KEY BISCAYNE! I KNOW THIS!" replied the driver, taking both hands off the wheel so he could make a gesture to indicate how irritated he was by this incessant jabber about the destination being Key Biscayne.

Seth turned to his Posse and said, "This guy doesn't know how to get to Key Biscayne."

"But he's a taxi driver," said Kevin.

"He's a *Miami* taxi driver," said Seth. He tapped the driver's shoulder and shouted, "STOP HERE! LET US OUT!"

"We're getting out here?" said Big Steve. "With our suitcases?"

"If we stay in this taxi," said Seth, "we could wind up in Belize."

They got out and unloaded the luggage. They refused to pay the driver, who, after shouting something incomprehensible, slammed his door and thumped slowly away in the thick traffic.

"OK," said Seth. "We need to find another taxi."

"You think there's more than one?" said Kevin.

They looked down Ocean Drive, surveying the bumper-to-bumper line of tourist-driven rental cars crawling past sidewalk café tables filled with tourists drinking fruit-festooned rum drinks and watching the passing pedestrian parade of still more tourists. There were no taxis in sight. They started walking, luggage in tow, weaving their way through the maze of sidewalk tables.

After a block and a half, they came to the Clevelander, a legendary South Beach bar bearing no resemblance to anything that has ever existed in Cleveland. On a small stage next to the packed bar a woman wearing a basically invisible bikini was writhing to inhumanly loud pounding music. Nearby, beneath a sign that said D.J. BOOGA WOOGA was a man wearing black lace-up boots and a purple thong held up by orange suspenders. He was shouting into a microphone: "LAST CALL FOR THE MISS HOT AMATEUR BOD CONTEST! LADIES, COME ON UP! FIRST PRIZE IS ONE HUNDRED DOLLARS! COME ON, LADIES! LET'S SEE WHAT YOU GOT!"

Standing near the DJ were a dozen young women wearing garments that, if all of them were combined, might have provided enough fabric to make a sock.

"We should stop here," said Kevin.

"No, we shouldn't," said Seth. "We need to get to the Ritz."

"We can't get to the Ritz," said Kevin. "Admit it. We tried and we failed."

"Plus," said Marty, "they don't have Miss Hot Amateur Bod at the Ritz, not to mention D.J. Booga Wooga."

Seth looked back out at Ocean Drive. Still no taxis.

"Maybe there's a bus to Key Biscayne," said Big Steve.

"Shut up, Steve," said Kevin.

"Come on, Seth," said Marty. "One drink."

"OK," said Seth, dragging his suitcase toward the bar. "One drink."

Three hours later, they were on their fifth pitcher of margaritas. The pitchers were $50 apiece, plus a generous tip for Vicki the bartender, with whom Kevin had fallen deeply in love. Kevin was also in love with Cyndi Friend Gonzalez, an outgoing young woman who had finished fourth in the Miss Hot Amateur Bod competition and who was wearing a dress made from roughly one square inch of some extremely stretchy material. At Kevin's invitation, Cyndi had joined the Groom Posse at the bar; she had in turn been joined by a friend of hers, a large bald man named Duane.

The Posse was not thrilled about Duane, but nobody told him to leave because in addition to being large, he had an eleven-foot Burmese albino python named Blossom draped over his shoulders. Duane made his living collecting tips from tourists who wanted to have their pictures taken with Blossom. He'd been doing this for eight years and considered himself a professional. He also considered himself an ambassador for Miami, and upon learning that Seth was about to get married, he had appointed himself as tour guide.

"This is my fuckin' town," he said. "*¿Se hablo españolo?* You need weed? Oxy?"

"I think we're good," said Seth.

Duane brandished Blossom. "You want to hold her? No charge for the groom, man."

"Maybe later," said Seth, leaning back to avoid Blossom's flicking tongue.

"Just say the word," said Duane, pouring Seth and himself another glass from the pitcher, finishing it. Kevin waved to Vicki for another.

The Clevelander was now very crowded and making far more noise than the entire state of Nebraska. The sea-salted night air was warm and sticky and thick with the aromas of spilled beer and cigar smoke and AXE body spray and billowing clouds of fuck-me perfume worn by women who were not wearing a whole lot else. Seth was staring at one of these women, wondering how she sat down in that dress and hoping she would attempt to do so soon, when he realized that Big Steve was shouting something into his ear, trying to be heard over the all-obliterating *boom-boom* issuing from the coffin-sized speakers of D.J. Booga Wooga.

"WHAT?" said Seth.

"THE HOTEL!" said Big Steve. He held up his phone so Seth could see the time: 9:30. Seth frowned. He swiveled toward Marty, grabbing the bar to keep from falling off the stool.

"MARTY!"

"WHAT?"

"WE NEED TO GET TO THE HOTEL!"

"WHAT?"

"THE HOTEL!"

Marty frowned deeply for several seconds, processing this concept, then said, "WHAT?"

"Never mind," said Seth. Realizing it was time to take matters into his own hands, he turned away from Marty and slid smoothly off the stool. He continued sliding smoothly until he found himself on all fours under the bar. He decided to remain that way for a bit, collecting his thoughts.

He'd been down there a while and had yet to collect any when he became vaguely aware of voices shouting above him in the thumping din. He heard his name and realized that the voices belonged to Marty, Big Steve and Kevin, who, apparently unaware that he was under the bar, were trying to figure out where he was.

"Hey!" said Seth. "Down here!"

They didn't hear him. Their voices were louder now and more concerned.

"Hey!" Seth repeated, again going unheard. He thought about attempting to stand up, but at the moment that didn't seem to be a good idea or even possible. He decided to collect his thoughts some more and soon fell asleep with his back against the bar.

He was awakened by the sudden absence of thunderous noise; D.J. Booga Wooga was taking a short break. It took Seth a few seconds to remember where he was. He rolled over and saw a forest of legs. He reached out an unsteady hand, his plan being to signal his location to his Posse.

"What the hell?" said a woman's voice from above. At the same moment, Seth felt a sharp pain, the result of being kicked in the forehead by the pointy-toed, high-heeled sandal of Hot Bod competitor Cyndi, whose ankle his hand had landed on.

"Sorry!" said Seth, crawling out from under the bar. He took hold of the barstool and began pulling himself upward. It was a struggle, and he would have failed if Duane hadn't grabbed his arm and helped him finish the job. He stood blinking, holding the bar for support.

"So *that's* where you were," said Duane, who still had Blossom around his shoulders.

Cyndi said, "Ohmigod, you're bleeding."

Seth touched a hand to his forehead, felt a stinging pain and sticky wetness.

"Shit," he said.

"Sorry I kicked you," said Cyndi. "I didn't know it was you."

"It's OK," said Seth, making a *Don't worry about it* gesture with his bloody hand. He looked around the teeming bar but saw no sign of his Posse.

"Where'd they go?" he said.

"They went looking for you," said Duane. "A while ago."

"Where?"

Duane waved his arm in the general direction of Miami.

"Shit," said Seth. "I gotta find them." He let go of the bar and went down on all fours again. Cyndi and Duane pulled him back to his feet.

"You better stay here for now," said Duane.

"I have to get married," said Seth. "I'm the groom."

"You should sit down," said Duane.

"I gotta get to the whaddycallit. Ricks Carleston."

"There's blood on your face," said Cyndi, dabbing at Seth's forehead with a napkin.

"My father-in-law has two helicopters, you believe that?" said Seth.

"Wow," said Cyndi, still dabbing.

"He thinks I'm a loser," said Seth. "I don't even know what the Commerce Clause does! You believe that?"

"I don't know what it does either, dude," said Duane.

Cyndi shrugged to indicate that she, too, was unfamiliar with the Commerce Clause.

"You think she thinks I'm a loser?" said Seth.

"Who?" said Cyndi.

"Tina."

"Who's Tina?"

"Tina is my bride. With whom I am getting married. To."

"Of *course* she doesn't think you're a loser," said Cyndi. "She's marrying you!"

"Yeah, but *why*?" said Seth. "Thass what I don't get. She's hot and she went to Harvard and she knows about the Commerce Clause. You wanna know what I do?"

"What?" said Cyndi.

"I tweet about douche!" To emphasize this point, Seth pounded the bar, accidentally knocking over the Miller Lite of the guy standing next to him, who turned and was about to say something but quickly turned back when he saw Duane and Blossom both giving him the eye, with Blossom adding some tongue.

"I'm sure she loves you," said Cyndi.

"Thank you," said Seth. He frowned at her. "Who're you?"

"I'm Cyndi."

"Thank you, Cyndi. You're ver' nice."

"Thank you."

"You're ver' beautiful."

"Thank you."

"I don't wanna throw up on you."

"Thank you," said Cyndi, stepping back.

Seth released the bar and took a staggering step toward Ocean Drive. He nearly fell again, but Duane caught him.

"Easy," he said.

"I hafta get to the hotel," said Seth. "The Ricks Carleson. Hotel. Key. Bickscayne. I hafta get there. I'm the groom. Of a *wedding*."

"OK," said Duane. "You got a car?"

Seth nodded.

"OK," said Duane. "Where's it parked?"

"Washington."

"Washington Avenue?"

"No. D.C."

"Your car is parked in Washington, D.C.?"

Seth nodded hard, almost falling over with the effort.

"OK," said Duane. "We'll find a taxi."

"We already tried that," said Seth. "It doesn't work."

"Let's try again," said Duane. He and Cyndi each took one of Seth's arms and they guided him out of the Clevelander and onto the sidewalk. Ocean Drive was now an unmoving mass of cars, so they made their way through the sidewalk crowd to Tenth Street, then over to Collins Avenue. Duane held on to Seth while Cyndi stepped into the street; she spotted a taxi rolling north and waved it over. She opened the door, then helped Duane push Seth into the backseat. She slid in next to him, followed by Duane.

The driver turned and looked at them.

"It's not him!" said Seth.

"Not who?" said Cyndi.

"That other guy," said Seth.

"Oh," said Cyndi.

"No snakes in the taxi," the driver said to Duane.

"It's a service snake," said Duane.

"A what?"

"Service snake. I need it for my emotional . . . needs. Federal law, you have to take this snake. We're going to Key Biscayne." He looked at Seth. "What hotel again?"

"The Rich Carlston," said Seth. "I'm the groom."

"That snake better stay back there," said the driver.

It was just after 11:30 p.m. when they pulled up at the main entrance to the Ritz-Carlton. With effort, Seth located his wallet and paid the driver the fare, plus a generous tip. He then doubled the amount to cover Duane and Cyndi's fare back to Miami.

They helped him out of the taxi. The instant they were outside, the driver stomped on the gas.

"Hey!" shouted Duane. "Wait!" But the taxi was gone.

"Asshole," said Duane.

A uniformed doorman emerged from the hotel. He paused at the sight of the newly arrived trio: Seth, standing unsteadily, blood oozing down his forehead; Cyndi, in her microdress and heels; and Duane, with Blossom coiled around him, her head hovering next to his.

"Checking in?" said the doorman.

"Yes," said Seth. "I'm the groom."

"Congratulations," said the doorman, with a little bow toward Seth, then Cyndi.

"Oh no," said Cyndi. "I'm not her."

"Ah," said the doorman. "Do you need any help with your luggage?"

Seth looked around, then took a staggering step backward.

"Oh shit," he said.

"What?" said Duane.

"My suitcase!" said Seth. "Did we bring my suitcase?"

"You had a suitcase?" said Duane.

"Yes! Oh Jesus! The ring's in it!"

"The wedding ring?" said Cyndi.

"Yes!"

"Oh man," said Cyndi.

At that moment a black stretch limo glided up and stopped. A dark-suited driver jumped out and hurried back to open the right rear door. Out stepped a tall, tan, distinguished, square-jawed, silver-haired man wearing a blue silk blazer, knit shirt and perfectly creased slacks. He wore tasseled Italian loafers without socks.

"Oh no," said Seth.

"What?" said Cyndi.

"That's Tina's dad. *Shit*."

The man, whose name was Mike Clark and whose net worth was estimated by *Forbes* at $3.7 billion, turned and held out his hand to assist in the graceful emergence from the limo of a tall, slim blonde woman in a pale pink designer dress and pearls. This was his wife, Marcia, who looked remarkably like Tilda Swinton in the role of the White Witch in *The Chronicles of Narnia*; the resemblance was so pronounced that despite Marcia's classic beauty, small children sometimes fled from her at malls.

The couple stood facing the limo as their three children emerged: Tina's sister, Meghan; their brother, Eric, a younger, even handsomer version of his father; and Tina. The family formed a tableau of perfection next to the limo, a real-life Ralph Lauren ad.

Tina's eyes fell on Seth and widened.

"Seth?" she said.

The others turned and saw Seth and his two companions, their faces registering varying mixtures of surprise and revulsion.

"Hey, Tina," said Seth. "Hey, Meghan, Eric." He turned to Tina's parents. "Hello, Mike. Marcia."

Mike responded with a one-micron nod. Marcia did not move. She was regarding Seth with the expression of a woman peering down the seat hole of a Porta-Potty into which she has just dropped her designer purse.

"You're bleeding," said Tina. "Are you OK?"

"I'm fine!" said Seth, attempting a jaunty wave, which turned into a sideways stagger requiring several steps to recover from.

"What happened to your head?" said Tina.

"My head?"

"Your head. Which is bleeding."

"Oh! Sorry. Cyndi kicked me. But it was totally my fault."

"Cyndi?" said Tina.

"I'm Cyndi," said Cyndi. "Congratulations, by the way."

Ignoring her, Tina said, "She kicked you in the *head*?"

"I didn't know it was him," explained Cyndi.

Meghan snorted. "Maybe your friends should have paid more than a hundred twenty dollars," she said.

"What did you say?" said Cyndi.

"Nonono," said Seth, waving his arms in the referee sign for a missed field goal. "She's not a stripper."

"Really?" said Meghan, staring at Cyndi. "So what *is* she?"

"What does *that* mean?" said Cyndi.

"Hey now, ladies," said Duane.

"And who are you?" said Tina.

"I'm Duane."

"Nice snake," said Eric. Meghan snorted again.

"Listen, Tina," said Seth, wishing desperately that he were less drunk. "This isn't what it looks like."

"Ah," said Tina. "So you're *not* bleeding from the head and hanging out with a Beyoncé look-alike and a *Jerry Springer* bouncer carrying a large snake."

"No, no. I mean, yes. But listen, here's what happened. We couldn't find the Ricks Carlson. I mean, the taxi couldn't find it. I mean, he *found* the Ricks Carlson, but it was the wrong one. So we got another taxi, but it was the *same* taxi. And he—"

"Seth," said Tina. "Forget it, OK? Like I said at the airport, just be ready for the rehearsal dinner."

"But really, Tina, this isn't . . ."

"Seth, it's OK. Really. I'm going in. You have fun at your bachelor party with your new friends."

"But these're not my . . ." Seth caught himself, glanced at Duane and Cyndi.

There was an awkward pause, ended by Mike, who did not get where he was in life by standing around idly during pauses. "Seth," he said. "I know this is your bachelor party, and I'm sure this"—he waved in the general direction of Cyndi and Duane without looking at them—"is all in good fun. I understand that. I'm all for having fun." He flashed a brief, dentally impeccable smile to indicate the extent to which he was in favor of fun.

"But remember, son, that the day after tomorrow you're going to be marrying my daughter and joining our family."

Behind Mike, Marcia shuddered visibly.

"So," said Mike, "I'm sure you won't do anything to embarrass your new family." He looked at Duane and Cyndi, then back at Seth. "Will you?"

"No, sir."

"Seth, I've told you to call me Mike."

"Yes, sir."

Another snort from Meghan.

"All right, then," said Mike. "We'll see you tomorrow."

"Absolutely," said Seth.

Mike and his acutely hygienic family headed for the hotel door, which was hastily opened by the doorman. The second-to-last thing Seth saw was Eric and Meghan laughing; the last thing was Marcia taking Tina's arm and leaning close, filling her daughter's ear with words that Seth suspected were not complimentary to him.

"Shit," said Seth.

"She's beautiful," said Cyndi.

"I know," said Seth. "And I lost the ring. Jesus. I hafta find my suitcase."

"Maybe your friends took it," said Cyndi.

"Ohmigod!" said Seth, feeling hope surge within him. "You think?"

"You could call them."

"Ohmigod! I could call them!"

"That's what I was thinking," said Cyndi.

"With my phone!"

"Right."

Seth dug out his phone, hit the speed dial for Marty, got voice mail, said, "Shit," speed-dialed Kevin, said "Shit" again, speed-dialed Big Steve.

"Come on, Steve, please," he said. The phone rang four times.

*"Please,"* said Seth.

"HELLO?" It was Big Steve, shouting over a roar.

"Steve! It's me! Seth!"

"HELLO?"

"This is Seth!"

"SETH?"

"Yes."

"WE'RE TRYING TO FIND YOU!"

"I'm at the hotel."

"WHAT?"

"The hotel."

"NO, WE'RE AT A CLUB!"

"No, *I'm* at the—"

"IT'S CALLED MEAT SOMETHING. PATROL. MEAT PATROL. YOU KNOW HOW MUCH A BEER COSTS HERE?"

"Steve, listen to me, OK? Do you have the suit—"

"FIFTEEN DOLLARS A BOTTLE! FOR MILLER LITE! I ASKED IF THEY HAD IT ON TAP, BUT THEY DON'T!"

"Steve, listen to—"

"FIFTEEN DOLLARS! FOR MILLER LITE!"

"Is Marty there?"

"WHAT?"

"Marty. Is he there!"

"NO, THIS IS STEVE!"

"No, I want to *talk* to Marty. Can you put him on? Steve? Hello? Steve? Hello?"

Seth looked at the phone: DISCONNECTED. He hit redial. This time he got voice mail.

"Shit!" he said.

"What?" said Duane.

Seth said, "They're at some club. Meat something."

"Meat Patrol?" said Duane.

"That's it."

"That's a hot club," said Cyndi. "Do they have your suitcase?"

"I don't even know if they have *pants*," said Seth. "Shit." He slumped to the ground directly in front of the hotel entrance. The doorman approached, apparently intending to tell Seth he couldn't sit there, but quickly retreated when Duane and Blossom turned to eyeball him.

"What am I gonna do?" said Seth. "I'm the *groom*."

"Tell you what," said Duane. "You go check in, lie down. I'll go find your friends and your suitcase, bring 'em back here."

"You would do that?" said Seth. The guilty thought occurred to him that if the situation were reversed, he probably wouldn't do the same for Duane.

"Sure," said Duane.

"Lemme give you some money for the cab," said Seth, getting unsteadily to his feet. He opened his wallet and handed two fifties to Duane. He noticed he had very little cash left. He'd scraped together $1,200 in carry-around money for his big wedding weekend and he'd managed to blow through almost all of it before he checked in.

Duane headed toward the wary doorman to see about a taxi. Seth, walking on legs he felt only a vague connection with, wobbled toward the hotel.

# 6

*I have to* drown my children.

The unthinkable thought seized Laurette's mind as the little boat, now too full of water to ride over the waves, was nearly flipped over by one. Laurette grabbed the side of the steeply tipping boat with one hand while she tried to cling to Stephane and the baby with the other. The next wave would almost surely throw them all into the water, and then there would be nothing for her to hold on to.

She made her mind up. When the time came, she would hold her children underwater and end this horror for them. She would not run the risk that she would lose them or be taken first and leave them alone in the cruel, indifferent sea. She would give her children the only comfort she could give them now, the comfort of death.

The boat leveled off in a trough between waves. She could see the next one coming, bigger than the last. She felt the boat lifting, then tilting wildly. She heard Stephane cry out to her as they tumbled into the sea. She clung to him, clung to the baby, determined to carry out her merciful plan.

But she could not. For years her reason for existing had been to protect her babies, and she could not overpower that instinct now. She grabbed each child with one hand and thrust them upward, trying to keep her head above water by kicking her feet. It was all she could do. She knew, as she felt the next wave coming, that it would not be enough.

# 7

Seth wobbled over to the hotel reception desk, behind which stood a clean-cut man whose name tag read ROBERT. He shot a concerned glance at Seth's oozing forehead but recovered quickly and welcomed Seth to the Ritz-Carlton with an expression conveying sincerely feigned warmth.

"I'm checking in," said Seth. "To the hotel."

"Excellent!" exclaimed Robert, smiling to show how delighted he was by this turn of events. "May I have a name, please?"

"You already have one," said Seth, pointing a wobbly finger at Robert's name tag. This struck him as a hilarious witticism, and as he laughed he attempted to pound the counter in mirth, missing by a good six inches.

Seth heard a giggle behind him and turned to see Cyndi.

"You're here," he said.

"Just making sure you get checked in OK," she said, hastily adding, "It was Duane's idea. Once you're set, I'll wait outside for him to come back."

"OK," said Seth.

"So," said Robert, getting back to business. "May I have *your* name, please?"

"I think you're better off with yours," said Seth, "seeing as how you already have the tag." This drew another giggle from Cyndi, and Seth was pleased that this time he was able to successfully hit the counter with his fist-pound of mirth.

Robert produced a polite nanosmile, then said, "But seriously, may I have the name on your reservation?"

"Weinstein," said Seth. "Seth Weinstein. I'm here for the Weinstein–Clark wedding, of which I am the groom."

"Congratulations," said Robert, shooting a glance at Cyndi.

"Oh no," said Cyndi. "I'm not her. I'm just here as a friend."

"She has another friend," added Seth. "Wayne."

*Duane,"* said Cyndi.

"Right, Duane," said Seth. "What's the snake's name again?"

"Blossom," said Cyndi.

"Right, Blossom," Seth told Robert. "She's Duane's snake."

"I see," said Robert. "Do you need assistance with your luggage?"

"Yes!" said Seth.

"Fine," said Robert. "Where is it?"

"Exactly."

"I'm sorry?"

"Where is it? That's what I need assistance with," said Seth.

"You need assistance *locating* your luggage?"

"Right. I don't know where it is."

"Ah," said Robert. "I'm afraid I don't, either."

"Shit," said Seth.

"All right, then," Robert said briskly, tapping on his computer. "I see we have a nice suite reserved for you, all expenses taken care of by Mr. Clark."

"I'm supposed to call him Mike, but I always forget," said Seth.

"I see."

"He has two helicopters, you believe that?"

"Huh," said Robert. "Here's your room key, Mr. Weinstein. I certainly hope you enjoy your stay." He handed Seth a folder containing the key card. Seth regarded it the way a dog might examine a quadratic equation.

"I'll give you a hand," said Cyndi, taking the card. "Which way to the elevators?"

"That way," said Robert, pointing and giving Cyndi a look that pissed her off. She took Seth's arm and led him to the elevators. They entered one; the doors closed. The ascent began in awkward silence.

"I'm really sorry about your head," said Cyndi.

"My head?" said Seth.

"Kicking it," said Cyndi.

"Oh, that's OK," said Seth, patting her arm, his hand touching her bare skin, a sensation they were both suddenly very aware of. He dropped his hand, and they moved a half step farther apart.

The doors opened. Cyndi led the way, checking the door numbers, Seth weaving behind. "Here we are," she said, handing the key card to Seth. He fumbled with it, trying to get it the right way into the door slot. She took the card back, their hands touching again just for a second. She unlocked the door and pushed it open.

"Wow," she said.

Seth stepped past her into the room. "Wow," he agreed.

They were in the foyer of a huge suite. To the right was a bar, with a bottle of champagne in a bucket of melting ice. Ahead was a darkened living room with sofas arrayed in front of a big-screen TV, which was showing an episode of *House Hunters* on the Home and Garden channel. In the distance was a dining area with table and chairs. To the left was a hallway leading to a bedroom.

"This is awesome," said Cyndi.

"Yeah," said Seth. "Tina told me they got me the Groom Suite, but I didn't know it was gonna be, like, a *house*."

Several seconds passed, then Cyndi said, "I guess I should go down and wait for Duane."

"You can wait here," said Seth. "I mean, it's huge."

"You think that . . . I mean, I don't want to cause any trouble."

"Nah," said Seth, waving away her concern, "I don't think I can get in any more trouble tonight."

Suddenly the suite filled with the harsh blatting sound of an extended high-decibel fart, which erupted from the direction of the sofas. Seth and Cyndi turned to look. A head appeared over the back of the center sofa.

"'Scuse me," said a deep-pitched woman's voice. "I fell asleep."

The woman rose, rubbing her eyes. She was African-American, light-skinned, pretty, quite large, wearing a tentlike garment. She yawned, looked at Seth and said, "You the groom?"

"Yeah," said Seth. "Who're you?"

"LaDawne," she said. "With an *e*."

"Um, how'd you get in here?"

"Oh, I know people here," she said. "They let me in."

"OK, but . . . why are you in my room?"

LaDawne, with a dramatic gesture, flung off her garment. Beneath it, she was wearing a fake-jewel-encrusted bikini, which was straining to hold in her massive, curve-a-licious womanliness.

"Honey," she said, "I'm the stripper."

"Wow," said Cyndi.

Seth sat on the floor, put his face in his hands. "No," he said.

"What?" said LaDawne.

Seth looked up. "I told Marty, no stripper."

"Well," said LaDawne, "that's not what Marty told *me*. He told me be here at nine and I was here at nine. So I been here a *lotta* hours, and I *am* going to get paid my money."

Seth pressed his face back into his hands. "How much?" he said through his fingers.

"Two hundred dollars," said LaDawne. "Plus usually I get a tip, because, honey, if you saw me dance, you would *want* to give me a tip."

"I don't have two hundred dollars," said Seth.

"Seriously?" said LaDawne. "Groom in a fancy suite, ain't got two hundred dollars? You sure you don't have the money and just promised it to this little girl here?"

"Hey," said Cyndi. "I'm not—"

"Honey, I don't care what you are," said LaDawne. "All I care about is, I want my money."

Seth pulled out his wallet. "I have, like, fifty. That's it. You can have that. I'm sorry."

LaDawne shook her head, setting off a wave of flesh movement that flowed down her body like a seismic event. "Unh-*unh*. I had an agreement with Marty and I showed up, and I want my money. So if you ain't got it, I suggest you get Marty over here right now with my money or I'm going to have to call Wesley."

"Wesley?" said Seth.

"My manager-slash-boyfriend," said LaDawne. "Believe me, you do *not* want me to call Wesley."

"No," agreed Seth. He shook his head. "*Marty*. Jesus."

"Maybe you could try calling him again," suggested Cyndi.

"Yeah," said Seth, getting the phone out of his pocket. He hit the speed dial for Marty, fearing he would again get voice mail. To his great relief, the phone was answered after a few rings.

By a woman.

"Hello?" she said.

"Is Marty there?" said Seth.

"He is busy," said the woman. She had an accent, not Spanish. Maybe Russian.

"Listen," said Seth. "This is important. I'm his best man. I mean, he's my best man. I'm the groom."

"The who?"

"Groom. I'm the groom. Just tell Marty I need to talk to him *right now*, OK? This is *really, really* important."

After a pause, the woman said, "OK, I ask."

Seth heard the phone being *clunk*ed down. LaDawne moved her massiveness over to the bar and pointed at the champagne. "You gonna drink this?"

Seth shook his head.

"You mind?" said LaDawne.

Seth made a *Be my guest* gesture. LaDawne lifted the bottle out of the melting ice. Seth heard somebody pick up the phone.

"Hello?" said Marty.

"Marty, this is Seth. Where the—"

"Seth! Where the fuck are you?"

"I'm at the—"

"We looked all *over* for you, man. You shouldn't just wander off like that."

"I didn't. I was under the—"

"Anyway, you gotta come to this place, man. This is *incredible*."

"What place?"

"It's a private club. We met these women at Meat Patrol—Seth, you would not *believe* these women. They make Tina look like Rosie O'Donnell, no offense. They invited us to a private party with them, so here we are."

"But where?"

"The something Hotel. Sea Monkey."

"The Sea Monkey Hotel?" said Seth.

"Yeah," said Marty.

"Uh-oh," said LaDawne.

Seth looked at LaDawne. "Uh-oh what?" he said.

"Your friends at the Sea Monkey?"

Seth nodded.

"With some girls speaking with a Russian accent?"

Seth nodded again.

"Who been giving them cocktails?"

"Marty," said Seth into the phone, "are they giving you cocktails?"

"Oh yes," said Marty. "Yum. Also they're serving paella."

Seth nodded at LaDawne.

LaDawne shook her head. "Your friends making a big mistake."

"Marty," said Seth into the phone. "You need to get out of there, OK? Right now. Marty? Marty?"

"He is busy," said a woman's voice.

"Hey!" said Seth. "Put Marty back on! Hello? Hello?"

Nothing.

"Shit," said Seth. "What's going to happen to them?"

"If they lucky," said LaDawne, "they wind up with a big bill on they credit card. I mean, *real* big. If they lucky, that's all."

"What if they're not lucky?" said Seth.

"You better hope they lucky," said LaDawne, pouring herself some more champagne. "Also you better find some other way to get me my two hundred dollars real soon. Wesley ain't gonna wait for me all night. He gonna come looking. You don't want that."

"Oh God," said Seth. "What am I gonna *do*?"

"Maybe there's an ATM machine," said Cyndi.

"Here?" said Seth, looking around the suite.

"No, like, in the lobby somewhere."

"Oh, right. OK, could you stay here? In case Duane comes back with my suitcase?"

"OK," said Cyndi.

Seth left the suite, weaved his way down the corridor, found the elevator, found—with some effort—the *L* button and finally returned to the lobby, occupied at that very late hour only by Robert, still manning the front desk. His eyes were wary as Seth approached, but his smile remained professional grade.

"May I help you, Mr. Weinstein?" he said.

"Yes," said Seth.

This was followed by a thirty-second pause, during which Seth tried to remember why he had come to the lobby.

Finally Robert, not giving up on the smile despite the fact that he was working a double shift and had been on duty for nearly ten hours battling a case of Irritable Bowel Syndrome that would bring down a water buffalo, said, "How, *specifically*, may I help you?"

"She's in my room," said Seth. "Whashername."

"The young lady?" said Robert.

"No," said Seth. "Another one."

"I see," said Robert.

"I didn't . . . I mean, *she* didn't," explained Seth. "At all. But Wesley will *not* be happy."

"And so . . ." said Robert.

"And so what?"

Robert sighed a sigh that was not one hundred percent professional. "And so how may I help you?"

"Oh yeah! Do you have an ATM machine? Here?"

"Yes, we do," said Robert. "You go down this corridor, then turn left, and it's in an alcove on your right just before the restaurant."

"Great," said Seth. He weaved his way into the corridor, trying to focus on the directions. Something about a restaurant. He made a left and there it was ahead, the restaurant, which was closed. There was an alcove to the right and a door to the left. Seth frowned, trying to remember the directions, then turned left, pushing the door open. He realized he was now outdoors. Had Robert said something about going outdoors?

"Hello, Seth."

Seth whirled, almost falling, searching for the source of the voice.

"Over here."

He saw her then, sitting on a bench alongside a walkway. Seth smelled the sweet aroma of weed.

"Hey, Meghan," he said.

"What's up?" she said.

"I'm looking for a cash machine."

"There's none out here that I know of," she said. She held out a glowing joint. "Have some."

Seth shook his head. "I don't think so," he said.

"Why not?"

"I'm already messed up. Plus . . ." He hesitated.

"Plus what?"

"There's a stripper in my room."

"I know. I met her."

"No, not her. Another one."

"Wow. Two strippers. You dog."

"No, they're not . . . I mean, OK, one is, but she didn't. But I have to pay her two hundred dollars. Which I don't have. Or Wesley will come."

"Wesley?"

"Her boyfriend. I don't want to meet Wesley."

Meghan took a hit, held it, eased it out, then said, "You want me to tell Mike?"

"What?"

"Daddy has these guys, for security. Believe me, however much you don't want to meet Wesley, Wesley doesn't want to meet Daddy's security guys even more."

Seth shook his head. "No," he said. "I don't want your dad to know about this." He rubbed his hair with both hands. "I just want the stripper to go away and whashisname to come back with my suitcase and Marty and Kevin and Steve to not be killed by the Russian women and please God just let this fucking night be *over*."

Meghan took another hit. "Sounds like somebody's not having the bachelor party of his dreams."

"No," said Seth.

"Sure you don't want some?" she said, holding the joint out again. "It'll calm you down."

"You think?"

Meghan nodded, exhaling.

"Maybe one hit," said Seth, taking the joint. He hadn't smoked weed for a couple of years; his recollection was that it made him fall asleep. He took a hit, held it. On the exhale, he said, "Is Tina asleep?"

"Not when I left. She was talking with Mother about the dinner. Something about forks."

"Forks," said Seth. He took another hit.

"I think it was the dessert forks," said Meghan.

"Ah," said Seth. "Got to have those. For the dessert."

Meghan smiled. "I bet you'll be glad when this is all over with."

"Yeah." Seth took another hit, handed the joint back to Meghan. "Can I ask you something?" he said.

"Sure."

"Why does Tina want to marry me?"

Meghan coughed out some smoke. "Seriously?" she said.

"Yeah."

"Because she loves you."

"But *why* does she love me? I'm a fuckup."

"No you're not."

"Meghan, look at me. I'm not even at my own bachelor party."

"OK, tonight you're kind of a fuckup."

"But also in general. Compared with all her genius lawyer friends. And perfect family."

"We're not perfect. Believe me. What we are is rich."

"That's another thing. I tweet about douche. I'll never make as much money as Tina. Never. And I'll never give a shit about half the shit she gives a shit about."

"Nobody will ever compete with Tina in the field of giving a shit."

"But I'm not even *close*. Meg, seriously, the truth, why does she want to marry me?"

"Well, why do you want to marry her?"

"Because I could never do better. She's smart and funny. At least she can be funny, when she's not managing forks. And she's *unbelievably* hot."

"You're not so hard on the eyes yourself."

"But there's lots of good-looking guys who'd marry her. Why'd she pick me?"

Meghan took a long, contemplative hit, then said, "OK, first of all, you're nice. A lot of these guys after her, they're assholes. You're not an asshole."

"That's it? She wants to marry me because I'm not an asshole?"

"If you knew the kind of assholes that were always swarming around Tina, and her money, and her dad's money, you'd give not being an asshole a lot more credit. Also, I think it kind of helps that you don't give a shit."

"What do you mean?"

"I mean, this way, she can be the one deciding what gets given a shit about. There's no conflict. She's in charge of a hundred percent of the shit giving. Tina really likes being in charge."

"So I'm, what, the faithful dog? The good little wife?"

"No," said Meghan, leaving it there, which Seth understood to mean, basically, yes.

"Shit," he said.

Meghan studied the tiny charred joint remnant, then flicked it onto the perfect Ritz-Carlton grass. "Kind of late to be thinking about this," she said.

"I know. Everything happened so fast once we decided to get married. I thought we'd talk more about getting married, but pretty much all we talked about was the wedding."

Meghan put her hand on his. "Listen, Seth, it's gonna be fine. Tina loves you, in her supergirl Tina way."

"Your parents hate me."

"They don't hate you. *Hate* is a strong word."

"They hate me."

"I admit you would not be their first choice."

"I'm Jewish."

"They have several Jewish friends."

"Any non-billionaire Jewish friends?"

Meghan thought about that. "No," she concluded.

"I'm a Jewish non-billionaire."

"They really don't . . ."

"I tweet about douche."

"OK, but . . ."

"They hate that their daughter is marrying a douche tweeter."

"Not for long."

"What?"

"Mike's going to set you up."

"I won't work for Mike. Tina knows that."

"Right, she does, and Mike does. But he'll set something up."

"Set what up?"

"I dunno. One of his rich, powerful friends will make you an offer you can't refuse."

"What if I don't want to do whatever it is?"

"Tina will want you to."

"So, what, it's all settled? Whatever I think?"

"Hey, Seth, relax. It's a good life. You'll be happy. Look at me. I'm happy." She lit another joint.

"You are? Really, you're happy?"

Meghan exhaled. "As a fucking clam." She held the joint out to Seth.

He shook his head, rejecting both the joint and the worry-free future.

"No thanks," he said. He stood, and suddenly the night was whirling around him. "Whoa!" he said, staggering backward.

"I know," said Meghan. "This is really good shit."

Seth grabbed the back of the chair and held on, oscillating gently back and forth, a feather in the breeze. "Can I ask you something?" he said.

"Sure."

"You remember when I came out here?"

"Here, outside? Like, just now?"

"Yeah."

She nodded. "I remember."

"OK, do you remember *why* I came out here?"

Meghan frowned. "You were looking for something."

"Right!" Seth was about to snap his fingers, then decided it was not worth the risk of releasing the chair. "But what?"

Meghan frowned harder, then brightened. "A cash machine."

Seth groaned. "Oh Jesus, that's right. The stripper."

"I'm telling you, Mike could arrange—"

"*No,*" said Seth. "No Mike."

"OK," said Meghan.

"I'll handle this. I just need to walk around a little first. Which way is the beach?"

"I think it's over there." Meghan gestured vaguely with the joint.

"OK," said Seth. He released the chair, turned and began weaving toward the humid darkness smothering the Atlantic.

"Be careful," said Meghan. "Can't have a wedding without the groom."

"Or dessert forks," said Seth, not looking back.

"Forks are important, too," said Meghan, taking another hit.

## 8

Big Steve, Kevin and Marty had no idea how they
wound up lying on the sidewalk in front of the Sea Monkey Hotel.
They remembered, vaguely, having drinks with some very hot Russian
women. But then . . . nothing.

Big Steve, the least wrecked of the three, noticed that a crowd had
gathered in front of them. People were standing over them, pointing,
laughing, shooting cell-phone video. *What was going on?*

With great effort, Big Steve sat up. He looked at Marty, lying next
to him.

"Ohmigod," he said. "Marty!" He shook Marty. "Marty!"

"What?" said Marty.

"You're naked!"

Marty got his head up just enough to look down at himself.

"Oh Jesus," he said.

Big Steve looked past Marty at Kevin. Kevin was not naked. But he
was missing his pants.

The crowd was growing. From the distance came the sound of
police sirens.

"We have to get out of here," said Big Steve. He struggled to his feet.
He then fell back down.

Kevin had his head up now.

"Marty," he said. "You're naked."

"I know!" said Marty. "I'm fucking naked!"

"We have to get out of here," said Big Steve, struggling to his feet again. "Kevin, give me a hand. The police are coming." Kevin also made it to his feet, and the two of them were able to prop Marty up between them and stagger away from the crowd, down to the corner and onto a side street.

Seconds later, a police car shot past on the main street, then another.

"I'm fucking *naked*," said Marty.

Kevin looked down. "Wait a minute," he said. "Where's my pants?" He stood up. "Where's my wallet?"

"Shit," said Marty. "My wallet's gone, too."

Big Steve felt his pockets, relieved to find he had both his phone and his wallet. He was less relieved when he opened the wallet. "My money's gone," he said.

"And where's our suitcases?" said Kevin.

"The Russians must have taken them," said Big Steve. "Maybe we should go back to the hotel, try to get our stuff back."

"No," said Marty, shaking his head violently. "We go back there, half naked and wrecked, we're gonna get arrested. We'll miss the wedding."

"So what do we do?"

"We have to get to the hotel. But first I need pants."

"You can wear Steve's shirt."

"I don't need a shirt. I need pants."

"I mean wear his shirt on your legs."

"Why *my* shirt?" said Big Steve.

"Because my shirt's too small, and besides if I give it to him, I'm down to just my underwear."

"I don't believe this," said Big Steve, pulling his knit shirt off over his head. He handed it to Marty, who turned it over and, with some effort, managed to get his bare legs into the sleeves. He pulled the bottom of the shirt above his waist and said, "OK?"

"Your balls are hanging out the neckhole," said Kevin.

Marty reached down and tucked them in.

"I can never wear that shirt again," said Big Steve.

They started moving away from the sirens, Marty walking awkwardly, trying to keep his testicles inboard.

"This is bad," said Kevin.

"We should've taken the hotel shuttle," said Big Steve.

# 9

**Seth was awakened** by a cold sensation on his legs. It took him a few seconds to realize it was the Atlantic Ocean.

"Shit," he said, sitting up quickly, an act that he instantly regretted.

When he'd lain down on the sand, the water had been a safe distance away; he'd planned to stay there for just a minute, clear his mind. But he'd fallen asleep to the whoosh and hiss of the waves coming and going, coming and going. Apparently, thanks to the tide, there had been more coming than going; his shoes and pants legs were soaked.

He groaned and pushed himself backward, higher up on the beach. He put his head in his hands as his brain rebooted, the firing neurons recovering, one by one, the unpleasant facts from which sleep had briefly liberated him.

FACT: There was a stripper—a large stripper—in his hotel room.

FACT: She wanted $200 cash.

FACT: Plus a tip.

FACT: She had a boyfriend whom Seth was not keen to meet.

FACT: Seth's suitcase was missing somewhere in Miami.

FACT: In the suitcase was the wedding ring Seth was supposed to place on Tina's finger at the wedding.

FACT: Which was *in two days*.

Here Seth frowned, realizing that the night was over and it was now Saturday. His neurons then issued the following:

CORRECTION: The wedding was *tomorrow*.

FACT: The person currently in charge of locating the suitcase was a man about whom Seth knew nothing other than that he went around carrying an enormous snake.

FACT: Seth was completely fucked.

He sucked in a lungful of sea air, exhaled, did it a few more times, trying to clear his head, trying to *think*. The first order of business, he decided, was to get rid of the stripper. He'd go to the ATM, get the money, get her out of there. He should have done that already. He'd been *trying* to do that when he ended up sharing Meghan's joint, which was idiotic. He had to stop being an idiot.

The suitcase was trickier. He'd call the bar . . . what was it called? . . . the Clevelander. Maybe they'd have the suitcase. Why wouldn't they? They probably would. He'd call them and he'd get it back and he'd have the ring, and Tina would never have to know it'd been missing.

Seth was starting to feel a little better. Maybe he wasn't *completely* fucked. Maybe he could make this work. He just needed to pull himself together, stop being an idiot, focus on the task at hand, the task of being the groom. No more distractions. No more Marty bullshit.

*Focus.*

With another groan, Seth got to his feet, brushing sand from his pants. In front of him, far out over the Atlantic, the black night sky was just starting to lighten to a dark gray. Seth turned to face the massive floodlit form of the Ritz-Carlton. He started trudging, his shoes squishing, toward the wooden walkway that led from the beach to the hotel lawn.

He heard a high-pitched sound and stopped, cocking his head. His first thought was that it was a seagull. He heard it again, and it didn't sound like a seagull. It sounded like a person, crying out in a voice hoarse with desperation.

It was coming from the ocean.

Seth stumbled down the beach to the water, peering into the darkness. The cry came again, from his left. He turned that way and saw something carried in the waves—a low silhouette. Another cry.

"Hello!" shouted Seth at the shape. "Is somebody there?"

A larger wave came, lifting the shape and tumbling it toward Seth. He saw now that it was a boat, upside down.

With a child clinging to it.

Seth plunged forward into the waves, stumbled and fell headfirst as the bottom dropped away suddenly beneath his feet. He got up, sputtering, and sloshed toward the boat, breasting a wave, then another.

He reached the boat and grabbed it, trying to steady it in the waves. He was on the opposite side from the boy, who was dark-skinned, gaunt, shivering in a soaked T-shirt. He was holding tight to the ridge along the boat's keel with one hand. His eyes were wide with terror.

Seth reached across to the boy and said, "Come on!"

The boy shook his head. He said something Seth didn't understand.

"Come *on*!" said Seth, reaching. The boy shook his head again. Another big wave made the boat rise, then settle. Seth, holding on to the boat, sloshed around the submerged bow, his intent being to grab the boy. But when he got to the other side he saw why the boy had refused to let go: there was another person with him, a woman. The boy was holding on to her dress with his other hand. Her head was barely above water. She didn't seem to be moving.

"Oh God," said Seth. He put his arms around the woman and lifted her farther out of the water. As he did, he realized she was holding yet another person. A baby.

"Oh God," said Seth again.

The boy let go of the keel and slid into the water with Seth, still holding the woman's dress. Together they carried her and the baby to the beach. Seth did most of the work; the boy could barely walk. The woman, like the boy, was extremely thin. To Seth her body felt like a bundle of sticks. When the water was knee-deep, he scooped her up and carried her in front of him the way a groom carries a bride across the threshold. Her head lolled sideways; neither she nor the baby made a sound.

Seth thought they were dead.

He carried the woman onto the beach, dropped to his knees and carefully laid her on her back on the sand. She was still clasping the baby to her chest. The boy crouched next to her, tugging at her dress, pleading in what sounded to Seth like French. The woman did not respond. The boy's tone became more urgent, his words rising to a wail. Seth's still-foggy brain raced to remember something, *anything*, about first aid for drowning victims.

*Blow into her mouth.*

Seth leaned close to the woman's face. In the early-morning light, her lips were a ghastly gray.

*Pinch her nostrils shut.*

Hesitantly, he put his hand on her nose and squeezed it. He put his mouth on hers. Her skin was cold.

*She's dead.*

He blew into her mouth, pulled his mouth away, waited a second, blew into her mouth again.

*You don't know what you're doing. She's dead.*

The boy was sobbing now, gripping the woman's dress with both hands.

Seth inhaled, blew into the woman's mouth again, paused.

He heard a moan. But not from the mother. From the baby.

The boy heard it, too. Quickly he snatched the baby, untangling it from the woman's arms. The baby started crying, its high-pitched squalls mingling with the boy's sobs.

Seth inhaled and leaned down to the woman again, putting his lips on hers, blowing his breath into her.

He felt her move, heard her make a retching sound. He pulled his head back as she jerked violently and vomited water, an astonishing quantity. The boy, still holding the baby, started shouting. The woman rolled on her side, vomited even more water. Her eyes opened. She looked at Seth, her expression fearful.

"It's OK," said Seth. "It's OK."

The woman looked around frantically. Her eyes fell on the boy and the baby. With a wail she reached for them, grabbing the boy, pulling him and the baby close, the three of them crying, two of them out of joy.

Seth watched for a few moments, then touched the woman's arm. She looked at him warily.

"I'll go get you some help," he said. "Stay here. I'll be right back, OK?"

The woman's expression was uncomprehending. Seth stood and made a *Stay here* gesture. He rose and ran up the beach toward the walkway. Ahead, up on the lawn, he saw a hotel maintenance worker holding a rake.

"Hey!" Seth yelled.

The man looked his way.

"I need help!" Seth shouted. "Some people almost drowned!"

The man dropped his rake and trotted toward Seth.

"Over here," said Seth, leading the man down the beach.

The woman was still holding the boy and the baby. She was still crying but calmer now, trying to quiet the baby. She looked up as Seth and the worker approached. Her eyes focused on the worker, whose skin, like hers, was dark.

He said something to her, not in English. She answered in a flood of words, interrupted by choking sobs. The man said something else; another long answer.

"What'd she say?" said Seth.

"She is from Haiti," said the man, pronouncing it *A*-tee. "She is looking for her sister."

"OK," said Seth, "but maybe we need to get her to a hospital?"

The man studied Seth for a few seconds, then said, "She does not want to go to the hospital."

"Why not? They can help her."

"Yes, they can help her, and then she will have to go back to Haiti."

Seth looked out at the pathetic little boat rolling in the surf upside down.

"Oh," he said.

"Yes," said the man.

"Then what does she want to do?" said Seth.

The man talked with the woman again.

"She wants to find her sister," he said. "Her sister lives here, in Miami."

"Where?"

"She doesn't know the address. She had it on a paper in her pocket, but she lost that in the sea. She was supposed to meet her sister, but the men who were supposed to bring her here did not take her to the meeting place. They just put her in that boat."

"Can we call the sister?"

"She doesn't have a phone."

"Then how can she find her?"

"She told me her sister's name. When I get off from work, I can ask some people in Miami. Maybe they will know where to find her."

"Can she go home with you? While she tries to find her sister."

"That is not possible," said the man.

"Why not?"

"I live here on the hotel grounds, in worker housing."

"Shit." Seth looked at the woman, crying softly, shivering, holding the baby. The boy was clinging to her dress.

"She can't stay here on the beach," said Seth.

"No," said the man. "The police will take her if she stays here."

Seth stared at the woman for a few moments. He ran his hands through his hair.

"I don't believe this," he said.

The man said nothing.

"What's your name?" Seth asked the man.

"Juste," said the man. "Carl Juste."

"I'm Seth," said Seth sticking out his hand. Carl shook it.

"OK, Carl," Seth said. "I have a room here in the hotel. A big room. Please tell her . . . what's her name, anyway?"

Carl spoke to the woman, then said, "Her name is Laurette."

"OK. Tell Laurette she can come up to my room for now. I'll try to find somebody who can help her. Meanwhile you can find her sister. Tell her that, OK?"

Carl spoke to Laurette. She became agitated, her voice rising again.

"What's the matter?" said Seth.

"She's afraid you will call the police," said Carl. "She is afraid she will be sent back to Haiti."

"Tell her I promise I won't call the police."

After more agitated conversation, Carl said, "She says, please, you must not tell anybody. *Anybody.* She says, please, you must wait until I find her sister, then she will be gone."

Seth and Laurette looked at each other for a few seconds, her eyes pleading.

"OK," said Seth.

Laurette burst into tears. She leaned over and pressed her forehead against Seth's soaking-wet left shoe, wailing. Seth reached down and patted her awkwardly on the shoulder. She looked up and said something to him in a sob-racked voice.

"She says you are an angel," said Carl.

"I don't believe this," said Seth.

They got her to her feet. She was unsteady, shivering. The baby slipped in her hands; she was too weak to hold it and walk. Seth reached out and took the baby from her. He looked at the baby's face, at its tiny nose and mouth, its tiny ears pierced with impossibly tiny earrings. A girl baby.

Seth had never held a baby before and couldn't believe how small and insubstantial she felt. He held her awkwardly in both hands, afraid of dropping her, equally afraid of squeezing her too tight. Walking very cautiously, he followed as Carl and the boy helped Laurette up the beach to the walkway. They made their way slowly across the lawn to the hotel. The sun was up but it was early, and there was nobody walking around yet.

Carl led them to the back hotel entrance. He stopped at the doorway.

"What is your room number?" he asked Seth.

Seth frowned, remembered, told him.

"OK," said Carl. "I will call you."

"Soon as possible," said Seth. "I can't . . ." He looked down at the baby. "I mean, I'm getting married this weekend."

"I will call you," said Carl. Then he was gone, leaving Seth with Laurette and the two children.

"All right," said Seth. "Come on."

He led them into the hotel, their clothes dripping seawater onto the sparkling marble floor. They walked through the corridor, turned right and approached the lobby. Seth poked his head around the corner. Seeing nobody at the front desk, he led Laurette and the boy across the main lobby and down the corridor to the elevator bank.

Seth used his elbow to push the up button. The elevator doors slid open. Seth nodded toward the opening. Neither Laurette nor the boy moved. It occurred to Seth that they had never seen, let alone ridden in, an elevator. He stepped into the car, nodding for them to follow. They stepped hesitantly inside. Their eyes widened as the doors closed. The car started moving. Laurette clutched the boy and whimpered.

"It's OK," said Seth.

The car stopped; the doors slid open. Seth led Laurette and the boy down the hall to his room. He realized he didn't have a key with him. He rapped on the door with his elbow, listened, rapped again, hoping Cyndi was still there, hoping LaDawne wasn't.

The door opened. He heard LaDawne talking before he saw her.

"It's about damn time you got back because I been waiting for . . ." She stopped, seeing the baby in Seth's arms, then Laurette and the boy.

"They were in the ocean," said Seth.

"Give me that child," said LaDawne, reaching for the baby, which Seth willingly surrendered. LaDawne held her confidently in one arm, reaching toward Laurette and the boy with the other. "You come right in here," she said.

"They don't speak English," said Seth. "They're from Haiti."

"You come right in," repeated LaDawne, pulling them into the suite. Seth followed.

Cyndi emerged from the bedroom, where she apparently had been sleeping. Seth was glad she hadn't left. Seeing the Haitians, she hurried across the living room toward them.

"Oh my God!" she said. "What happened?"

"I was on the beach," said Seth. "They were in this little boat, turned over."

"The poor things!" said Cyndi. "They're soaking wet!" She ran into the bedroom, returning a few seconds later with towels and robes. As the two women fussed over the Haitians, Seth wandered into the suite. He stopped short when he spied an enormous man in an enormous workout suit reclining on the sofa, holding the remote control, which almost disappeared in his enormous hand. The man was watching SportsCenter, which was showing a series of escalatingly impossible basketball shots. He did not look at Seth.

"Hello," said Seth. The man did not respond.

"That's Wesley," said LaDawne. "He came to get me. And the money. You got my money, right?"

"I . . . um, no, not yet," said Seth. "Because of . . ." He gestured toward the Haitians. "But I'll go down and get it right now."

"Thousand dollars," said Wesley, not taking his eyes off of SportsCenter. His voice sounded like what a large male bear's voice would sound like if large male bears could talk.

"A *thousand*?" said Seth. "She said two hundred!"

"For an hour. She here overnight. Overnight is a thousand."

"But she never . . . I mean, she didn't even . . ." Seth stopped because now Wesley was looking at him in a way that somehow—despite the fact that Wesley was eight feet away and not in physical contact—made Seth's face hurt.

"A thousand," said Wesley.

"I can't get a thousand from the ATM," said Seth.

Wesley shifted his weight very slightly. It was all Seth could do to keep from yelping.

"OK, OK," he said. "Just give me time to figure something out." Eager to escape the force field of Death Star Wesley, he walked back over to where LaDawne and Cyndi were ministering to the Haitians. LaDawne was still holding the baby; Cyndi was looking with concern at Laurette.

"She doesn't look too great," she said. "I think maybe she should see a doctor."

"She doesn't want to do that," said Seth.

"How you know that?" said LaDawne.

Seth told them what Carl had told him. "They're just hiding out here temporarily," he concluded. "Until Carl can find her sister."

"All right," said LaDawne. "But they gotta eat."

"I'll order room service," said Cyndi, heading for the phone.

"Get pancakes," said LaDawne. "And bacon. Lotta bacon. I'm hungry, too. So is Wesley."

While Cyndi called room service, LaDawne shepherded the Haitians into the master bedroom and got them situated in the king-sized bed. They looked small, almost doll-like, propped against the complex edifice of decorative pillows that, in the tradition of top-tier hotels, covered forty-five percent of the bed. The Haitians were still dazed, but seemed to be responding to the relentless 250-pound round mound of mothering that was LaDawne.

Seth went to the opposite end of the living room from Wesley and slumped on another sofa. He was beyond exhausted but saw no hope of sleep. He longed to take a shower and change clothes. But his clothes were in his suitcase. With the ring.

"Breakfast will be here in twenty to twenty-five minutes," said Cyndi, hanging up the phone.

"Any word from Duane?" Seth asked her. "About my suitcase?"

She shook her head. "Sorry. I'm sure Duane is . . ." Her voice trailed off because they both knew she had no idea what Duane was up to.

"I'm never gonna see that suitcase again," said Seth.

"You might," said Cyndi, coming over and sitting next to him.

Seth shook his head. "No," he said. "I'm not. I'm going to have to tell Tina that I lost it. She planned this whole giant wedding, every detail, invitations, forks, bridesmaids' favors, nineteen million things, on spreadsheets, everything perfect. *Perfect.* And you know what I did?"

"What?"

"I LOST THE FUCKING RING!"

LaDawne's angry face appeared in the bedroom doorway. "We got a baby sleeping in here," she hissed.

"Sorry," said Seth as the face disappeared.

"I'm sure Tina will understand about the ring," said Cyndi. "I mean, you can get another ring, right?"

Seth groaned and shook his head.

"Why not?"

Seth looked at her, inhaled, exhaled. "Do you know what a cake topper is?" he said.

"The thing they put on top of the wedding cake. The, like, little statue of the bride and groom."

"Correct. So there's lots of places that sell cake toppers on the Internet. You can buy any kind of cake topper you want—traditional cake topper, gay cake topper, Labrador retriever owner cake topper, gay Labrador retriever owner cake topper, you name it—all ready-made. You can get a really nice one for a hundred bucks."

"OK," said Cyndi.

"So guess where we got our cake topper."

"Where?"

"Italy."

"Seriously?"

"Tina found out that there was this supposedly master cake topper maker in Florence, so she flew there with her mom to personally supervise the making of our cake topper."

"Wow."

"Yeah. The little bride doll is wearing a dress made from a piece of Tina's mom's actual wedding dress. The groom's is made from her dad's wedding tuxedo. The bride doll is wearing a little diamond tiara, and they are *not fake diamonds*. You want to know how much that cost? Including flying over there? And the hotel?"

"How much?"

"I have no fucking idea. A LOT, though. Thousands and thousands of dollars. For the *cake topper*. So imagine what she did for the ring."

"What?"

"She got all this precious family jewelry, her parents' wedding rings, her grandmother's locket, all these other old heirloom pieces that have been in her family for, like, two hundred years. Then—and this was a huge deal because she had to talk her family into letting her do it—she had a jeweler take little teeny-tiny slivers from each piece where it wouldn't show. And then she had the slivers made into a ring that she had specially designed by the finest ring guy in the entire world, who is in Paris, which was a whole nother trip with her mother."

"Wow."

"So to answer your question, no, we can't get another ring. This is a very, very special, one-of-a-kind Tina-designed ring that there will never be another one of. It's like the *Lord of the Rings* ring, except it probably cost more."

"Oh."

"And that was the *one thing* she trusted me with. Everything else, she handled. She handled it *perfectly*. All I had to do was bring the ring, because that's supposed to be the groom's job. So now I have to explain to Tina that I don't have the ring because I couldn't manage to get from the airport to the hotel without getting lost in Miami Beach and then getting drunk and losing my suitcase with the ring in it, because I am a FUCKING MORON."

LaDawne's disapproving face reappeared in the doorway.

"You watch your mouth. We got young ears in here."

"They don't even speak English," said Seth.

"That's right, and I don't want them learning it from you."

The face disappeared. Seth sighed. There was a knock on the door and a voice calling, "Room service."

"I'll get it," said Cyndi, heading for the door.

The suite phone rang. Seth answered and, fearing that it would be Tina, winced as he said hello.

"Seth!" said the voice of Big Steve. "Thank God. I've been trying to call your cell."

"Hang on," said Seth. He reached into his still-soaking-wet pants pocket and pulled out his phone. The screen was lifeless. "Shit," he said. "I drowned my phone."

"Listen," said Big Steve. "We need you to come get us."

"Where are you?"

"We're on Miami Beach."

"You're *still there*?"

"Yeah. We got robbed by these Russians. They got all our money."

"Did you call the police?"

"Um, no."

"Why not?"

"We're kind of afraid they might arrest us. We don't look that great, Seth. We're kind of hiding out on the beach behind a hotel. But we're getting some looks because Marty and Kevin don't have pants."

"*What?*"

"Well, Kevin has his boxers. But all Marty has is my shirt, and his balls keep falling out. People are starting to notice us."

"You don't have other clothes? In your suitcases?"

"We lost those, too."

"Jesus."

"Yeah. So can you come get us? Like, right now? Please?"

"You can't take a taxi? I'll pay the guy when you get here."

"We tried that. The taxi drivers won't even slow down for us. Seriously, man, you gotta get over here."

"How? I don't have a car."

"Can you borrow one? We really can't stay here."

Seth sighed. "What's the hotel?"

"The Delano."

"OK. I'll try to figure something out. I'll call you back."

"Hurry up, OK?"

Seth hung up. Across the suite, a room service waiter had wheeled a cart into the dining area and, with Cyndi's help, was transferring platters of pancakes, bacon, eggs and sausages to the table. LaDawne was busily preparing plates for the Haitians. Wesley, drawn by the smell, had risen from the couch, which made him look even more enormous, like a vending machine with a head. He lumbered over to the table, picked up a platter of bacon, lumbered back to the couch, picked up the remote.

"Everything OK?" Cyndi asked Seth.

"No," said Seth. "My friends are stuck on Miami Beach with no money. They want me to come get them, but I don't have a car, and . . . Holy shit, that's Marty."

Wesley had changed from ESPN to a channel showing the local morning news. On the screen was a wobbly video, obviously taken with a phone, showing Big Steve, Kevin and Marty lying on the sidewalk, Marty naked but with his genitals digitally blurred.

"Oh God," said Seth.

The video ended, replaced by a pair of concerned-looking TV anchorwomen. Superimposed on the screen below them were the words SOUTH BEACH DRUG EPIDEMIC.

"Oh God," said Seth again.

"Those your friends?" said Wesley.

Seth nodded. "They're supposed to be in my wedding. Tomorrow."

Wesley chuckled. Even his chuckles were scary.

LaDawne's face appeared in the doorway. "This baby needs some Huggies," she announced. "Wesley, you go get this baby some Huggies."

Wesley shook his enormous head. "I ain't going to get no Huggies." He was not a Huggie-getting man.

LaDawne immediately turned to Seth. "I need you to go get the baby some Huggies."

"I don't have a car."

"You can take Wesley's car."

Seth looked at Wesley, who was very still. "Is that, um, OK with Wesley?"

"Wesley don't make the payments on that car. *I* make the payments on that car. Wesley, give him the ticket."

Without taking his eyes off the screen, Wesley pulled a valet parking ticket from a pocket and held it out to Seth, who, as he took it, suddenly understood who wore the enormous pants in this relationship.

"Huggies and formula," she said.

"What kind of . . . I mean, are there, like, sizes?" Seth said.

LaDawne rolled her eyes and looked at Cyndi. "Can you go with this man?"

"Sure."

"Listen," said Seth. "Do you think it'd be OK if I picked my friends up while we're out? They need a ride."

From the couch, Wesley chuckled.

LaDawne frowned. "All right," she said. "But make it fast. I got that baby's little butt wrapped in a towel."

While Seth and Cyndi pondered that image, the phone rang again. Seth answered. "Hello?"

"Seth?"

"Mom? Oh God, Mom! You're here!"

"We're at the airport. We landed an hour ago. We tried to call your cell phone but we got a message."

"Mom, I am SO sorry. My phone is broken, and it got a little crazy here, and I . . . uh . . . I just . . ."

"You forgot you were going to meet us at the airport."

"No! Not at all!"

"It's fine, you're too busy, we'll just get a taxi. Although your father, with his hip, if he falls again Dr. Gersten says he might never walk again. But it's fine, you're too busy for us. We'll just get a . . ."

"No! Stay there! I have a car! I can pick you up." He looked pleadingly at LaDawne, who rolled her eyes but nodded *OK*. "I'm on my way right now. Stay right there. Bye, Mom." He hung up. "I'll be right back, I swear."

"You *better* be right back," said LaDawne. "With Huggies and formula."

"And two thousand dollars," said Wesley.

"Wait a minute," said Seth. "You said *one* thousand."

"We now in a overtime situation."

Seth looked at LaDawne, who made an *It's out of my hands* gesture and headed back into the bedroom. The phone rang again. Seth picked it up.

"Hello?"

"You got to get over here," said Big Steve. "There's a lot of people on the beach and we're attracting attention."

"All right, all right, I'm coming." Seth hung up, beckoned to Cyndi and headed for the door. As he passed the bedroom, he looked inside. The three Haitians were still in the bed, surrounded by half-finished room service plates. The boy was asleep, as was the baby, wrapped in towels and nestled in her mother's arms. Laurette's eyes were open, barely; they widened when Seth came into view. She said something, too softly for him to hear.

"What'd she say?" said Seth.

"She says *Mêci*," said LaDawne. "It's Creole. It means thank you."

"You're welcome," said Seth.

Laurette smiled a weary smile, then closed her eyes.

"Don't take long," said LaDawne. "These people counting on you."

# 10

**Seth and Cyndi** stood in the driveway of the Ritz as Wesley's car, a black Cadillac Escalade with gleaming twenty-two-inch chrome rims that, by themselves, cost more than a midrange Kia, glided to a stop. As the parking valet held the door for Seth, he said, "I couldn't figure out how to turn it off."

Seth climbed in and saw what the valet was talking about: There was a high-definition video screen—one of six in the vehicle—mounted on the dashboard directly in the driver's field of vision, a location of dubious legality. The monitor was showing a porn movie involving a male actor, portraying a cable installer, who was at the moment installing his cable in a female actor while simultaneously using his tongue, which was inhumanly long, like some kind of exotic mouth-dwelling, legless purplish tropical lizard, to probe a second female actor, who was emitting the kinds of rhythmic, high-decibel moans associated with either sexual ecstasy or severe gastrointestinal distress.

Seth studied the dashboard control panel, a complex of buttons, knobs, indicator lights and touch screens that looked more suitable for the cockpit of a 747. Trying to turn off the video, he stabbed a series of screens and buttons, but he succeeded only in turning on the Escalade's custom audio system, which featured four 2,000-watt subwoofers capable of pulverizing concrete at seventy-five yards. It began blasting a bass-intensive song titled "Butt Sweat," which as it happened was a composition by none other than D.J. Booga Wooga.

"I can't turn it off," said Seth, stabbing more screens and buttons.

"WHAT?" said Cyndi.

"SEE IF YOU CAN TURN IT OFF!" said Seth. He put the Escalade in gear and pulled out of the driveway. He lowered his windows, hoping the breeze would help dry his clothes. Cyndi managed, by trial and error, to lower the sound system's volume, but she had no luck with the video playing directly in front of Seth. The plot was thickening: A third woman had entered the scene and was urinating on the cable installer, who appeared to welcome this development.

A glorious South Florida morning was unfurling as they drove across the bridge to the mainland, Biscayne Bay glittering on both sides, a line of massive white cruise ships being serviced at the port off to the right, the city skyline ahead, jutting into a cloudless blue sky.

"It's supposed to be nice tomorrow, too," Cyndi said over the yips and moans of the video. "You're gonna have a nice wedding day."

"If I have a wedding," said Seth.

"Oh, you will," said Cyndi. "You love her, right?"

"Right."

"You want to be with her?"

"Of course."

"That's what matters. Your life together. The wedding isn't important. A wedding is just a party. Believe me. I've been there."

"You're married?"

"I was. For, like, three months."

"Oh."

"He cheated on me. I mean, right from the start. *Before* the start he was cheating on me."

Seth looked over at her. The breeze from the open windows was blowing her long dark brown hair around. Her skin was glowing bronze in the early-morning sun. He noticed, for the first time, that she had green eyes.

"He was an idiot," said Seth.

"Thanks," she said, smiling a wan smile and touching his arm just for a second. "But the point is, I had a big wedding. A Cuban wedding, the *abuelos* and *abuelas* and all the *tios* and the *tias* . . ."

"You're Cuban?"

"Yes. Why?"

"No, nothing, I just didn't get the impression, I mean . . ."

"Because I sound American?"

"No, I didn't mean it like . . . Well, yeah."

She laughed. "My parents came on a boat, *Marielitos*. But I was born here, grew up here."

"You speak Spanish?"

"Of course. I speak Spanish, English, Spanglish. I'm American *and* Cuban, like everybody in Miami. If you meet somebody here with blond hair and blue eyes, maybe he looks like he's a *gringo*, but you better not say something bad about Cubans because suddenly he could be cursing you out, talking bad about your mother, in Spanish. You never know who's a Cuban here or who's married to one."

"I'll keep that in mind. So, anyway, you had a big wedding . . ."

"Yeah, it's the happiest day of my life, right? Everybody's telling me how beautiful and happy I look in my beautiful white wedding dress that cost seven hundred and forty-eight dollars from Nordstrom and that I saved up for for *six months*. And meanwhile my maid of honor, my best friend, she's sitting there at the same table drinking champagne with me and my brand-new husband, who I later found out she slept with *two nights before* the wedding."

"Wow. Your best friend?"

"I thought she was. She ended up getting pregnant and marrying that asshole, and guess what?"

"What?"

"Now he's cheating on her. And guess what else?"

"What?"

"He tried to cheat on her with *me*."

"You're kidding."

"No. He calls me up, this is, like, two months ago, and he's, like, 'Oh, Cyndi, I made a big mistake, I still love you, I want to get back with you.' And I'm, like, 'Aren't you married to Lizette now and she's pregnant?' And he's, like, 'Yeah, but it was a mistake, she's not right for me, you're what I want, baby, we got to get back together.' He's, like, crying on the phone."

"So what'd you say?"

"I said OK."

"*What? Really?*"

"Really. I said, 'Friday night, eleven, meet me at Liv.' That's a night-club at the Fontainebleau, real expensive, way too expensive for my ex, but I told him my friend Paulo works the door there, he's gonna take care of it. So my ex goes there, and Paulo lets him in, takes him to this table, the same table Diddy sits at, A-Rod, those kind of people. It costs, like, five thousand dollars just to sit there. Paulo tells him he can order whatever he wants. So he orders Belvedere, which they charge you, like, four hundred fifty dollars a bottle."

"Wow."

"So I let him sit there an hour, drinking his Belvedere, then I show up wearing the shortest dress I have, shorter than this one, very low-cut, and I am looking *hot*."

"I bet," said Seth, taking what he hoped was a subtle gander at her dress, wondering how she could wear a shorter one and still sit down.

"So he sees me and he's, like, 'Cyndi, baby, you look so good, I love you, blah blah.' So I go, 'Really? You really love me?' And he's, like, 'Yeah, baby, I want you back so bad.' And I say, 'What about Lizette?' And he goes, 'I told you, baby, that was a mistake, I'm leaving her.' And I say, 'What about the baby?' And he says, 'I don't care about the baby.' And I go, 'Anything else you got to say before I put this on YouTube?' That's when he sees I'm holding my iPhone next to my purse, recording him. Which he didn't notice before because he's staring at my boobs."

"You didn't!" said Seth, taking care not to look at her boobs.

"Yes I did."

"So what'd he do?"

"He jumps up, he's yelling, 'You fucking bitch, give me the phone,' but Paulo was watching, and he comes right over, and he's a big guy, so my ex sits right back down. Paulo asks him how he plans to settle the bill and my ex says, 'Wait a minute, you said it was comped.' And

Paulo says, 'I said you could order whatever you want, I didn't say it was comped.' Next thing, there's two bouncers standing over him, ex-Dolphins, telling him he has to go with them to sign some papers so they can take the bill out of his paycheck. He's begging them to let him go, crying like a baby. I walked away nice and slow, let him get a good look at what he had and threw away."

"Wow. Did you post the video on YouTube?"

"Of course. You do not mess with a Cuban woman."

"I'll keep that in mind also."

For a few seconds the car was quiet, except for the frenzied bleatings of the video cast, who had been joined by a woman wearing a strap-on appliance the size of a pool noodle. They were on the mainland now, Seth taking the ramp to I-95 toward the airport.

"My point," said Cyndi, breaking the silence, "is the wedding doesn't matter. I had a great wedding. I looked great, he looked great, everybody had a great time. It didn't mean shit. When I get married the next time, it's gonna be just me and him, and if we're still happy ten years later, *then* I'll buy another seven-hundred-and-forty-eight-dollar dress from Nordstrom and we'll have a big party."

Seth nodded, thinking about Tina's dress, which cost $137,000, plus a trip to London, and featured pearls that had once been worn by Elizabeth Taylor, and those were not even the most important pearls it featured. "I get what you're saying," he said. "But can't you have both things? A really nice wedding *and* you're really in love?"

"Of course you can. I'm sure you will. I'm just saying, I know it's a nice ring, but she's marrying *you*, not the ring, right?"

"Right," said Seth, "but . . . *Jesus*." He swerved to avoid a motorist, who, having missed his exit, was backing up on the interstate. "Did you *see* that?"

"Welcome to Miami," said Cyndi.

"OK, but what I'm saying, about the ring," said Seth. "She put a lot of time and effort into that ring. Into this whole wedding. It's very important to her. She's the kind of person who, whatever she does, she wants to do it perfectly. That's what makes her happy. I want her to be happy."

"Right, and because you care so much if she's happy, that will make her happy. Not the ring. The caring. She's a smart lady. She'll see that. She'll see she's lucky to have a man like you who really cares. That's more important than the dress, the ring, the wedding."

"So let me ask you something," said Seth. "The day you got married, let's say your groom—this is when you were still in love with him before you knew he was cheating on you—let's say that right before the wedding, you're about to go down the aisle, let's say he spilled ketchup all over your seven-hundred-thirty-eight-dollar wedding dress."

"First of all, it was seven hundred and forty-eight dollars, and, second of all, why would he have ketchup when we're about to walk down the aisle?"

"Don't try to wiggle out of this. You know what I mean. If your groom did something stupid that messed up your wedding, would you be, like, hey, I don't care, I'm not marrying the dress, I'm just happy to be with this man I truly love? Or would you be pissed off? The truth."

She thought about it a few seconds, then said, "I would have killed him."

"*Exactly.* So I appreciate the pep talk. But I gotta get the ring. Can you maybe call whatshisname . . ."

"Duane."

"Duane, right, can you call him and see if he had any luck at all?"

"Sure," said Cyndi, pulling her phone from her purse.

They had reached Miami International Airport. Seth pulled up to the curb in front of Arrivals and left Cyndi with the Escalade while he ran into Baggage Claim to find his parents.

He spotted their luggage first. In his youth it had embarrassed him on many a family trip: plastic suitcases from the pre-wheels era in a violently pink hue, like large radioactive wads of bubble gum, purchased from Sears on sale during the Carter administration. Sitting statue-still on a bench next to the suitcases were Seth's parents, Sid and Rose, wearing their standard travel attire: matching purple velour tracksuits, also obtained at a steep discount, and pristine white sneakers. It was unclear to Seth why two people who could take as long as ten minutes to walk across their own living room needed to dress as though at any moment they were going to strip down and compete in the 100-meter high hurdles. But he was long past questioning such things.

He put a smile on his face and strode forward, arms wide. "Mom! Dad!"

His mother turned and registered his presence, her face adopting the expression she had shown him as long as he could remember— love tempered by the disappointment of a woman who had had just the one child, relatively late in life, and had decided that motherhood was not all that it had been cracked up to be.

"What happened to you?" she said.

"I'm really sorry, like I told you, I just got all hung up with wedding stuff and I . . ."

"No, I mean, you look terrible. You look like you were in an accident. Were you in an accident?"

Seth looked down at his wrinkled, still-damp clothes, rubbed his stubbled face, attempted to straighten his salt-encrusted hair. "No, no accident, I just . . . I've been running around since we . . ."

"Was he in an accident?" said Sid.

"He says he wasn't," said Rose. "But he looks like he was. He's a mess."

"What kind of accident?" said Sid. Sid, though nearing eighty, could see and hear reasonably well if he had to. But he preferred to perceive the world through the ever-present interface of Rose so that his impressions and opinions would always be completely in sync with hers; this, Sid had learned over the years, was the key to a peaceful marriage, if not necessarily a happy one.

"I didn't say he was in an accident," said Rose. "I said he *looks like* he was in an accident, but he says he wasn't in an accident."

"Does he need to see a doctor?"

"Why would he need to see a doctor if he didn't have an accident? What he needs is a bath, unless he wants to get married looking like a homeless person."

"I know, Mom. As soon as we get back to the hotel I'm gonna clean up. It's just been . . ."

"I have to go to the bathroom," said Sid.

"No you don't," said Rose. "You just went."

"OK," said Sid.

"All right, then!" said Seth. "The car's outside. I'll get these."

His parents rose. He hefted the suitcases, which, to judge from their weight, contained railroad ties. He took a few steps toward the exit, then glanced back to make sure his parents were following. He continued to the door, then looked back again; his parents did not appear to have made any progress. They had the mysterious ability that some older people have to walk without making any visible progress. Sometimes, even though they clearly intended to go forward, they seemed to be going very, very slowly backward.

Seth put down the suitcases and sighed.

"Well, look who's here," said a voice. "The lovely groom."

Seth turned and saw Customs Agent Roberto Alvarez and his partner, Vincent Peppers, who was holding the leash of Sienna the drug dog.

"Nice luggage," said Alvarez, smirking at the pink blobs.

"It's my parents'," said Seth, nodding toward Rose and Sid.

Alvarez looked over and said, "They potheads, too?"

"Easy," said Agent Peppers.

"This is what you do?" Seth said to Alvarez. "Hang around the airport hassling people?"

"Just doing my job," said Alvarez. "Some of us have to work, you know. Can't all marry rich girls and have their daddies take care of us."

"Easy," repeated Peppers, edging between Alvarez and Seth.

Sid and Rose were finally getting close to the exit. Rose noticed the presence of the police officers and, following procedure, relayed this information to Sid.

"Seth is talking with two police," she said.

"Is he in trouble?" said Sid.

"Are you in trouble with the police?" said Rose.

"No, Mom," said Seth. "It's fine."

"He says he's not in trouble," Rose informed Sid. "But I wouldn't be surprised. You go around looking like a homeless person, you get in trouble with the police."

"What kind of trouble is he in?" said Sid.

Before Rose could update Sid, Sienna started whimpering, her nose pressed against one of the pink suitcases.

"Well, well, well," said Alvarez.

Seth stared at the dog. "You have got to be kidding me," he said, more to Sienna than anybody else. He looked at the Customs agents and pointed to his parents. "I mean, seriously. Do you *see* these two people?"

"What I see," said Alvarez, "is a highly trained U.S. Customs Service drug detection dog alerting on a suitcase. Which is what is known as probable cause."

Seth turned to Agent Peppers. "Seriously?" he said.

Peppers frowned, his eyes on Sienna, his mind on the phone call he received the day before from somebody very high up the totem pole that he was very near the bottom of—somebody who could make Peppers's last seventeen months before retirement extremely unpleasant.

"Come on," Peppers said, pulling the whimpering Sienna away from the suitcase.

"No way," said Alvarez.

"I said, come *on*," said Peppers, walking away.

"Jesus," said Alvarez. He stared at Seth for a few seconds, Seth staring back, two guys meeting their testosterone quotas. Then Alvarez was gone, too.

"I don't see why they allow dogs in an airport," said Rose. "It's unsanitary."

"I have to pee," said Sid.

"No you don't," said Rose.

Seth sighed, picked up the suitcases and resumed leading the long, slow march to the car.

## 11

Cyndi was standing outside the Escalade, phone in hand. She was smiling.

"I got hold of Duane," she said.

"And?" said Seth.

"He found your suitcase."

"Yes!" said Seth. He put down his parents' suitcases and hugged her, their bodies pressing together for two seconds.

"Where is it?" said Seth.

"Well, that's the thing," said Cyndi.

"Is there a problem?"

"OK, what happened is, Duane got to the Clevelander and they had the suitcase and he got it, but then he couldn't bring it back to the Ritz because he had to go to an emergency at work."

"I thought his job was walking around with a snake."

"That's his main job. But he works part-time at Primate Encounter."

"Primate what?"

"Encounter. It's this tourist attraction, they have, like, monkeys and gorillas, but also some snakes. Duane fills in sometimes for the main snake guy, who's sick today, so Duane had to go down there right away because one of the snakes, I think he said anaconda, swallowed this lady's backpack. She set it on the wall so she could take a picture and it fell into the . . ."

"But he definitely has my suitcase? At Primate Adventure?"

"*Encounter*. Right. He has it in his brother's truck, which he drove out there."

"So he's going to bring it to the Ritz?"

"Well, here's the thing. He's going to try to make the snake throw up the backpack because the lady's freaking out because all her stuff is in there, her passport and money and credit cards, plus Duane says it's not really that good for the snake, so he's gonna try to get it to eat a rat that has some medicine inside it that will make it throw up. I don't mean the rat will throw up. I mean the medicine will make the *snake* throw up. But Duane has to figure out how to get the rat to eat the . . ."

"OK, so when he's done with the snake, can he bring the suitcase over here?"

"Well, that's the thing. He was gonna bring it here, but he got *another* call, from the Miccosukee casino, which is also having a snake emergency. You know those pythons? In the Everglades? There's like a million of them out there, breeding like crazy, and one of them got into the casino and it . . ."

"So my suitcase is at the casino?"

"No, he's gonna leave it at Primate Encounter because he says it'll be crazy at the casino, and after he catches the snake he might have to take it somewhere else."

"So where is Primate Encounter?"

"It's in the Redlands."

"Is that close to here?"

"No, it's way down in South Dade. It's, like, maybe an hour."

"Damn. I'll have to go get it after I take everybody back to the hotel. Could you tell me how to get there?"

"Sure. I can ride down there with you, if you want."

"That'd be great."

Sid and Rose had finally tottered all the way to the Escalade.

"It's hot here," said Rose. "How do people live here, in this heat?"

"What?" said Sid.

"I said, it's hot," said Rose.

"I know it's hot. I'm standing right here. You think I can't feel how hot it is?"

"Would you like me to get you some water?" said Cyndi.

"Who're you?" said Rose.

"I'm Cyndi," said Cyndi, extending her hand.

Rose ignored it, turned to Seth. "Who is she?"

"She's a friend," said Seth. "She's helping out with the wedding."

"Helping out doing what?" said Rose, eyeballing Cyndi's dress.

"Is there water?" said Sid.

"I can get you some," said Cyndi.

"He doesn't need water," said Rose. "He had some before."

"What about my medicine?" said Sid.

"When we get to the hotel you'll get your medicine."

"Mom," said Seth, "if he needs his medicine . . ."

"I gave him his heart medicine and his blood pressure," said Rose. "He wants the brownies from the suitcase."

Seth's head jerked around. "He wants the *what*?"

"The brownies from your Aunt Sarah in California. She sends them to your father. For his gout. He likes them."

Seth lowered his voice: "Mom, do you know what's in those brownies?"

"Of course I know. It's marijuana."

"Ohmigod, Mom," said Seth, shooting a glance back toward the terminal entrance. "You brought *marijuana*? In your *suitcase*?"

"It's *medical* marijuana," said Rose. "For his gout. Sarah told me it's perfectly legal. She gets it from a place."

"In *California* it's legal," said Seth. "Here it's not legal."

"Who is she?" said Sid, noticing Cyndi.

"I'm Cyndi," said Cyndi, extending her hand.

Sid turned to Rose. "Is she the one he's marrying?"

"Of course not," said Rose. "He's marrying the other one. This one is helping with the wedding. He says."

"OK, Mom, Dad, let's get in the car, OK?" said Seth.

"I have to pee," said Sid.

"No you don't," said Rose.

This was followed by several minutes of departure preparations supervised rigorously by Rose: getting Sid settled into the backseat; making sure that Seth had put the luggage in the back; fastening the seat belts; adjusting the seat belts because they were too tight; re-adjusting the seat belts because they were too loose; readjusting the seat belts because they were once again too tight; insisting that Seth go back and check to make absolutely sure that he had put the suitcases into the back; reminding Seth that he should not make any sudden starts or stops or drive like a maniac because he could give his father a heart attack. Finally Seth was given clearance by Rose to actually leave the airport. He started the Escalade.

". . . yes yes oh yes that's right fuck me baby yes yes fuck me hard you fucking fucker *fuck me hard!*" moaned the porn-video actress, add-ing, "FUCK ME WITH THAT BIG COCK!!"

"OK!" said Seth, stabbing frantically at the dashboard controls as he drove. "Maybe we can have some music! Cyndi, can you put some music on loud right now please?"

"YES! YES! YES! I'M COMING, BABY! FUCK ME!!!!"

"What is all that racket?" said Rose, leaning forward.

"Nothing!" said Seth, hunching close to the video to block her view.

Cyndi managed to get the audio going. That was the good news. The bad news was, the song currently playing was a tune by 50 Cent titled "I Smell Pussy." Fortunately, the shouted rap lyrics, intermingled with the porn sound track, filled the Escalade with an incoherent cacophony of obscenity.

"Who is that shouting?" said Sid.

"Music, they call it," said Rose.

Finally, as they reached the expressway, the porn actors achieved a spectacular fake climax and the video ended. Cyndi was able to stab the audio off just as the rap artist David Banner launched into "Play," a romantic ballad that begins, "Cum girl, I'm tryna get your pussy wet."

"You call that music?" said Rose.

"So!" said Cyndi brightly. "How was your flight?"

"That's not what I call music," replied Rose.

They rode in silence to Miami Beach, Seth pulling to the curb near the entrance to the Delano.

"Is this the hotel?" said Rose.

"No, Mom," said Seth. "I'm just picking up Marty and Kevin and Steve. It'll just be a minute." She started to ask another question, but Seth was already out of the car, leaving Cyndi to her futile efforts at making small talk with his mother.

Seth entered the Delano Hotel and walked through its desperately hip lobby, consisting of random weird spaces sparsely decorated with unattractive yet at the same time uncomfortable furniture, then through the pool area, then down to the beach. He spotted the Groom Posse immediately: Big Steve on his feet, looming nervously over the wretched, sprawling, sunburned, semi-comatose figures of Kevin and Marty. Kevin was wearing boxers and a T-shirt; Marty was wearing only Big Steve's shirt as pants. Although the beach was filling with sunbathers, the Groom Posse was in the middle of an empty circle of sand ten yards in diameter, nobody wanting to get close.

Big Steve saw Seth approaching. "Finally!" he said.

"Jesus, Seth," said Kevin, getting to his feet. "What took you so long?"

"Oh, right," said Seth. "My bad, failing to anticipate your need to be rescued after you left me, the groom, unconscious at the bar and went off and got robbed and all ended up fucking naked."

"Objection," said Marty, struggling to rise. "We weren't all naked. Just me. And Kevin had no pants."

"Jesus, Marty," said Seth. "Will you please put away your balls?"

"Oops," said Marty, tucking himself back into the neckhole of Big Steve's shirt.

They made their way back through the Delano lobby. "Where'd you get this?" said Kevin as they approached the Escalade.

"It belongs to the stripper's boyfriend," said Seth.

"The stripper showed up?" said Kevin.

"She did," said Seth. "And she's in my room with her boyfriend, who's the size of a post office, and Marty's going to get rid of them both or I'm going to kill Marty."

"Not a problem," said Marty, dismissing the matter with a wave of the hand he was not using to keep his balls inside Big Steve's shirt.

"There's another thing," said Seth. "There's these Haitians in my room."

"There's *what*?" said Big Steve.

"I'll explain later," said Seth. They had reached the car. Seth pasted on a smile as he opened the door and said, "Mom! Dad! Look who's here!"

"It's an oven in here," announced Rose. "Are you trying to kill us in this heat?"

"It's Marty, Kevin and Steve!" said Seth.

Rose peered at the Groom Posse and said, "Were they in an accident?"

"Sort of," said Seth. "But they're fine. Guys, you remember Cyndi from last night?"

Cyndi waved from the front seat.

"Cyndi from last night is still here?" said Kevin, brightening.

"Yeah," said Seth. "It's complicated."

"He *says* she's helping with the wedding," said Rose. "He doesn't say how."

"I can think of lots of ways Cyndi could help," said Kevin.

"Kevin's married," said Seth.

"I can tell," said Cyndi. "Hey, don't forget you need to get diapers and formula."

"Damn, that's right," said Seth. "OK, we'll stop on the way back."

"Diapers and formula?" said Big Steve.

"Just get in," said Seth.

Kevin, Marty and Big Steve clambered back into the third-row seat. Seth started the Escalade and discovered, to his horror, that the video system had rebooted and was now displaying the opening scene of the porn movie in which the cable installer knocks on an apartment door, which is opened, as so often happens in apartment life, by a woman wearing only a lavender thong. To blot out the video sound track Cyndi quickly got the audio system going again, which proved to be a mixed blessing inasmuch as the selection currently playing was the singer

Riskay's plaintive love ballad about a woman who suspects that her boyfriend is unfaithful, titled "Lemme Smell Yo Dick."

They pulled away from the curb encased in a cocoon of cacophonic cursing. There was no conversation, other than Sid asking Rose what all the shouting was and Rose informing Sid that maybe some people called it music but she, Rose, did not call it music.

# 12

Mike and Marcia Clark, impeccably attired in casual yet very expensive resort wear, stood outside the entrance to the Ritz-Carlton, waiting. A few yards away, their security guards, looking as unobtrusive as possible for men the size of forklifts, kept an eye on the surroundings.

Mike, for the twentieth time, glanced at his scarily complex, $380,000 Swiss watch, which had so many dials on it that it took real determination to decipher the actual time. The Clarks were not used to waiting. They were used to having people wait for them, inasmuch as, being Mike and Marcia Freaking Clark, their time was exponentially more valuable than the time of anybody they were likely to encounter. They were waiting for a man named Wendell Corliss, who resided in Greenwich, Connecticut, where he ran a hedge fund worth more than most member nations of the European Union.

But that was not why Mike was waiting for him. He was waiting because Corliss was in a position to give him one of the few things he wanted but could not buy. It happened that Mike belonged to a fanatically exclusive and secret group of powerful businessmen called the Group of Eleven. The Group of Eleven, as the name suggested, was limited by its charter to eleven members. If you wanted to join, you had to wait for somebody to die—assuming you even knew (and very few people did) that the Group of Eleven existed. It was almost impossible just to be considered for membership, let alone be admitted. Warren Buffett had been deemed too *nouveau*. Donald Trump's letters were returned unopened.

The members of the Group of Eleven gathered periodically at fabulously luxurious undisclosed locations for retreats, during which they talked frankly about the kinds of things that men at their level of achievement have on their minds, such as golf and the cruising ranges of their helicopters. There was one topic, however, that the Group of Eleven did not discuss, although it was never far from their thoughts when they got together. It was too painful to bring up, too sensitive even for these tough, commerce-hardened men. For the truth was that despite the fact that they seemed to have everything a man could want—immense wealth, power, influence and spectacular surgically enhanced second or third wives—there was one thing they did not have, and because they did not have it, it was the one thing they wanted above all else.

They wanted to belong to the Group of Six.

This was an even *more* exclusive group, a group so secret that the only people on the planet who knew it existed, outside of the men who actually belonged to it, were the deeply envious members of the Group of Eleven. They had to live with the knowledge that, although they were treated like gods by the mortals around them, they had not reached the pinnacle. There was a higher peak, upon which wealthy men were holding helicopter range discussions to which they were not privy. This gnawed at their guts like a cancer.

It especially gnawed at Mike Clark. He had become obsessed with the Group of Six, consumed by the desire to join it, and now he saw his chance. A prominent eighty-seven-year-old industrialist had recently died; Mike was pretty sure the man had been a member of the Group of Six. That meant there was an opening, and Mike intended to fill it.

The key to his plan was Wendell Corliss, the man Mike was waiting for outside the Ritz. Mike was fairly certain that Corliss was one of the five surviving members of the Group of Six. Corliss had the personal charm of an iguana, but that did not deter Mike, who had cultivated Corliss relentlessly—bringing him in on lucrative business deals, contributing massively to his pet charities, sending him fawning congratulatory notes for every minor achievement, kissing up to him at social events.

His boldest move had been to invite Corliss to his daughter's wedding. To his delight, Corliss had accepted. This was Mike's big chance: He would spend quality time with Corliss, show him what kind of man he was, what kind of family he had. He would not mention the Group of Six explicitly—that would be a serious breach of etiquette—but by the end of the weekend, Corliss would think of Mike as a man he could confidently recommend for membership. Tina's wedding had created the perfect opportunity; now it was a matter of closing the deal. And nobody closed a deal better than Mike Clark.

"Is that his car?" said Marcia, pointing down the driveway.

Mike looked and saw a maroon Bentley Mulsanne approaching, followed by a black SUV.

"Shit," said Mike.

"What is it?" said Marcia.

"I should've brought the Bentley."

"But I thought you said—"

"I *know* what I said." What Mike had said was that he didn't want to bring the Bentley fearing that Wendell Corliss would find it pretentious. Instead, Mike had gone with a rented stretch limo. But here Corliss was, arriving in his Mulsanne, which he must have had flown down from Greenwich. "Shit," said Mike again, wondering if there was time to have *his* Bentley flown in. Or maybe his Maybach, so Corliss wouldn't think he was mimicking him.

No time to think about it anymore; the Bentley was pulling up, a Ritz doorman hustling toward it, only to back quickly away when confronted by two massive bodyguards who'd jumped out of the trailing SUV. Mike was glad he had thought to have his security on hand for the Corliss arrival, even though he didn't really expect to need them. Good to show Corliss how he rolled.

One of the Corliss bodyguards opened a rear door of the Bentley. Out stepped Wendell Corliss, a tall, gaunt, bald man with ice-blue eyes that remained intensely predatory no matter what the rest of his face was doing. Emerging behind Wendell was his third wife, Greta, a tall, Amazonian Swede who had begun her climb to social prominence by working as the Corliss family *au pair* and who compensated for her humble origins by treating all forms of hired help like cockroaches.

Mike and Marcia put on welcoming smiles and stepped forward to greet their guests. Manly handshakes and delicate air kisses were exchanged, followed by a flurry of *How was your flight?*s and *So thrilled you could make it*s and *Delighted to be here*s. Standing at a discreet distance to either side, the Corliss and Clark security details eyeballed each other appraisingly. A team of bellmen, supervised by the Corliss chauffeur, was transferring the Corliss luggage to a cart. Wendell Corliss himself seemed to be in a good mood. Mike was also pleased; so far, things were going smoothly.

And then they heard it, a series of booms, like casinos being rhythmically imploded in the distance. Heads turned toward the source: a black Escalade pulling up to the hotel. The booms were in fact the bass line to a tune by the rap artist Dirt Nasty titled "Fuck Me I'm Famous," a phrase repeated often in the lyrics, which came through loud and clear as the Escalade doors opened.

The first person to emerge, to the slack-jawed horror of the Clarks, was their future son-in-law, looking as though he had not slept, shaved or bathed since they saw him the night before, which in fact he had not. Next out was Cyndi in her very tight, very short dress, carrying a grocery bag and a large package of Huggies. Then came Rose and, with Seth's help, Sid, in their matching tracksuits. Then came Big Steve; then Kevin, in his boxers; and finally Marty, still wearing only a shirt, but not in the manner a shirt was intended to be worn.

The Clarks and the Corlisses regarded the new arrivals with frozen faces. A bellman hefted the pink suitcases out of the Escalade and then a valet drove it away, the speakers still blasting Dirt Nasty.

Seth caught sight of the Clarks, did a double take. "Mike!" he said. "Marcia!"

The Corlisses' heads swiveled toward their hosts, their eyes asking *You KNOW these people?*

"I don't think you met my parents," said Seth. "This is my mom, Rose, and my dad, Sid. Mom, Dad, these are Tina's parents, Mike and Marcia."

The two sets of parents approached each other warily. Mike extended his hand.

"Sid!" said Rose. "Don't stand there like an idiot! Shake his hand!" She turned to the Clarks. "He's tired from the trip, he can't get comfortable on the plane. He has a hip condition, plus he has a sore on his leg that won't heal. You see that stain? On his pants? That's from the oozing. He's in an experimental program for that, they pay all the medical expenses and give him this drug that's supposed to help, but he still has the oozing. You wouldn't believe how much I spend on laundry detergent. Sid, I said SHAKE HIS HAND!"

"My God," said Marcia, quietly but audibly.

"So!" said Seth, herding his parents toward the door. "I'm sure Mom and Dad want to freshen up. We'll see you at the rehearsal dinner! Really looking forward to it!"

"Why are you pushing?" said Rose.

"Who was that?" said Sid.

They disappeared into the hotel, followed by Cyndi, then the Groom Posse. Greta Corliss recoiled visibly as Marty walked past.

There were several seconds of utter silence.

"So," said Wendell carefully, "he's marrying your daughter?"

"Yes," said Mike. "But he's not usually . . . He usually doesn't look like that.

"He's really a fine young man," said Mike.

"He is," said Marcia.

"The one who wasn't wearing pants," said Greta. "Who was that?"

"A friend," said Mike. "Not of *ours*, of course. He knew Seth in college. But he's not really anybody. We don't really know him."

"At all," said Marcia.

"And the woman carrying the . . . with the diapers?" said Greta.

"Nobody," said Marcia.

"I see," said Greta.

"It's just the usual pre-wedding bachelor hijinks," said Mike, smiling to indicate how comical it all was. Neither Greta nor Wendell smiled back.

"So!" said Marcia. "I'm sure you two want to freshen up after your trip."

Greta and Wendell said they definitely wanted to freshen up.

# 13

Seth, having finally got his parents checked in, was back in the elevator, blissfully alone for the moment. His plan was to check on the situation in his suite, maybe grab a quiet nap, then head down to Primate Whatever—to retrieve his suitcase and the ring. He slumped against the wall, exhausted, closing his eyes and fantasizing, briefly, that when he got to his room everything would be all right and he could simply go to sleep.

This was not the case, of course. Wesley, remote in hand, was still overflowing the sofa in front of the flat-screen, surrounded by plates; apparently there had been more deliveries from room service. The bedroom—theoretically, Seth's bedroom—was a combination hospital and nursery. Cyndi and LaDawne had put Huggies on the baby; LaDawne had it cradled in her arm and was feeding it formula from a bottle. Stephane, eyes wide with wonder, was sitting on the floor, watching *SpongeBob SquarePants* on TV.

Laurette, her dark skin in sharp contrast to the fluffy white Ritz bathrobe, was sitting up in bed, looking a little better than before but still very weak. When she saw Seth, she smiled and reached out her hand to him. He went over and hesitantly reached his own hand out; she took it in hers and spoke to him in Creole, her voice soft and raw from swallowing seawater.

"I think she's thanking you again," said Cyndi.

"You're welcome," said Seth to Laurette. He gently pulled his hand away and turned to LaDawne. "Did anybody call here?"

LaDawne nodded. "A man called, a Haitian man said you knew him from the beach."

"What'd he say?"

"He said tell you no luck so far."

Seth's shoulders slumped.

"He's still looking," said LaDawne. "He'll come over here later."

"How much later?"

"He didn't say."

Seth rubbed his weary face with his weary hands. "This isn't gonna work," he said. "I'm getting married tomorrow."

"So, you get married tomorrow."

"But I can't have . . ." Seth gestured toward Laurette. "I mean, I feel bad for her and everything, but she can't stay here."

"Really? You gonna kick her out? With two babies? In her condition? She can't hardly stand up, you really gonna kick her out?"

Seth looked at Laurette, who was looking at him fearfully, picking up on his gestures, his tone. He made himself smile at her. "No," he said. "I'm not gonna kick her out."

"'Course you ain't," said LaDawne. "By the way, somebody else called."

"Who?"

"Girl named Tina. With a attitude. Wanted to know who I was."

"What'd you tell her?"

"Talking to me like that? I told her none of her damn business who I was."

"Oh God. That's my *fiancée*."

"Well, she got a mouth on her."

"Did she say anything else?"

"I don't know. I hung up."

"Oh God," said Seth.

A minute later he was knocking on the door to Tina's suite. It was opened by Meghan, wearing a bathrobe.

"Call me old-fashioned," she said, "but I believe it's traditional for the stripper to leave at some point before the actual wedding."

"Listen, I can explain . . ."

"You don't need to explain to me," said Meghan, waving Seth into the suite. "I'm just the pothead younger sister."

"Where is she?"

"On the balcony. Good luck."

Seth walked through the suite, which was even bigger than his, and found Tina outside on a lounge chair, tanning in a white bikini, looking stunning as always.

"Babe, I'm sorry," he said, leaning over to kiss her.

She accepted the kiss but did not return it. "I'm not insecure," she said.

"I know that. You're the most not insecure person I've ever met. But this—"

"I was fine when I saw the stripper last night—"

"OK, she's not really a—"

"Let me finish."

"OK, sorry."

"I was fine with the stripper you were with last night because it was your bachelor party and I knew she was just some tramp Kevin and Marty hired and you would never do anything to jeopardize our relationship. Also she is nowhere near as hot as I am."

"Of course not. But listen, she's not even—"

"Let me finish. So even though you embarrassed yourself last night in front of me and my parents with the bimbo and the snake guy, I was OK with it because I understand guys get drunk and act like idiots for their bachelor party, and, above all, I trust you. OK, so that was last night. Now it's today, the bachelor party is over and it's the day of our rehearsal dinner. I call your room and a woman answers, apparently a *different* woman, definitely a rude woman, and she won't tell me who she is and she hangs up on me. A woman *in your room* hangs up on *me*."

"Tina, I can explain this."

"Good. Because, as I say, I'm not an insecure person. But I really, really would like an explanation."

"OK. There's Haitians in my room."

"Haitians!"

"Right. Three of them. A mother and two kids. One's a baby."

"And that's who hung up on me? The Haitian mother?"

"No, that was LaDawne."

"And LaDawne is?"

"A stripper. But I swear to God she didn't strip. She was there when I got back last night because Marty hired her, which I told him not to. But she never took her clothes off. Thank God."

"But she's still in your room."

"She's taking care of the Haitians. With Cyndi."

"Who's Cyndi?"

"She's the woman who was with the snake guy. But she's not a stripper. She's just helping out with the Haitians."

"OK," said Tina, "exactly *why* are there Haitians in your room?"

Seth quickly summarized what happened—his falling asleep on the beach, hearing the child's cry. Tina sat up, hands over her mouth, when Seth told her about pulling the Haitians out of the ocean. When he was done, she said, "Ohmigod, Seth, why didn't you call an ambulance?"

Seth explained about Laurette's fear of the authorities. When he was done, Tina said, "I need to talk to Daddy about this." She reached for her phone.

Seth put his hand on her arm. "No."

"Why not?"

"I promised Laurette."

"Laurette?"

"The Haitian woman. She's terrified she'll get sent back. I promised her I wouldn't tell the police."

"My father's not the police. He knows a lot of people. He can fix things. He can help this woman."

Seth thought about Laurette, the way she'd looked at him. He shook his head again. "Teen, I promised her. She trusts me. I know your father's a powerful man, but the kind of people he knows are exactly the kind of people this woman's afraid of. Listen, she has a sister here in Miami. A guy who works for the hotel, a Haitian guy, is looking for the sister. When he finds her, she can take Laurette and the kids and they'll be gone. Let's just let that happen, OK?"

It was Tina's turn to shake her head. "Seth, this is our wedding weekend. We have family and guests here from all over the country. There's a rehearsal dinner in a few hours. We're getting married tomorrow. *Tomorrow*, Seth. We've been planning this wedding for the better part of a year. I think it's great what you did for this woman and I'm happy to give her some money, or maybe we can pay this Haitian man to help her out. We can get her a lawyer . . ."

"She doesn't want a lawyer. She doesn't want to deal with anybody official. She just wants to find her sister."

"OK, fine, but she can't stay here, Seth, not during our wedding. She's a distraction, and she's also, to be honest, a legal risk. Technically, you're harboring a criminal, Seth. She has to go."

Seth stared at her for a few seconds. "Wait a minute. You're worried that I'm breaking a law?"

"I'm just saying that, technically, that's what you're doing."

"The way you were at the airport with Meghan's weed in your suitcase?"

"That's hardly the same thing. That's an idiotic law."

Seth thought about that, then said, "OK, remember the time we were going to the Giants–Redskins game?"

That stopped the conversation for a moment, Tina and Seth both remembering. It happened right after they got engaged. A friend had given Seth a pair of tickets to a Giants–Redskins game, great seats. Seth, a passionate, lifelong Giants fan who rarely got to see his team play live, was pumped. He and Tina were walking to the Metro, Seth in his vintage Lawrence Taylor jersey, exchanging some mostly good-natured smack with Redskins fans also heading for the game, when they came upon a protest demonstration at a bank branch that had an ATM lobby open Sundays.

There were about a dozen protesters, mostly youngish males, their attire traditional urban protest scruffy, in some cases accessorized with bandannas. They had signs and a bullhorn and were chanting slogans critical of this particular bank, which according to them was exploiting The People.

The protesters were blocking the entrance to the lobby, which did not make them popular with several local residents who wanted to get inside and use the ATMs. Particularly unhappy was a fiftyish woman, who, as Seth and Tina paused to watch, was trying to push her way past the line of protesters.

"Let me through!" she shouted. "You people have no right to block this door!"

"This bank has no right to *exist*," said the bullhorn holder, speaking through the bullhorn despite the fact that the woman was perhaps eighteen inches away. "Do you know how this bank does business?"

"I don't care! My money is in there and I want to take some out."

"Let me explain something to you about the foreclosure practices of—"

"I don't want you to explain anything to me! I want you to get out of my way so I can get my money!"

The woman lunged forward; the protesters closed ranks. It was getting ugly. A police car arrived and two officers emerged. This was when Seth said, "Let's go, Tina," and Tina replied, "Just a minute."

The officers waded in, told the protesters they had to let the woman use the ATM. The protesters said no. The police told them they had to step aside or get arrested. Four of the protesters locked arms in front of the door; the rest whipped out cell phones and began recording video. The police got on their radios and called for more police. That was when Seth said, "Tina, we really have to go if we're gonna make the game," and Tina again replied, "Just a minute."

Ten minutes later, she was on her way to jail. She'd gotten into it with the cops, and they'd told her to step aside and she'd told them they couldn't tell her to step aside. She wound up getting arrested along with the Armlock Four, and Seth wound up going to the police station, where he waited uselessly until Tina, with the help of her father, was released. She got out fairly quickly, as these things go, but nowhere near quickly enough for Seth and Tina to make it to the Giants–Redskins game.

Outside the police station, Tina told Seth she was sorry but she hoped he understood why she had to do what she did. Seth told her that, to be totally honest, he did not understand. Tina explained that sometimes you have to stand up for what you believe in even if it was inconvenient, and she was not going to just walk away and let the police run roughshod over a bunch of people who were trying to make a difference by fighting against injustice. And Seth, who usually did not argue with Tina about issues, or really about anything, but who had just missed his first chance to see the Giants live in *fifteen fucking years*, said that it didn't look to him like they were fighting injustice, that it looked to him more like they were a bunch of self-righteous punks with expensive phones who claimed to care about regular people but were in fact keeping regular people from getting their own money out of an ATM. And Tina said, yes, maybe some people were temporarily inconvenienced, but the protesters were creating public awareness of a greater injustice. And Seth asked who, exactly, the protesters were creating this awareness *in* since the only people watching the protest were the police and the people trying to use the ATMs, all of whom clearly thought the protesters were assholes. And Tina, whose cheekbones at this point were deep red, said that was *exactly* the kind of cynical thinking that prevented anything from ever getting changed and if Seth truly felt that it was more important to go to some stupid football game than to stand up for what you believe in, even if it meant getting arrested, then maybe he would be happier being with somebody else because she, Tina, did not ever want to be the kind of person who would just walk away. And Seth, who was still trying to get used to the idea that a person as hot and smart and sought after and (usually) funny as Tina was willing to commit herself exclusively to a guy like him, elected at that point to back right down, telling Tina that he was sorry and that he respected her for standing up for her convictions and getting arrested. Tina asked if he really meant that, and he, not one hundred percent sincerely, said yes, and she said she really was sorry about making him miss the game, and he said, again not one hundred percent sincerely, that it was fine, and that night they had *unbelievable* sex.

Now, on the balcony of her suite, Tina said, "I remember that."

"And remember what you told me outside the police station? About doing the right thing no matter what?"

A pause, then a soft "Yes."

"OK. I'm just trying to do the right thing here."

Tina nodded. "OK," she said. "But you have to *swear* to me you're not going to screw up the wedding."

"Teen, I swear."

"This is really, really important to me, Seth. And my family."

"I know, baby. Me too."

"If you would just let my father . . ."

"Baby, no. I made a promise."

"OK. But I'm serious: Don't screw us up."

"I won't. Laurette will find her sister, she'll leave, we'll get married. It'll be great."

"You swear."

"I swear."

"OK. Now, get out, because I have to get my hair done for the rehearsal and the dinner. And you need to get cleaned up, OK? Because for a good-looking guy, you look like complete shit."

"Thanks." Seth leaned over and kissed her, this time getting something in return. On his way out of the suite, he passed Meghan, who was sitting on a sofa, rolling a joint.

"You lovebirds all patched up?" she said.

"I think so."

"So Daddy won't have to kill you?"

"I'm hoping not."

"I'm kidding. He wouldn't kill you. He'd have one of his thugs kill you. Still kidding. Sort of." She held up the finished joint. "Care to join me?"

"No thanks. I got into enough trouble doing that last night."

"I don't know," said Meghan, lighting the joint, inhaling. "Seems to me if you hadn't done this last night, those people could have drowned."

"You were eavesdropping on me and Tina?"

Meghan exhaled. "Of course. For the record, I think you're right, and I admire the way you stood up to her. People usually don't."

"Thanks." Seth headed for the door. "See you at the rehearsal."

"Be careful," said Meghan.

Seth stopped halfway out. "Of what?"

"There's a reason people don't stand up to her."

"I know, but in this case I think she really agrees with me."

Meghan took another hit. "Sure she does."

Seth hesitated a second, then closed the door.

# 14

Primate Encounter was the kind of tourist attraction that traditionalists loved because it was old but that tourists generally shunned because it was old.

It was started in the twenties during one of Florida's land booms, way out in the southwest Dade County Redlands near the Everglades. Its founder was a man named Dan Seckinger, who was drawn to South Florida primarily because of its distance from Duluth, Minnesota, where he was wanted for passing bad checks, bigamy and assault with a hockey stick. Seckinger, in the great Florida tradition, was looking for a way to get money from people without doing a great deal of work and hit on the idea of running a tourist attraction.

His first enterprise was called Snake Village. It was a roadside hut with a dozen small cages inside; for ten cents, tourists could gawk at a variety of snakes, all of which, according to the signs Seckinger had made, were EXTREMELY DANGEROUS. This was highly inaccurate: All of the snakes were harmless. Several of them, in fact, were dead. Seckinger found them on the roads, squashed by cars; he cleaned them up and put them in the darker cages, posing them so that the tire marks didn't show. When tourists asked why these snakes didn't move, Seckinger explained that they were "night feeders."

Snake Village enjoyed modest success, prompting Seckinger to dream bigger. He changed its name to Reptile City and added lizards, turtles and alligators to the menagerie. All of the new additions were alive; the problem, from a showmanship perspective, is that most of the time they were no more animated than the roadkill snakes. The alligators were especially disappointing. Although Seckinger's signs described them as FEROCIOUS MONSTER LIZARDS OF THE SWAMP, they spent days on end lying inertly in the muck like logs, but less animated.

In an effort to liven things up, Seckinger brought in Chief Brave Savage, billed as "A Noble Seminole Indian Warrior, Raised in the Darkest Heart of the Vast Trackless Everglades Swamp." In reality he was a Cuban immigrant named Carlos Penin, who took the job to earn tuition money so he could study civil engineering.

As Chief Brave Savage, Carlos would wrestle an alligator four times a day on weekdays and six times on Saturdays and Sundays. This required him to wade into the pen and engage in what Seckinger billed as a "Death Struggle with an Alligator," which required considerable acting on Carlos's part because the alligators were not at all interested in wrestling. They were interested in the same activities they had been interested in for millions of years: eating and, very occasionally, mating. But since they were fed regularly, they had no desire to eat Carlos, and they definitely did not find him sexually alluring.

Thus the wrestling show consisted of Carlos dragging an extremely reluctant alligator around in the muck, looking less like a man engaged in a Death Struggle than like a man moving a roll of waterlogged carpet. Meanwhile Seckinger, from the crowd, sought to add drama by shouting warnings such as, "Watch out, Chief! He almost got you there!"

The Death Struggle, with a succession of non–Native Americans playing the role of Chief Brave Savage, carried Reptile City for several decades. But by the seventies, business had slacked off badly. Tourists wanted the spectacular flash and dazzle of Disney World, where they could see semi-lifelike animatronic alligators; they weren't going to stop at some run-down roadside shack to look at real ones. In the eighties, Reptile City, now operated by Seckinger's descendants, tried to revive itself by capitalizing on the popularity of *Miami Vice* by obtaining two chimpanzees, dubbed Crockett and Tubbs. Costumed in tiny pastel sport jackets, they starred in a show wherein they shot toy guns, and occasionally flung real feces, at actors portraying drug dealers, while the PA system blared Phil Collins wailing "In the Air Tonight."

The *Miami Vice* craze ended, but Crockett and Tubbs stayed on, and over time were joined by a variety of monkeys donated to Reptile City by naïve South Floridians who had thought they were bringing home a fun family pet, only to find themselves sharing their home with a hyperactive, poo-flinging banshee. By the nineties, Reptile City had again reinvented itself, this time as Monkey Adventure, which became, in the environmentally sensitive twenty-first century, Primate Encounter, its signage now rife with buzzwords such as HABITAT, RAIN FOREST, ECOSYSTEM and SUSTAINABILITY, although it was still basically a roadside shack exhibiting critters in crates.

These critters still included snakes, one of which—an anaconda named Trixie—had this day swallowed a lady tourist's backpack, which is how Duane, as Primate Encounter's backup snake guy, got the emergency call. He'd driven out in his brother's truck and, with effort, managed to get Trixie to swallow a doctored rat, which eventually caused her to regurgitate both the rat and the backpack. Neither came back out in great shape, but that was not Duane's problem.

Duane's plan had been to retrieve the backpack, then drive over to the Ritz and give Seth his suitcase. But he'd received another emergency call, this one from Miccosukee Resort & Gaming out by the Everglades, where a seriously large python had somehow got onto the casino floor and wrapped itself around a *Wheel of Fortune* slot machine, where it apparently intended to stay. This had attracted a lot of attention, none of which was proving to be good for business; even the seriously dedicated slot players—people who had been known to continue feeding quarters into their machines while a neighboring player keeled over with a heart attack—were giving the python a wide berth. This meant many machines were going unused; hence the casino's urgent summons to Duane, who had developed a reputation as one of Miami's go-to python wranglers.

And so it was that Duane elected to leave Seth's suitcase at Primate

Encounter. He entrusted it to a man named Gene Singletary, whose official title was Director of Operations, in which capacity he spent the bulk of his day picking up monkey shit. Duane had told Gene a guy named Seth would be coming by for the suitcase, but as the day wore on, no Seth appeared, and closing time was looming. Gene tried to call Duane but got voice mail. After giving the matter some thought, he called Duane again and left a message, saying that he'd leave the suitcase under a tarp behind the animal cages so his friend could pick it up after hours. He said it'd be safe enough because to get back there after hours you had to go through the security gate, which had a key-pad lock. Gene included the code in the message to Duane.

And so as dusk approached, Seth's suitcase was sitting on the ground under a tarp next to a cage occupied by an orangutan named Trevor, who had a lot of time on his hands.

# 15

**Seth woke up** in a chair in the living room of his suite, looked at his watch and said, "Shit." He'd meant to close his eyes for just a few minutes, then go get the suitcase. But instead, despite the noise in the suite—LaDawne and Cyndi mothering the Haitians, the baby fussing, Wesley watching SportsCenter—Seth had fallen sound asleep. Now it was too late to go for the suitcase. He'd have to get it after the rehearsal dinner.

He rose and stretched, surveying the suite. Little had changed. The inert mass of Wesley was still on the sofa, surrounded by still more room service platters. Tina's parents were paying for the suite; Seth hoped they wouldn't look too closely at the bill. Wesley had been joined in front of the TV by Stephane, the two of them watching ESPN's top ten plays. At the moment, LeBron James, in open defiance of the laws of physics, was leaping over another player's head to snare a pass from Dwyane Wade, then slam the ball through the rim.

"You see that?" said Wesley, nudging Stephane with a forefinger the size of a salami. "Lemme see Kobe do *that*."

Stephane, eyes wide, looked at Wesley, then back at the screen.

Seth crossed the suite and poked his head into the estrogen festival that was the bedroom. The TV was tuned to *Say Yes to the Dress*. LaDawne and Cyndi were sitting on opposite sides of the bed, Cyndi holding the baby. Laurette was between them, propped up in the pillow forest. When she saw Seth, her face lit up with a radiant smile, brilliant white teeth against dark skin, eyes shining. She said something in Creole, holding both hands out toward Seth. He responded with an awkward wave.

"She thinks you're Superman," said LaDawne.

"I wish," said Seth.

"The Haitian guy called," said LaDawne. "Carl. While you was asleep."

Seth brightened. "And?"

"He said he's still looking."

Seth's shoulder's sagged; he put his face in his hands. "Great."

"He said don't give up," said LaDawne. "He's still looking. He'll be here later."

"Duane called, too," said Cyndi.

Seth looked up. "Don't tell me there's a problem with the suitcase."

"No, it's at Primate Encounter." She relayed Duane's message that the suitcase had been left under a tarp in back of the animal cages. Duane also told Cyndi the code to the security gate, which she'd written down.

"I'll have to get it after the rehearsal dinner," said Seth. "Are you still up for showing me where that place is?"

"Sure," said Cyndi. "I can wait here until your dinner's over and we'll go."

"Thanks," said Seth. He glanced at his watch again. "Jesus, the rehearsal's in an hour."

"You gonna wear that?" said LaDawne, looking at Seth's wrinkled, stained clothes, which he'd been wearing for more than a day.

"All my other clothes are in my suitcase."

"The hotel store sells clothes," said Cyndi.

"Like, clothes that I could wear to the rehearsal dinner?" said Seth.

"Anything is better than what you got on," said LaDawne.

It took Seth ten minutes to rouse the Groom Posse, who were sound asleep in a darkened suite reeking of BO and farts. Seth herded them down to the hotel store, Marty and Kevin wearing hotel bathrobes, as neither had pants. The store had a limited selection of men's clothes, so they ended up buying overpriced golf outfits, which Seth, wincing, charged to his room. They went back to the Groom Posse suite to shower and change, after which Seth headed to his parents' room to escort them to the rehearsal.

He paused outside their door, put a smile on his face, knocked.

Rose opened the door, wearing a Hawaiian Punch–red pantsuit and what looked like a pound of matching lipstick. Her hairstyle had been sprayed to the point where it could deflect rifle fire.

"Hi, Mom!" said Seth.

"This is what you're wearing?" she said. "A bowling outfit?"

"It's really more golf, but—"

"Who is that?" said Sid. Sid was wearing the brown suit he had worn to Seth's bar mitzvah.

"It's Seth," said Rose. "He's wearing a bowling outfit."

It took several minutes, but Seth managed to get his parents moving toward the door. They'd almost made it when Sid declared that his gout was acting up and he needed his medicine.

"You don't need it now," said Rose.

"I'm telling you," said Sid, "this gout is killing me."

"He just wants a brownie," Rose informed Seth. Seth had forgotten about the brownies.

"I do *not* just want a brownie," Sid declared. "I have a *medical condition.*"

"All right, already," said Rose. "You'll get your brownie, but not until after you eat your dinner. Seth, go get the brownies from your father's suitcase."

"Mom, I don't know if that's a good idea."

"So now you're a doctor? In your bowling outfit?"

Seth sighed and rummaged through Sid's suitcase, where he found a shoe box–sized plastic box with a pharmaceutical label on it. He opened it and stared: There were several dozen individually wrapped brownies inside. He started to take one out.

"Just give me the whole box," said Rose.

"What? There's a *lot* of brownies in here, Mom."

"I don't want to leave them in the room," she said. "The people who work in these hotels, you never know. Plus I might need one later also, for my digestion."

Seth stared at her. "You eat these things, too?"

Rose showed a trace of embarrassment but quickly recovered. "It's *medical*. Now, give it to me."

Seth handed her the box. She put it into her enormous black purse, from which Seth had seen her pull a wide variety of objects over the years, including air fresheners, a spatula and, once, a fire extinguisher. Seth looked at his watch again: They were late for the rehearsal. He started down the hall. Halfway to the elevator, he looked back; Rose and Sid had managed to move about five feet. Seth sighed, turned and trudged toward them.

"Are we going back already?" said Sid.

## 16

Trevor was a mature male orangutan. He weighed 250 pounds, and though he stood just a little over five feet tall, he had an arm span of nearly eight feet. He was, like all orangutans, very strong compared to humans—stronger than five large, fit men.

Trevor had been imported illegally to South Florida from Malaysia as an infant. He spent his early years in the possession of a series of dimwits in the narcotics business who thought it would be cool to have an orangutan as a pet. All of them had quickly learned otherwise. Several had been hospitalized; one lost an ear. Trevor had suffered retaliations, having been stabbed twice and shot once in the leg. He recovered each time, but had developed a deep-seated distrust for men.

Women were a different matter. There were no female orangutans in Trevor's life and he had his needs. He was attracted to human females and found that they treated him much better than males, although, with the exception of one incident involving the very wasted girlfriend of an Oxycontin dealer, they had resisted his efforts to mate with them. But Trevor was an incurable romantic: He never stopped trying with the ladies.

After five years of being passed from dimwit to dimwit, growing larger and stronger all the time, Trevor had been dumped late one night at Primate Encounter in a packing crate. He was received enthusiastically by management and soon became a star attraction, although he was a headache for the animal handlers—hostile to the men, always hitting on the women.

Trevor lived alone in a large cage with ropes, a tire swing and a log climbing structure for his amusement. By the standards of Primate Encounter, it was fairly lavish. But orangutans are not goldfish; they know when their recreational options are limited. There are only so many times an orangutan can swing on the same tire or climb up the same log before it thinks the orangutan equivalent of *Fuck this*. Trevor had reached that point. And he was only five years old. In captivity, he could live to be sixty. Basically, he was serving a fifty-five-year life sentence with no possibility of parole. He didn't know this exactly; neither law nor math was his strong suit. But he did know he was bored shitless.

And so when the male human who smelled like a snake went around behind his cage and left something there, Trevor perked up. This was new, and new was interesting. When the humans had left Primate Encounter, Trevor went to the back of his cage and peered through the bars. He saw the tarp several feet away in a clump of tall grass. He studied it for a few moments, then reached his right arm through the cage. With effort, he managed to get his hand on the edge of the tarp and pull on it. It came easily.

Trevor pulled the tarp through the bars and into the cage. He held it up to his huge moony face and smelled it. It was not particularly interesting. He tossed it aside.

Trevor went back and peered through the bars. He saw the suitcase. He reached his arm through the bars but could barely touch the suitcase with his fingertips. He shifted his position and reached his arm through again, straining. This time he was able to get enough purchase with his fingers to pull the suitcase an inch closer. He strained again and grabbed it this time, dragging it up to the bars.

The suitcase was too big to pass through the bars. But it was made of fabric, so it could be squashed. And Trevor was strong. He got both hands on it and gave a hard yank. The suitcase came through the bars. Trevor studied it, sniffed it. He could tell there were things inside it. He didn't know yet how to get to those things. But he had plenty of time.

## 17

The wedding rehearsal was held on the putting-green-perfect lawn behind the Ritz, overlooking the ocean; this was where the ceremony would take place the next day, in the Wedding Gazebo, currently being decorated for the occasion by workers.

In charge of the rehearsal was the wedding planner, Blaze Gear, a tall, thin woman with short-cropped black hair who, when she woke up in the morning, inserted her Bluetooth earpiece even before she went to the bathroom. She was dressed completely in black, as were her two assistants, Traci and Tracee.

Blaze, clipboard in hand, was explaining the wedding procession.

"All of you will be starting out from inside the hotel, except our officiant," she said. "Where is our officiant, Mr. . . ." She looked at her clipboard. "Mr. Dazu?"

A short, balding man with an unkempt gray beard stepped forward. He was wearing sandals and a white robe with a suit jacket over it. "I am Banzan Dazu," he said. He had been born Norman Cochran, in Avalon, New Jersey, and had worked as a record promoter in Philadelphia in the seventies before he discovered how much easier it was to get laid if you were a holy man.

"And how shall I address you?" Blaze Gear asked Dazu.

"You may call me Your Holiness," said Dazu. He smiled at Blaze with an expression reflecting wisdom and deep inner tranquility. He practiced in the mirror.

Tina's parents had not been happy about having Dazu do the ceremony. They wanted an Episcopalian priest, because they belonged to an Episcopal church, which they attended faithfully every other Christmas. But in this matter, as in virtually every matter involving the wedding, Tina got what she wanted, and she wanted Banzan Dazu, whom she regarded as her spiritual mentor.

She had met Dazu at a lecture by the Dalai Lama, whom Tina regarded as the wisest person alive. After she and Seth got serious, she'd taken him to a Dalai Lama lecture in Switzerland. Seth had not been impressed. As far as he could tell, the Dalai Lama message boiled down to: *Be nice.* This didn't strike Seth as particularly profound. It was pretty much the same lesson he'd been taught by his preschool teacher, Mrs. Wheatley, the difference being that people didn't fly around the world and pay big bucks to hear Mrs. Wheatley say it.

Of course Seth didn't express this view to Tina. Nor did he object when Tina declared that she wanted their wedding ceremony to be performed by Banzan Dazu, although Seth thought he was kind of creepy, always looking up Tina's skirt during their premarital counseling sessions.

"All right, Your Holiness," said Blaze Gear. "At the start of the ceremony, you'll be positioned on the Wedding Gazebo, facing the procession. Now I need my groom and his parents."

Seth shepherded Rose and Sid forward.

"There you are!" said Blaze. She extended her hand to Rose. "You must be Seth's mother. I'm Blaze Gear."

"Blaze *what*?"

"Gear."

"That's your name?" said Rose.

"That's my legal name, yes. I originally—"

"Who's she?" said Sid.

"She says her name is Blaze Gear," said Rose.

"That's her name?"

"I just want you to know," said Blaze, soldiering on, "that my job is to make this wonderful occasion as enjoyable for you as possible, so if there's anything you need, anything at all, just let me know, OK?"

"I could use a glass of water," said Sid.

"Certainly," said Blaze, signaling. "Tracee, would you—"

"He doesn't need it," said Rose.

"OK!" said Blaze, waving Tracee off and turning away to avoid any further interaction with Rose and Sid. "Now, where's my maid of honor?"

She got them lined up in processional order. Behind Seth and his parents were the groomsmen—Kevin, Big Steve and Tina's brother, Eric. They were paired up with Tina's bridesmaids, all old friends of Tina's, all bombshells. Behind them were Meghan, the maid of honor; and Marty, the best man.

Kevin was paired with Tina's Harvard roommate, a blonde named Kirsten. In heels, she was a good three inches taller than Kevin, a fact that did not deter him in the least.

"It looks as though we'll be spending some time together," he said. "My name's Kevin. And you are . . ."

". . . well aware of your reputation," said Kirsten.

"Whoa whoa whoa," said Kevin, raising his hands. "What've you heard about me?"

"That you're married, for one," said Kirsten. "Also that you'll try to stick your dick into pretty much any warm orifice."

"Not true!" objected Marty, listening from behind them. "It doesn't have to be warm."

"Anyway," said Kirsten, shaking Kevin's hand formally, "I'm Kirsten. And please don't take this the wrong way, but the total amount of time we'll be spending together is however long it takes to get up and down the aisle, OK?"

"We'll start there," said Kevin, holding on to her hand, "and see what develops. By the way, you have fantastic skin."

"Wow," said Kirsten, pulling her hand away.

Behind Marty and Meghan were Tina and her parents, dressed elegantly for dinner. Mike and Marcia did not look pleased about the attire of the groom and his groomsmen, but they didn't say anything.

Behind the Clarks, standing a few yards apart from the group and looking bored yet observant, were Mike's two massive bodyguards, Ron Brewer and Paul Castronovo, wearing khaki slacks, polo shirts and navy blue sport jackets. Brewer and Castronovo were former New York City Police detectives, veteran partners who had left the force under the cloud of an Internal Affairs investigation arising from the unusual number of cases wherein suspects whom they were about to apprehend elected instead—according to Brewer and Castronovo's official reports—to leap voluntarily to their deaths from the roofs of tall buildings. This had happened often enough that the other detectives had—not without a certain amount of respect—nicknamed Brewer and Castronovo the Tinker Bells, in recognition of the magical power they had to enable people to fly, at least for brief periods.

The Tinker Bells liked working for Mike Clark. He paid a lot better than the NYPD and he wasn't picky about how they handled problems as long as it stayed out of the news. In fact, Brewer and Castronovo got the impression that Mike had hired them specifically because of their reputation. He seemed to enjoy it when they got physical with people who dared to approach him in public or simply happened to be in his way.

With the wedding party lined up in processional order, Blaze Gear led everyone across the lawn to the Wedding Gazebo, which overlooked the section of beach where Seth had pulled Laurette and her children out of the waves. The beach was dotted with groups of sunbathers, kids shouting, random music coming from various devices. Motorboats cruised past offshore; closer to the beach, two young men on Jet Skis chased each other in ever-tightening circles, jumping each other's wakes.

Blaze gathered the wedding party around her and began going over the timetable for the ceremony. The Jet Skis got closer, engines snarling.

"I can't hear a thing," Rose announced.

"What?" said Sid.

"I SAID I CAN'T HEAR A THING!"

"I CAN'T HEAR YOU!" said Sid.

The truth was, at that point, nobody could hear much over the din of the Jet Skis.

"Maybe we should do this inside," said Seth.

"What if they're here tomorrow?" said Tina. "They'll ruin the wedding."

"No they won't," said Mike. He walked over and said something to Brewer and Castronovo, nodding toward the Jet Skiers. Immediately the two big men started lumbering toward the wooden walkway to the beach.

"What're they gonna do?" said Kevin. "Swim out there and punch them?"

As the wedding party watched from the gazebo, the Tinker Bells crossed the beach, stopping at the water's edge. Brewer waved an arm over his head, getting the attention of the Jet Skiers, who were now about twenty yards offshore. Brewer made a shooing gesture: *Get out of here.* The Jet Skiers thought that was pretty funny. One of them gave Brewer the finger. The other revved his engine and moved closer, laughing, beckoning mockingly at Brewer: *Come and get me.*

What happened next happened quickly and went unnoticed by almost everyone outside of the wedding party. Brewer said something to Castronovo, who stepped a little to the right, shielding Brewer. Brewer unbuttoned his jacket and shifted his position slightly. Then there was a faint popping sound, barely detectable over the roar of the engines and the other beach noises.

"What the hell?" said Kevin.

As he spoke, the closer Jet Ski began sputtering and emitting smoke. Its driver, no longer cocky, dove off and swam frantically to the other machine. He scrambled onto the back, barely making it aboard before the driver gunned the engine and took off at full speed toward the horizon. Both driver and rider looked back repeatedly and fearfully. The remaining Jet Ski bobbed in the swells. It coughed out a last plume of smoke and died.

Brewer and Castronovo turned and walked calmly back up the beach, Brewer buttoning his jacket. A dozen or so sunbathers were looking at them; several were applauding.

For a few seconds, the wedding party stood in stunned silence. Then Big Steve said, "Did he just *shoot* at them?"

"Of course not," said Tina.

"Definitely," said Meghan.

"Wait, he *shot a Jet Ski?*" said Kevin. "Even in Miami, that has to be against the law."

"Well," said Marty, "legally, he—"

"Legally, he works for Mike Clark," said Meghan. "That's really all you need to know."

Seth was looking at Tina. "Seriously?" he said.

"First," she said, "we don't really know what happened."

"I think we do. I think your father's bodyguard just—"

"*Second,*" said Tina, "nobody got hurt. And third, those idiots were disturbing the peace and operating illegally close to the beach in a designated swimming area."

"Illegally?" said Seth.

"Yes," said Tina. "Somebody could've gotten hurt."

Seth stared. "You're kidding, right?"

"Seth, I don't want to talk about this anymore. This is supposed to be our wedding rehearsal, so let's just focus on that, OK? We've already had enough distractions." She looked pointedly in the direction of the hotel.

Seth hesitated, then said, "OK."

Blaze Gear resumed the briefing, which was pretty simple: Everybody would walk from the hotel to the platform, Banzan Dazu would perform the ceremony, everybody would walk back to the hotel. It was going to be wonderful, Blaze declared. A perfect day. She asked His Holiness Banzan Dazu if, as officiant, he would like to say a few words about the ceremony and he said he would.

First he held his arms out and turned his face toward the sky, eyes closed, looking holy. He held that pose for quite a while, long enough to make everybody else uncomfortable. Then he opened his eyes and beamed at the group, especially at Mike and Marcia Clark, who were paying his fee plus expenses, including first-class airfare. He found Tina with his eyes, beckoned and said, "Come here, my child."

Tina came over and stood next to her mentor. Seth figured that, as the other half of the wedding couple, he would be beckoned next and had taken half a step forward when Dazu instead beckoned to Meghan. She came over and stood on his other side, she and her sister forming a holy-man sandwich.

Dazu put his arms around the sisters' waists and squeezed them in a manner that could be seen as affectionate and paternal but also could be seen as a way that an older man subtly puts his hands on two attractive young women's asses. Holding them tight, Dazu beamed at the group again—he was a skilled beamer—and began to speak.

"We are all seekers," he said. "We seek love and we seek happiness. We know that love is not happiness and happiness is not love. But without love, it is not possible to be happy. And without happiness, it is not possible to love. And so we seek them both." He beamed again. Tina was nodding a nod that said *So true, so true.* Everybody else was trying to look thoughtful, except for Sid, who whispered loudly, "What did he say?"

"I don't know," said Rose.

"As we seek," said Dazu, "as we walk on this journey of life, we ask, Why are we here? Who are we? Who am I, and who are you? Who are the people we meet along the way?" Here he gave Tina and Meghan a squeeze; Seth noted that the holy hands had drifted lower.

"But when we ask these questions," Dazu continued, "we only make it more difficult to find the answer. Because if we are always seeking, we are never finding. We must understand that it is only when we *stop* seeking something that we can find it. But we must not *try* to stop seeking. For to *try* is to fail. It is only when we learn *not* to try to stop seeking, to simply allow the stopping of the seeking to *be*, that we will succeed. Then we will understand that we did not need to succeed at all, for what we are seeking has been with us all along."

"Is this the wedding?" said Sid.

"Be quiet," said Rose.

"You ask me, What is the purpose of life?" Dazu said, although in fact nobody had asked him that. "I answer you with another question: What is the purpose of having a purpose?"

Out of the corner of his eye, Seth saw someone waving at him. He looked over; it was Carl Juste, the Haitian groundskeeper. Seth slipped away from the wedding party, getting a look from Tina. He went to Juste and stood close, the two of them whispering.

"Did you find the sister?" said Seth.

"There is a problem," said Juste.

"What kind of problem?"

"The sister was arrested."

"*What?*"

"Yes. But I talked to the sister on the phone. She has a lawyer. She thinks maybe she can get out by tomorrow. Then she can take Laurette and the children."

"But I'm getting *married* tomorrow." Seth glanced over at Tina, still in the clutches of Banzan Dazu but looking his way. "This is getting ridiculous."

"The sister asked me to tell you, Please, just one more day. Please."

Seth looked over at Tina again. Now she was glaring.

"I have to go," said Juste.

"But what am I supposed to do?"

"Please, just one more day," said Juste. He turned and walked away before Seth could say anything.

Seth trudged back to the wedding party. Dazu was still dispensing insights.

"And so," he was saying, "what you will find, when you finally reach your destination, is this: You have been there the whole time."

"Kind of like in *The Wizard of Oz*," said Meghan. "When Dorothy discovers there's no place like home."

This drew a glare from Tina, but Dazu was delighted.

"Exactly!" he said, giving Meghan's ass a congratulatory squeeze. "Now, if I may continue, the journey that we are on . . ."

"Oh my goodness!" interrupted Blaze Gear, staring with fake surprise at her watch. "This has been so fascinating that I totally lost track of the time! I'm sorry, Your Holiness, but we really do need to get to the rehearsal dinner."

Dazu reluctantly released the sisters, and the wedding party, relieved to be done with having its consciousness raised, started moving toward the hotel. Tina went straight to Seth, looking unhappy.

"Did you really have to do that?" she said.

"Do what?"

"Go over and talk to that janitor when Banzan was speaking."

"He's not a janitor. He's a groundskeeper."

"Whatever. Did you have to interrupt the rehearsal for that?"

"Teen, he's the guy trying to find Laurette's sister."

"*Trying?* He hasn't found her?"

"Not yet, but he says that by tomorrow—"

"Tomorrow? *Tomorrow?* Seth, you swore you wouldn't let this screw up the wedding."

"I know, and I won't."

They had stopped on the walkway to the hotel, letting the rest of the wedding party go ahead.

"Then why can't you get rid of this Lornette?"

"Laurette."

"*Whatever.* Why can't the groundskeeper take her home?"

"Teen, she's not a stray dog."

"I *know* that. I'm just asking why the fucking groundskeeper can't take her until he finds the sister?"

"He lives here, in hotel housing. He can't take her. And it's not really his responsibility."

"Well, why the fuck is it *your* responsibility?"

Her raised voice had drawn the attention of the rest of the group up ahead. Mike turned and walked back to Tina and Seth.

"Is there a problem, baby?" he said.

"We're OK," said Seth.

"I didn't ask you," said Mike. "I asked my daughter. She doesn't look OK to me. What's wrong, baby?"

Tina sniffed and shook her head. "It's nothing. I just want . . . It's nothing."

"You just want *what?*"

"I just want everything to be perfect."

"Of course everything's going to be perfect. What's not perfect? What's the problem?"

Tina and Seth exchanged a look, Seth shaking his head very slightly. "It's nothing," Tina said.

Mike studied her for a few seconds. "OK, baby. Whatever it is, I'll let it go for now. But"—he looked pointedly at Seth, then back at Tina—"if you need anything, anything at all, you just tell me, and I will make it right for you. OK, baby? *Anything.*"

"OK, Daddy."

"That's my girl."

With a last hard look at Seth, Mike rejoined his wife, saying something quietly to her that made her look at Seth.

"They hate me," said Seth.

"No they don't," said Tina.

"They don't look at me like I'm their future son-in-law. They look at me like I'm a giant tapeworm."

"That's ridiculous. They love you."

"Then why are they looking at me that way?"

"Because they think you're making me unhappy."

"Am I making you unhappy?"

"Right now, yes."

Suddenly her perfect blue eyes overflowed, tear tracks cascading down her perfect pink cheeks. She was not normally a crier, and rarely looked so vulnerable. To Seth, she had never looked more beautiful. He reached out and pulled her to him, felt her sobbing into his shoulder.

"Teen," he said. "I'm sorry."

"I know you're just trying to be a good guy," she said, her voice wavering. "I know that. You're a nice guy, and you want to be nice to everybody, and you're being nice to the Haitians and I understand that." She pulled back so she could look at him. "But this is my wedding. This is *our* wedding. Why can't we have our wedding be just for *us*?" She went back to his shoulder and resumed sobbing.

Seth held her for a while, feeling awful, every sob a punch to his heart.

Finally he said, "OK."

Tina looked up at him. "OK what?"

"OK, you're right. This is insane. I can't be the only person in Miami who can help these people. There has to be someplace else they can go. I'll just tell them I'm sorry but I'm getting married and they have to leave."

"You will? Really?"

"Really."

"When?"

"Tonight. After the rehearsal dinner."

"Really?"

"Really. I'll just tell them they have to go. It'll be OK. They'll just . . ." He trailed off because he had no end to that sentence.

Tina smiled hugely, hugged him hard. "Thanks, baby." She took his arm, and they resumed walking toward the hotel, a handsome, happy couple once again. Seth glanced over at Tina; she was smiling at her parents. Her cheeks were dry; her tears were gone.

# 18

In the end, Trevor solved the problem of how to open the suitcase by simply ripping it apart. He dumped the contents onto the dirty cement floor of his cage and began going through them. Most of them were clothes, and they smelled like a man. This displeased Trevor, so he urinated on them.

With that taken care of, he found Seth's toiletries kit, which he also ripped open. Out spilled a variety of interesting things, including a tube of Crest toothpaste, which Trevor tore open and ate. *Not bad.* He then picked up a Right Guard deodorant stick and managed to get the cap off. He sniffed the gel, took a bite, then spat it out. *Bad.*

Something caught Trevor's eye on the floor: a small red-velvet-covered box that had been tucked in among the clothes. He picked it up and sniffed it. It had a little bit of man scent on it, but much more of a woman scent. Trevor inhaled deeply. He liked it. This was something he would treasure.

# 19

The rehearsal dinner was held in a private banquet room in the hotel's upscale Italian restaurant. On hand, besides the wedding party, were several of Tina's relatives, as well as Wendell and Greta Corliss, who were included as part of Mike Clark's full-court press on Wendell. The diners sat at one long table, with the Clarks and Corlisses at the end farthest from Seth's parents.

The dinner, which was paid for by the Clarks, was first class. The wine was both expensive and plentiful; as it flowed, the lingering tension of the rehearsal receded from the room. Seth and Tina sat at the center of the table, the two of them feeling closer than they had since they'd arrived in Miami.

The food came in courses, each more delicious than the last. Finally, when everyone was stuffed, it was time for the serving of the Groom's Cake.

The Groom's Cake is allegedly an old Southern wedding tradition that nobody ever heard of until about five years ago when the wedding industry, always on the lookout for ways to make weddings more expensive, started hyping it. The idea is to have a special cake just for the groom, reflecting some special thing about him. Tina had commissioned a high-end New York cake designer to produce a cake shaped like a football, sporting the logo of the New York Giants and an amazingly lifelike portrait, in frosting, of Eli Manning. This cake was to be a surprise, presented to Seth by Tina at the end of the dinner. For now, it was hidden under a silver dome on a cart near the end of the table.

Also at that end of the table were Rose and Sid. They had been fairly well behaved for most of the meal, but now Sid, declaring that his back was bothering him, had started pestering Rose for his medication, by which he meant one of the brownies that Rose's sister Sarah sent them from California. Rose was inclined to let Sid have one; she was thinking she wouldn't mind having a brownie herself.

Rose and Sid had both become quite fond of these brownies. Sarah baked them herself using high-grade medical marijuana, which she added in far larger quantities than the standard recipe called for on the theory that if some medicine is good for you, then more medicine must be better for you. These were potent brownies. Both Sid and Rose had found that no matter what was ailing them, they felt a lot better after eating one. Sometimes they completely forgot what had been ailing them in the first place. Once Rose had gone to the kitchen to get Sid a glass of water and had become fascinated by the water running out of the kitchen faucet. She wound up staring at the glittering cascade for more than an hour, barely moving. Sid, sitting in the living room, had not minded; he was engrossed in listening to the subtle and fascinating interplay of droning sounds made by the vacuum cleaner, which Rose had left running.

As the rehearsal dinner approached the dessert course, Rose decided it was time for her and Sid to take their medicine. She opened her massive purse and took out the plastic box filled with brownies. She set it on the serving cart next to her and began rummaging through her purse, looking for her reading glasses so she could unwrap the brownies.

"I have to go to the bathroom," said Sid.

Rose was about to give her automatic response to Sid, which was that no he didn't have to go to the bathroom, when it occurred to her that maybe he did, as it had been some time since his last trip. She decided she had to go, too. So she closed her purse, stood, and told Sid to come on. The two of them toddled slowly from the room.

On their way out, they passed a waiter coming in. The waiter's name was Miguel; he had been assigned the task of unveiling and serving the Groom's Cake when given the signal by Tina. He positioned himself by the serving cart in the corner and noticed the plastic box sitting next to the silver dome. This did not look right to Miguel. He opened the box and saw that it was filled with brownies individually wrapped in plastic. He assumed that these, like the cake, had been provided by the wedding party; he also assumed that they were meant to be part of the dessert offering and somebody had failed to unwrap them.

Miguel was a man with initiative. Using his body to shield the cart from the rest of the room, he lifted the dome and set it aside, exposing the football cake, which lay in the center of a silver platter. Working quickly, Miguel unwrapped the brownies and positioned them artfully around the cake, making a nice display. Miguel was pleased with his work and his quick thinking. He stuffed the wrappings into the box and tucked it out of sight on the cart's lower shelf. Then he replaced the dome and turned just in time to see Tina signaling him that she was ready to begin.

Tina tapped her water glass with a teaspoon, bringing the table to silence. She rose and made a short, graceful speech, thanking the wedding party for being there. She then signaled Miguel, who rolled the cart to the middle of the table and, with a flourish, lifted the dome. Everyone *Ooh*ed at the Groom's Cake; Seth stood and kissed Tina. Tina noticed the brownies arranged around the cake. She hadn't ordered brownies but assumed the hotel had provided them. Seth also noticed the brownies but assumed Tina had ordered them.

Miguel sliced and served the cake, putting a brownie on each plate next to the cake slice. Everyone agreed the cake—Seth's favorite, orange sponge cake with chocolate frosting—was delicious. They also raved about the brownies, especially Wendell Corliss, who considered himself a serious chocolate connoisseur. He declared he had never tasted brownies quite like these. Miguel served him a second one, which he ate. He then asked Mike if he planned to eat his brownie, which was untouched; Mike, who did not like chocolate, said sure, and Wendell wolfed that one down.

The brownies were all consumed; the room was now abuzz with

conversation and laughter. More wine arrived, and a selection of liqueurs. Miguel wheeled the dessert cart out. He passed Rose and Sid, reentering the room after the long, slow toddle back from the restrooms. Upon reaching her seat, Rose said, "Where's my brownies?"

Seth's head whipped around. "They're not in your purse?" he said.

"No," said Rose. "I put them right here, on a little table. But now it's gone."

"Oh God," said Seth.

"What?" said Tina.

Seth lowered his voice. "You didn't order brownies to go with the cake?"

"No. I think the hotel gave us those."

"Actually, I think they were my mom's."

"Oh! Well, that was very nice of her. I didn't eat one, but people seem to really like them."

Seth opened his mouth, about to reveal the true nature of the brownies. Then, seeing how pleased Tina was with how the dinner was going, he closed his mouth, figuring he'd already subjected her to enough stress for one evening. Besides, the dinner *was* going great. The guests, aside from Rose and Sid, were happy to the point of giddiness, especially down at the Wendell Corliss end of the table.

Wendell was not known for his sense of humor; he rarely smiled, except for business reasons, and pretty much never laughed. But now, suddenly, he was downright jovial. This did not go unnoticed by the brownie-free Mike, who decided that now might be a good opportunity to subtly steer Corliss toward the topic of—without directly mentioning it—the current vacancy in the Group of Six.

"I was really sorry to hear about Herb Wentworth," Mike said, bringing up the name of the recently deceased industrialist who had been, Mike believed, a member of the Group. "What a shock."

"A shock?" said Wendell.

"Yes," said Mike.

"You were shocked that Herb died?"

"Well, yes. I mean, no, he was definitely getting on in years, but, I mean, he was . . . it was quite a loss."

"Herb Wentworth," said Corliss, "was the deadest person I have ever met who was not technically dead."

"Really?" said Mike, surprised to hear Corliss talking about the late business legend this way.

"Really. You'd be with him and there would be times when he wouldn't say anything, wouldn't do anything, wouldn't *move*. He was like a corpse."

"Huh," said Mike.

"One time," said Corliss, "I was sitting next to Herb at dinner and I swear he didn't say a word, didn't eat anything, didn't move a muscle, for five minutes. I couldn't really tell if his eyes were open or shut. So I was kind of watching him out of the corner of my eye and I'm thinking, *I wonder if old Herb has kicked the bucket here.* I was thinking about nudging him, but this is Herb Wentworth we're talking about. You don't nudge Herb Fucking Wentworth."

"No," agreed Mike, a bit shocked by Corliss's language, but not saying anything.

"So I'm watching him," continued Corliss, "and I see this fly walking around on his head. Herb had a *huge* head, totally bald, and this fly is just strolling around on it, very casual, for a fly. And then, while I'm watching, the fly walks *into his ear.* All the way in. And I didn't see it come back out. Can you imagine?"

"Having a fly walk into my ear?"

"No, being the fly. Being *that* fly and walking into Herb Wentworth's ear. I mean, to the fly, that earhole was the size of the Lincoln Tunnel. But the fly just walked in there as if it knew exactly what it was doing. Think about it. Think about the *confidence.*"

Mike tried to think about it, but had no luck.

Corliss said, "But at that point, what do you say? Do you say, 'Wake up, Herb! A fly just walked into your ear'?"

At this point, Corliss emitted what could only be described as a giggle. Mike couldn't believe it. Wendell Corliss did not giggle.

"How do they do that, anyway?" said Corliss.

"How does who do what?" said Mike.

"Flies. How do they walk around on a smooth surface like Herb's head? Or a wall? Or a *window*, for God's sake? I mean, it's *glass*. What holds them on?"

"I think they have little suction cups on their feet," said Marty, who'd been listening and who had eaten a brownie.

"Seriously?" said Corliss, turning with interest toward Marty, to the visible annoyance of Mike. "Suction cups?"

"No no no," said Big Steve, another brownie consumer weighing in. "They have like little hooks."

"Hooks?" said Corliss, fascinated now.

"On their feet," said Big Steve.

"But getting back to Herb Wentworth," said Mike.

Corliss ignored him. "How can they attach themselves to glass with hooks?" he asked Big Steve. "What do they hook onto?"

"That's the thing," said Big Steve. "Even really, really smooth surfaces have tiny irregularities. The hooks can hook onto them."

Corliss picked up his water glass. "So what you're saying is, there are tiny irregularities in this glass?" He held the glass up close to his face and peered at it. "My God," he said.

"You can see them?" said Marty.

"See what?"

"The irregularities?"

"No . . . The light. Look at the *light!*"

Marty and Big Steve both raised their glasses to their eyes and both said, "Whoa."

Corliss turned to his wife, who had also consumed a brownie and had been staring straight ahead for several minutes without blinking. "You have to see this," he said, extending his glass. "The *light.*"

She looked at him and said, "Do you think we could get a pizza?"

"That is an *excellent* idea," Corliss said.

"What?" said Mike.

Ignoring him, Corliss signaled a waiter, who hustled over.

"We'd like to order a pizza," said Corliss.

The waiter, who had just finished serving these very people a lavish, multi-course Italian meal, from antipasti through dessert, said, "A pizza?"

"It's a flat, round piece of baked bread dough topped with tomato and cheese," said Corliss. This absolutely slayed Big Steve, Marty and Greta, all of whom began giggling uncontrollably. Corliss beamed; he *never* made people laugh, especially not his wife.

"Sir," said the waiter, "I'm afraid we don't have pizza on the menu."

"Then you need to order one," said Corliss.

"Order one?" said the waiter.

"Yes. A delivery pizza."

"You want to have a pizza delivered here? To this restaurant?" said Mike.

"Exactly!" said Corliss.

"OK," said Mike, who was not about to contradict Wendell Corliss even though Corliss was acting weird. In fact, Mike was noticing that almost everyone was acting weird. Even his wife, Marcia, was behaving oddly: she had risen from her seat and was now intently studying a picture on the wall. Meanwhile, farther down the table, Banzan Dazu was leading Kevin, the bridesmaids and the rest of the Clark relatives in some kind of chant.

"So what's the best pizza around here?" Corliss asked the waiter.

"On Key Biscayne, that would be Stan's," said the waiter. "But they don't deliver."

"Of *course* they'll deliver," said Corliss. He withdrew an iPhone from his pocket, tapped at the screen for a bit, then held it to his ear.

"Hello, this is Wendell Corliss," he said. "I'd like to speak to the owner. Corliss. C-o-r-l-i-s-s. Yes, I'll hold."

"You know what you're like?" said Marty.

"What?" said Corliss.

"The fly."

"Which fly?"

"The one who walked into the guy's ear."

Corliss frowned. "How so?"

"Well, like you said, the fly was *confident*. It's walking around on this dude's head and it sees the hole, and instead of being scared of the hole, the fly is, like, 'I'm going *in* there.' Which is dangerous. I mean, what if the dude goes, 'Shit! There's a fly in my ear,' and he slaps his hand over it and the fly is trapped? That's a huge risk. But the fly goes in there anyway. The fly doesn't stand around thinking about the danger. The fly just *does* it. He takes the risk and that's how he gets the reward."

"But what *is* the reward?" said Big Steve. "I mean, what's inside the guy's ear that a fly would want?"

"I don't know," said Marty. "Maybe flies eat earwax. Flies will eat a lot of things."

"Earwax could be a source of protein," said Big Steve.

"There you go," said Marty. "But the point is"—here he pointed at Corliss, who was following the conversation with deep fascination—"you're like the fly. You want a delivery pizza, so you *act*. The rest of us, we're all walking around on the outside of the head. But you, you went *right into the fucking earhole*."

Corliss stared at Marty for a moment, then said, "What do you do?"

"Do?"

"For a living."

"I'm an attorney," said Marty.

"Where?"

"I'm in between positions."

Corliss held up a finger and spoke into the phone. "Hello, yes, is this the owner? Stan? Stan, my name is Wendell Corliss. C-o-r-l-i-s-s. I would like to order a delivery pizza. No, I understand that. But I am prepared to make this worth your while."

"Tell him pepperoni," said Greta Corliss.

Corliss nodded, holding up a *Wait a second* finger. "Stan, I don't think you understand. I'm aware that you have a no-delivery policy. I respect that. But here's what I'm saying, Stan. I'm saying that if you can find a way to deliver a pizza to us here . . ."

"With pepperoni," said Greta.

". . . a pizza *with pepperoni*, Stan, then you would find that the upside, financially, would be extremely rewarding. *Extremely*, Stan. Are you familiar with the Transglobal Financial Capital Funding Group?"

Mike listened to this with his mouth open. Wendell Corliss was a man who could alter the financial stability of entire nations, a man who could, and routinely did, leave heads of state waiting on hold. And here he was cajoling the owner of a *pizza joint*. Mike tapped Corliss on the arm and said, "Listen, why don't you let me just send one of my guys over there to get the pizza, OK?"

Corliss shook his head firmly. "I can't do that."

"But why not?"

Corliss pointed to Marty and said, "Explain it to him." He went back to talking to Stan.

"He's inside the hole now," Marty explained to Mike.

"What the hell are you *talking* about?" said Mike.

"He's committed," said Marty. "He's all the way in."

"He's after the wax," said Big Steve. "And the wax, for him, is getting this guy to deliver a pizza."

"With pepperoni," said Greta.

"With pepperoni," said Big Steve. "That's his earwax."

Mike shook his head, wondering why suddenly everybody in the room seemed to be insane. He rose and went over to Marcia, who was still staring at a picture on the wall.

"Marcia," he said. "There's something—"

"Look at this," she said, pointing at the picture.

Mike looked. It was a reproduction of a painting of a cocker spaniel.

"That's nice," he said. "Listen, there's—"

"No, Mike, really *look*." Marcia was pointing at the cocker spaniel. "Look at his *eyes*."

Mike looked at the cocker spaniel's eyes. "What?" he said.

"Don't you *see*?"

Mike looked again. "See *what*?" he said. "It's a dog."

"Yes!" said Marcia. *"Exactly."* She resumed staring at the picture.

"Mike!" shouted Corliss from the end of the table.

"What?" said Mike.

Corliss pointed at the phone. "I'm buying it. You want in?"

"You're buying a pizza?"

"No. I'm buying Stan's."

"You're *buying the restaurant?*"

"I am. Cash deal. Stan's coming over here right now so we can iron out the details. But we're good on the price." Corliss looked at Marty and said, "What's your name again?"

"Marty."

"Right. Marty here is going to handle the paperwork. Stan's going to bring a pizza with him."

"With pepperoni," said Greta.

"Correct. With pepperoni, right, Stan?" Corliss listened to the phone. "Stan wants to know if we want garlic rolls." Corliss looked around, saw lots of nods, including from the chanters. "Definitely, Stan, garlic rolls. Mike, you in?"

"I don't eat garlic."

"No, are you in on the purchase deal? I can let you have twenty-five percent. Marty's taking ten percent in lieu of a fee."

"I . . . I'll be right back," said Mike, suddenly feeling desperate for fresh air. He walked quickly from the dining room, then paused outside and looked back. Marcia was still staring at the cocker spaniel. The chanting of Banzan Dazu, Kevin and the others was getting louder. At the end of the table, Wendell Corliss—the man who never smiled—was engaged in an animated conversation with Marty and Big Steve, the three of them erupting in hysterical laughter.

*What the hell was happening?*

Back in the dining room, Seth knew what was happening but he still hadn't told Tina, who believed that rehearsal dinner guests had simply consumed a lot of wine.

"I think it's going really well, don't you?" she asked Seth. "Look at Marty and Big Steve hitting it off there with Wendell. What on earth are they talking about?"

"I have no idea," said Seth. "I heard Marty saying something about earwax."

"What?"

"I swear that's what they were talking about."

"Well, whatever, they're definitely enjoying themselves."

"Yeah," agreed Seth. "Nobody seems to want to leave."

This was true. Sid and Rose, having reluctantly accepted that the brownies had disappeared, had toddled off to bed. But the rest of the group appeared to be just getting started. This presented a problem for Seth: He needed to get out of there so he could go retrieve his suitcase and the wedding ring.

"So listen," he said to Tina. "Would it be incredibly impolite if I snuck out? I've got something I need to take care of."

Tina's face got serious and she nodded. "I know you do."

"You do?"

"Yes, and I know it's hard, because you promised them. But I'm sure they'll be OK. This really is for the best."

"Right," said Seth, realizing that Tina was talking about the Haitians and remembering his promise to evict them tonight.

"So you go ahead, do what you have to do," said Tina. "I'm not planning to stay here too much longer myself. Baby, we're getting married tomorrow! Do you believe it?"

"I know!" said Seth, trying to look more excited than he felt at the moment, wondering how he was going to tell Laurette she had to leave.

Seth and Tina kissed and Seth left, waving good-bye to the rest of the group, none of whom noticed his departure. On his way out of the restaurant, he passed a middle-aged man in jeans and a T-shirt talking to the maître d'. The man was holding a pizza delivery box; it looked as though he was delivering a pizza *to* the Italian restaurant. Seth found that odd.

# 20

When he reached the elevators, Seth heard a voice call his name. He turned and saw Carl Juste poking his head through the doorway to the hotel's back patio.

"I've been waiting for you," said Juste. He was not wearing his groundskeeper uniform. He looked nervous. "I am not supposed to be in the hotel now."

"What's going on?" said Seth.

"I spoke again with Laurette's sister."

"What'd she say?"

"She can't be released tomorrow because it's a Sunday."

Seth started shaking his head.

"But she has a hearing Monday," Juste continued quickly. "Her lawyer hopes she can be released then."

"Hopes? He doesn't know?"

"No. It's complicated. But if you can just wait one more day, maybe the sister will be released, and maybe she can . . ."

"No," said Seth. "I'm sorry. No more maybes. They have to leave tonight. Right now."

"Now? But you said—"

"I know and I'm really sorry. But it has to be now. I'm glad you're here because I need you to come talk to her. It'll be better if she understands the situation."

"I'm not supposed to be here."

"It'll just be a minute. It's right up these elevators. I'll give her what money I have. But you have to talk to her, explain what's going on, OK?"

Juste looked around nervously, then came inside and followed Seth into an elevator. The doors closed.

"I'm really sorry about this," said Seth. "But this whole thing has gotten way out of hand."

Juste said nothing.

They reached the room. LaDawne greeted them at the door, finger to lips, *Shhh*. She pointed toward the living room, where Wesley was asleep sitting up, snoring in front of the TV, which was showing *Dancing with the Stars* with the volume muted. Stephane was next to Wesley, leaning up against his massive form, also asleep. Cyndi sat on the other sofa, holding the baby. Next to her was Laurette, still in a Ritz bathrobe, smiling shyly at Seth.

Seth, whispering, introduced Juste to LaDawne and Cyndi. They nodded at each other.

Seth took a deep breath.

"They have to leave now," he said.

"Who does?" said LaDawne.

"Everybody," said Seth, gesturing at the group. "You too. I'm sorry. But you all have to go."

"You gonna throw her out?" said LaDawne, pointing at Laurette. "With these two babies?"

"I'm sorry, I really am. But I think I've been incredibly patient."

"Where they gonna go? Where is this woman supposed to go with two babies, she doesn't speak English, she's not legal, she doesn't have a penny in her pocket? She doesn't even have a *pocket*."

Laurette's smile was gone. Her worried eyes were darting back and forth between Seth and LaDawne.

Seth said, "Why don't *you* take her home, if you're so concerned?"

"Because she's still sick from being half drowned and I live in West Palm, which is two hours away, and she doesn't need to get dragged all the way up there in her condition when she's trying to find her sister, who's down here. Otherwise, hell yes, I'd take her. She just needs a little more time. Why can't you give her that?"

"Because according to Carl, her sister's in jail right now, and we don't really know when she's going to get out." Seth's voice was rising. "And I'm getting *married*. Doesn't anybody *get* that?" The outburst awakened Wesley, who stirred and half opened his eyes.

"Yeah, we get that," said LaDawne. "You're getting married. So go ahead, get married. But let this poor woman stay here one more night. Tell you what: You let her stay tonight, you don't owe me and Wesley anything. Ain't that right, Wesley."

From somewhere deep in his massive body, Wesley made a rumbling noise that could have indicated agreement or indigestion.

Seth shook his head. "No," he said. He turned to Carl. "Please tell her. Tell her I'm really sorry but I'm getting married tomorrow and I need everybody to clear out of here. Tell her I'll give her some money."

Carl nodded and spoke to Laurette for about a minute. She listened, motionless, expressionless. When Carl was done, she spoke, her voice soft and wavering, her eyes now on Seth. She spoke for several minutes, at one point almost losing control, then fighting back sobs and continuing.

"She says of course she will leave," Carl said. "She says she is sorry to be so much trouble for you before your wedding, and she thanks you for everything you have done. She says she cannot take money from you. She wishes she could give *you* money, to thank you, because you saved her life, saved her two babies, and carried her to the land, to America. Her situation was very bad in Haiti. She lost her husband and her oldest child, a daughter, in the earthquake. She had no house and had to live in a dangerous place. Her babies were always hungry and there were bad men around. That is why she came here. No matter what happens, it will be better here. So she says please do not feel bad for her. She says you helped her more than anyone, pulling her from the water. Without you, she would not be here."

When Carl finished, Laurette rose from the couch, walked over to Seth and gave him a shy, tentative hug.

"*Mêci*," she said.

"You're welcome," he said, patting her back awkwardly.

Laurette let him go and went into the bedroom. She walked slowly, uncertainly, each step a chore. The living room was silent for a few seconds, then LaDawne said, "Well, I guess we're going, then."

"You're going to take them?" said Seth.

"Who else is gonna take them?" said LaDawne.

"Where?" said Seth. "To West Palm?"

"I don't know yet," said LaDawne. "But it's not your problem, right? Wesley. Wake up that boy."

LaDawne bustled about, gathering stuff. Seth stood absolutely still, staring at the floor. Cyndi set the sleeping baby down gently on the sofa and came over to Seth. She put her hand on his arm.

"Don't feel bad," she said.

"How can I not feel bad?"

"You did what you could."

"It's not like her staying here one more night will solve anything."

"No."

"It's just that Tina has spent so much time planning this wedding and she really wants for it to be about *us*. And if I'm caught up in all this"—he gestured toward the sleeping baby—"I can't be focusing on what should be the most important thing in my life right now. You know?"

"Of course."

Seth stared at the floor again, then turned to Carl. "Is there some way I can find out what happens to them?"

"You can ask me," Carl said. "And if I know, I will tell you."

"Do you think she'll be OK?"

Carl shrugged. "I don't know. If her sister is released, maybe she can find a place for her to stay that will be safe."

"But the sister might not be released."

"No," said Carl. "But maybe I can find somebody else to help her."

"Maybe."

"Maybe."

"What if she gets picked up?"

Carl shrugged again. "Nobody knows. It keeps changing, the law, the politics. Maybe she gets lucky and she can stay."

"But maybe not?"

"Maybe not."

"And if she's not lucky?"

"She have to go back to Haiti."

"Where she has nothing."

"Many people in Haiti have nothing. It's why they come here."

Laurette emerged from the bedroom wearing the clothes—rags, really—she'd had on when Seth had pulled her from the sea. She picked up her baby. Wesley guided the sleepy Stephane over to her. Carl, LaDawne and Wesley stood behind them. They were ready to go.

Seth could see the bones in her arms and legs. He remembered carrying her out of the ocean, the way she'd felt like a bag of sticks. He remembered when he thought she'd died, and when, with his breath in her lungs, she came to life.

*Without you, she would not be here.*

Laurette turned to Seth and spoke.

Carl said, "She hopes you have a beautiful wedding and a happy life."

"Thank you," said Seth.

She touched his arm. *"Mêci."*

She turned and started toward the door.

"Wait," said Seth.

She stopped.

"Shit," said Seth.

"That's it?" said LaDawne. "That's what you wanted to say?"

"Tell her she can stay tonight," said Seth.

"You serious?" said LaDawne.

"Are you sure?" said Carl.

"Yes," said Seth. "Tomorrow morning, maybe I can call somebody. A lawyer or somebody. I don't know. But I can try. I haven't really tried."

"You're getting married tomorrow," said LaDawne.

"In the afternoon. I can try in the morning."

Carl was explaining the new plan to Laurette, who was weeping and saying, *"Mêci, mêci."* Wesley, with Stephane in tow, was already lumbering back to the sofa.

"What about Tina?" Cyndi said.

"You know what?" said Seth. "I really think she'll understand. The thing is, she cares more about stuff like this, about issues and helping people, than I do. *Way* more. I just haven't explained this situation to her clearly enough, is the problem. Plus she's been under a lot of stress. I'm going to explain this whole thing to her better. I'm going to bring her here and have her actually meet Laurette and then I know she'll understand why I can't just kick her out tonight, in her condition. Once Tina sees that, she'll probably even want to help, you know?"

"Mm-mm," said LaDawne.

"I'm sure she will," said Cyndi. "Listen, I've been here forever and I need to get home. Do you still want me to help you get your suitcase from Primate Encounter?"

"Oh Jesus, that's right," said Seth. "Are you still up for doing that?"

"Sure."

"I really appreciate it. Wesley, I hate to do this, but do you think I could borrow your car again?"

Wesley made a noise that either meant yes or no, or something else.

"You can take the car," said LaDawne, "seeing as you decided to do the right thing." She walked Seth and Cyndi to the door of the suite. "I'll tell you the truth, when I met you I thought you was just another one of these rich white boys that hire me for their parties, watch me dance while they get drunk and act stupid, say things about me with me right in front of them like I was deaf." She paused. "And, don't get me wrong, I still think you probably are one of those white boys. But you got some heart in you. You could turn out to be a good man when you grow up."

"Thank you," said Seth, "I think."

"Go get your wedding ring," said LaDawne.

## 21

The final negotiations for the purchase of Stan's Pizza of Key Biscayne, represented by owner Stanley Karpimsky, and Transglobal Financial Capital Funding Group, represented by CEO Wendell Corliss, with Marty acting as legal counsel, took place on the beach behind the Ritz-Carlton.

The negotiations had begun in the restaurant, but the manager had finally asked the wedding party to leave, both because he needed the private dining room and also because the chanting was bothering the other diners. And so the group had flowed out of the restaurant, a giddy, giggling amoeba of mellowness. The lone points of normalcy were Tina and her father, neither of whom had partaken of Aunt Sarah's special California medication, and both of whom were baffled by the wildly euphoric mood of the rest of the group.

Stanley Karpimsky was also brownie-free, but he was ecstatic because he was in the process of selling his pizza joint to the famous Wendell Corliss. Stanley had Googled Corliss on his phone and learned that he was fully qualified to purchase Stan's Pizza, and, if he felt like it, the rest of Key Biscayne. Stanley didn't know why a world-famous financial genius wanted to buy Stan's Pizza; apparently it had something to do with earwax. All Stan knew for certain was that Corliss was willing to pay him a ridiculously good price, a price that would enable Stan to retire in comfort and—more important—tell his

father-in-law, who owned twenty-five percent of Stan's Pizza and there-
fore felt entitled to walk into the kitchen whenever he felt like it and
tell Stan there was too much oregano in the tomato sauce, that he
could go fuck himself.

The chanting group had flowed through the hotel lobby, getting
stares from other hotel guests, then out the back and down to the
beach. At the moment, Stan was sitting cross-legged in the sand, forming a triangle with Wendell and Marty. All three were now barefoot.

Mike Clark had been standing with Tina, who seemed to Mike to
be the only other sane person there. But Tina had just left, saying she
wanted to get a good night's sleep before her wedding day. So now
Mike stood alone, a few feet away from where Wendell, Stan and
Marty were sitting. Mike felt awkward, not wanting to be too far from
his prized guest Wendell but definitely not part of whatever the hell
was going on. Mike was hating the way Wendell was hitting it off with
these two losers.

A few yards down the beach, Banzan Dazu and the chanters—who
had been joined, to Mike's alarm, by his wife, Marcia—were lying on
their backs in the sand, staring at the stars. Also on the beach, but
keeping a discreet distance from the wedding party, were the Clark
bodyguards, Castronovo and Brewer.

The Stan's Pizza deal was done. Wendell had just made a phone call
to somebody in New York, who had made a phone call to somebody in
Miami; at that very moment, the money was on its way, to be delivered
by courier to the beach behind the Ritz, in cash, in a briefcase. Stan
had wanted it that way because he'd seen it in the movies so many
times, the scene where the guy opens the briefcase and sees all the
cash. In fact the bulk of the negotiations for the sale of Stan's Pizza
had consisted of Stan and Marty hammering out exactly what kind of
briefcase it would be while Wendell stared at his feet.

"I don't want one of those soft-side things," Stan had said.

"You mean like a messenger bag?" Marty had said.

"Right. Not that. There's no lid on those."

"Exactly. There's just a flap."

"Right. I don't want a flap."

"Right. You don't want to *unflap* the money, with the briefcase vertical. You want the briefcase to be horizontal. You lay it down, unlatch it, and you lift the lid, and there's your money, all lined up."

"*Exactly.* Horizontal. With latches."

"And it needs to be a hard lid."

"Right. The whole briefcase has to be hard."

Marty, having reached what he felt was a critical point in the negotiations, turned to his client and said, "Is that good with you, Wendell? A hard briefcase?"

Wendell was staring at his bare toes, half buried in the sand.

"What?" he said.

"Stan wants it to be a hard briefcase, with latches. No flap."

"No flap?" said Wendell.

"Correct."

Wendell, a man who had once personally caused the Dow-Jones industrial average to drop 247 points, stared at his toes a few seconds more and said, "Rocks are really hard."

Marty and Stan nodded.

"But when you think about it," said Wendell, "what is sand?"

Marty and Stan thought about it, but had no answer.

"Sand is tiny rocks," said Wendell.

"Jesus Christ," said Marty. "That's true."

"And sand is really soft," said Wendell.

"He's right," said Marty.

Stan, not about to screw up his retirement, nodded in agreement.

"So, Wendell," said Marty, getting back to the issue at hand. "About the briefcase."

Wendell looked at him.

"Is hard good with you?" said Marty. "Instead of soft?"

Wendell stared at him for several seconds. "That's exactly my point," he said. "Hard and soft are the same thing."

Marty chose to interpret this as a yes. He stuck his hand out to Stan and said, "Do we have a deal?"

"Hell yes," said Stan.

At that point Wendell—who, despite being high as a weather satellite, still possessed an innate ability to get things done when a deal was on the line—had made the call to New York. Now they were just waiting for the cash. At least Stan was. Wendell Corliss, legendary financial visionary, was moving on.

"I like the name," he was saying. "Stan's Pizza."

"Legally," said Stan, "it's Stan's Pizza of Key Biscayne."

Wendell nodded. "What would you think of this," he said. "Stan's *Transglobal* Pizza of Key Biscayne."

"Transglobal?" said Stan.

"Transglobal," said Wendell.

"The thing is," said Stan, "it's pretty much a Key Biscayne operation. Every now and then, somebody picks up a pie, takes it back over to Miami. Maybe even once or twice Broward. But I don't think we get farther than Fort Lauderdale."

"Yeah," said Marty. "You don't usually think of pizza as being global, let alone *trans*global."

Wendell looked at Marty. "Maybe that's the problem," he said.

"Whoa," said Marty.

Mike Clark, standing nearby, listening in, was going crazy. What the hell was Corliss up to? It has to be something. Corliss was one of the financial world's most brilliant strategists. He did not do things for no reason. He was seeing something here that Mike was not seeing. *What was it?*

Mike edged closer to the trio in the sand, cleared his throat.

"Wendell," he said.

Wendell looked up. "Yes?"

"Um, you remember, back in the restaurant, you mentioned the possibility of my participating in this?"

"Yes," said Wendell.

Several seconds passed awkwardly.

"You mentioned twenty-five percent," said Mike.

"Yes."

More awkward seconds.

"I was just wondering," said Mike, "if that option is still open."

Wendell looked at Stan, then Marty, then back up at Mike.

"I don't think so, Mike," he said. "I think we're good."

Mike couldn't believe it. He, Mike Clark, whose name regularly appeared in *Fortune* magazine, who had been to the White House four times and once golfed with the president, was being turned down for *a twenty-five percent interest in a pizza joint.*

What the hell was happening?

Furious and frustrated, Mike spun and stalked away from the trio. He walked over to Marcia, who was still with the chanters, lying on her back in the sand between Greta Corliss and Banzan Dazu, all of them gazing upward, watching as a large cloud, which had been directly overhead, drifted away, revealing a night sky dense with stars.

"Shining star, come into view," said Dazu. "Shine its watchful light on you."

"Oh my God," said Marcia. "That's beautiful."

"Thank you," said Dazu modestly. He had good reason to be modest, as the lines he was taking credit for were lyrics from Earth, Wind & Fire's funktastic 1975 hit "Shining Star," which Dazu had promoted in the Philadelphia market back when his name was Norman Cochran.

Mike leaned over Marcia and said, "I'm going back to the room."

"OK," said Marcia.

"So let's go."

"I'm staying here."

"You're not coming?"

"Could you move?" said Marcia. "You're blocking the stars."

"You're a shining star," said Dazu. "No matter who you are."

"Oh my God," said Marcia.

"I don't believe this," said Mike, straightening up. He turned and started trudging up the beach toward the hotel, Castronovo and Brewer following. Behind him, Mike could hear Wendell and his two new friends laughing.

Mike reached the wooden walkway leading up to the hotel lawn.

Three men were coming down. The ones in front and back were large, the one in the middle was carrying an attaché case—hard-sided, with latches.

Mike watched the men pass, then started up the walkway. A minute later, as he was crossing the back lawn, he heard a joyous whoop from the beach, the sound of a man who had just opened a lid and found a glorious, father-in-law-free future.

# 22

Tina had gotten as far as the bar in the hotel lobby. She'd intended to go to her room but decided she'd have a glass of wine to help her sleep.

She found an empty table and sat down. A waiter appeared immediately, as waiters always did when Tina entered an establishment. She looked at the wine list and selected a glass of the most expensive *sauvignon blanc*. The waiter bustled off.

Tina glanced around and saw men at the bar noticing her, as men always did. She knew from experience that eventually several of them would offer to buy her a drink and she would have to rebuff their advances. This did not concern her. She was an excellent rebuffer. And although she would never admit it to anyone, she took pleasure in the power that her looks gave her over men.

Her wine came; she sipped it, enjoying the temporary solitude, thinking about the next day, her wedding day, mentally running down her checklist. All was going well, she decided. The rehearsal dinner had ended a bit weirdly—her mom was *not* the kind of person to lie on the beach in dress clothes—but Tina had decided the strange behavior could be explained by the wine. Aside from that, everything appeared to be going smoothly, now that Seth had agreed to deal with the ridiculous situation with the people in his room.

She frowned, thinking of her confrontation with Seth. She'd been troubled by his reaction when she told him the Haitians had to go—the way he brought up the time she got arrested on the way to the Giants game, throwing that in her face. As if he was saying she didn't care about the Haitians. *Of course* she cared about the Haitians. She was infinitely more aware of the plight of undocumented immigrants than Seth could ever hope to be. She had *marched in rallies*, for God's sake. But there was a time and a place, and this was neither. This was her *wedding*. And instead of understanding that, Seth had challenged her, almost *lectured* her. That bothered Tina. That was a side of Seth she hadn't seen. She would have to keep an eye on that.

The waiter approached and said, "The gentleman at the bar would like to buy you a drink."

Tina glanced toward the bar and saw him smiling at her—good-looking, in a Latin way, but not her type. She gave him the barest of smiles, a smile that said *I understand, but: In your dreams.* "Please tell the gentleman thank you but no."

"Of course," said the waiter, backing away.

Tina went back to thinking about Seth. She sincerely believed he was the right choice for her. He was good-looking and funny, a nice guy, a thoughtful and sensitive lover. He wasn't well educated, but he was smart enough. And unlike the many highly educated guys who had pursued her—and who would have made her parents much happier—Seth was not obsessed with succeeding.

This suited Tina perfectly. She had dated enough high-achieving, self-worshipping Law Review assholes to know she did not want to be in a relationship with an ambitious man. She had more than enough ambition for two, with a detailed plan mapped out in her mind for a career as a humanitarian and leader of causes. *She* would be the achiever in her relationship. Seth's role would be as supporter, sounding board, confidant. Some day, at a banquet honoring her for some prestigious award—she had pictured this in her mind more than once—she would dance with Seth, the two of them on the floor looking great, everybody else watching, and the song playing would be "Wind Beneath My Wings," and she would kiss him, and everyone would agree that they were a terrific couple, perfect for each other.

She would make a gracious speech about how she could never have done it without him. Everybody would cry.

Tina believed that Seth, on some level, shared her vision for their future; that he understood and accepted his subordinate role as the price he willingly paid for a prize so many other men wanted, namely, her. She was also confident that, once they were married, he would swallow his pride and leave his stupid tweeting job for some position set up by her father. In time they would have children—beautiful, smart, exceptional children—and Seth would be busy with his duties as father. He would be a good father. He would be deeply involved with his family, and as a couple they would make new friends. Seth would drift apart from Marty and Kevin and Big Steve, who were entertaining enough in their way, but losers, not suitable for the long term.

The waiter, looking apologetic, approached again. "I'm sorry to bother you," he said, "but there's another gentleman at the bar who would like to buy you a drink."

Tina glanced over and saw another smiling man, even handsomer than the first, raising a glass hopefully, looking at Tina the way men did, letting her know she could get them to do anything she wanted them to do, anything.

"Tell him no thank you," said Tina, turning away. She took a last sip of wine, signed the check and rose to leave.

She had reached the doorway when she saw Seth on the far side of the lobby, emerging from the hallway that led to the elevators.

He was with a woman. It was the same woman she'd seen him with the night before when he'd also been with that hideous man with the snake. But the snake man wasn't here now, just this woman. She was still wearing the tight, short, low-cut dress she'd been wearing the night before. She was pretty enough—Tina wouldn't say beautiful—and she seemed to be in decent shape, although a bit too meaty for Tina's sensibilities.

As Tina watched, Seth and the woman went out the front door. Tina took a few steps into the lobby so she could see through the doorway. Seth and the woman stood by the driveway, waiting, for about a minute. A pimped-out black Cadillac Escalade pulled up, bass thumping. Seth and the woman got in, Seth driving. The Escalade pulled away.

Tina, in shock, stood utterly still, trying to come up with an explanation. No good one came to mind. She found it almost impossible to believe that Seth would be cheating on her—on *her*—on the night before their wedding, especially with a cheap-looking woman like that. But why would he have left the hotel with her? Where would they be going?

She took her phone out of her purse and dialed Seth's number. She got voice mail. She hung up and thought some more about what she'd seen. She still had no explanation, at least no acceptable one. The more she thought about it, the unhappier she got.

*Maybe it had something to do with the Haitians.* Tina turned that over in her mind. Seth had promised he'd get them out of his suite. She assumed he'd done so, but now, suddenly, she wanted to know for sure.

Walking quickly, she crossed the lobby, went to the elevators, rode up to Seth's floor. She marched down the hallway to his suite door and pressed the doorbell button.

Thirty seconds later, the door was opened by LaDawne.

"Can I help you?" she said in an unhelpful tone.

Tina looked past LaDawne's massive form. She saw Wesley on the sofa with Stephane next to him. Laurette walked into the room, carrying the baby.

"What are you people doing here?" said Tina.

"*You people?*" said LaDawne.

"Yes. What are you doing in this room?"

"Who the hell are you?"

"I'm the fiancée of the person who's the registered guest in this room. And you people have no business being here."

"Well, then, maybe you need to talk to your fiancé," said LaDawne. "Because he knows *we people* are here and he said it's fine with him."

"I don't believe you," said Tina.

LaDawne stepped closer. "Are you calling me a liar?"

Tina did not back up. "I guess I am."

"Then I'm calling you a skinny-ass bitch," said LaDawne, slamming the door.

Tina stared at the door for several seconds, her eyes suddenly burning, her brain not believing this was happening. People simply did not, *ever*, slam a door in the face of Tina Clark. She turned and ran back down the hallway to the elevators. She punched the down button furiously, over and over, until an elevator came. She rode it down to the lobby, tears streaming down her face.

The doors opened. Standing there, waiting for the elevator, was Mike Clark. Behind him loomed Castronovo and Brewer.

Mike looked at Tina's anguished face, held out his arms as she stumbled toward him.

"Baby," he said, his voice a mixture of concern and fury. "Tell Daddy what's wrong."

# 23

It took a lot of experimentation, but Seth and Cyndi had finally managed to subdue both the video and audio systems in Wesley's Escalade. They now rode in welcome silence, the windows down, letting the cool and salty night sea air flow through the car.

"I really appreciate you going with me to do this," said Seth. "After we get the suitcase, I can drop you off at your house, if you want."

"No, I'll come back, if that's OK," said Cyndi. "At this point I really want to see they're OK. I feel kind of, like, *responsible* for them, you know?"

"Yeah," said Seth.

"It was really nice what you did, letting them stay."

Seth nodded. "I just hope Tina feels the same way."

"I'm sure she will."

"The thing is, I told her I'd tell them to leave. She's really not happy, me having all these people around, the distraction. But when I saw Laurette walking out the door, with those two kids, me sitting in that big suite . . ."

"I know. You did the right thing. And Tina will understand. I know she has to be a good person or you wouldn't be marrying her."

"Yeah."

They rode for a while in silence, which was broken by Cyndi.

"This whole thing is making me think," she said.

"About . . ."

"About me. What I'm doing with my life. Like, I'm almost embarrassed about how you met me."

Seth frowned, trying to remember. It seemed like decades ago. He smiled when it came to him. "At the Clevelander," he said. "The Miss Hot Amateur Bod contest!"

Cyndi put her face in her hands. "I can't believe I did that. And I didn't even *win*."

"Hey," he said, "I'd have given you first place."

Cyndi blushed. "Thanks, but that was stupid. I'm too old to be out there getting drunk and acting like that. I think maybe it's because of what happened with my marriage, my husband cheating on me . . . Like, I have to prove it wasn't my fault, that I can still look good."

"You don't have to prove that. You definitely still look good."

"So why am I trying to prove it? I mean, the guys I meet on South Beach, going to clubs every night, getting wasted . . . they're not the kind of guys I want to meet anyway. I want to meet nice guys. Guys like . . . OK, like you."

This time they both blushed.

"Well, thanks," said Seth. "But I have to point out that you met *me* over there on South Beach and I was totally wasted. I was so wasted, I lost my suitcase, which is how come now we're driving over to Primate Encounter."

"Right, but that was your bachelor party. That's different. And besides, if you think about it, if things didn't happen the way they did, you wouldn't have ended up on that beach last night, and you would never have pulled Laurette and her kids out of the ocean. They probably would have drowned."

"Maybe."

"Anyway," she said, "the point is, you're a good guy. Tina's very lucky to have you."

"I hope she feels the same way."

"I'm sure she does," said Cyndi. She touched Seth's arm, then pulled her hand away.

# 24

"You did *what?*" said Meghan.

"I told Daddy about the Haitians," said Tina.

The sisters were back in their suite, getting ready for bed.

"Why'd you do that?"

"Because Seth told me he'd get rid of them, and he didn't."

"I'm sure he's trying to, Tina, but it's probably—"

"And I saw him leaving the hotel in a car with that bimbo he was with last night, the one with the boobs hanging out who was with the snake idiot."

"OK, maybe he was driving her home. Tina, it's *Seth*. He *loves* you. He's *crazy* for you. He can't believe you're marrying him. He thinks he won the lottery. He would *not* mess that up, especially not the day before the wedding. I'm sure there's a totally innocent explanation for all of this."

"There fucking better be," said Tina, though as she thought about it she realized Meghan was probably right. Seth was just driving the bimbo home, because that was the kind of nice guy Seth was.

"You shouldn't have told Daddy about the Haitians," said Meghan.

"Why not?"

"Because Seth asked you not to."

"Seth had his chance to take care of this, and he couldn't. These people are taking advantage of him the way I'm sure the bimbo did. You know how he is. He's a pushover. So when this kind of person shows up, they just walk all over him."

"When *what* kind of person shows up? Drowning Haitians?"

"You know what I mean. And it's not just them. There was this huge African-American woman in his room. She called me a bitch. *She slammed the door on me.* That fat fucking black bitch."

"OK, Tina, whoever's there, the point is that Seth promised this Haitian woman—"

"I don't care what he promised her! He promised *me* he'd get rid of them! We're getting married tomorrow!"

Meghan sighed. "So what is Daddy going to do?"

"He's going to take care of it."

"Meaning what?"

"Meaning he's going to get them out of there."

"Meaning his two thugs are."

"They're not going to do anything bad to them. I made Daddy promise that."

"So what *are* they going to do?"

"They're going to take them to the federal immigration people."

"But Tina, that's exactly what he doesn't want to happen."

"That's exactly what the law says is *supposed* to happen," said Tina. "They're here *illegally*, Meghan. Don't you get that?"

"I thought the term you used was *undocumented*," said Meghan. "You know, when you're marching in your rallies."

Tina reddened. "Don't try to make me into the bad guy here, Meghan. They're going to be perfectly fine. They'll be well treated."

"Until they get sent back to Haiti."

"You don't know that's what will happen. There are procedures that have to be followed. They'll have legal representation. And why the hell are you being so self-righteous about this anyway? When have *you* ever cared about this kind of thing? What have *you* ever done to help undocumented immigrants?"

Meghan was silent for a few seconds, staring at the wall.

Tina let her words hang in the air for a while. Then she rose and said, "I'm going to bed."

"Sleep well," said Meghan.

"I'll sleep just fine," said Tina.

## 25

Wendell and Marty were now alone on the beach. One by one, the members of the wedding party had drifted off to bed. Stan, former owner of what was now Stan's Transglobal Pizza of Key Biscayne, had also departed, literally skipping up the beach, firmly holding his attaché case.

Now it was just Wendell and Marty, bare toes in the sand, listening to the whoosh of the waves and staring at the fat moon rising over the Atlantic.

Neither had spoken for more than a half hour when Marty chuckled and said, "You realize what you did, right?"

Wendell, still looking at the moon, said, "What did I do?"

"You bought a pizza restaurant."

"I know!" Wendell burst out laughing.

"And the *whole entire reason* you bought it was so you could have a pizza delivered."

"I know!" Wendell was laughing so hard he was gasping. "And you want to know the worst part?"

"What's the worst part?"

"I didn't even get a slice!"

"Seriously?"

"Seriously. Greta ate the whole thing."

"You're kidding."

"Nope. That woman hardly eats anything. And she *never* eats carbs. But she scarfed down the entire pizza. She was a pepperoni piranha."

"Wow."

They stared at the moon some more, catching their breath. Then Wendell said, "You know what?"

"What?"

"I'm still hungry."

"Me too," said Marty.

"You think there's any place around here that sells Chinese food?"

Marty looked at Wendell. "Are you serious?"

"I could really, seriously, eat some Chinese food right about now."

"Chinese sounds good," said Marty.

# 26

**Seth and Cyndi** were driving through the Redlands, having left behind the dilapidated strip malls and ragtag housing developments along the U.S. 1 corridor. Now they passed clapboard houses scattered among palm tree nurseries, mango groves, horse farms and U-PICK-'EM tomato fields, the air smelling of damp grass and soil and manure. It was still Dade, but a world away from Miami.

With Cyndi giving directions, they took a series of lefts and rights, zigzagging south and west on the narrow, arrow-straight rural roads, getting ever closer to the Everglades. Finally the Escalade's headlights illuminated a big, faded PRIMATE ENCOUNTER sign looming over an unlit dirt parking area next to a dense stand of trees. Seth pulled in and killed the motor and the headlights. The lot was dark, the trees blocking most of the light from the rising moon.

"Maybe there's a flashlight," said Cyndi. She opened the glove compartment and started rooting around.

"Hmm," she said.

"What?"

"There must be twenty condoms in here. Also a box of Cheez-Its. Also rolling papers, and . . . Whoa, here's a *large* jar of Vaseline."

"Wesley's prepared."

"He actually is," said Cyndi, producing a metal-bodied, three-cell flashlight, the kind favored by law enforcement because it could be used for both illumination and, when necessary, busting the heads of suspected wrongdoers. She handed it to Seth, who found the switch. The Escalade filled with a bright white light.

"That'll work," said Seth, switching it off. "So where'd Duane say the guy left my suitcase?"

"In the back, behind a big cage. He said you go in through a gate around the side to the left. He gave me the code to get in."

"Is there a night watchman?"

"I don't know. Duane didn't say either way."

"Well, if there is, let's hope we don't run into him. We'll just grab the suitcase and go."

They got out of the car. The night air was thick with humidity and the sweet smells of tropical vegetation. They crossed the parking lot, Seth leading. He left the flashlight off; there was just enough moonlight leaking through the trees for them to see their way.

They reached the front entrance to Primate Encounter and turned left, following a high wooden fence. The fence turned right, and they followed a path alongside it, barely visible in the filtered moonlight. To their left was a thick wall of foliage. From inside the fence, they heard animal noises—rustling, grunting, chittering, a moaning sound. Suddenly a high-pitched shriek pierced the night. Cyndi grabbed Seth's hand.

"That was a monkey, right?" she said.

"I'm thinking zombie," said Seth.

"Very funny. Ha-ha."

She was still holding his hand.

They kept moving along the fence and came to a steel gate with narrowly spaced vertical bars. Seth turned the flashlight on. Above the gate latch handle was a numeric keypad. Cyndi got a scrap of paper out of her purse and read the code to Seth. He punched it into the keypad, heard a click, turned the handle and pushed the gate. It swung open. They went inside. Behind them, the gate swung closed with a dull clang.

Seth shined the flashlight beam ahead, illuminating a walkway lined with animal cages, each with a sign out front identifying its occupants. From inside some of the cages, pairs of glowing eyes stared out at Seth and Tina. Seth swept the beam to the right, toward the entrance, then to the left. At the far left end the beam found a cage quite a bit larger than the others.

"That must be it," whispered Cyndi.

"Why are you whispering?" said Seth.

"I don't want to attract the zombies."

"Ha-ha."

But she was still holding his hand.

They walked to the big cage at the end. The air there held a musky aroma. Seth flashed the light beam through the bars, illuminating a large log play structure and a tire swing, but no living creatures.

Seth and Tina walked around to the back of the cage, a grassy embankment leading down to a drainage ditch. Seth shined the flashlight back and forth, a sick feeling growing in his gut.

"It's not here," he said. "Are you sure this is the right cage?"

"He said the big cage in the back."

"Well, this is definitely the big cage in the back." He walked along the embankment, flashing the beam back and forth.

"Shit," he said. "Where the hell *is* it?"

"Duane said it'd be here."

Seth, still moving the light beam around, said, "Well, apparently Duane was . . . Hey."

"What?" said Cyndi.

"Look here." Seth was shining the light on a clump of tall grass close to the cage. The grass had been pressed down; the stalks were pointing toward the cage. "Looks like something got dragged."

Seth stepped closer to the bars and shined the light inside. Close by he saw a dirty gray tarp lying on the floor in a rumpled heap. He reached through the bars, grabbed an edge of the tarp and pulled it. There was nothing under it. He moved the light beam around some more, then stopped.

"Oh shit," he said.

"What?" said Cyndi.

Seth trained the light on a ragged black cloth lump about six feet into the cage. "I think that's my suitcase," he said. "At least part of it."

"Oh no," said Cyndi.

Seth was moving the beam around the cage floor. "Oh God. That's my tuxedo jacket. There's my dress shoes, my shirt . . . My clothes are all over the place." He kept moving the beam. "*Damn.* I don't see the ring. It's in a red jewelry box. It's gotta be in there somewhere." He took a breath, let it out. "I have to get in there."

"I don't think that's a good idea. Whatever's in there . . . look what it did to your suitcase."

"Yeah, but there doesn't seem to be anything in there now. I'm thinking they move whatever it is to a sleeping area at night."

"You don't know that."

"I know I don't. What I *do* know is, I have to get that ring. There has to be a door to the cage, right? For the trainers to get in?"

He moved left along the cage wall. The door was almost at the end, in a steel frame welded into the cage bars. The door had a digital keypad that looked identical to the one on the fence gate.

"Do you think they'd use the same code?" said Cyndi.

"Let's hope," said Seth. He punched the code into the keypad, heard a click. "*Yes.*" He turned the latch and pushed. The door swung open. Seth reached down to the side of the doorway and pulled out a thick clump of grass. He wedged it between the door and the frame to keep the door from closing and latching shut behind him. Then he stepped inside the cage. Cyndi followed, not happy about going inside but not wanting to stay outside alone.

The musky aroma was stronger inside the cage. Seth, with Cyndi staying close behind, walked back along the cage wall to where his clothes were strewn. He played the light beam over the scattered garments, kicking them aside. They were damp and reeked an eye-stinging odor.

"I don't like this," whispered Cyndi.

"It has to be here," said Seth, his eyes on the cage floor. "It *has* to."

He moved a little deeper into the cage, sweeping the flashlight beam back and forth across the floor.

"I *really* don't like this," said Cyndi.

"You want to wait for me outside?" said Seth.

"No. I want us *both* to be outside."

"I'm sorry but I gotta do this."

They were nearing the log structure. The flashlight beam fell on a wadded clump of clothing near its base. Seth stepped closer. The musky aroma was very strong now. Seth reached out his foot to probe the clothing.

A noise.

It came from the log structure, a low rumble.

"What was that?" said Cyndi.

Seth raised the flashlight, swept it across the structure, the beam illuminating the logs right to left.

Seth caught a glimpse of something as the light swept past it. He stopped the beam, moved it back.

Cyndi screamed.

# 27

"I don't want them to get hurt," said Mike Clark. "I promised Tina they wouldn't get hurt."

Brewer and Castronovo nodded. They were in the lobby, sitting on some chairs in a quiet corner.

Brewer said, "So what do you want us to do?"

"First, I want you to take them out of the room, *quietly*. I don't want a scene. And be careful. Tina said there are some other people in the room, too. More black people. Apparently my idiot future son-in-law has a fucking United Nations going on in there. And *I'm paying* for this."

Castronovo said, "You want them out, too?"

"Yes, definitely, get them out. I don't care how, just don't make noise about it. I don't give a shit about them. Just get them out of the hotel."

Brewer said, "What about the Haitians? What do we do with them?"

"That's trickier. The most important thing is, I don't want them to be connected with me or Tina's wedding. I don't need some asshole do-gooder immigration lawyer somehow finding out my name is connected with these people and going to the newspaper with some sob story about how the big mean billionaire Mike Clark had these poor Haitian boat people arrested. They *should* be arrested, for God's sake; they're breaking the fucking law. But I don't want this thing blowing up into a PR disaster that ruins the wedding. So there can be *no connection* between them and me, understand? I want you to take them out of Miami, drive them north. Past Boca. Maybe to Delray Beach. Or north of there, but at least that far. Drop them off near the water, somewhere where the cops will find them. They'll get picked up and it'll look like they came ashore there. Even if they say they were down here, nobody's going to believe them. How would Haitian boat people get into the Key Biscayne Ritz? So that's the plan, OK?"

Castronovo and Brewer nodded.

"One thing," said Mike. "If Tina asks you about this, tell her you took the Haitians to the federal immigration authorities and they took them into custody. That's what I told her I was going to do. They'll end up getting picked up by the feds anyway. I just don't want anybody connected with me to be directly involved."

Brewer said, "What about Seth? Does he know we're going to be doing this?"

"He's not in his suite. Tina said he's out right now." Mike's tone of voice made it clear he did not want to discuss that matter any further.

Castronovo said, "Do you care when we do this?"

"Soon as possible without creating a scene."

"OK," said Brewer, looking around. "Best time is early morning, not too many people out."

"All right," said Mike. "Just get it done. I want them gone."

"They'll be gone," said Castronovo.

# 28

Your mature male orangutan is not a looker. His head is dominated by huge cheek pads—wide flaps of black flesh that extend outward from the face, surrounding it and joining at the forehead, forming a sort of hood over the eyes, which are deep-set and absurdly close together. The nose is small, almost dainty; it's perched high over a wide, purse-lipped mouth, beneath which is a scraggly beard and a huge chin pouch. These features give the male a moon-faced, dopey, comical appearance. Until he feels threatened or angry. When that happens, he will open his mouth—which is much larger, and much more powerful, than a human mouth—and reveal a fearsome set of teeth, dominated by long, fang-like canines. Then the male orangutan does not look comical at all. He looks like a powerful, badass animal capable of inflicting great harm, which he is.

It was that badass face that Trevor was showing to Seth and Cyndi as he emerged from beneath his log structure. He was standing up, showing his full height, which was more than five feet, although his powerful arms still reached almost all the way to the cage floor. He was covered in long, unkempt reddish brown fur.

He was advancing toward the intruders, and he was clearly pissed off.

Cyndi had stopped screaming, but only because she was now too terrified to breathe. She was clinging to Seth, a little behind him. Seth

was also terrified, but, being the guy in the situation, he felt an obliga-
tion to pretend he wasn't. He held his hand up and told Trevor, "Stay!"

Trevor, who was unfamiliar with "Stay!" and not inclined to obey
commands anyway, continued to advance.

"OK," Seth whispered to Cyndi. "We need to back up toward the
door. Slowly."

"OK," said Cyndi in a hoarse, squeezed-throat voice.

They started backing up. Trevor kept coming. He had dropped
down a little, walking on both his feet and his huge hands, still showing his teeth. He was moving faster than they were. He was going to
get to them before they got to the door.

"Oh God," whispered Cyndi.

Seth flashed the light into Trevor's face.

Trevor, blinded by the brilliant light, turned away.

"Go!" said Seth, turning, pushing Cyndi toward the door.

They stumbled toward the door. Seth grabbed it and pulled; his
clump of grass had prevented it from latching, so it swung open. He
pushed Cyndi through the doorway and followed her, pulling the door
behind him.

In his haste, he did not notice that the grass clump was still jammed
against the frame.

Outside the cage, Seth and Cyndi stood for a moment, breathing
hard.

"Jesus," said Cyndi.

"Yes," agreed Seth.

"What *is* that thing? A gorilla?"

"I dunno. Gorilla, baboon, one of those things. Definitely not
friendly."

"Definitely not."

Warily, Seth approached the cage bars, shined the light inside. The
beam found Trevor sitting near the pile of clothes, facing Seth and
Cyndi. He was holding something to his face, sniffing at it. Seth put
the light on it.

"Oh no," he said.

"What?" said Cyndi.

"No no no. No."

"What?"

"That thing has Tina's ring."

"No."

"Yes. Look. See the red thing he's holding? That's the box. The ring's in there."

"Oh man."

"Yeah. I think I have to go back in there."

As if on cue, Trevor bared his teeth.

"Or maybe not," said Seth. "Jesus. What the hell am I gonna do?"

"OK," said Cyndi. "Here's an idea. In the morning, the people who run this place, they're going to be arriving here, right? Like the animal handlers."

"Right."

"So you come back in the morning, first thing, so you're here when they get here. You explain what happened, how the gorilla ripped apart your suitcase and got hold of the ring. Then a handler goes in there and gets it back."

"That's an excellent idea."

"Thank you."

Seth looked at his watch. "So, for now, I guess we should go back to the hotel."

"I guess."

They headed away from the cages, back to the side gate leading to the pathway around the fence. They didn't need a code from this side of the gate; they simply pushed the latch and it swung open. They exited without looking back. So they did not see Trevor make his way over to the cage door and give it a tug, as he had thousands of times before.

The difference was, this time it opened.

# 29

As it happened, Primate Encounter did have a night watchman, of sorts. His name was Artie Kunkel, and he had been forced to take the job after a spectacularly unsuccessful career as a real-estate investor left him deep underwater on four houses.

Artie hated the watchman job. He hated the animals, hated the smells, hated being out in the middle of nowhere alone in the dark late at night. He was not supposed to carry a gun, but he did anyway, having bought one for $35 from a guy in the parking lot of a Party City in Hialeah. It was a .25 caliber pistol of the type sometimes called a Saturday night special. The entire training Artie had received on it came from the seller, who told him, "You have to push this thing up before you can shoot it."

Artie had not shot his pistol so far. But he was glad he had it, and he always carried it with him on his rounds. He was supposed to make his rounds every hour, but in fact he did it only once per night, preferring to spend the rest of his shift watching Internet porn on the Primate Encounter office computer.

Artie disliked making rounds because the animal stink was worse near the cages, and the animals seemed to hate him as much as he hated them. Especially the orangutan. It went batshit whenever Artie walked past, showing its teeth, jumping around, making weird noises. Artie sometimes drew his gun when he passed that cage. Lately he had taken to stopping and pointing his gun at the orangutan, imagining what it would be like to shoot it. He would have loved to have a reason to shoot it. He *hated* the fucking orangutan.

On this night, Artie has just finished watching a video titled *Classy Redhead BBW Takes It Up Ass on Piano*. He looked at the wall clock and decided it was time. He cleared the computer's browser history, rose, stretched, burped, farted. He patted his windbreaker pocket, felt the reassuring hard angular mass of the pistol.

He headed for the exit, pausing at the door to fart once more. He preferred to do his farting in the office. When he was finished, he headed out the doorway.

Artie Kunkel on patrol.

# 30

Wendell and Marty were still barefoot on the beach behind the Ritz-Carlton. Marty was on his back, staring up at the fat full moon, now high in the sky. Wendell was on his cell phone talking with Mr. Woo, the owner—for the time being—of a Chinese restaurant in North Miami Beach called the Majestic Rooster.

Marty and Wendell had done some research, Googling *best chinese restaurant miami*. After reading a bunch of reviews, they had settled on the Majestic Rooster, which apparently had a sensational dong bo pork. By the time Wendell called, the restaurant was closing for the night, the last of the customers paying their bills. Wendell had asked to speak to the owner.

Mr. Woo proved to be a tougher nut to crack than Stan of Stan's Pizza. For one thing, Mr. Woo had never heard of Wendell Corliss or the Transglobal Financial Capital Funding Group. For another thing, Mr. Woo did not want to sell. He had, in fact, hung up on Wendell before Wendell had gotten a chance to really get into negotiation mode.

A less determined man might have at that point given up on the Majestic Rooster and pursued another target, such as the Imperial Moon Harvest or the Jade Dragon Bamboo Palace. But Wendell Corliss was a man who did not accept failure. He was also a man who was very fond of dong bo pork.

So when Woo hung up on him, Wendell immediately placed a call to Shanghai. He spoke to a friend and business associate of his who happened to be the most influential banker in China, and thus, basically, the world. That man had in turn placed a call to Beijing. And so it was that less than twenty minutes after Mr. Woo had hung up on what he believed to be an annoying drunk, his personal cell phone rang and he found himself speaking to the Paramount Leader of the People's Republic of China. The Paramount Leader had politely yet firmly urged Mr. Woo to be receptive to Mr. Corliss, in the spirit of friendship and cooperation between nations, as well as for the continued well-being of Mr. Woo's many relatives still living in the People's Republic.

Thus when Wendell called the Majestic Rooster the second time, he got a completely different Mr. Woo, a can-do Woo who was eager to find ways to accommodate Mr. Corliss. Although he had not been planning to sell his restaurant, he quickly came to see the benefits, especially when Wendell offered not only an extremely generous cash purchase price but also the option of staying on in the position of CEO of what would become the Majestic Transglobal Rooster.

The tricky point in the negotiations came when Wendell stated that one of the conditions—the key condition, really—was that a takeout order of dong bo pork be delivered within forty-five minutes to the beach behind the Key Biscayne Ritz-Carlton. Mr. Woo said he was very sorry, but he did not think that was possible. He could make the order himself, but that would take at least thirty minutes. That left fifteen minutes for the delivery and, with the Saturday-night traffic, there was no way to get from North Miami Beach to Key Biscayne in such a short time.

"Just make the order," said Wendell. "Have it at the front door of your restaurant in thirty minutes."

He hung up the phone and turned to Marty, still lying on his back. "Marty," he said.

"What?"

"Do you see any reason why a helicopter couldn't land on this beach?"

Marty thought about that, staring at the moon.

"No reason at all," he said.

# 31

Seth and Cyndi reached the Escalade, still shaky from their encounter with Trevor. They had opened the doors and were about to get in when Seth said, "Maybe I should leave a note, in case they get here before we do in the morning. I could tell them to call me, tell them it's urgent."

"That's a good idea," said Cyndi.

"Do you have something to write with?"

"I think so." She dug around in her purse, produced a pen. She looked in the glove compartment and found a Wendy's wrapper. "You can write on this."

"Great, thanks," said Seth. Leaving the car door open, he started toward the front entrance. Cyndi, not wanting to be left alone, followed.

Neither of them noticed the dark shambling shape coming around the corner of the fence.

At the front gate, Seth handed the flashlight to Cyndi, pressed the paper against the wall. "Can I use your phone number?" he said. "I just remembered, my phone's broken."

"Sure." Cyndi gave him her number. Seth started to write.

"FREEZE!" shouted Artie Kunkel.

Cyndi screamed and dropped the flashlight. Seth dropped the pen and Wendy's wrapper.

"Put your hands up where I can see them!" said Artie, this being a command he had heard used by law enforcement personnel on television.

Seth and Cyndi raised their hands. Seth said, "Listen, this isn't—"

"Shut up!" said Artie, emerging from the shadows next to the main entrance. He was holding the gun out in front of him with both hands, also as seen on television.

"You don't need to point a gun at us!" said Cyndi. "We're just trying to—"

"I told you to shut up!" said Artie. "Now, what the hell is going on here?"

"Do you want us to answer?" said Seth.

"Of *course* I want you to answer."

"Well, how come you keep telling us to shut up?"

Artie ignored that, as it was accurate. "What are you doing here?" he said.

"OK, listen," said Seth. "One of your gorillas has my wedding ring."

Artie frowned. "What?" he said.

"My wedding ring—actually, my fiancée's wedding ring—was in a suitcase behind the gorilla cage."

"A suitcase?" said Artie.

"Duane left it there," said Cyndi. "You know Duane? He helps out here sometimes with the snakes. He was here today because one of them ate a lady's backpack."

"The gorilla did?" said Artie.

"No, the snake."

"Then why do you keep talking about a gorilla?"

"No, no, wait," said Seth, waving his arms to clear the air of confusion.

"Keep your hands up!" said Artie.

"They *are* up," said Seth. "I'm just waving them."

"Well, stop waving them!"

"OK," said Seth, holding his arms still. "Please just listen to me. My fiancée's wedding ring was in a suitcase, and the gorilla got into it."

"So now we're back to the gorilla."

"Right, the gorilla," said Seth. "Just forget about the snake, OK?"

"I'm not the one who brought up the snake," said Artie. "*You're* the one who brought up the snake."

"Actually," said Cyndi, "I brought up the snake. I was just trying to ex—"

"NEVER MIND ABOUT THE SNAKE!" said Seth, fighting desperately against the urge to wave his arms again. "The point is, the gorilla has my fiancée's wedding ring and I'm just trying to get it back, OK? That's all that's happening here."

Artie frowned, thinking hard. There was something fishy about this story, something that didn't add up. *What the hell was it?*

Suddenly it came to him. He smiled what he believed was a hard-bitten smile.

"Nice try, asshole," he said.

"What?" said Seth.

"There *is* no gorilla here," Artie said triumphantly. He knew this because, out of desperate boredom, he had read every sign in Primate Encounter at least fifty times and he knew he would have remembered a gorilla. He was about to explain this to the suspects the way detectives sometimes did on television when they had cracked a mystery. But when he opened his mouth, what came out instead of an explanation was more of a girlish scream.

Because it was at that moment that Trevor attacked.

Trevor had been observing the humans from the darkness of the parking lot. He recognized all three of them. Two of them had just been in his cage—the male, whom Trevor on principle did not like, and the female, whom Trevor found intriguing.

But the human who most had Trevor's attention was the other male. Trevor knew him very well and disliked him intensely. He was the one who came to Trevor's cage every night and threatened him from the other side of the bars. He was making the same threatening gesture now.

But now there were no bars.

And so Trevor launched himself at Artie, coming out of the darkness with a bloodcurdling howl, teeth bared.

Artie, still screaming, had about a second to react. And react he did, in the form of closing his eyes and pulling the trigger.

The gunshot terrified everyone about equally, including Artie. Seth and Cyndi both had the same reaction: *Run*. They turned and sprinted into the parking lot. Trevor, after being stunned for a moment by this terrifying new noise, did the same, taking an arcing path to the side of Seth and Cyndi, moving considerably faster than they were. Another shot rang out, then another, then another. Artie's eyes were still closed, but, given his marksmanship skills, this actually increased the chance that he would hit somebody.

Trevor, a fast-moving blur in the dark, reached the Escalade first, going around to the far side, looking for safety. He saw the passenger-side door open, as Cyndi had left it, and darted inside, clambering over the front seat into the second row, then the third, huddling down in the footwell, seeking safety from the awful sounds.

Seth and Cyndi, who had not noticed Trevor, reached the Escalade just as a fifth shot rang out. This one, by random chance, actually hit the car, putting a hole in the left rear door.

"Get in!" said Seth.

Cyndi raced around to the passenger side and hurled herself into the seat, slamming the door as Seth slid behind the wheel and started the engine. A sixth shot rang out as Seth yanked the shift lever into drive and stomped on the gas pedal. The Escalade shot forward, rear tires spewing dirt. Seth wrestled with the wheel, fighting to keep the SUV from slamming into the PRIMATE ENCOUNTER sign support as it swerved, screeching onto the road, almost going into a ditch on the other side, before Seth got control of it. Straightened out now, he accelerated, glancing nervously in the rearview mirror.

"Holy shit," he said.

"Yes," said Cyndi.

"That guy is *insane*."

"Yes."

"And that thing . . . what *was* that?"

"I think it was the same gorilla, or whatever it is, we were in the cage with. It must have got out."

"Did you see if it still had the ring?"

"I didn't get a good look."

"Shit." Seth pounded the steering wheel with his palm. "If that thing is running around loose in the woods with Tina's ring, I'm *never* going to get it back."

"Should we go back and see if we can find it?"

Seth shook his head. "Not with that maniac back there with the gun." He shook his head. "I have totally, *totally*, screwed this up. Totally. I'm going to have to tell Tina I lost the ring." He pounded the steering wheel again. "I'm an *idiot*."

They rode in silence for a few minutes.

Then Cyndi said, "Do you smell something?"

# 32

The suite's door buzzer sounded.

LaDawne, dozing on the sofa next to the snoring Wesley, sat up with a start and looked at her watch. "Who in the world is that this late?" she said.

Wesley continued snoring.

Another buzz.

"All right! All right!" said LaDawne, rising and heading for the door.

Another buzz. Insistent.

"All *right*," said LaDawne, opening the door. "You don't need to—"

Brewer was pushing past her into the room, Castronovo right behind him.

"Hey! Don't you *touch* me!" shouted LaDawne. "Wesley, wake up!"

Wesley opened his eyes, saw the Tinker Bells, sat up.

"Who are you?" said LaDawne. "What are you doing in here?"

"Hotel security," said Brewer.

"You can't just come in here like that."

"Yes we can."

Castronovo was drifting over toward Wesley, the two big men eyeing each other.

"What do you want?" said LaDawne.

"We want you to leave the hotel."

"*What?*"

"You have to vacate these premises," said Brewer. "Right now."

"You can't tell us to leave."

"Yes I can."

"We're guests."

"No you're not."

"OK, but the person who *is* a guest knows we're here. He said it's OK. You can ask him."

Brewer made a show of looking around. "Where is he?"

"He's not here right now."

"Then you're going to have to leave. Right now."

"Wesley, get up and tell these men they can't do this to us!"

With a sigh and a grunt, Wesley lifted his massive form from the sofa and stood. Castronovo faced him and unbuttoned his jacket so Wesley could see inside.

"They got guns," said Wesley.

"What are you gonna do, *shoot* us?" said LaDawne.

"Like I told you," said Brewer, "we just want you to leave. Now. You leave now and nobody's going to get hurt."

"There's people we're taking care of," LaDawne said. "In the other room. There's a mother in there with two kids. We have to stay here with them."

"We'll take care of them."

"That woman is sick."

"We'll make sure she gets medical attention."

"We're *not* going to leave them," said LaDawne. She started toward the bedroom door. Brewer quickly blocked her path. "Wesley!" she said.

Wesley was still looking at Castronovo, who now had his hand inside his jacket. "Baby," Wesley said, "they got guns."

Castronovo nodded toward the door and said, "Move." Wesley started walking.

Brewer took LaDawne by the arm. "You're leaving now," he said.

"Don't you *touch* me," she said. She tried to yank her arm away, but Brewer held on, his grip hurting her. He pushed her toward the door.

"You can't *do* this," she said, her tone changing, closer to pleading now. "That poor woman—"

"We're done talking," he said. "You'll leave quietly. You don't stop in the lobby. You keep moving, all the way off the hotel grounds. If you stay around the hotel, or you make any trouble, we'll call the police, and you'll get arrested for trespassing, and you'll go to jail." He opened the door and pushed her into the hallway.

Wesley, with Castronovo behind him, followed LaDawne. He turned in the doorway and said, "How are we supposed to get back to Miami? My car's not here."

"What are you going to do with that woman and those kids?" said LaDawne.

Castronovo closed the door in their faces.

# 33

"I think it's coming from inside the car," said Cyndi.

They were in the vast Miami-Dade suburban blob called Kendall, approaching U.S. 1. They had opened all the windows, but the smell in the Escalade was still there. It was a distinct aroma, and although neither had said so out loud, they both found it disturbingly familiar.

Cyndi turned and looked toward the back of the Escalade. It was dark back there. But she saw movement.

"I think there's something back there," she said.

"What is it?" said Seth. They were making a left turn onto U.S. 1.

"I don't know," said Cyndi. "Could you turn on the inside light?"

Seth fumbled around with the controls. "I can't find the switch."

"I'm going to open my door for a second to make the light go on," she said. She opened the door, looked back.

"Oh God!" she said, slamming the door. "It's back there!"

"What is?"

"The gorilla!"

"*What?*"

"It's in the backseat. It must've got in when we left the doors open back there."

Seth looked in the rearview. He saw a large, round, shaggy head silhouetted in the headlights of the car behind.

"Jesus," he said. "What do we do?"

"Maybe if you stop the car and we open the door, it'll get out."

"Good idea." Seth saw a parking lot to the right and veered the Escalade into it, screeching to a stop next to the entrance to a low concrete building with no windows and a large neon sign on the roof that said CHUCKLETROUSERS.

Chuckletrousers was what is sometimes called a gentlemen's club, although it wasn't really a club, and none of the patrons could by any definition be considered a gentleman. Late Saturday night was the busiest time, during which management employed six bouncers, all exceptionally large individuals clad in tight black Chuckletrousers T-shirts that emphasized their cartoon biceps.

The bouncers' main function was to ensure that the patrons did not touch the performers unless they had paid for this privilege up front. When necessary, the bouncers escorted unruly patrons off the premises, a chore that the bouncers had turned into a sport, the object being to see who could throw a patron the farthest through the air before any part of the patron's body made contact with the parking lot. The current Patron Toss record, marked by a discreet white line spray-painted on the parking lot asphalt, was eight feet, four inches. It was set by a veteran bouncer named Juan "Fig" Figueras, a former Florida State University offensive tackle with approximately the same physical dimensions as a three-bedroom condominium.

On this particular night Fig had been assigned to door duty, which meant his job was to refuse admission to underage males, puking drunks, psychopaths and hardcore sexual deviants, unless, of course, they were politicians or judges. The bouncer on door duty was also supposed to keep an eye on the parking lot, which was why Fig witnessed the high-speed arrival of the Escalade, which skidded to a halt directly in front of the entrance only a few feet from the door. It had barely stopped when the front doors flew open and Seth and Cyndi jumped out.

Fig opened the door and stepped outside.

"You can't park here," he said.

"We're not parking," said Seth. "We're just trying to get something out of our car."

"Well, get it out someplace else. You can't put your car here."

"This is kind of an emergency," said Seth. "There's a gorilla in there."

"A gorilla," said Fig.

"We don't actually know if it's a gorilla," said Cyndi.

"OK, but it's definitely big," said Seth.

Fig, who was not new to the bouncing profession, assumed that this was simply another case of two idiots with too much money who had consumed too much of some illegal substance—Fig was guessing Ecstasy, but he wasn't ruling out ketamine. He decided to try reason first.

"I don't see a gorilla," he said.

"It's in the way backseat," said Cyndi. "The third row."

Fig peered into the rear window. He saw something, but the dark tinting on the Escalade's window kept him from seeing exactly what. So he opened the rear door and leaned inside. He saw a strange-looking, head-like shape in the backseat and leaned in closer to get a better look. He got close enough to see a large raggedy mass beneath the head, but before he could make out what it was a long furry arm shot out and a powerful hand grabbed him by the hair, slammed his head sideways into the doorframe and flung him out of the Escalade. He landed on his back in the parking lot, out cold.

"Ohmigod!" said Cyndi, running over to where Fig lay. "He's hurt! He's bleeding! Seth, get some help!"

Seth opened the door to Chuckletrousers and went inside, where he was assaulted by flashing lights and thunderous bass pumped from nuclear Death Star speakers. In the distance he saw naked women dancing on a bar, clumps of men watching them. He took a few steps forward.

Seth felt a hand on his arm. "Hi!" said a perky voice. He turned and saw that he was attached to an extremely redheaded woman who was wearing only a G-string and sporting a pair of breasts that were far too large and high up to be human. Nevertheless, they *were* breasts, and so Seth, being a male, had no choice, despite the urgency of his mission, but to stare at them.

"Wanna have a drink with me?" she said.

Seth, fighting off the hooter-induced brain paralysis, said, "I need help. There's a guy hurt outside."

The redhead rolled her eyes; there was always some asshole getting beat up in the Chuckletrousers parking lot. She dropped Seth's arm and went off in search of better prospects. Seth looked around and spotted an extremely large man in a Chuckletrousers T-shirt. This man was a bouncer, Paul "The Planet" Pino, who currently held second place in the Chuckletrousers Patron Toss competition with an effort of seven feet, four inches.

Seth trotted over and tapped The Planet on the shoulder. It was like tapping on a Dumpster. The Planet did not like being tapped. It's a fact about strip clubs: The bouncers don't like to be touched any more than the performers do. The Planet turned slowly, the way a cruise ship turns, and looked down at Seth in an unwelcoming manner.

"What," he said.

"There's a guy hurt outside," said Seth, shouting to be heard over the bass. "He needs help."

"Tell the bouncer at the door," said The Planet.

"That's the guy who's hurt."

"Who is?"

"The bouncer. That's who's hurt."

The Planet looked toward the front entrance, did not see Fig at his usual post. He started walking quickly in that direction, Seth hurrying in his wake. The Planet shoved the front door open and saw Fig, who was now sitting up, bleeding from the side of his head, looking dazed. Cyndi was standing next to him.

"What the hell happened?" said The Planet, crouching next to Fig. "You OK? Who did this?"

"I don't know," said Fig, his voice weak.

"There's a thing in the car," said Cyndi, pointing toward the Escalade. "In the back."

The Planet rose and looked at the dark Escalade windows. "What kind of thing?"

"It's like a gorilla."

The Planet looked at Cyndi. "You're saying you have a gorilla in your car."

"We're not sure it's a gorilla," said Cyndi. "But it's a gorilla type of animal."

"I know that sounds weird," said Seth.

"It sounds very weird," agreed The Planet. "And you're saying the gorilla knocked this man out." He pointed at Fig.

"Yes," said Seth. "We're very sorry. It's not our gorilla."

The Planet frowned, pondering. On the one hand, he did not believe there was really a gorilla in the Escalade. Like Fig, he assumed he was dealing with idiots on drugs. On the other hand, there was Fig, on the ground, bleeding. The Planet did not believe that a guy like Seth was capable of putting Fig on the ground. But somebody had, and The Planet figured that whoever it was might be in the back of the car.

He approached the rear door, which was still open. It opened on to the second row of seats; to see back into the third row, he would have to lean his head inside.

"Be careful," said Cyndi.

The Planet did not like being told to be careful by a woman, especially an idiot woman on drugs. He gave Cyndi a look that said *I can take care of myself*, then stuck his head into the rear doorway of the Escalade to see what was what.

Two seconds later, he was lying on the ground next to Fig, moaning and bleeding from the head.

Seth and Cyndi stared at the fallen bouncers, then at each other. Cyndi said, "I'll go get help." Before Seth could answer, she had opened the front door and plunged into the thumping darkness of the club. Seth stood awkwardly near the two fallen bouncers, keeping his distance from the Escalade. As he waited, a pickup truck pulled off of U.S. 1 into the Chuckletrousers lot. Two men got out.

The club door opened and Cyndi emerged with a third Chuckletrousers bouncer, a short but wide and very muscular man with dark curly hair. This was Eddie Friedman, who held the title of head

bouncer, and who, in recognition of his Jewish heritage, was sometimes called, but only by his friends, The Big Bagel.

Eddie saw Fig and The Planet on the ground. He said, "What happened here?"

Cyndi said, "There's a gor—"

"Wait," said Seth, cutting her off. "Let me try to explain it." He had
decided that the problem was the word *gorilla* and wanted to try
another term. "There's a wild animal in the back of the car," he said.

"What kind of wild animal?" said Eddie.

"We don't know," said Seth. "But when these guys tried to grab it, it
knocked them down."

The two men from the pickup truck were approaching the entrance.
They saw Fig and The Planet lying on the ground. They turned around
and went back to their truck.

Eddie looked at Fig and The Planet, then the Escalade, then Seth.
He said, "Why did you bring a wild animal to a strip club?"

Cyndi started to speak, but Seth cut her off.

"It was a mistake," he said. "We're very sorry."

Eddie started toward the open Escalade door.

"Don't look in there," said Cyndi. "That's what happened to the
other two guys."

Eddie stopped, looked down at Fig and The Planet again. They
were both sitting up now, still looking shaky. Eddie moved to the rear
of the Escalade and put his face to the window, but couldn't make out
anything clearly.

"Wait here," he said. He went back into the club. Thirty seconds
later he came out again, holding a flashlight. He went to the rear
window of the Escalade, pressed the flashlight lens against the glass,
then pressed his face against it to peer inside. Immediately he jumped
back.

"Holy fucking shit," he said. Cautiously, he brought the flashlight to
the glass again and leaned in for another look. Seth and Cyndi leaned
in next to him. Cyndi gasped. Looking back at them, from six inches
away on the other side of the glass, was the huge, weird, pie-shaped

face of Trevor. He seemed to be looking at Cyndi. He raised his left hand and pressed it against the glass next to her face, displaying a thumb and four impossibly long, strong fingers designed for sure-handed swinging from limb to limb.

"That's a *gorilla*," said The Big Bagel. "You people have a fucking *gorilla* in your car."

"We're not sure it's a gorilla," said Cyndi.

"Well, whatever the fuck it is," said Eddie, straightening up, "it injured these two men."

"We're very sorry about that," said Seth.

"I'm sure you are," said Eddie. "But I'm still calling the police."

"Wait, no," said Seth. "You can't do that."

"Yes I can," said Eddie, pulling a phone out of his pocket.

"Please," said Seth. "Listen. I can't get involved with the police now. I'm getting married tomorrow morning." He looked at his watch. "Today, actually."

"You two are getting *married* today?" said Eddie.

"Not *both* of us," said Cyndi. "Just him. To a different woman."

"But the wedding is today," said Seth.

Eddie stared at him for a moment. "OK," he said. "Just so I have this straight, for my own personal understanding. You came to a strip club with a woman who is not your fiancée, *and* a gorilla on your wedding day."

Seth took a breath, raised his hands, dropped them at his sides. "I know it sounds crazy," he said.

"It does," said Eddie.

"But if you give me a minute, I can explain it," said Seth.

"You can explain it to the police," said Eddie. He started tapping the screen on his phone

"Please don't do that," said Seth. He reached out and grabbed Eddie by his massive forearm.

Big mistake. You did *not* grab The Big Bagel. In a lightning-quick, well-practiced move, Eddie shot out an elbow, putting some weight behind it, driving it deep into Seth's solar plexus. With a high-pitched

*Unhh*, Seth folded like a cheap lawn chair and staggered backward, trying desperately to breathe.

Cyndi was on Eddie instantly, inches away, right in his face. "Don't you hit him!" she said, stabbing her forefinger into his chest.

"I won't hit him if he stays away from me," said Eddie. "You better keep back, too." Eddie grabbed her by the arm and shoved her hard sideways.

Big mistake.

Trevor shot from the Escalade, teeth bared. He slammed into Eddie, a furry red, 250-pound muscle missile, knocking Eddie backward a good six feet and onto his back, his cell phone clattering across the parking lot. All three bouncers were on the ground now. Trevor stood over them, showing his teeth and making a range of scary noises that a male orangutan makes to let other males know he is prepared to bite their faces off to defend his female. None of the bouncers spoke orangutan, but they knew they did not want to mess with this hairy fanged banshee. All three scrambled backward toward the door to Chuckletrousers.

Cyndi saw her chance. She ran to Seth, who was on his hands and knees, gasping and retching.

"Get up!" she said, putting her arms around him, pulling him to his feet. She dragged him to the Escalade, pushed him in through the driver's-side door, shoved him across the seat and jumped in behind him. She felt for the keys—*Thank God, he left the keys in the ignition*—started the engine, slammed the gearshift into drive and hit the gas. The Escalade lurched forward, the motion causing all the open doors to slam shut. She glanced sideways, saw the bouncers on their feet now, shouting. She glanced into the rearview mirror.

And screamed.

Trevor was in the backseat.

She almost slammed on the brakes, but another sideways glance told her that the bouncers were now running after the car. She looked into the rearview again. Trevor had not moved. She was on U.S. 1 now, gaining speed. From somewhere behind her came the sound of a siren. She kept driving, her eyes darting at the rearview every second or two.

Trevor was looking at her, but he had not moved. Beside her, Seth was still bent over but was breathing more normally and could finally speak.

"Thank you," he said.

"I think we're in trouble," she said. "I think they called the police."

"That's all we need," said Seth, slowly sitting up. "Maybe we can . . . HOLY SHIT THAT THING IS IN THE BACKSEAT."

"I know," said Cyndi. "It jumped back in."

Seth was staring at Trevor. Trevor gave Seth a look that Seth interpreted, correctly, as unfriendly.

"Jesus," said Seth, "what're we gonna do?"

"We can't stop, at least not now. I think there's police behind us."

Seth was still staring at Trevor, who was squatting on the seat, his ridiculously long arms folded in front of him.

"Holy *shit*," said Seth.

"What?"

"He still has the ring."

# 34

Quite a few of the guests in ocean-facing rooms at the Ritz-Carlton were awakened by the helicopter. It sounded as though it was right outside their windows. This was because it *was* right outside their windows.

Those who got out of their beds and went to the window to investigate saw the helicopter land on the lawn behind the hotel. They saw a man leap out, holding a large brown paper bag. He ran toward the beach, ducking down as he passed under the spinning rotors. The helicopter engine kept running. A minute later, the man returned empty-handed. He climbed back into the helicopter, which immediately took off.

Those who were curious enough called the hotel's front desk. They were informed that the helicopter had been making an emergency medical delivery and the Ritz-Carlton regretted any inconvenience. A few people wondered what kind of emergency medical supplies would need to be delivered to a beach in the middle of the night. Eventually these people decided that this was just another one of those strange things that seem to happen in Miami.

In the end, everybody went back to bed.

Except for Meghan. She'd left Tina sleeping soundly in the bedroom of their suite and gone to the living room window to see what the racket was. She wasn't particularly surprised to see a helicopter; she lived in a world where people often came and went by helicopter. She watched it leave, but she didn't feel like going back to bed. She hadn't been sleeping anyway; too much on her mind.

She'd started out by being angry at Tina for ratting out the Haitians to her father. But the more she thought about it, the more she directed her anger at herself. In her mind she kept replaying Tina's words: *And why the hell are you being so self-righteous about this anyway? When have* you *ever cared about this kind of thing?*

The truthful answer, Meghan knew, was: Never. Tina was always the one who cared about things. Meghan had never really cared about anything. She'd always been perfectly content just being a rich man's daughter. She'd grown up knowing that she would never have to work, and she'd never given much thought to what else she might do with her life. She had managed, thanks to a generous donation from Daddy, to scrape through a mediocre college with shitty grades, and since then she had done . . . nothing, really. She traveled wherever and whenever she felt like going, bought whatever caught her eye, occasionally dated men as rich and shallow as herself, watched television, smoked weed. In fact the more she thought about it, the more she realized that, in terms of time and effort, the main thing she had done with her adult life was smoke weed. She had no interest in anything else. She didn't really know what else there was.

She thought about this, staring out the hotel window at the darkness over the ocean, and it made her depressed. More and more these days, that was how she felt. But she knew what to do about it.

She crept into the bedroom, put on jeans and a T-shirt, slipped on some sandals. She opened a dresser drawer and felt beneath her bras and panties, found the baggie and her lighter, stuck them in her pocket.

Then she went out to smoke some weed.

# 35

Laurette had been asleep in the bedroom with her children when the two big men opened the door, banging it hard against the wall. They turned on the bright lights, and one of them grabbed Laurette's shoulder and shook her awake. They were speaking to her in harsh voices. She did not understand their words, but she knew she had to do whatever it was they wanted her to do or they would hurt her. There were men exactly like these in Haiti.

They yanked her off the bed onto her feet. The baby woke and started crying, which annoyed the men. Laurette picked the baby up quickly, tried to quiet her. One of the men went over to the other side of the bed and yanked Stephane out from under the covers. He half fell to the floor, then scrambled over to stand next to Laurette. He was crying, too, but quietly.

The men were talking to Laurette, but she didn't understand them. This also annoyed them. She struggled to understand what they wanted her to do so they would not hurt her or her children.

They were pushing her toward the bedroom doorway. They wanted her to leave. She wished she could ask them to wait just a moment, to let her take the diapers for the baby, and some milk, but she didn't know how to ask them and she didn't want to make them angrier. She held the baby in one arm and guided Stephane with the other, gently pushing her terrified son ahead of her, whispering to him that he should not cry, that everything would be all right, although he knew she did not believe it.

She looked around the big room. It was empty; LaDawne and Wesley were not there. Laurette was very afraid now. She hadn't understood much of what LaDawne had said to her—and LaDawne almost never stopped talking—but Laurette knew LaDawne cared about her and her children. She was a warm and strong woman. She made them feel safe. Laurette knew that LaDawne wouldn't have left them without being forced to go by these men.

These were bad men.

Where were they taking her and her babies?

## 36

The Escalade was still headed north on U.S. 1. Cyndi was still driving, staring straight ahead, trying not to think too hard about the fact that Trevor was less than a yard away. He was still squatting in the second seat, motionless, his gaze locked on Cyndi, ignoring Seth. Trevor was still holding the red velvet ring box in his right hand. Neither Seth nor Cyndi had yet come up with a plan for getting the ring away from him.

Seth was looking back, past Trevor, through the rear window of the Escalade. He saw blue lights flashing in the distance, caught the faint whoop-whoop-whoop of a siren.

"There's a police car coming," he said. "I'm pretty sure it's coming after us."

"What do we do?" said Cyndi.

Seth looked forward. They were approaching a twenty-four-hour drive-through convenience store on the right. He looked back. The lights were gaining fast.

"Pull in there," he said, pointing to the convenience store.

Cyndi veered right. The drive-through window was on an alley between the store and the building to the right.

"Pull forward to the window," said Seth. He looked back; the Escalade was well off the highway and partially concealed by the building next door. He hoped the police wouldn't look to the right as they went by. He stared out the back window. The siren was getting louder.

A Lexus convertible pulled in behind them, driven by a guy wearing a Marlins cap. Seth was glad; the Lexus would further block the view of the Escalade from the highway. Cyndi lowered the window, preparing to speak to the store clerk.

Then she went rigid.

"Oh God," she said.

"What?" said Seth.

"It's touching me."

Seth looked and saw Trevor reaching out his left hand and touching Cyndi's hair with the tips of his long fingers. He was touching her gently, with a slight downward stroking motion. She was vibrating with fear. Seth started to reach out his hand toward Trevor's arm. Trevor turned and looked at him. Seth pulled his hand back.

"I don't know what to do," Seth said. "It doesn't *seem* to want to hurt you."

Cyndi remained rigid, saying nothing.

The siren was getting louder.

"Can I help you?" The clerk, a man in his fifties, was leaning out of the drive-through window.

Cyndi kept staring straight ahead, as if in a trance.

"Miss, can I help you?" said the clerk.

Cyndi said nothing.

Behind them, the Lexus's horn honked. Seth looked back. Marlins cap guy was holding both hands in the air in a *What the hell?* gesture.

"Look, miss," said the clerk, "if you're not going to buy anything, you have to move your car."

The siren was louder.

"Cyndi, order something," said Seth. "Anything."

Cyndi was frozen.

The clerk opened the half door under his window and stepped out. "Miss," he said, "you're blocking the drive-through." He stepped close to the car and leaned in toward Cyndi.

Big mistake.

Trevor leaned forward, his head suddenly appearing in the window behind Cyndi's. He showed the clerk his fangs.

The clerk emitted a non-masculine whimper and stumbled backward.

The Lexus honked again.

The clerk, keeping his eyes on the snarling Trevor, reached back, feeling for the cash register. He found it, glanced back quickly, punched a button. The cash drawer opened. His eyes on Trevor again, the clerk scooped out some bills. Keeping his distance, he tossed them through the window onto Cyndi's lap.

"Please," he said. "That's all I have. Please."

On U.S. 1, the police car shot past, not slowing down, the siren now growing fainter.

The Lexus honked again—a long, angry honk.

"Cyndi!" said Seth. "Go, OK? Just go!"

This time he got through. Cyndi, still facing rigidly forward, put the Escalade in gear and pulled ahead. Trevor, having driven off his rival for the affection of the female, settled back into his squat, no longer touching Cyndi's hair.

Cyndi drove around behind the convenience store and onto a side street. She pulled to the side, put the car in park and looked down at her lap strewn with random bills. She was shaking. "What just happened?" she said.

"I think we just committed a robbery," said Seth. He nodded toward Trevor. "Or he did."

Cyndi was still looking at the money. "Oh God. We should give this back."

"I think that's a bad idea right now. He's gonna call the cops. We need to get out of here. Listen, you're pretty shook up. I'll drive." Seth got out and hustled around to the driver's side. Cyndi slid over and Seth got in. In the backseat, Trevor moved over, too, so he was still behind Cyndi. Seth put the Escalade in drive and got back onto U.S. 1 northbound. He checked the rearview. For the moment there were no flashing lights.

"We're like in serious trouble, aren't we?" said Cyndi. "With those guys back at the strip bar, and now this . . ."

"Yeah," said Seth. "And the whole mess back at the monkey place."

"So what do we do?"

Seth thought for a moment, then said, "OK, here's what we do. We stop at the next place we see that looks safe, like a gas station, and you get out, and you call a cab and go home. I'll take the car and the gorilla and park somewhere near the hotel, see if I can figure out how to make it let go of the ring. It seems to be kind of getting used to me."

"What about the police?"

As if on cue, a police car appeared ahead on the southbound side, speeding, lights flashing. Seth and Cyndi held their breaths as it reached them. But it shot past and kept going, apparently heading to the convenience store. Seth and Cyndi exhaled.

"I'll just hope for the best," said Seth. "But look, there's no reason why you should be involved in this. This is totally my mess. I really, really appreciate the way you've helped. Especially getting me out of that parking lot back there. But I don't want you getting in trouble. I am so sorry you got dragged into this."

"What about the Haitian woman? And her kids?"

Seth shook his head. "I just have to hope her sister comes through. It's all I can do." He pointed ahead. "OK, here's a Shell station. I'll let you off here." He pulled into the brightly lit service plaza, stopped toward the back, near the air pump. He put the Escalade in park and turned to Cyndi.

"OK," he said. "I really don't know how to thank you. But . . . thank you."

Cyndi looked straight ahead. She shook her head.

"No," she said.

"No what?"

"No, I'm not getting out. I'm staying."

"Cyndi, this isn't your problem."

"Maybe it didn't used to be. But I feel like it is now. I want to make sure Laurette's OK. And her kids." She paused, looked down. "And I want to make sure you're OK."

"You don't have to—"

"I know I don't have to. I *want* to. Listen, Seth, you're a really nice guy. You didn't have to help those people but you did. You didn't have to let them stay. A lot of people wouldn't have. But you did, even with the wedding and everything else. You did it because it was the right thing to do. I want to do the right thing, too."

She raised her head, turned toward Seth. "I'm staying."

Seth turned toward her. Her eyes were shining. To Seth, even in the garish light of the Shell station she looked beautiful. He reached out and rested his hand gently on her arm. Her skin was smooth and soft. "Thank you," he said, his voice strained. Cyndi smiled and put her hand over his hand. Her hand was warm. She left it on his. Seth hesitated for a moment, the two of them looking into each other's eyes. Then he leaned closer to her, and she leaned closer to him, and in that instant they both knew that, wrong as it was, they were about to kiss.

Trevor made an unhappy noise.

They quickly pulled their hands apart and sat upright. Seth, smiling ruefully, shook his head, put his hands on the wheel. "I guess he's right," he said.

"It's like having an *abuela*," said Cyndi.

"A what?"

"An *abuela*. A Cuban grandmother. If you're a Cuban girl from an old-school family, when you go on a date your *abuela* goes with you to chaperone. She rides in the backseat, keeps an eye on you, makes sure nothing happens."

"Did that happen to you?"

"Absolutely. I went on dates when I was sixteen, seventeen years old, some boy driving me, my *abuela* sitting right behind us. And, trust me, she was at least as scary as that thing is."

Seth snorted, his first laugh in many hours. Then he said, "You really sure about this? You don't want to get out now?"

"I'm sure."

Seth put the Escalade in gear and pulled out of the gas station. "Listen," he said. "Back there . . ."

"Don't worry about it," said Cyndi. "It's been a crazy night."

"Yeah," agreed Seth. "Crazy night."

They drove on, neither talking, both thinking.

# 37

Meghan had settled on her bench by the lawn on the ocean side of the hotel. The night was pleasant—warm, but not too sticky, an easy breeze carrying the salty tang of the Atlantic. She sat for a few minutes staring at the sky, then dug the baggie out of her jeans, fished out the papers and began to roll a joint. She took her time getting it right. She enjoyed rolling joints, anticipating the buzz to come.

She finished the joint and pocketed the baggie. She was just about to light the joint when the hotel door opened, the one that led to the elevator lobby. Meghan saw the massive form of Brewer emerge. Behind him loomed Castronovo. Between the two big men were the much smaller figures of a woman and a boy, both very thin and dark-skinned. They passed by a pathway light, and Meghan saw that the woman was carrying a baby. She and the boy looked frightened.

Brewer left the path, turning right; the others followed, Castronovo herding the Haitians. They were going around the side of the hotel apparently to avoid going through the main lobby. They hadn't seen Meghan on the bench. They disappeared in the darkness. Meghan guessed they were headed for the parking lot.

She inserted the joint in her lips, dug into her jeans, pulled out a butane lighter. She flicked it, brought the flame up, anticipating taking the first hit, sucking the sweet smoke deep into her lungs, holding it, letting it blend with her blood, feeling the mellow descend . . .

She held the lighter an inch from the tip of the joint, staring into the yellow-blue flame.

She released her thumb. The flame went out. She lowered the lighter and said, "Fuck." She stuck the joint into her bra, stood up and started walking quickly around the side of the hotel.

She caught up with them on the hotel driveway, heading toward the parking lot.

"Wait," she called.

The group stopped and looked at her. Laurette and Stephane still looked scared. Castronovo and Brewer looked annoyed, although they kept their voices grudgingly respectful when they spoke to the boss's daughter.

"Meghan," said Castronovo. "What are you doing out here, this hour?"

"That's what I want to ask you," said Meghan. "What are you doing?"

"This doesn't concern you," said Brewer.

"Don't tell me what concerns me. I want to know where you're taking these people."

"Listen, Meghan," said Brewer, "we're just carrying out your father's wishes here. These people were staying in Seth's room and they weren't supposed to be there, no legal right. So your father asked us to . . . to relocate them."

"Does Seth know you *relocated* them from his room?"

"It's not his decision," said Brewer. "Your father's paying for the room."

"So that means it's OK for you to just yank them out of there in the middle of the night? A woman with two kids? With a baby?"

"They're going to be fine," said Castronovo. "Nobody's going to hurt them."

"They don't look fine to me," said Meghan. "They look terrified."

Brewer stepped closer to Meghan, looming over her, putting his large frame between her and the Haitians. A big-man intimidation move.

"Meghan," he said. "Your father's not going to like this, you interfering with us. Why don't you just go back to your room and chill out, OK?"

"You mean just go smoke a joint? Get stoned?"

"I didn't say that."

Meghan stepped around Brewer, went to Laurette, who was watching her uncertainly. She put her hand on Laurette's shoulder. She could feel the bones through her thin, worn blouse.

"Are you OK?" Meghan said.

Laurette didn't answer.

"They don't speak English," said Castronovo.

"So you haven't explained what's happening to them?"

Castronovo shrugged.

"Where are you taking them? Are you taking them to the police?"

"No," said Castronovo. "We're taking them to Delray B—" He stopped, seeing Brewer shake his head.

"They'll be fine," said Brewer. "We're just getting them out of this hotel, where they're not guests and where they have no legal right to be, OK? We're doing this at your father's request because he doesn't want their presence here to interfere with your sister's wedding. You don't want these people to ruin your sister's wedding, do you?"

"Right," said Meghan. "God forbid anything should interfere with Tina's wedding."

"OK, so if you don't mind, we're going to—"

"I *do* mind," said Meghan. "These aren't animals you take to the shelter and dump. These are *people*."

"They're illegals."

Meghan snorted. "And of course you care *deeply* about the law. Like when you shot the Jet Ski from the beach. No law against *that*, right?"

Brewer said nothing.

"Listen," said Meghan. "Just leave this woman and her kids with me, OK? I'll get them a room. I'll pay for it with my money."

Brewer shook his head. "Sorry," he said. "We do what your father tells us to do."

"What if my father told you to kill them? Would you do that?"

"Meghan, come on. We're just doing our job here."

"I'll call my father."

Brewer smirked. "Go ahead, call him."

Meghan reddened. She knew what would happen if she called Mike. He'd tell her to go to bed and stay out of this. She felt helpless and foolish, resorting to a child's threat. *I'll tell my daddy on you.*

"Let's go," Brewer said to Castronovo. "Good night, Meghan."

They turned away from her and resumed walking toward the parking lot, herding Laurette, with the baby, and Stephane. The Haitians went docilely. Meghan stayed where she was. Laurette turned and looked back at her, their eyes meeting for a moment. Then Brewer said something, and Laurette turned her head forward again.

When they were almost out of sight, Meghan started following. She reached the edge of the parking lot in time to see Brewer and Castronovo putting the Haitians into the backseat of a black Lincoln Navigator. The men got into the front seat, Castronovo driving. He started the Navigator and backed out of the space. Meghan went a few steps closer, next to one of the palms that lined the edge of the lot. The Navigator started forward. As they went past Meghan, Brewer, in the front passenger seat, glanced at her, shook his head and looked away.

Laurette, in the backseat, met her eyes again.

This time it was Meghan who looked away.

# 38

**Wendell and Marty** had finished the dong bo pork. They both agreed it was delicious, totally worth the effort involved in persuading Mr. Woo to sell the newly named Majestic Transglobal Rooster.

They were no longer hungry. They were content now to lie on their backs in the sand and watch the moon's leisurely journey across the sky.

They had been utterly silent for more than half an hour when Corliss said, "We're high, aren't we?"

Marty said, "I do believe we are."

"But not from drinking wine."

"No. I think we're baked."

"Baked?"

"We're on the choongs."

"On the *what*?"

"Choongs. We're stoned. High on pot. Or as the kids today call it, with their crazy slang lingo, *marijuana*."

"But we didn't smoke marijuana."

"Correct."

"So how did we get on the choongles?"

"Not the choongles. Just the *choongs*."

"The choongs. How did we get on them?"

"I think it was when we ate dessert."

"You can get high from dessert?"

"You can if it's brownies and somebody puts pot in them."

"Somebody put pot in the brownies?"

"I think maybe somebody did."

"Who would have done that?"

"I dunno. Maybe Seth, as a joke. Maybe Meghan. She likes pot. But whoever it was, pretty soon after we ate the brownies was when I started to feel the buzz."

Wendell thought for a while, then said, "I had three of those brownies."

"Whoa. Really? Then you are seriously baked, sir, because that was some strong weed. I only had one and I'm still buzzed. Or, as the kids say today, on the choongles."

"That would explain how come Greta ate the whole pizza despite the carbs."

"It would. Also why you bought two restaurants."

They both burst out laughing, thinking about the Transglobal restaurant empire.

"Seriously," said Marty, when they'd settled back down, "are you starting to feel buyer's remorse? I mean, you're Wendell Fucking Corliss."

"I am indeed. I am Wendell Fucking Corliss."

"So when you wake up tomorrow and you are no longer high and you still have two restaurants, are you going to feel like you, Wendell Fucking Corliss, made a stupid mistake?"

Wendell pondered it. "I don't care," he said.

"Seriously? It's a lot of money."

Wendell made a farting noise with his mouth.

"Come again?" said Marty.

"Do you know how much money I spent tonight on restaurants?"

"Including the helicopter?"

"Sure, include the helicopter."

"A million dollars?"

"No. It was about seven hundred and twenty thousand. But let's say, for the sake of argument, that it was a million. Let's say I spent a million dollars tonight so we could have some dong bo pork and a pepperoni pizza."

"Which you did not get any of."

"Which I did not get any of. Now, let's say I do that again tomorrow night."

"Buy two restaurants?"

"For a million dollars."

"OK."

"And then let's say I do it the next night, and the next, and the next. And I keep doing it."

"OK."

"Do you know how long it would take me to run out of money? Take a guess."

"OK, spending a million a night." Marty frowned, trying to do some mental calculations, which he was not good at even when he was not baked. "I dunno," he said, "five years?"

"Longer."

"Ten years."

"Longer."

"*Twenty* years?"

"The answer," said Wendell, "is just about a hundred years."

Marty sat up. "Are you shitting me?"

"I am not shitting you. I am constipating you."

"You're what?"

"Shouldn't that be the opposite of shitting somebody? Constipating them?"

"I guess it should."

"My point is, the money is nothing. It has no material effect whatsoever on my life. It does not matter. What matters is, this was the most fun I've had in as long as I can remember. And you know why?"

"Why?"

"Because it was *ridiculous*. There was no logical upside to it. Which is *extremely* uncharacteristic of me. The one principle I've lived my life by is: Don't do anything ridiculous. Always pursue the upside, always avoid the downside. Take risks, but always *calculated* risks. Everything I have ever done has been calculated. When I was at Harvard, you know what I did?"

"What?"

"I studied! I studied *all the time* so I could get better grades than everybody else, so I could get into Harvard Business School and get better grades than everybody there and get my MBA and go out and make more money than everybody else. You know what I did not do at Harvard?"

"What?"

"I never got high. Not once. This was in the early seventies. *Everybody* got high then. There were people in my dorm who were never *not* high, as far as I could tell. I walked by their rooms, smelled the pot, heard them playing the same Van Morrison album over and over and over again, and I thought they were idiots. It wasn't a moral thing. It was a rational calculation. Drugs diminish your mental capacity and distort your sense of reality, and when your mental capacity is diminished, you make foolish decisions."

"Like buy a restaurant just to get a pizza delivered."

"Exactly. So I never did anything like that. I was extremely disciplined and focused all through college and graduate school. Then I went out and excelled at rational risk taking, and I became very wealthy and influential. I became Wendell Fucking Corliss. A complete prick."

"Oh come on. Not a *complete* prick."

"Yes! Complete! Ask anyone who has ever negotiated with me. 'What a prick,' they'll say. And they'll be right! I *am* a prick. I am *proud* of my prickitude. I can out-prick *anybody* in a business situation. This is the essence of being Wendell Fucking Corliss."

"Yeah, but that's a pretty good thing to be, right? You have a mansion and a jet and a helicopter and probably a giant boat."

"Actually, I have several of each of those things."

"Right. And you can go anywhere you want in the world and do whatever you want."

"True, I *can* do whatever I want. But in the course of becoming, by discipline and focus and careful calculation, Wendell Fucking Corliss,

I have somehow become very limited in my ability to imagine things that I might enjoy doing because I automatically rule out anything that's irrational or might be viewed as ridiculous. So I end up doing basically the same things that all extremely wealthy people do, and I do them with other extremely wealthy people. I have come to simply assume that only extremely wealthy people are worthy of socializing with me. And you know what I have found?"

"What?"

"I have found that extremely wealthy people can be fantastically boring. Not all, but many. Because it turns out that, in most cases, the only thing they're really good at is getting rich. I've been bored to death in some of the most fabulous places on the planet. And yet these are the people I associate with as a matter of policy. May I be frank with you?"

"Please."

"I was standing outside this hotel with the Clarks when you and your friends arrived. Do you remember?"

"Dimly."

"Unless I'm mistaken, all you were wearing at that time was a shirt. Except you were wearing it as pants, with your legs in the sleeves."

"Oh yeah. That was Steve's shirt. My balls kept falling out the neckhole."

"That they did. Do you want to know what my initial impression of you was?"

"I'm guessing not positive."

"Correct. I thought you were an idiot, a clown. I was appalled that I, Wendell Fucking Corliss, would be attending the same social event as a repulsive buffoon such as yourself. No offense intended."

"None taken."

"And I was also appalled when I realized that you were going to be at the rehearsal dinner."

"I totally understand."

"And you may have noticed that I didn't say a word to you or your friends until the brownies arrived. And if they hadn't arrived, I never would have talked to you. I would have ended up talking to Mike Clark about the relative merits of our helicopters. Do you know how many evenings I've spent in fabulous places having boring conversations with boring people about helicopters?"

"A lot?"

"A *lot*. But that would have been the topic. That would have been my evening. Instead, thanks to the brownies, I got on . . . I've forgotten—is it the *choongs* or the *choongles*?"

"The *choongs*."

"I got on the choongs and I've had a very enjoyable time chatting and laughing and noticing things I never would have noticed before and making truly absurd yet strangely pleasurable financial decisions. I believe Greta enjoyed herself, too."

"I believe she did."

"But here's the thing. On the one hand, this has been a remarkably pleasant evening. But on the other hand, it has been troubling."

"Why troubling?"

"Because I'm wondering why I have so few evenings this enjoyable. I'm wondering if I didn't take a wrong turn long ago when I walked self-righteously past the pot smokers' dormitory door. Maybe instead of walking past, I should have opened the door and gone inside and gotten high and listened to Van Morrison over and over. I'm wondering if I haven't missed out on a whole lot of life because I've always been so busy being Wendell Fucking Corliss."

"So you're saying the door is, like, a metaphor."

"Exactly. A metaphor for an opportunity missed. I think I should've opened the door."

Marty shook his head. "Nope."

"Nope what?"

"Nope, you're wrong."

"Why do you say that?"

"Because I was on the other side of that door."

"*You* went to Harvard? No offense."

"None taken. I went to the University of Delaware. But, *metaphorically*, I was on the other side of that door. I spent the vast majority of my college days high, listening to Phish."

"You listened to *fish?*"

"It's a band. They were my Van Morrison. I listened to them all the time and I went to see them whenever I could. What I didn't do very often was study or attend class because I found that those activities interfered with getting high. After college I continued to get high—a *lot*. I did manage to get into a shitty law school, where, thanks to my ongoing policy of getting high a lot, I did shittily. There's no way I will ever pass the bar exam unless they change it to include a lot more questions about World of Warcraft."

"World of what?"

"Warcraft. It's a video game you play against other people on the Internet. That's basically what I'm doing with my life. I'm a grown man and I have no job and I live at home with my parents. I have very little money and nowhere to go, so I sit in my parents' family room and play World of Warcraft online against thirteen-year-old boys and other unemployed loser stoners like myself. And I get excited, sometimes *very* excited, when I am able to outwit some thirteen-year-old boy. *That's* what happens to you when you spend your college days on the other side of the door getting high and listening to Van Morrison or, in my case, Phish."

"So you're saying pot is bad?"

"Fuck no. Pot is *great*. It's the only fun thing I do. I'm just saying I wish that back when you were walking by the door, I heard your footsteps and put down the bong and opened the door and followed you to whatever class you took where you learned to make ginormous piles of money so that now I'd be rich, except maybe not as rich as you because I would have continued to get high but in *moderation*. So that today I'd be combining the benefits of being able to afford a big house and a jet and a trophy wife, no offense . . ."

"None taken."

". . . with the benefits of being able, if I was at some fabulous location and some boring wealthy asshole started to talk to me about his helicopter, to tell him to shut the fuck up and let me enjoy the fabulous location, and maybe fire up a doobie. Do you follow me?"

"Incredibly, I think I do."

They both stared at the sky for a minute. Then Wendell said, "Is this profound?"

"Is what profound?"

"What we're discovering here about ourselves. That I would be happier if I had been less obsessively rational and disciplined and smoked pot more. And you would be happier if you had smoked pot less and been more disciplined in pursuing a career. That each of us would be happier if he were more like the other. Is that profound?"

Marty thought about that. "No," he said.

"Why do you say that?"

"Because we're high. When you're high, you're always thinking you've discovered some mind-blowing insight. Then the next day you realize that what you discovered boils down to something pretty obvious, like that the universe is really fucking big. Or something that doesn't really matter, like that you have way more bacteria cells inside you than actual human cells."

"Not really."

"Oh yeah, really. It's a Science Fact. Your body contains like ten times as many bacteria as human cells."

"That can't be true."

"It is totally true. Google it, if you don't believe me."

"But if that's true, what you're saying is, we're not really human. I mean, we *are*, but only a tenth of us is. We're really just hosts for all these other living things. That's incredible. *We're not really human. We're essentially hybrids.*"

"That's exactly my point."

"That we're essentially hybrids?"

"No, that you think shit like this is profound. Trust me, tomorrow you'll be, like, 'Yeah, OK, so there's a lot of bacteria inside us. Ho-hum.' Then you'll forget about the bacteria and go ahead and order breakfast just like you always do."

"Really?"

"Really. Nothing will come of it. I've had many, many amazing pot insights, including about the bacteria, and every single one of them turned out, upon further review, to be stupid. That's the thing about pot: It's fun, but nothing really important ever comes out of it. That's how come you had all those millions of Grateful Deadheads smoking all that pot and listening to all those endless songs for all those decades and the only tangible result of all that, in the end, was a lot of ugly T-shirts."

"So this isn't profound, this conversation."

"I seriously doubt it."

"It's just us talking."

"Nothing wrong with talking."

"I wasn't a prick, right? When I negotiated with Stan and Mr. Woo?"

"Not at all. Can I be honest?"

"Please."

"You were more of a pussy."

"Seriously?"

"Seriously. Right now, Stan and Mr. Woo are both sitting around counting their money and going, 'That was Wendell Fucking Corliss? What a pussy.'"

Wendell snickered. It was his first snicker in perhaps forty-five years. "I guess you're right," he said. "Those were the worst negotiations I've ever been involved in. I violated all of my principles. But I have to say, I've enjoyed it. The whole night. I really enjoyed it."

"Me too."

Several more minutes passed in silence. Then Wendell said, "So the brownies are all gone?"

"I believe they are."

"Do you think it would be difficult to get more?"

"Are you kidding? This is Miami. You can get anything you want. For the right money you could have the mayor come out and fuck a manatee right here on the beach."

"As appealing as that sounds, I'm really just interested in the brownies."

"Believe me, that is not a problem."

Wendell stared at the sky. Out over the Atlantic, the horizon was just starting to change from deep black to light gray, the first hint of the new day coming.

"One more question," he said.

"What?"

"How hard do you think it would be to get hold of Van Morrison?"

# 39

Seth turned in to the driveway of the Ritz just as a black Lincoln Navigator was pulling out. The atmosphere inside the Escalade was still tense, but since the convenience store Trevor had been well behaved in the backseat, sitting quietly directly behind Cyndi, mainly staring out the window.

He still held the red ring box in his right hand. Seth and Cyndi had not come up with a plan for getting him to part with it. They had decided to stop the car in a deserted part of the hotel parking lot and try to figure out their next move.

As Seth steered into the lot, he saw a woman standing next to a palm tree up ahead. Drawing closer, he recognized Meghan. She looked agitated.

"That's Tina's sister," he said.

"What's she doing out here?"

"I dunno." He pulled up next to Meghan and lowered his window. "Meghan, you OK?"

"Seth!" she said. She glanced past him, registering the presence of Cyndi. "There's a big problem."

"What?"

"The people in your room. The Haitians."

"What about them?"

"My father's bodyguards, Brewer and Castronovo. They took them."

"What? What do you mean, *took* them?"

"They went to your room and made them leave, the mom and the two kids. They were here just now in the parking lot. They left maybe two minutes ago."

"Were they in a black Navigator?"

"Yes."

"I saw them leave. Where are they taking them?"

"Delray something? Castronovo started to say the name but Brewer stopped him."

"Delray Beach," said Cyndi.

"Why would they take them there?" said Seth.

"I don't know. I tried to stop them, but Brewer and Castronovo don't listen to me. They do what my father says."

"But why did your father tell them to do this? How'd he even know they were in my room?"

Meghan started to say something, stopped, shook her head. "No idea," she said.

Seth stared at his hands, gripping the wheel. *"Damn,"* he said. "That poor woman has to be terrified."

Meghan nodded. "They looked really scared."

"Maybe we should call the police," said Cyndi.

"No," said Seth. "That's exactly what Laurette *doesn't* want. That was the point of this whole thing, her staying in my room. *Damn.*" He looked at Cyndi. "How would they go to Delray Beach?"

"Ninety-five, probably. It's, like, an hour, hour and a half."

"I still don't get why Delray Beach. What would they do with them up there?"

"Maybe they just want them far away from here," said Meghan. "So they won't mess up the wedding."

Seth looked at the sky, which was getting lighter. He put his forehead on the steering wheel. "Today," he said. "I'm getting married *today*. Look at me. Look at this situation. How did everything get so fucked up?"

Cyndi said, "Don't worry. It's OK."

Seth, his head still on the wheel, looked sideways at Cyndi. "How is it OK?"

"It just is. You get out of the car, walk into the hotel, get some sleep, wake up and have your wedding. It'll be a wonderful day."

"What about Laurette and her kids?"

"You did everything you could. She wouldn't even be alive without you. This is not your fault. She knows that. Everybody knows that. You're a good person and you did the best you could. But now it's your wedding day and you need to just think about that."

Seth sat up. Suddenly he felt desperately tired. He looked toward the hotel, where he had a nice big room with a nice big now-empty bed. He put his hand on the door handle.

*She wouldn't even be alive without you.*

He took his hand off the door handle.

"We could follow them," he said.

"What?" said Cyndi.

"Wait a minute," said Meghan. "No."

Seth looked at his watch. "There's time. The wedding's not until this afternoon. If we leave now and drive fast, we can catch up on I-95. We can follow them to Delray Beach."

"And do what?" said Meghan. "They're violent men, Seth. They have guns."

"I'm not going to confront them. Just follow them and make sure they don't do anything bad to Laurette and the kids."

"And if they do?"

"I don't know," said Seth. "Call the police, I guess."

"But she doesn't want the police to know about her," said Cyndi.

"OK," said Seth. "I don't have an exact plan. But I'm not just gonna let those two assholes take those people away and do whatever they want with them." He started the engine. "I need to get going. You can get out if you want."

Cyndi shook her head. "I'm going," she said.

Seth put the car in gear.

"Wait," said Meghan. "I'm going, too." Before Seth or Cyndi could respond, she opened the back door, slid inside and pulled the door closed.

Then she screamed.

Then she said: "THERE'S A FUCKING ORANGUTAN IN THE BACKSEAT!"

"It's OK," said Cyndi.

"WHY IS IT OK?"

"He's been pretty calm lately."

Despite this assurance, Meghan sat rigidly still, staring at Trevor. Trevor was staring back at her. He reached out his left hand and very gently touched her hair with his left forefinger. Meghan did not move. Trevor stroked her hair for a moment, then pulled his hand back and resumed staring at her.

Meghan felt a little calmer. "Why," she said, "is there an orangutan in this car?"

"It's kind of a complicated story," said Seth.

"Is that what it is?" said Cyndi. "An orangutan? Because we've been calling it a gorilla."

"No, it's definitely an orangutan. A full-grown male. I'm an animal person. I was going to be a veterinarian before I found out there would be actual study involved. What do you mean, it's a complicated story?"

"Well," said Seth, "to cut right to the chase, bottom line, it has Tina's wedding ring."

"The *orangutan* does?"

"Yeah. He's been holding on to it. I don't know why, but he seems to like it."

Meghan looked at Trevor's hands. The right one was wrapped around the red ring box. "But how—I mean, why—*why* does the orangutan have Tina's wedding ring?"

"I can explain that," said Seth. "But if we're going to catch those guys, we have to get moving. Are you still in?"

Meghan looked at Trevor. He was still looking at her.

"I've dated worse," she said. "I'm still in."

Seth hit the gas.

# 40

Rose and Sid were up early. They were always up early, because, as older people tend to do, they spent a substantial chunk of each morning in the bathroom, laboriously striving to execute bodily functions that younger people take for granted.

At the moment, it was Rose's turn on the throne. As was her habit, she was keeping Sid up to date on her progress by yelling through the door.

"I'LL BE OUT SOON," she was saying. "I THINK I'M ALMOST FINISHED. BUT IT COULD BE A LITTLE LONGER. SID? SID?"

"OK," said Sid, this being what he always said in response to Rose's morning play-by-play. Sid was sitting on the edge of the bed exactly where Rose had left him. He was watching the TV channel Rose had selected for him after she had spent ten minutes on the phone with a hotel employee who explained to her, with great patience, how to operate the remote control.

At the moment, the channel was showing the local news. On the screen was a thin but perky woman named Lisbeth Renaldo, who could have been pretty, but who also could have been Mike Tyson. There was no way to tell because she was wearing roughly a cubic yard of makeup.

"If you're just joining us this morning," she was saying, "we're following one of those weird stories that makes you shake your head and say, 'Only in Miami.'" To emphasize this point, Lisbeth shook her head. Her hair did not move a micron. "Miami-Dade Police are telling us that early this morning, the Primate Encounter tourist attraction in the Redlands was broken into by a man and a woman . . . who apparently stole an orangutan. Yes, you heard that right: They stole an orangutan! According to police, the pair allegedly used the animal to assault a security guard—an assault that led to gunfire. And, believe it or not, there is still more to this story. Police are now telling Action 5 that a short while after the assault at Primate Encounter, the alleged suspects then used this same orangutan to attack three bouncers at a gentlemen's club on U.S. 1 in Kendall and then rob a convenience store a short distance away. Action 5 has exclusive coverage of this bizarre crime spree. We'll begin with crime reporter Trace Finn, who is live on the scene at Primate Encounter. Trace, what's the situation down there?"

"I'M ALMOST DONE," shouted Rose from the bathroom.

"OK," said Sid.

On the screen now was a suit-wearing blond man who appeared to be about twenty-three years old. He was standing in front of the roadside Primate Encounter sign, holding a microphone, his brow slightly furrowed to indicate seriousness. Standing next to him was the blobular form of Artie Kunkel, still wearing his security guard uniform, which featured armpit stains the size of Frisbees.

"Lisbeth," said Trace Finn to the camera, "it almost sounds like a joke—robbers stealing an orangutan and using it to attack a security guard. But there's nothing funny about what happened here if you were the victim of that attack. I'm standing here with Primate Encounter security guard Arnie Krunkle, who—"

"Artie," said Artie.

"Sorry, Artie Krunkle, who—"

"*Kunkel.* There's no *r.* Just Kunkel."

"OK, fine," said Trace Finn, trying without complete success to hide his annoyance. "Can you tell us exactly what happened here last night?"

"ALMOST FINISHED," called Rose from the bathroom.

"OK," said Sid.

"Well," said Artie, "I was making my rounds, which I do every hour. I go around and check on things. I do this every hour. I follow a certain route that I'm prescribed to take where I go from one thing to another. So, basically, I'm almost always out patrolling. I start at the back, and then there's this path that goes around all the animal cages, starting with the monkeys, and then over to the birds, and then over to—"

"So can you tell us when you saw the alleged assailants?" said Trace Finn, moving things along.

"Right," said Artie. "So I was making my rounds and I heard some noise out by the front gate and I went to investigate, which is when I saw the alleged assailants."

"And it was a man and a woman?"

"Right, a man and a woman. I ordered them to halt, which is when Trevor attacked."

"Trevor?"

"Trevor is the orangutan."

"It attacked you?"

"Yes, which is when I had to defend myself, in self-defense. With the gun."

"So you had a gun?"

Artie, with a glance at the camera, said, "No."

"You *didn't* have a gun?"

"I'm not supposed to carry a gun. So I don't."

"But shots *were* fired, right?"

"Right. Shots were fired."

"So who fired them?"

Another glance at the camera. "I did."

"So you *did* have a gun."

"Not at first. Eventually I did have a gun, yes."

"JUST ANOTHER MINUTE," said Rose.

"OK," said Sid.

"How did you eventually get a gun?" said Trace Finn.

"I took it away from him," said Artie.

Trace Finn's brow furrows deepened.

"Wait, are you saying the *orangutan* had a gun?"

"No, the guy. The assailant. I took his gun."

"How did you get it away from him?"

"I don't really remember."

"OK," said Trace Finn, determined to get this thing done, "so you got the gun, and then what?"

"I fired it. In self-defense."

"Did you hit the assailant? Or Taylor?"

"Who's Taylor?"

"The orangutan."

"No, he's *Trevor.*"

"OK, did you hit him? Or anybody?"

"I don't know. It was dark."

"Then what happened?"

"They jumped in the car and drove away."

"Were you hurt in the struggle?"

"What struggle?"

"To get the gun."

"Oh. No. I was just doing my job."

Trace Finn looked into the camera again.

"So there you have it, Lisbeth. An eyewitness account from security guard Artie Krunkle."

*"Kunkel,"* said Artie. "There's no *r.*"

"JUST ANOTHER MINUTE," said Rose.

"OK," said Sid.

Lisbeth Renaldo was back on the screen. "Thank you, Trace," she said. "Police told Action 5 News that the assailants left Primate Encounter in a late-model black Cadillac Escalade. They then apparently drove to Chuckletrousers, a gentlemen's club located on U.S. 1."

The TV screen showed the exterior of Chuckletrousers.

"It is not known why they went here, but what is known is that the orangutan attacked three Chuckletrousers bouncers in this parking lot. All three were injured, although police say that fortunately none of them were hurt seriously. Meanwhile the assailants took off again in the Escalade."

"ONE MINUTE," said Rose.

"OK," said Sid.

The TV screen was now showing the convenience store.

"A short while later," said Lisbeth, "they used the orangutan to threaten the cashier at this convenience store a little farther north on U.S. 1. They forced the cashier to open the register and give them an undetermined amount of cash."

The screen was showing Lisbeth again, her expression letting the viewers know she still couldn't believe how *crazy* this all was.

"Police have released this video from a surveillance camera in the Chuckletrousers parking lot," she said.

The screen showed a grainy, dimly lit image. In the foreground, scooting backward toward the camera on the ground on their butts, were three large male figures. Advancing on them, teeth bared, was Trevor.

"This was moments after the orangutan attacked the bouncers," said Lisbeth. "You can see them on the ground with the orangutan still threatening them."

Several feet behind Trevor, a shadowy female figure could be seen helping a shadowy male figure to his feet next to a dark-colored car.

"The two suspects are in the background," said Lisbeth. "You can see the female suspect helping the male suspect get up; apparently he was knocked down at some point during the attack, although the details of that are not clear."

The female figure was pushing the male toward the passenger car, shoving him into the open doorway. As he got in, he turned sideways and for just a second he was looking toward the camera.

Sid frowned and leaned forward.

"I'M DONE," said Rose. There was a flushing sound. "SID? SID?"

"OK," said Sid.

On the screen, the female figure jumped in after the man, pushing him over to the passenger side. She threw the car into gear. At the instant it lurched forward, Trevor, showing amazing quickness and agility for his size, darted into the car via the back doorway. As the car accelerated forward and disappeared off camera, the doors slammed shut. The video ended with the bouncers scrambling to their feet.

Lisbeth was back on camera, now looking Serious. "The couple— and the orangutan—are still at large. They were last seen driving a late-model black Cadillac Escalade northbound on U.S. 1 in South Miami. Miami-Dade Police are asking anyone with any information on the suspects to call Crimestoppers. But police are warning people not to approach the suspects, who are believed to be armed and danger- ous. Police are especially warning people not to approach the orang- utan, which as you saw in the surveillance video can be a very dangerous animal. Action 5 will be following this story closely and we'll have continued reports throughout the morning. But right now we're going to take you to Coral Springs, where yesterday a motorist drove his car into a community swimming pool."

The screen showed a large swimming pool with a 1998 Buick Le- Sabre fully submerged in the deep end.

"You can go in now," said Rose, emerging from the bathroom. She looked at the TV screen. "Is that a car in the swimming pool?"

"I think I saw Seth," said Sid.

"Quiet," said Rose, pointing to the TV. "I want to hear."

"Police say the driver, an eighty-seven-year-old Margate resident, was attempting to park his car in the community center parking lot when he apparently confused the accelerator with the brake," said Lis- beth. "His car went through a fence, then across a lawn and a pool deck before plummeting into the pool. Fortunately, a community cen- ter employee with lifeguard training saw the mishap. He dove in and was able to rescue the driver, who was taken to the hospital but appar- ently did not suffer any serious injuries and has been released. Ironi- cally, police said the man had gone to the community center to attend court-ordered driving school for numerous previous driving infrac- tions, including parking on a bicycle rack." Lisbeth shook her head to emphasize the irony of this. "Stay tuned, because when we come back we'll have a story about the chaos yesterday at the Miccosukee casino, where a twenty-three-foot python wrapped itself around a slot machine."

The screen began showing a commercial for a law firm, informing viewers who had pain or injuries that they were entitled to compensation.

"What an idiot," said Rose. "He drives his car into a pool! How do these people get driver's licenses?"

What crossed Sid's mind then was the fact that six months earlier Rose had, while driving in a funeral procession, rammed the hearse so hard that its rear door opened and the casket fell out onto the Garden State Parkway. But Sid, not being an idiot, refrained from mentioning this. Also he had something more important on his mind.

"I think I saw Seth," he said again.

"Saw him where? Did he come to the room? Why didn't you tell me?"

"No. I think I saw him on the TV."

"Seth was on the TV? When?"

"Just now."

"That wasn't Seth. That was a car in a swimming pool."

"No, before that. There was another story about a whaddycallit. Like a baboon."

"A baboon."

"Some kind of big ape. These people were driving around with this ape in their car robbing people and the police are trying to catch them. A man and a girl."

"So what does this have to do with Seth?"

"They showed the man on TV. I'm pretty sure it was Seth. He was with the girl. They got into the car and the baboon got in with them."

"You saw Seth on the TV with a girl and a baboon."

"No, I remember now. It was an orangutan."

"And the police are chasing Seth and this girl and this orangutan."

"According to the TV. For robbing people."

Rose studied Sid for a moment, then said, "You found another brownie, didn't you?"

# 41

LaDawne and Wesley stood on the side of Crandon Boulevard, the main road connecting Key Biscayne with the mainland, trying to decide what to do.

They had been walking briskly from the Ritz-Carlton, anxious to put some distance between themselves and Castronovo and Brewer. LaDawne was still seething about being evicted from Seth's room, and worrying about what would happen to Laurette. Roughly every forty-five seconds she declared she was going to call the police, but each time Wesley quashed the idea. For a variety of reasons, Wesley did not want to interact with the police.

LaDawne had just re-declared her intention to call the police, and Wesley was just about to re-quash it, when they saw their Escalade go rocketing past in the direction of the hotel. After some debate, they turned around and started back toward the hotel, hoping to reclaim their car. They had almost reached the beginning of the hotel driveway when they saw the Escalade again, exiting the driveway at high speed and turning in their direction. Wesley had waved and shouted, "Hey!" but the Escalade shot past without slowing.

"Where the hell they going with my car?" said Wesley.

"Did you see in the backseat?" said LaDawne. "With the window down?"

"No," said Wesley, who'd been focusing on the driver's side. "Who was it?"

"Not who. *What.* There's a *monkey* in that car."

"You serious?"

"As a heart attack. It was looking out the back window. Like it was sightseeing. A monkey."

Wesley looked down the road. The Escalade was out of sight now. He turned to LaDawne, shook his massive head.

"White people," he said.

# 42

The baby was crying. The men did not like the noise, and they did not like the smell in the car. They were turning around in the front seat, giving Laurette stern looks, saying things to her. But she did not understand their words. She understood only that they were angry at her and the crying baby.

Laurette was doing her best to comfort the baby. But the baby was hungry, and Laurette, in her exhausted and weakened state, was having trouble breastfeeding her. Also, she had just filled her Huggie with poop, which was making her uncomfortable and the atmosphere inside the Navigator pungent. Laurette wished the men had let her take the formula with her and some more diapers. But they had pushed her and her children out of the room without giving them time to take anything.

Next to her, Stephane was whispering, *Mama, where are they taking us?*

*I don't know.*

*Are they going to hurt us?*

*Don't worry.*

*Are they going to make us go back in the boat?*

Stephane's eyes were filling with tears. He did not want to go back in the boat.

*No, we won't go back in the boat.*

*How do you know?*

*Just don't worry.*

*But how do you know?*

One of the men turned around, glaring. He said something in a harsh, deep voice. Laurette and Stephane stopped talking. The baby was still crying. Laurette looked out the window. They were driving on a wide, smooth road, much grander than any road in Haiti. It rose into the air and flew over the city, which Laurette thought must be Miami. On both sides were glass buildings that rose even higher than the road, much higher than any buildings in Port-au-Prince. In the distance to the right, she saw a line of fantastically huge cruise ships, gleaming white in the morning sun. On the left, the rows of buildings stretched into the distance farther than Laurette could see.

Somewhere in this city was her sister, Marie. She could be very close. Maybe in one of these buildings. If only the men would just stop the car, let her and her children out, maybe she could look for Marie. But the men were not stopping. The car was soaring over the city on the flying road. She hugged the baby, hugged Stephane, protecting her children as best she could without knowing what she was protecting them from.

Where were the men taking them?

# 43

Tina, in pajamas and a bathrobe, sat on a sofa in her suite, across the room from a big flat-screen TV, which was on with the sound turned down. Her mother sat in an adjacent armchair. Marcia was having coffee; Tina was sipping a glass of imported water. All the bridal magazines said it was important to stay hydrated. They routinely printed horror stories of brides keeling over on the Big Day, including one woman who passed out facedown in her own cake.

Nothing like that was going to happen to Tina.

Standing in front of Tina and Marcia, not quite at attention but almost, was Blaze Gear, flanked by Traci and Tracee, the three of them clad in black. They were not having anything to drink; they had breakfasted at dawn and were now in all-out Wedding Day Plan Execution Mode. Blaze, reading from an iPad with an app that displayed a wedding day timeline, was going over the schedule for the Big Day. They had been at it for fifteen minutes and had just reached the bride's manicure.

The manicure had been a contentious issue during the wedding planning. Tina had originally wanted to get her nails done the day of the wedding so they would be perfect. But her mother felt—and Blaze Gear agreed, and so did Tina's New York–based manicurist, Rochelle— that waiting for the wedding day posed too great a risk in case something went wrong, or the schedule got too tight.

After much argument, the trio had convinced Tina that she should get her manicure done three days before the wedding, but have Rochelle flown down to Miami (first class) so that she could do a wedding day touch-up immediately before Tina saw her hairstylist, Miguel, who also had been flown in from New York. The timing of Miguel's session with Tina was critical; it had to be scheduled so that there was absolutely no possibility that Miguel would come into contact with Tina's makeup specialist, Konstantin, who, it goes without saying, had also been flown in first class from New York.

Miguel and Konstantin loathed each other. Several years ago they had worked in the same salon/spa, where they had found themselves competing for the affections of an aromatherapist named Douglas. The competition became so intense that it ultimately erupted in violence; in a confrontation still talked about in New York salon circles, harsh chemicals had been deliberately, if inaccurately, thrown. So it was essential that Miguel and Konstantin be kept separated today, lest they upset each other and be rendered incapable of doing their most perfect work for the bride.

All of this was noted on Blaze Gear's app.

With the manicure plan reviewed and reapproved, the group moved on to the issue of the hair and makeup schedules for the bridesmaids and maid of honor, Meghan. It was during this discussion that Marcia Clark asked where Meghan was. Tina said she assumed her sister was in her bedroom, sleeping off her usual pot-induced stupor. Marcia decided to check. She went to the bedroom door, knocked, got no answer. She opened the door and looked in.

"She's not there," she said.

"Really," said Tina.

"Maybe she went for an early breakfast," suggested Tracee.

Tina snorted. "I don't think Meghan has ever eaten *breakfast*, let alone an *early* breakfast."

"So where could she be?" said Marcia.

"She's due for hair at ten forty-five," said Blaze.

"I'll call her." Tina picked up her cell, pressed the speed dial number for Meghan. From the bedroom came the voice of Bob Marley singing "Jammin'," this being Meghan's ringtone. "Her phone's here," she said.

"Where could she be?" said Marcia.

"Tracee," said Blaze, pointing to indicate that she meant Tracee and not Traci, "go find Meghan."

As Tracee left, Blaze resumed her review of the timeline, with the next major element being the putting on of the $137,000 environmentally sustainable fiber wedding dress, which would be accomplished with the assistance of the dressmaker herself, who had of course been flown in from London along with her assistant, both first class. It was at this point in the timeline that the transformation of Tina from civilian to bride would be complete and she would be ready to make her appearance, in all her radiance, at the photo session, where a photographer, who had been flown in first class from Milan with his four—yes, four—assistants, would take formal portraits of Tina with various combinations and permutations of wedding participants—her bridesmaids, her maid of honor, her flower girls, her ring bearer, her parents, her siblings, Banzan Dazu and various others. Including, of course, the groom.

Seth's name did not come up until fairly late in the timeline and then he was discussed only briefly. His job was laughably simple, especially compared with the daunting list of interconnected, time-critical obligations facing the bride. All the groom had to do, noted Blaze Gear, was put on his tuxedo and show up with the ring. "Basically," she said, "the bride is coordinating the Normandy invasion and the groom is remembering to zip up his fly."

The women in the suite were amused by this remark and allowed themselves a chuckle. But it was only the briefest of chuckles, for time was of the essence. This was D-Day and there was much to be done if they were going to successfully storm the beachhead of holy matrimony. They could not be frittering away their limited wedding timeline review time thinking about the groom.

It was just after the chuckle subsided that Traci happened to glance over at the TV screen. It was displaying the Action 5 News logo and a headline that said ROBBERS GO APE! As Traci watched, the logo disappeared and was replaced by a low-resolution video showing some kind of gorilla standing over three men on the ground. The gorilla was jumping around and looking menacing; the men were backing away from it. In the background were two dark figures, a man and a woman. The video stopped and zoomed in on them until their faces, dim and grainy, filled the screen, over which were superimposed the words ROBBERY SUSPECTS.

Traci stared at the screen, frowning.

"Traci!" said Blaze Gear. "Are you with us, or are you watching television?"

"Sorry," said Traci. "I just thought . . ."

"You just thought *what*?"

"Nothing," said Traci, looking away from the screen. "I'm sorry."

With a *Don't let it happen again* glare at Traci, Blaze turned back to Tina and Marcia and resumed the review of the next critical element in the timeline, which was delivery of the bridal bouquet by the floral installation artist, Raul, who had been flown in first class from Los Angeles, along with two assistants.

## 44

"It's definitely a black Navigator, right?" said Seth.

"Right," said Meghan.

Seth peered ahead through the windshield. "Still nothing," he said.

They were northbound on I-95, passing through downtown Miami. Seth and Cyndi were still in the front seats, Trevor and a wary Meghan were in the middle seats. Trevor was still clutching the red velvet ring box in his right hand. Other than emitting a loud, stenchadelic orangutan fart that forced them to open all the windows and the sunroof, Trevor had been reasonably well behaved, mostly looking out the windows. In the past few minutes, however, he had reached out his left hand and touched Meghan's hair several times. He did this gently, but Meghan was not thrilled by the attention.

"I'm wondering if maybe we can distract this thing," she said. "Is there any food in this car?"

"There's some Cheez-Its," said Cyndi. She opened the glove compartment and handed the box back to Meghan.

"Nobody tell PETA about this," said Meghan. She opened the box and handed a Cheez-It to Trevor. He reached out, took the bright orange square between a long, slender finger and thumb, held it to his nostrils, took a sniff, then put it in his mouth. He chewed thoughtfully, then swallowed. He held out his hand for another one.

"He likes them," said Meghan, giving Trevor a second Cheez-It. "Thank God. So you guys were going to explain to me how this happened, you ending up with an orangutan who has the ring."

"Right," said Seth. "OK, short version: I left my suitcase on South Beach with the ring in it. Cyndi's friend Duane, the snake guy, picked it up for me, but he couldn't bring it to the Ritz because he had to go work at this place called Primate Encounter, so he left the suitcase there. So Cyndi and I went down there to get it, but somehow the orangutan got the suitcase into his cage and he tore it open and got hold of the ring."

"So Cyndi just happened to be around and she went down there with you," said Meghan, handing Trevor a third Cheez-It.

"That's right," said Cyndi, not liking Meghan's tone. "I went there to help Seth get his suitcase back. Is there something wrong with that?"

"I suppose not."

"You suppose not?" said Cyndi, still not liking the tone.

"Well, it's the night before his wedding day and he goes off with a woman wearing, no offense, a really skimpy dress."

"Now, wait a minute," said Seth. "There is absolutely . . ."

"Yes, *wait a minute*," said Cyndi. "I'm wearing this skimpy dress because I haven't been home since I went to the Clevelander two nights ago because I've been helping out with this poor woman and her kids and—"

"I'm not accusing you of anything," said Meghan, handing Trevor another Cheez-It. "I'm just—"

". . . *and* trying to help this nice man, who loves your sister very much, try to get his wedding ring back so he can marry your sister, who, I repeat, he loves very much, and I don't appreciate you suggesting that there's anything else going on."

"Meghan," said Seth, "there is absolutely nothing going on."

"He has been a perfect gentleman," said Cyndi.

Meghan handed Trevor another Cheez-It. "OK, I'm sorry," she said. "It's just that she's my big sister, and last night she saw you two leaving the hotel together and it got her really upset."

"She saw us?" said Seth. "Oh *man*."

"I told her I was sure it was nothing," said Meghan, handing Trevor another Cheez-It.

"But you didn't mean it," said Cyndi.

"No, I trust Seth."

"But not me."

"Look, I didn't know you, OK? I was just looking out for my sister. I apologize. I'm sure you're a perfectly good person."

"In a skimpy dress."

"Well *look* at it."

"OK, OK," said Seth. "Let's not beat this to death. Meghan, is Tina still upset?"

"About you and Cyndi, I don't think so. But she was pretty pissed about the Haitian people still being in your room, and some large black woman."

Seth frowned. "Did she happen to mention that to your father?"

Meghan didn't answer that. She gave Trevor another Cheez-It.

Seth was about to say something, but just then Cyndi touched his arm and pointed at the road ahead.

"Is that a black Navigator?" she said.

# 45

Edward and Margery Costigan, whom everybody called Ed and Marg, always timed their annual spring drive from the Florida Keys back to Traverse City, Michigan, so that they passed through Miami on a Sunday morning. They figured this was when all the drug addicts, robbers, murderers and cannibals would be sleeping, giving them their best chance of making it through this legendarily violent urban hellhole alive.

Ed and Marg had topped off the gas tank of their custom forty-two-foot El Domestico motor home in Homestead, which meant that even though the "El Do" got essentially the same fuel economy as the Lincoln Memorial, they would be able to get all the way past West Palm before they would have to even think about stopping for more gas. They had the doors and windows locked, and they had been monitoring the local news via their satellite dish TV. What they had seen so far this morning had only reinforced their conviction that Miami was an insanely dangerous place—criminals going around robbing people with an *orangutan*, for God's sake. What kind of depraved criminal lunatic would even *think* of that?

Ed, at the wheel as always, was on Full Alert, constantly checking the sideview mirrors as well as the video screen showing the road directly behind. He spotted a black car coming up fast in the far left lane. He frowned.

"Marg," he said. "What kind of car was it that the police were look-ing for, with those orangutan robbers?"

Now Marg frowned. "An SUV," she said. "Black."

Ed nodded. "Well, there's one coming up on the left fast."

"I'll take a look," said Marg. She put down *Fifty Shades of Grey*, unbuckled her seat belt, swiveled in her captain's chair and, moving quickly for a woman of 257 pounds, went back to the dinette nook window behind Ed and peered out. "I see it," she said. Then: "Oh my God, Ed! That's them! I see the thing!"

Ed looked sideways as the Escalade pulled alongside. It was past him in half a second, but he saw the big red furry figure clearly through the open rear window on the passenger side.

"Jesus, Marg!" he said. "Call the police!"

Marg was already tapping on her cell.

## 46

"I can't stand this anymore," said Brewer.

"What do you want me to do about it?" said Castronovo. "Throw the baby out the fucking window?"

"OK by me," said Brewer.

"Seriously, it's a baby. They shit their diapers and they cry. That's what babies do."

From the backseat, the sound of the baby's anguished wails intensified.

"Seriously," said Brewer, "I cannot fucking take this all the way to Delray, the smell *and* the fucking noise."

"She needs to change the diaper," said Castronovo, who had four children, although he personally had never changed any of them. "Maybe feed it."

"Well, can she do that?"

"Not without food or diapers."

They rode another half mile, the baby's ceaseless wails drilling deeper into their brains.

"OK," said Brewer, "we gotta stop."

Castronovo looked over. "Mike didn't say we could stop."

"Mike isn't in this car listening to this and smelling this."

"But Mike doesn't like us to change the plan. I dunno."

"I *do* know. We get off at the next exit, find a supermarket, a drugstore, something. One of us stays with them, the other one goes inside and gets diapers and baby food. We're back on the road in two minutes. Mike never knows it happened."

Castronovo thought about it, although the baby's frantic, increasingly high-pitched screams made thinking difficult.

"Fuck it," he said and put on the turn signal.

## 47

"They're getting off at this exit," said Seth.

"Why here?" said Cyndi, looking at the exit sign, which said MIAMI GARDENS DRIVE.

"I don't know," said Seth, putting on his signal.

"Have we thought about what we're going to do when they stop?"

"I've been thinking about it," said Seth.

"And?"

"And I have no earthly idea what we're going to do."

"Good plan," said Meghan.

"Do *you* have a plan?" said Cyndi.

"I'm going to keep feeding Cheez-Its to the orangutan."

"Well, then," said Seth, "I guess we're ready."

# 48

**Miami-Dade Police** Officer Christopher Delgado, a seventeen-year veteran of the force very much looking forward to retirement, was not happy about getting the radio call dispatching him to check out the reported sighting of the alleged orangutan. For one thing, he was supposed to go off duty in half an hour after a long overnight shift. For another thing, he was almost certain the investigation would be a waste of his time. Thanks to the TV news assholes yammering all morning about "ROBBERS GO APE!" there had already been a flurry of reported sightings of the wanted orangutan, and, as far as Officer Delgado could gather from monitoring the police radio, all of these animals except one had turned out to be dogs. The one exception turned out to be a pet monkey.

Pet monkeys were quite common in Miami, as were many other kinds of exotic pet animals, including—but by no means limited to—tigers, tarantulas, llamas, vampire bats, venomous lizards the size of dogs and constricting snakes the size of fire hoses. Officer Delgado had, in the line of duty, been bitten by two Rottweilers and a ferret, and once had to fatally shoot an extremely hostile ostrich outside a day care center in front of a playground full of traumatized toddlers. He had more than once, upon arriving home after a day on patrol, asked his wife why Miamians couldn't just get a fucking hamster like people in normal cities.

So Officer Delgado hated animal calls. But it was his bad luck that his happened to be the closet patrol car to Miami Gardens Drive when 911 got a call reporting a suspicious black SUV exiting at that location with a suspected orangutan on board. Delgado, a professional, kept the annoyance out of his voice as he radioed the dispatcher that he was responding. He would check it out because that was his job. But he was pretty sure, as he approached the exit, that he would soon be explaining to some baffled motorists why he had stopped their car to look at their dog. And then he would go home, kiss his wife, and go to bed, one day closer to retiring and getting the hell out of this insane city.

# 49

"Over there," said Brewer. "The drugstore."

To the right, in a strip shopping center, was a CVS Pharmacy. Castronovo turned in and pulled up to the curb in front of the store. He put the Navigator in park and said, "You go. I'll stay here with them."

"No," said Brewer, shaking his head. "I don't know shit about diapers. You're the one with kids. You go, I'll stay here."

Castronovo almost argued but decided he wouldn't mind getting away from the screaming baby for a couple of minutes. He opened the door and climbed out of the Navigator.

From Miami Gardens Drive, Seth, Cyndi and Meghan saw the Navigator park in front of the pharmacy, watched as Castronovo went inside. Seth turned into the parking lot and stopped about fifty feet away. They could see the heads of Laurette and Stephane in the backseat of the Navigator and Brewer's in the front. Brewer was not looking their way.

"Whatever we're going to do," said Meghan, "we should do it now, while Castronovo is out of the car."

"So what are we going to do?" said Cyndi.

"How about this," said Seth. "I'll pull right up behind the Navigator, with the bumpers touching, so they can't drive away."

"Then what?" said Cyndi.

"Then . . . OK, then we jump out real quick and open the doors and get Laurette and the kids out of there. There's three of us, and right now only one of him."

"But he has a gun," said Cyndi.

"He's not gonna use the gun once he sees who it is," said Meghan. "I'm the daughter of the guy he works for."

"That's great," said Cyndi. "So he won't use the gun on *you*."

"We better do this now," said Seth, pulling forward, "while the other guy is inside." He pressed the accelerator. The Escalade started rolling.

Castronovo stood in front of the Huggies display. He personally had never purchased diapers—that was his wife's job—and he had not expected the selection to be so large. There were Huggies Pure & Natural, Huggies Little Snugglers, Huggies Overnites, Huggies Snug & Dry, Huggies Little Movers and Huggies Little Movers Slip-On. Next to these were equally large and baffling selections of Luvs and Pampers.

"Fuck me," observed Castronovo, grabbing a package of Huggies Little Snugglers. He stalked off, looking for baby formula.

Eastbound on Miami Gardens Drive, Officer Delgado spotted a black Escalade in the distance, crossing a nearly empty parking lot. He thought about requesting backup, but decided not to. He didn't want to deal with the mockery he'd get from his fellow officers if he called in backup to assist in the apprehension of a dog.

No, he would handle this alone.

Castronovo now stood in front of the Enfamil baby formula display, trying to decide whether to get Enfamil Newborn, Enfamil Infant, Enfagrow Toddler, Enfagrow Older Toddler, Enfamil Gentlease for Fussiness & Gas, Enfamil ProSoBee for Fussiness & Gas (Soy-based), Enfamil A.R. for Spit-Up or one of the many other products in the Enfamil line, not to mention the array of offerings from Gerber. Feeling the beginnings of a migraine, Castronovo reached out a meaty hand and grabbed a package at random. It turned out to be Enfamil Nutramigen with Enflora for Cow's Milk Allergy. His shopping done, Castronovo headed for the checkout register.

Trevor had made his decision.

He had originally thought that he would be fighting the male in the front for the female in the front. But then this new female had gotten into the back, causing Trevor to rethink the situation. He found both females attractive, and they both had an acceptable, if somewhat odd, aroma. But the one next to him had been feeding him. That told Trevor that she was receptive to being his mate. He decided that he was fine with this. It meant he would not have to fight the male in the front after all. In his heart, Trevor was more of a lover than a fighter.

There was only one checkout register open in the drugstore and there was only one customer in line ahead of Castronovo. Unfortunately for him, she was the nightmare customer to be stuck behind: a woman with coupons. Worse, she was an *elderly* woman with coupons, of which she was clutching a stack the thickness of the Dayton, Ohio, telephone directory. She had several items in her basket. At the moment, she and the cashier, a studious-looking young man in horn-rimmed glasses, were focusing on the first of these, a tube of toothpaste.

"OK," the woman was saying, "I have a coupon for that one. I think it's fifty cents off." She started going through her coupon stack. Behind her, Castronovo shifted his feet, rolled his eyes, looked at his watch.

"Here it is," said the woman, handing the coupon to the cashier.

The cashier looked at it and said, "OK, this is for Crest Complete Multi-Benefit Extra Whitening with Tartar Protection—Clean Mint."

"Isn't that what I have?" said the woman.

"No," said the cashier. "You have"—he picked up the toothpaste box and read from it—"Crest Complete Multi-Benefit Extra White + Scope Outlast—Lasting Mint."

"Outlast what?" said the woman.

"Lasting Mint," said the cashier.

"Jesus Christ," said Castronovo, mainly to himself but not totally.

"OK, is this it?" said the woman, handing the cashier another coupon.

"No," he said. "This is for Crest Pro-Health Clinical Gum Protection Toothpaste—Invigorating Clean Mint."

"That's a different one?"

"Yes. Also it's not a cents-off coupon. It's a buy one, get one free."

"I get one free?"

"Yes, but you have to buy one."

"I *am* buying one."

"No, you're buying Crest Complete Multi-Benefit Extra White + Scope Outlast—Lasting Mint."

"OK," said the woman. "Let me see if I have a coupon for that."

"I don't believe this," said Castronovo.

**Brewer didn't hear** the Escalade coming because the baby's wails drowned out all other sounds. But he felt the jolt when its front bumper connected with the Navigator.

"What the fuck?" he said. He turned around and saw the

dark-tinted windshield of the Escalade. He opened the door and quickly got out, striding around to the driver's side of the Escalade.

"Hey, asshole," he said. "What the fuck do you—" He stopped, seeing Seth getting out of the Escalade. "What the hell are you doing here?"

"We're here to get those people," said Seth, pointing to Laurette and her children.

"No," said Brewer. "We can't let you—"

He stopped, mouth open, as Meghan emerged from the rear of the Escalade. "Meghan? What the hell?"

Meghan ignored him, striding toward the Navigator. "No, wait, hold it," said Brewer, blocking her path.

"Get out of my way," she said.

"Meghan, we discussed this already. Your father gave us orders and we . . . Hey! Don't do that!"

He was yelling at Cyndi, who had emerged from the other side of the Escalade and was opening the Navigator's rear door.

"Come on," Cyndi said to Laurette, pulling on her arm. "Get out. Quick." Laurette climbed out of the car, holding the wailing baby. Stephane got out behind his mother.

Brewer, seeing things getting out of hand, made a decision. He reached into his jacket. He wasn't going to shoot anybody, but he needed to scare them. His hand was on the butt of his gun, about to pull it from the holster, when he spotted the Miami-Dade Police cruiser pulling into the parking lot.

"Shit," he said.

"Oh no," said Seth.

The cruiser stopped about ten yards away from the rear of the Escalade. Officer Delgado put it in park, got out and surveyed the scene. On the surface it looked like a minor traffic accident, a fender bender. But Delgado, who had handled hundreds of fender benders, found this one odd, even by the standards of Miami driving. Why had the Escalade bumped the Navigator in an almost empty parking lot? And what was this strange, mismatched, obviously tense collection of people?

Delgado stood near his cruiser, his right hand not quite touching the Glock 17 holstered on his hip.

"What's going on here?" he said.

"Nothing," said Brewer, holding out his arms to indicate nothingness.

"Nothing," agreed Seth.

Officer Delgado nodded toward the two SUVs, touching nose to tail. "Did you have an accident?"

"No," said Seth and Brewer in unison.

"Then why are the cars parked that way up against each other?"

"Oh," said Seth, as if he had just noticed. "That was me. It was a mistake."

"A mistake."

"Yes. I didn't mean to . . . do it."

"You drove into this parking lot, with all these empty spaces, there's only one other car here, and you somehow hit it."

"Yes. Sir. But gently."

"It's just a tap," said Brewer. "No damage. No harm done. I'm willing to just forget about it and be on my way."

Officer Delgado studied Seth and Brewer for a moment, then turned his attention to Meghan.

"Can you explain what's going on here?" he said.

"Nothing's going on here," said Meghan. "Everything here is fine."

Delgado looked over at Cyndi, with the Haitians.

"Really," Cyndi said. "We're fine."

Delgado turned his gaze to Laurette. She didn't look fine to him. She looked terrified.

"Are you all right?" Delgado asked her.

She didn't answer, only held her crying baby closer.

"She doesn't speak English," said Cyndi.

Delgado inhaled, exhaled, abandoning the hope that he'd be heading home soon. Something was going on here, and as much as he wanted to pretend he believed the bullshit these people were handing him, he was too good a cop to just walk away. He thought again about calling for backup, but again decided he couldn't really justify it. So far he had nothing remotely approaching probable cause for charging any of these people with anything other than acting weird.

He looked back toward Brewer and Seth.

"I want to see your licenses and registrations," he said.

"Is that really necessary, Officer?" said Brewer. "I mean, there's no—"

"Yes," said Delgado. "I want to see them now."

As Brewer and Seth dug out their wallets, Meghan edged closer to Seth. Turning away from Delgado, she whispered, "We have to get out of this. We can't get arrested. We'll wreck the wedding *and* ruin everything for the Haitians."

"I know," whispered Seth. "You got any ideas?"

"I'm thinking," said Meghan.

"Shh. Here he comes."

Delgado was walking toward Seth and Brewer to get their paperwork. His wary cop eyes were mainly watching the two men, but he kept glancing round to keep track of everyone else. As he neared the Escalade, he thought he saw movement through the dark-tinted rear window. It occurred to him that he didn't know whether or not there were more people inside the car. He decided he needed to check that out before he did anything else.

He reached down and unsnapped the holster strap securing the Glock.

"I have a coupon for that, too."

Having finally succeeded in knocking fifty cents off the price of her toothpaste, the elderly woman had moved on to her next purchase item, a package of dental floss. She went through her stack of coupons and selected one, which she presented to the cashier.

"OK," he said, reading it. "This is for the Reach Total Care ninety-yard."

"That's not what I have?" said the woman.

"Oh for Christ sake," said Castronovo.

"What you have here is the Reach Cleanburst Waxed fifty-five-yard," said the cashier.

"Is that different?"

"Yes."

"Because of the yards?"

"The yards are different, but also one is Total Care and one is Cleanburst."

"And which one do I have?"

"The Cleanburst."

"Let me see if I have a coupon for that."

"I do *not* fucking believe this," said Castronovo.

Delgado was about ten feet behind the Escalade. The left rear door from which Meghan had exited was open, but from his angle Delgado couldn't see inside. He moved to his left to get a better view. As he did, he saw a look pass between Meghan and Seth.

Then he saw Trevor.

*Fucking animal calls.*

Delgado put his hand on the Glock.

"Wait a minute!" said Meghan. "Don't *shoot* it! That's a harmless animal!"

Delgado, ignoring her, used his free hand to key the police radio microphone clipped to his collar. He identified himself, then requested backup and gave his location. When that was done, he started side-stepping toward Seth, Brewer and Meghan, keeping his eyes on Trevor.

"Now," he said, "I want to know what's going on here."

"I never saw that thing before in my life," said Brewer. This was true; he had not noticed Trevor until Delgado had, and he was just as surprised. Also just as unhappy. Like Delgado, Brewer was not a fan of animals.

"There's a perfectly innocent explanation," said Seth.

"I'm listening," said Delgado, eyes still on Trevor.

"OK, it's a long story, but, basically, I'm getting married today."

Delgado shot him a glance. "And so that's why you're driving around with an ape in your car?"

"I know it sounds weird."

"It does," said Delgado. "But we're going to get it sorted out."

From the distance came the faint whoop of sirens.

"Here's the problem," Meghan said to Delgado. "I'm in the wedding, too. My sister's the bride. I'm the maid of honor."

"Congratulations," said Delgado.

"But the thing is, we really can't stay here and get involved in a whole big production. We have to get ready for the wedding. We really have to leave right now, OK?"

"I'm afraid you can't do that," said Delgado.

"Why not?" said Meghan. "What right have you got to keep us here?"

Delgado nodded toward Trevor. "I have probable cause to believe that this animal may have been involved in a robbery," said Delgado. "Among other things."

"*What?*" said Meghan. "That's the stupidest thing I ever—" She stopped, feeling Seth's hand on her arm.

"What?" she whispered.

"We had an incident last night," he whispered back. He glanced toward Trevor.

She stared at him, then whispered, "Did you *rob* somebody with that thing?"

Delgado was looking at them.

"I'll explain later," whispered Seth.

"Holy shit," said Meghan.

The sirens were still distant but getting louder.

**The elderly woman** and the cashier were focusing on her third item, which was a tube of ChapStick. The problem, as the clerk was explaining, was that she had selected a tube of ChapStick Medicated and the coupon she had was good for only ChapStick Moisturizer, ChapStick Ultra 30 or ChapStick Lip Shield 365.

"OK," the woman said, "is moisturizer similar to medicated? Could I just switch them maybe?"

"They're really two different purposes," the cashier said. "But I think there's an offer, with the medicated, where you can get a one-dollar mail-in rebate."

"What do I have to mail in?" said the woman.

"A proof of purchase," said the cashier.

"How do I get that?"

"You have to buy the ChapStick."

"Which one do I have to buy?"

"I'm going to fucking kill myself," said Castronovo.

The entire sequence of events took seventy-one seconds. It began when Meghan made a civilian mistake.

Meghan, being rich and pretty and in possession of a healthy pair of breasts, was used to getting her way, especially with men, even when what she wanted was not technically allowed. People bent the rules for Meghan, and she was able, thanks to the fact that she was also funny and charming, to make them feel good about doing it. It was rare for Meghan to be told no.

Right now it was very important to Meghan that she and Seth not get arrested because that would wreck her sister's wedding. It was also important to her that Laurette and her kids not get taken into custody by the authorities. And it was important to Meghan, although less so, that the orangutan not be harmed.

Meghan saw that the way to achieve all three of these objectives was to persuade this police officer to simply let them all go right now, before more police arrived, which, to judge from the sound of the sirens, would be soon. Meghan, who had talked her way out of countless speeding tickets, including the time she had been clocked going 102 miles per hour in a 55 zone, sincerely believed she could do this. She even believed that, with a little luck, she could do it in such a way that the Haitians got into the Escalade with her, Seth, Cyndi and Trevor and they would drive off, leaving the assholes Castronovo and Brewer behind.

This was Meghan's plan. The key was for her to work her charm on the officer. Quickly.

She walked up to Delgado, smiling what she knew from experience was a winning smile suggesting warmth and just a hint of sexuality. "Look, Officer," she said, putting a little huskiness in her voice. "First of all, I'm very sorry about yelling at you."

Meghan reached out her hand. She had found that physical contact had a positive effect on people, especially men. She rested her hand on Delgado's right forearm. This was the forearm connected to the hand that was resting on the butt of the still-holstered Glock.

That was Meghan's big mistake.

"So what you're saying," the coupon woman was saying, "is that if I buy the one I'm buying, the medicated, you'll give me a dollar rebate?"

"No," said the cashier. "I give you proof of purchase and you have to mail that in to get the rebate."

"Mail what in?"

"Excuse me," said Castronovo, tapping the woman on her shoulder. She turned around and looked at him.

"Let me show you how a normal, non-retarded human being buys things at a drugstore," he said. "Let's say you wanted to buy this"—he reached past the coupon woman and put the Huggies on the counter—"and this"—he put the Enfamil on the counter. "Now, watch closely. What you do is, you get out your wallet"—he got out his wallet, opened it, removed a $100 bill—"and YOU PAY FOR IT WITH NORMAL FUCKING MONEY." He slapped the bill on the counter, picked up the Huggies and the Enfamil and started walking toward the exit.

For a moment, the woman and the cashier watched him.

Then the woman said, "Wasn't I ahead of him?"

"Sir!" called the cashier.

Castronovo stopped, looked back.

"The Huggies Little Snugglers are buy one, get one free," said the cashier.

Castronovo gave him the finger, then resumed walking.

Police officers do not like to be touched. They especially do not like to be touched by civilians when they are in high-stress situations that they believe pose a threat of physical harm, such as when they are operating solo and are surrounded by suspicious-acting individuals, some of them males. Not to mention an orangutan.

When Meghan's hand touched Officer Delgado's arm, he wasn't looking at her, wasn't expecting the contact. He was focusing most of his attention on Trevor, but he was glancing frequently at Seth and Brewer—especially Brewer, who hadn't done much but who looked to Delgado like a potential problem. Delgado didn't like this situation, not at all. Outside, he was a calm and experienced cop waiting for backup; inside, he was a piano wire tightened to its limit.

So when Delgado felt Meghan's hand on the arm he planned to use to defend himself if something went down, he reacted forcefully, with the survival instincts of a streetwise cop. Without even turning his head, he threw his right elbow out sideways, getting Meghan's hand off his arm and sending her staggering away.

That was Officer Delgado's big mistake.

Trevor, who had been intently watching as his female approached this unfamiliar male, launched himself from the Escalade, using both his legs and his extremely powerful arms to cover the distance between him and the rival male in less than a second. It was a testament to Delgado's alertness and reflexes that he was able to get his Glock clear of the holster. But he had no chance to aim and fire before one-eighth of a ton of irate great ape slammed directly into his chest, sending him backward, airborne, the Glock flying high into the air, spinning against the brilliant blue sky like the bone in *2001: A Space Odyssey*.

Officer Delgado landed on his back in the parking lot, his head banging hard on the asphalt. By the time his Glock came clanking down twenty feet away, Brewer had his hand inside his sport jacket and was pulling out his Smith & Wesson Model 64, the six-shot revolver he'd carried ever since he started out at the NYPD. He got it clear from the holster and swung it toward Trevor.

That was Brewer's big mistake. Trevor, who hated guns, and especially hated having guns pointed at him, launched from where he stood and landed on Brewer before he could squeeze the trigger. The two of them went down, the gun clattering away on the asphalt. As Brewer landed on his back, Trevor, on top, sank his teeth into Brewer's nose. Brewer emitted a high-pitched, un-bodyguard-like yelp.

Ten seconds had passed.

Meghan, seeing Delgado out cold and Brewer battling a pissed-off orangutan chomping on his face, shouted, "Get in the car! Get in the car!" She shoved Seth toward the driver's seat of the Escalade and started around to the passenger side. Meanwhile Cyndi, quickly picking up on the plan, grabbed Laurette and Stephane and pushed them into the backseat.

Fifteen seconds had passed. Seth started the engine. Meghan was halfway around the front of the Escalade.

Trevor was blocking her path.

He'd seen her running and he was definitely not about to let her go, not after defeating *two* males so he could have her. So he'd jumped up from biting Brewer's face and shot around in front of Meghan, preparing to make the traditional mating noises that instinct told him would win her heart.

Twenty seconds had passed. Brewer, blood pouring down his face from his wounded nose, was starting to get up, looking around for his revolver.

Meghan, trying desperately to get around Trevor, danced left, then right, then left again. Trevor stayed right in front of her, moving with her, interpreting her actions as receptive and flirtatious. Trevor was starting to get a boner.

It went away instantly when Brewer fired the first shot.

The shot missed; Brewer, ordinarily an excellent marksman, had been shaken by Trevor's attack and his hands were trembling with rage. He started toward Meghan and Trevor, gun extended. They both turned and took off across the parking lot, Meghan running, Trevor bounding along using his arms. Meghan's goal was to reach Officer Delgado's police cruiser and use it as a shield. Trevor's goal was to get away from the scary noise.

Brewer walked around the front of the Escalade, stopped, steadied himself, inhaled and squeezed off another shot. Trevor yelped in pain and fell. Brewer started walking again.

Thirty-three seconds had passed.

Meghan heard the second shot but did not turn; she kept running, thinking only of getting away. She reached the cruiser and ran behind it. Delgado had left the driver's-side door open and the engine running. Keeping herself low, Meghan peeked over the roof of the car. In an instant her terror turned to rage. "GET AWAY FROM HIM!" she shouted.

Brewer, approaching the fallen Trevor, stopped and looked up at her. His face, shirt and sport jacket were drenched in blood. He looked away from Meghan and resumed walking toward Trevor, holding his revolver out in front with both hands.

"No you fucking will *not*," shouted Meghan. She jumped into the cruiser, slammed it into gear and stomped the accelerator, yanking the wheel hard right. The cruiser fishtailed, and Meghan fought the wheel. She got it straightened out just as she reached Brewer, who was standing next to Trevor, aiming down. He saw her just in time to jump, landing on his side on the hood of the cruiser. Meghan drove straight ahead, carrying him ten yards, almost to the pharmacy entrance. Then she slammed the brakes and spun the wheel hard right, sending Brewer sliding off the hood and tumbling toward the building.

Forty-six seconds had passed.

Meghan circled the cruiser, tires screaming, back to where Trevor lay. She jumped out to look at him. He was bleeding from his right leg. He was not moving but his eyes were open. He looked at her and blinked.

She could hear the sound of sirens, much closer now.

"Meghan!"

She looked up and saw Seth, who'd driven the Escalade over, shouting out the window.

"Get in!" he said. "If the police get here, we're totally fucked."

Meghan stood up, took a step toward the Escalade.

Sirens.

"Come *on*, Meghan," said Seth.

She looked down at Trevor. He blinked again.

"I don't believe I'm doing this," she said. She ran behind Trevor, got her arms under his, started dragging him toward the cruiser.

"Meghan!" shouted Seth. "What are you *doing?*"

Meghan was in good shape, but Trevor was heavier than he looked. Meghan, grunting, got him a few feet closer to the cruiser, then opened the rear door. She went to drag him again. He suddenly seemed to grasp the plan and helped her, using his good leg and his arms. Together they got him into the cruiser. Meghan closed the door. She could see flashing lights coming from the east on Miami Gardens Drive. She jumped back into the driver's seat, then leaned out the doorway and shouted to Seth. "NO MATTER WHAT, GET BACK TO THE HOTEL, OK? JUST MAKE IT TO TINA'S WEDDING."

Before Seth could answer, she slammed the door. The cruiser engine roared, the tires smoked, and Meghan and Trevor shot across the parking lot, making a screaming right onto Miami Gardens Drive. The Escalade was close behind.

Seventy-one seconds had passed since Meghan had touched Officer Delgado's arm.

**Castronovo emerged from** the pharmacy, holding the Enfamil and the Huggies. The first thing he noticed was a police cruiser and a black Escalade leaving the parking lot at a high rate of speed.

The second thing he noticed was the sound of sirens.

The third thing he noticed was Brewer, slowly getting to his feet, blood all over his front.

"What the fuck?" said Castronovo.

"Get in the car!" said Brewer, limping toward the Navigator and yanking open the passenger door. "We have to get the fuck out of here *now.*"

Castronovo got into the driver's seat and tossed the diapers and formula into the back. This was when he noticed the fourth thing, which was that the backseat was empty.

"Where are the Haitians?" he said.

"Not now!" said Brewer. "Just go! GO!"

Castronovo reversed it fast and swung out into the parking lot. That was when he noticed the fifth thing, which was a Miami-Dade police officer getting unsteadily to his feet. He looked over at Brewer and said, "What the fuck *happened* out here?"

*"Later,"* snapped Brewer. He pointed east. "That way."

Castronovo turned right out of the parking lot on Miami Gardens Drive. Less than a minute later, the first of the backup Miami-Dade Police units arrived from the west and pulled into the parking lot and screeched to a halt next to Officer Delgado, who was standing on wobbly legs, looking around for his weapon, knowing he was not going to be getting home anytime soon.

# 50

**Blaze Gear checked** her watch and allowed herself a small smile. They were wrapping up the bridal timeline briefing, and they were right on schedule. They were now reviewing the cake-cutting ceremony, which would be personally supervised by the internationally renowned master cake maker who had created the cake and who had been flown in with an assistant first class from Paris.

Marcia had just raised a concern regarding the cake forks when Tracee reentered the suite and reported that she had been unable to locate Meghan in the hotel or on the grounds. Marcia frowned at this news, but Tina only smiled.

"She'll show up," said Tina. "She's just punishing me because we had an argument last night. She probably took a walk down the beach. But she'll be here."

"I suppose you're right," said Marcia. She was feeling strangely mellow today after a night of deep sleep, which was rare for her.

"Of course I'm right," said Tina. "Mom, it's Meghan. Right now she's sitting under a palm tree, smoking a joint."

Marcia sighed. That would be Meghan, all right.

They resumed their discussion of Marcia's fork concern. Nearby, on the screen of the muted TV, Action 5 News anchorperson Lisbeth Renaldo was frowning into the camera over a superimposed headline that said APE GANG STRIKES AGAIN. But none of the women were looking in that direction. They were on a tight schedule.

## 51

For the fiftieth time in two minutes, Meghan glanced at the rearview mirror of the police cruiser. The Escalade was still behind her. That was reassuring. She turned her head and took a quick look back through the metal prisoner grille. Trevor was curled up on the backseat, not moving, but his eyes were open and they met hers for a second.

"I'm sorry," she said.

The police radio was active, emitting a constant stream of exchanges, most of which Meghan did not understand. She found the volume knob and turned it all the way down. She was crossing West Dixie Highway. Signs ahead told her that the road was about to dead-end into Biscayne Boulevard. Meghan wasn't sure where exactly she was, but figured that heading south would put her in roughly the direction of Key Biscayne, so as she approached the traffic light she pulled into the right-hand lane and put on the cruiser's right-turn signal. Behind her, Seth did the same in the Escalade. They turned southbound on Biscayne Boulevard and came to another light, which was red, with several cars stopped. Meghan pulled up behind them and glanced into her rearview.

"Shit," she said.

About a quarter mile behind her she saw a black Navigator turning from Miami Gardens Drive onto Biscayne Boulevard. She looked up at the light; it was still red. Behind her, the Navigator had made the turn and was coming fast.

"Shit," she said again. She looked around the cruiser dashboard. Next to the radio was a panel of red toggle switches, including one labeled SIREN and one labeled LIGHTBAR. She stuck her left arm out the window and made a *Follow me* gesture to Seth. Then she flipped the siren and lightbar switches. She flinched at the sudden loud whoop of the siren, then swerved right onto the right shoulder, passing the cars waiting at the light. She waved again for Seth to follow, muttering, "Come *on*." Two seconds later she saw Seth coming around on the shoulder. She accelerated. Cars were pulling aside to let her by. She glanced into the rearview and saw that Seth was keeping up. At the moment, she didn't see the Navigator.

She gripped the wheel and stared ahead, heart pounding, trying to visualize a map of Miami, and a way to get from here back to the hotel.

## 52

"I don't believe this," said Castronovo. "She's using the fucking siren."

"Go around," said Brewer. He was holding a Huggies Little Snuggler disposable diaper to the oozing wound Trevor had inflicted on his nose. "We can't lose them."

Castronovo drove onto the right shoulder and past the clot of cars. "What're we gonna do?" he said.

"I'm gonna kill the fucking monkey."

"OK, but what about the rest of them?"

Brewer thought about that. "First priority, we get the Haitians back," he said. "Those were Mike's orders, get rid of the Haitians. We can't admit we lost them because we stopped to buy fucking diapers."

"Which was your idea."

"All right, it was my idea, but we're both fucked if Mike finds out."

Castronovo nodded. "So what's our plan?"

"We stop the Escalade, get the Haitians back, get rid of them."

"Get rid of them how?"

"Whatever's quickest."

Castronovo gave him a look.

"I'm not saying that," said Brewer, "necessarily. I'm saying we get them back and dump them somewhere quick. Mike doesn't have to know we never made it to Delray. What we *can't* do is let Seth take them back to the Ritz."

"What about Seth and Meghan? They'll be pissed off, we take the Haitians away. If they keep trying to be heroes out here"—Castronovo glanced at his watch—"they could miss the wedding."

"Not our problem. We report to Mike. If Meghan and Seth want to fuck up Tina's wedding, that's on them. But they're not gonna do that. Once they realize this stupid little game they're playing is over, they'll go back to the Ritz. She's not gonna piss off her daddy and he's not gonna pass on all that money."

"Do we call Mike? Tell him what's going on?"

"Definitely not," said Brewer. "Not until we have the Haitians back."

"There they are," said Castronovo. In the distance they could see the flashing lightbar of the police cruiser. Castronovo put a little more pressure on the accelerator. The Navigator surged forward.

Brewer dabbed his oozing nose with the Little Snuggler and said, "I'm gonna kill that monkey."

## 53

Mike Clark was feeling pretty good. He'd slept well. The weather was spectacular. Castronovo and Brewer had taken care of the idiotic Haitian distraction. Marcia had just called from her meeting with Tina and the wedding coordinator, reporting that everything was on schedule. The only bit of bad news was that Meghan was nowhere to be found. But Meghan was always disappearing; Mike was sure she'd be back.

And there was one more piece of excellent news that Mike had just gotten from his personal assistant: The governor of Florida was coming to the wedding. It had been uncertain, but now it was definite. Mike was pretty sure the governor was coming because he'd found out that Wendell Corliss was there. But that was fine with Mike. It was a huge feather in his cap. *The governor of Florida.*

So this was shaping up to be a very good day. And Mike was determined, as he strode down the corridor to the Corliss suite, to make it a great one. He and Wendell had a breakfast scheduled for this morning, a power meal, just the two financial titans. It would be their only time alone together this weekend, and Mike did not intend to let it go to waste. He had decided that he was going bring up the topic of membership in the Group of Six.

The conventional wisdom among Mike's fellow multibillionaires in the Group of Eleven was that it was bad form to lobby for membership in the Group of Six, and that any such effort would result in being permanently blackballed. But Mike, while flossing this morning, had gotten to thinking about something Corliss had said at the rehearsal dinner the night before. It had happened when Mike, in a coy effort to refer indirectly to the Group of Six vacancy, had mentioned the death of industrialist Herb Wentworth. Corliss had responded with a weird story about watching a fly walk into Wentworth's ear and then marveling at how *confident* the fly would have to be to do that. At the time Mike had assumed that Corliss had simply drunk too much wine, although he wasn't known to be much of a drinker.

But then this morning a startling thought struck Mike: *What if Corliss had been trying to tell him something?* What if he'd been saying to Mike: *Hey, if you want to join the Group of Six, you have to be confident.* You have to plunge into the dark unknown of the earhole.

The more Mike thought about it, the more certain he became: Corliss was daring him to make the bold move.

And by God, he was going to make it.

He reached Corliss's suite and pressed the door buzzer. From inside he heard a shout, which sounded like Corliss, and then a laugh, which sounded like another man. Mike frowned: This was supposed to be a one-on-one breakfast. He waited at the door. Nobody came. He heard more shouts and laughter. He pressed the door buzzer, leaving his finger on the button longer this time.

He heard footsteps. The door opened. Mike's jaw dropped. It was Marty, wearing only a huge bathing suit the color of a traffic cone, his pasty white belly drooping over the waistband.

"Look who's here!" said Marty.

"Who's there?" replied Wendell from inside the suite.

"The father of the bride!" said Marty.

"Who?" said Wendell.

"Mike," said Marty.

"Ah," said Wendell.

Mike stepped into the suite, which was huge. To the left, beyond a barrier of sofas, the TV was showing *SpongeBob SquarePants*. In the distance, Wendell, in a bathrobe, was seated at the dining-area table, frowning at the screen of a laptop computer. The table was strewn with coffee cups, dirty plates and ravaged stainless-steel platters of bacon, toast and potatoes. In the middle was a large Styrofoam takeout container containing two pancakes.

"So," said Mike, approaching Wendell, "are we—"

Wendell raised a hand, stopping him. "Marty," he said, "how do you capture a graveyard again?"

"Which graveyard?" said Marty.

"Snowfall."

"No no no," said Marty, waving his arms. "Do *not* capture Snowfall Graveyard."

"Why not?"

"We don't want to re-spawn out of the battle."

"Ah," said Wendell.

"What's going on?" said Mike.

"World of Warcraft," said Marty. "Ever play?"

"No," said Mike, trying not to look at Marty's vast mayonnaise-white belly. He turned to Wendell. "So, are we still on for breakfast?"

Wendell looked up at Mike. His eyes were bloodshot. "You have *got* to try the pancakes," he said. "There's a couple left."

Mike looked at the pancakes, then back at Wendell. "I'm cutting down on gluten," he said.

Wendell nodded. "Is it just me," he said to Marty, "or does it seem like everybody's cutting down on gluten?"

"It's not just you," said Marty. "Five years ago, I never even *heard* of gluten. Then all of a sudden it's the worst thing in the world. It's the Nazi Party of food ingredients. People are scared to death of gluten. You could rob a bank with it. The bank people would be like, 'Do whatever he says! He's got gluten!'" Marty burped. "What the fuck *is* gluten, anyway?"

"It used to be trans fats," said Wendell.

"Gluten did?" said Marty.

"What I mean," said Wendell, "is that it used to be you weren't sup-posed to eat anything with trans fats. Or maybe you were *supposed* to eat things with trans fats. I don't remember which. You never hear anybody talk about them anymore. They're over."

"Like Myspace," said Marty. "Or global warming."

"Or Deepak Chopra."

"Who?"

"Exactly."

"What about carbs?" said Marty.

"What *about* carbs?" said Wendell.

"Are they still bad?"

Wendell frowned. "I think so," he said. "But not as bad as gluten. Or lactose! Lactose is *evil*. Lactose is *death*. Lactose is Glenn Close, in that movie where she stalks whatshisname."

"Who?"

"Whatshisname. You know. She boils his daughter's rabbit."

"Who does?"

"Glenn Close."

"Glenn Close boils a *rabbit*?"

"You never saw this movie?"

"No. Why did she do that?"

"She was in love with whatshisname."

"So she boils a fucking *rabbit*?"

"Yes."

"How?"

"How does she boil it?"

"Yes."

"In a pot."

Marty thought about that. "Why doesn't it jump out?"

"Of the pot? They don't explain that."

"That's a plot flaw. I mean, a rabbit is not a lobster. You put a lobster in a pot, it stays in the pot. But a rabbit would definitely jump out."

"Yes, but if she boiled a lobster, nobody would care. I mean, as a viewer you'd be thinking, *Big deal, a lobster*."

"No, I understand that. It couldn't be a lobster. But it could be a small dog."

"Dogs can jump."

"OK, maybe a chicken."

"No, because there you have the lobster problem all over again. A chicken boiling in a pot, the viewer goes, *Well, it's only a chicken.*"

"So you're saying it has to have fur."

"No, I'm not ruling out feathers entirely. For example, it could be a parrot, but it has to have some personality. Like earlier in the movie it says some comical words or phrases so the viewers get to know it, and their reaction is, *Oh no! Glenn Close boiled Polly!*"

Marty thought about that. "Why wouldn't the parrot just fly out of the pot?"

"Excuse me?" said Mike, trying not to show how pissed off he was getting.

Wendell and Marty looked at Mike, whom they had both forgotten about.

"So, Wendell," said Mike, "about breakfast."

"Absolutely," said Wendell. "You should try these pancakes. They're gluten-free."

"Seriously?" said Mike.

"No. But they're very special pancakes."

Wendell gave Marty a look, and Marty snickered. That did it for Mike. He was Mike Clark, and nobody treated him this way, not even Wendell Corliss. He was about to deliver a cold good-bye and stalk out when suddenly it hit him what was going on here: *Corliss was testing him.* He was deliberately trying to annoy him by talking nonsense with this idiot Marty, to see if Mike would give up and walk away.

Well, fuck that. Mike Clark didn't get where he was by giving up. This was his opportunity and he wasn't going to let it slip away: *He was going into the earhole.* He pulled out a chair and sat down at the table.

"Wendell," he said. "Let's cut the bullshit here."

Wendell looked at Mike, suddenly interested in him. "OK," he said.

Mike looked at Marty, who was listening while at the same time reaching inside his gigantic orange swim trunks and scratching himself.

"Can we speak privately?" said Mike.

Wendell looked at Marty, then back at Mike. "I think whatever we have to discuss, we can discuss it in front of Marty."

"Fine by me," said Marty. He then farted.

"All right, then," said Mike. Clearly this was part of the test. He took a breath, exhaled. "Wendell, I—"

"Michael Douglas!" said Wendell, snapping his fingers.

"What?" said Marty.

"It was Michael Douglas whose daughter's rabbit was boiled."

"Which one is he?" said Marty.

"Michael Douglas," said Wendell. "You know, he's married to whatshername."

"Glenn Close?"

"*No.* Whatshername."

"*Excuse* me," said Mike.

Wendell looked at him.

"I want in," said Mike.

Wendell blinked. "You want in."

"That's right. I want in, and I think I belong."

Wendell nodded thoughtfully. Several seconds passed.

"He wants in what?" said Marty, in a stage whisper.

"I have no idea," Wendell whispered back. "I'm just nodding thoughtfully to stall for time."

From across the room, a woman's voice called, "Are there any more pancakes?"

Mike looked and saw Greta Corliss's head poking above the sofa in front of the TV. Mike hadn't noticed her before.

"There's two," said Marty.

"Could you toss me one?"

Marty reached into the foam container, picked up a pancake and flung it, Frisbee style, across the room. Greta—New York society superstar Greta Corliss, famed for her elegance, her poise, her fashion savvy and her lavish yet exquisitely tasteful dinner parties—caught the pancake one-handed, stuffed the entire thing into her mouth, then sank back onto the sofa to resume watching *SpongeBob SquarePants.*

Mike was shaken. But he was not going to quit.

"The Group of Six," he said.

"What?" said Wendell and Marty both.

"I want to join the Group of Six."

"Ah," said Wendell, suddenly realizing why he'd been invited to the wedding.

"What's the Group of Six?" said Marty.

Wendell turned to Marty, his face solemn. "You must not tell any-one what I am about to reveal to you," he said.

"OK," said Marty.

"The Group of Six," said Wendell, "is a very secret, very exclusive organization of highly successful men who get together from time to time for the express purpose of hanging around with other highly suc-cessful men."

Marty arched his eyebrows. "Is that where you talk about your helicopters?"

"Exactly." Wendell turned to Mike. "So you want in."

"I do," said Mike.

"Are you sure? You *really* want in?"

Mike fought to hide his excitement. He had passed the test. *This was going to happen.* "I'm sure," he said. "I really want in."

Wendell's eyes met Marty's for a half second. Then he stood, put his hands on Mike's shoulders and said, "There's a sort of initiation."

## 54

"Where does this road go?" said Seth. The Escalade was still southbound on Biscayne Boulevard, Seth doing his best to keep up with Meghan in the police cruiser. She was using the siren and lights as needed, turning them on to blast through red lights or force slower drivers to get out of her way.

"It goes right into downtown Miami," said Cyndi.

"Can we get to Key Biscayne this way?"

"Yeah," said Cyndi. "You go through downtown, then down Brickell Avenue to the causeway."

"I guess that's what Meghan's doing. I just hope we can make it there without getting stopped by some real cops."

"Or getting caught by those guys," said Cyndi, turning to look through the Escalade rear window. "They're still after us."

Seth glanced in the rearview mirror and picked up the Navigator about a half mile back, weaving through traffic. Castronovo and Brewer had gotten hung up at a couple of intersections, but they weren't giving up.

"How're they doing in the backseat?" said Seth.

Cyndi looked back at Laurette, holding her fussing and aromatic baby, huddling close to Stephane. She gave them what she hoped was an encouraging smile.

"They look kind of in shock," she said.

"Can you blame them?" said Seth.

"No," said Cyndi. "What are we going to do with them when we get back to the hotel? We can't just let those guys grab them again."

"I've been thinking about that," said Seth. "Maybe we could put them in Marty and Kevin and Steve's room. They could hang out there until tomorrow, and by then maybe Carl will have some good news for them."

Cyndi nodded. "That might work."

"On the other hand," said Seth, "we might all be getting arrested soon, after last night and what just happened in that parking lot back there."

"But we didn't *do* anything, really, when you think about it."

"I don't think the police would agree. Especially now that Meghan stole a police car. They really frown on that."

"She was just trying to save the orangutan. That guy was *shooting* at it."

"I know that, and you know that. But I don't see the police being sympathetic." He glanced at her. "Listen, Cyndi, this could get bad, and you really don't have to be part of it. I could pull over and stop for a second and you could just get out and walk away."

Cyndi shook her head. "Nope."

"You sure? We could be in some pretty serious trouble. The cop back there was talking about robbery."

"I know, but it *wasn't* a robbery. And anyway"—she glanced back at Laurette—"this is going to sound pathetic, but this is the first time in my life where I felt like I was doing something that actually matters. OK, maybe not *doing* it. Maybe actually screwing everything up. But at least I'm *trying* to do something that actually matters. You know what I mean?"

"I know exactly what you mean," said Seth.

Ahead, Meghan whooped the siren and shot through yet another red light. Seth kept the Escalade right behind.

"Do you have your phone?" he said.

"Yes."

"OK, we need to call the hotel, let Marty and those guys know we're coming so they can let us into their room. I don't know the hotel number."

"I'll Google it," said Cyndi, tapping her phone.

"Of course," said Seth, "I'm assuming we're going to even *make* it to the hotel." He glanced at the rearview.

The Navigator was gaining.

## 55

Big Steve had been on the hotel phone for twenty minutes, slowly driving the Ritz-Carlton room service order taker insane.

"So if I order two eggs any style," Big Steve was saying, "I get toast, potatoes and a choice of bacon or sausage, is that right?" (Pause) "What if instead of the potatoes, I wanted bacon *and* sausage?" (Pause) "How much of an extra charge?" (Pause) "OK, what if I had bacon *and* sausage, but didn't have *either* toast *or* potatoes?" (Pause) "How much?" (Pause) "So it's the same amount extra even if I'm giving up the potatoes *and* the toast?"

"Will you *place the fucking order*?" said Kevin, grabbing the remote and turning on the TV. "I'm starving."

Big Steve held up a *Shush* finger. "OK," he said, consulting the room service menu, "I have some questions about the three-egg omelet. I get a choice of three omelet ingredients, plus toast and potatoes, right?" (Pause) "OK, now what if I want *four* ingredients, but I *don't* want the potatoes?"

"Steve," said Kevin. He was staring at the TV screen.

"Just a minute!" said Big Steve, annoyed. "OK, so you're saying there's an extra charge for the fourth omelet ingredient regardless of whether—"

"Steve!" said Kevin, *"Hang up the phone."*

"Will you please just—" Big Steve stopped, staring at the TV. "Holy shit," he said. He hung up the phone. "Is that *Seth*?"

"It sure looks like him," said Kevin.

On the screen was a freeze-frame from the Chuckletrousers park-ing lot surveillance video. In the foreground were Trevor and the three downed bouncers. In the background were two shadowy figures next to a car. A white circle was superimposed around the face of one of the figures. As Kevin and Big Steve watched, the face was expanded so it filled most of the screen.

Seth's face.

"Holy shit," said Big Steve.

Seth's face was replaced by Action 5 News anchorperson Lisbeth Renaldo. Superimposed in the upper right corner of the screen was a logo featuring a cartoonish picture of a King Kong–like beast, snarling, fangs bared. Next to it were the words APE GANG CITYWIDE RAMPAGE.

"So to recap the latest development in this bizarre story," Renaldo was saying, "the so-called Ape Robbers have apparently struck again, this time in the parking lot of a North Miami Beach drugstore, where they were involved in some kind of shooting incident that left a police officer injured and his police cruiser stolen. Police are telling Action 5 News that the alleged robbers are still at large, and one of them may be driving the police cruiser."

The phone rang. Big Steve picked it up. "Hello? Seth? Seth!"

Kevin hit the mute. Seth's picture was back on the screen, along with an APE GANG logo and the words CALL CRIMESTOPPERS.

"Jesus, Seth," said Big Steve, "what the hell have you *done*? Yes! You're on the TV news *right now* with a picture of a gorilla . . . OK, whatever. It says the police are after you. How the hell did you end up with a . . . OK. OK, give me the number." He snapped his fingers at Kevin, made a writing gesture. Kevin got him a hotel pad and pen. "All right," said Big Steve, writing. "OK." He hung up.

"What'd he say?" said Kevin.

"He said it's complicated."

"I bet. What is he doing with a fucking gorilla?"

"He says it's an orangutan."

"What's he doing with a fucking orangutan?"

"He says it's complicated."

"Well, that clears *that* up."

"He's coming here now."

"What? Here? Now?"

"Yes. He wants us to be here in the room, because he has to hide some people here."

"*What?* What people?"

"He didn't say."

"Hide them from *what?*"

"He didn't say that, either."

"Is that his phone number?"

"No, it's that woman from the bar. Cyndi. She's with him."

"She's with him and the ape? What the fuck is he *doing?*"

The phone rang again. Warily, Big Steve picked it up. "Hello? Oh hi, Tina." Big Steve shot an *Oh shit* look at Kevin. "Seth? He's . . . ah . . . he's . . ."

Kevin snatched the phone away from Big Steve. "Hey, Tina," he said. "How's the beautiful bride doing on the big day? Right. Right. No, he's not in his room, that is correct. And the reason for that is simply because he is . . . out. I mean, he's out*side*. He's walking. He's taking a walk out—No, because he didn't take his cell phone on his walk. He just wanted a quiet walk. But he's on his way back . . . No, I just . . . OK, I'm just *assuming* that he's on his way back, because he went for a walk, and then he would walk back to here, where he started. No, I'm completely sober. For the big day. You must be very excite—Meghan? No. Not a clue. Right. Definitely. I'll have him call you. Right. Immediately. Right. Bye."

Kevin hung up. "Lawyers," he said.

"Did she believe you?" said Big Steve. "About the walk?"

"I dunno. But Seth better get here soon. Where's Marty?"

"He went down to the rich guy's room. Corliss."

"I'm thinking maybe we might need him."

Big Steve stared at Kevin. "*Need* him? Need *Marty?*"

"Desperate times," said Kevin. "Desperate measures."

# 56

*Where are they* taking us? asked Stephane.

*I don't know,* said Laurette. *But we will be safe.*

*Will those men shoot at us?*

*No.*

*Will the monkey bite us?*

*No. We are safe now.*

*How do you know?*

*Just be quiet. We are safe now.*

Laurette wondered if they would ever be safe again. She had been terrified back in the parking lot when the policeman was attacked by the animal, and one of the big men started shooting. She was glad to be away from the big men, and glad to be in the car with the man who had rescued her from the sea and the woman who had helped take care of her and her children at the hotel. She knew they were trying to help her. But she didn't know where they were taking her, driving so fast. She didn't understand what was going on. And she was beginning to wonder if all Americans were crazy.

# 57

**Meghan was starting** to think they were going to make it. They were in downtown Miami now, still slicing through traffic and stoplights thanks to the police cruiser's siren. The Escalade was still right behind her. She'd caught a few glimpses of the Navigator in the rearview mirror, but none for the last few minutes. She wasn't sure exactly where the bridge to Key Biscayne was, but she was pretty sure that if she stayed on Biscayne, she'd come to it.

She glanced into the back of the cruiser. Trevor hadn't moved; he was lying on his side. There was blood on the seat. His eyes were still open; his gaze met hers.

"Hang in there," she said.

She saw a red light up ahead, a major intersection, four lanes of cars crossing. She reached for the SIREN and LIGHTBAR switches, flipped them up, heard the now familiar whoop-whoop-whoop.

Then she saw the Miami Police cruiser. It was to her right, on the cross street, four cars back in the line of cars that had stopped to allow Meghan to lead her two-car motorcade through the intersection. She caught the barest glimpse of the officer at the wheel, a female, staring at the speeding cruiser.

"Oh shit," said Meghan. She shut the lights and siren off, glanced in the rearview. The Escalade was still right behind her. She accelerated, glancing every few seconds into the rearview, holding her breath.

"Oh shit," she said again.

In the distance behind her, the police car was turning south on Biscayne Boulevard. It was following her.

Meghan stomped on the gas.

## 58

It was a busy Sunday morning at Bayside Marketplace, a flamboyantly tacky, tourist-infested waterfront shopping-dining complex on the bay in downtown Miami. Five huge cruise ships were in the nearby Port of Miami, and many cruise passengers, both arriving and departing, had made their way to Bayside to kill some hours before their ships or planes were due to depart. They were eating at outdoor restaurants serving cuisines ranging from Cuban to Hooters. They were wandering among the stores and stalls selling souvenirs of the Caribbean manufactured in Asia. Some were boarding sightseeing boats or listening to the salsa band on the outdoor stage. Others were prolonging or getting a head start on their vacations by getting hammered on rum drinks. A few were paying to have their pictures taken with exotic birds or, if they were feeling adventurous, an eleven-foot albino Burmese python.

That python was Blossom, beloved pet and business partner of Duane, who liked to work at Bayside on mornings when the cruise ships were in port. It was a tricky gig because Duane and Blossom—especially Blossom—were not welcome at Bayside. This was the result of an incident several years earlier when four very large and very intoxicated Ohio State football players on spring break decided it would be fun to shoot a video of themselves forming Blossom sequentially into the letters *O-H-I-O*. They had gotten as far as the *H* when

Blossom wrapped herself several times around the neck of one of the players, an offensive tackle, apparently intending to asphyxiate and then consume him. It was several minutes before the other players were able to pry her free from their now-unconscious teammate. The consensus of eyewitnesses was that Duane had done little to help. This was true: Duane, a loyal University of Miami fan, detested the Buckeyes.

Since that incident, Duane and Blossom had been officially banned from Bayside, though this did not stop Duane from going there. His strategy was to position himself at the end of the gangplank for the *Barco Loco*. This was a charter boat built to look, vaguely, like a pirate ship. It had a black hull with four cannons sticking out of gunports; it flew the Jolly Roger atop its mainmast, from which were suspended purely decorative sails. The *Barco Loco* was chartered for parties— occasionally corporate events but mainly children's birthdays. The crew dressed in pirate costumes and motored the boat around Biscayne Bay, shouting *"Arrr!"* a lot while serving the kids mass quantities of microwaved chicken nuggets and occasionally firing the *Barco*'s propane cannons, which emitted loud *BOOM!*s.

When it wasn't being chartered, which was most of the time, the *Barco Loco* was docked at Bayside and manned only by its live-aboard captain, the nautically named Bobby Stern, who happened to be a longtime drinking buddy of Duane's. So when Duane was working the Bayside crowd and he spotted a security guard heading his way, he would grab Blossom and hustle across the gangplank and into the *Barco*, where he would hang out and sip tequila until Bobby told him the coast was clear.

On this particular day, no security guards had appeared. That was the good news for Duane. The bad news was that business was bad. For whatever reason—this always was a mystery to Duane—some people just didn't see the fun in coming into close physical contact with ninety pounds of cold-blooded, constricting reptilian muscle. Duane—who was tired anyway, having been up late dealing with the slot-machine python—was thinking of knocking off early. Some days were like this: nothing going on.

## 59

Derek Tritt, governor of Florida and rising political
star, hadn't wanted to go to Tina Clark's wedding. He didn't know Tina
Clark at all, and his relationship with her father, Mike, consisted
entirely of pretending to like him in exchange for campaign contribu-
tions. So Tritt had initially responded to the wedding invitation by having his people inform Mike Clark's people that, unfortunately, on the
big day the governor was scheduled to meet with a trade mission from
Belgium. This was actually true, provided that the words "meet with a
trade mission from Belgium" were defined as "play golf."

But then Clark's people had informed the governor's people that
among the guests at the Tina Clark wedding would be Wendell Corliss. That changed things. Corliss was a whole different level of billionaire from Clark. Corliss wasn't just ridiculously wealthy; he was also
hugely influential. He was a man who could determine which states
would be granted huge federal contracts and who would be on the
short list for the vice presidential nomination and—above all—who
got Masters tickets.

Derek Tritt did not become a rising political star by passing up
opportunities to kiss the asses of men like Wendell Corliss. So Tritt
had his people get back to Clark's people to let them know that, somehow, the governor was going to find a way to reschedule the Belgians,

because he would not miss Tina's big day for the world, provided that he was seated next to Corliss at the wedding dinner.

Thus a deal was struck. And thus it was that the limo carrying Gov. Tritt and his administrative assistant was now arriving at the Ritz-Carlton, followed by the Chevrolet Tahoe carrying the governor's Florida Department of Law Enforcement security detail. Waiting to greet the governor on behalf of the Ritz were the hotel manager and a squadron of hotel bellmen. Also in the welcoming party were Wendell Corliss, Marty (still in his orange swim trunks) and a six-foot-tall flamingo.

The governor, thrilled to see Wendell—Wendell Corliss!—waiting for him in person, opened the limo door himself and stepped out, beaming.

"Governor Tritt," said the hotel manager, stepping forward, "on behalf of the Ritz-Carlton, I want to wel—"

"Thank you, great, thanks," said Tritt, shaking the manager's hand and making sincere eye contact for approximately seven nanoseconds before withdrawing his hand and thrusting it at Wendell. "This *is* an honor, Mr. Corliss," he said. "I don't believe we've met."

"Definitely not," said Wendell, shaking Tritt's hand. "This is my associate Marty . . ." He turned to Marty. "What's your last name, anyway?"

"Kempfelmeyer," said Marty.

". . . my associate Marty something," said Wendell.

Gov. Tritt shook Marty's hand. "Good to meet you, Marty."

"Please," said Marty, "call me Marty."

"And this," said Wendell, turning to the flamingo, "is our host, Mike Clark."

"What?" said Tritt.

"Great of you to come, Governor," said the flamingo, sticking out a pink-sheathed arm.

"Mike?" said Tritt.

The flamingo lifted its beak, and Tritt saw that the man inside the costume was in fact Mike Clark.

"I can explain," said Mike.

"No you can't," said Wendell.

"No I can't," said Mike. "But there is an explanation."

"Great to be here," said Tritt, who, being governor of Florida, was not unaccustomed to weirdness. He shook the flamingo's hand.

"I'll be out of this costume soon," said Mike.

"Maybe," said Wendell.

"Maybe," amended Mike.

"So, Governor," said Wendell, "we have some time. Why don't we go inside, maybe have a drink before the wedding?"

"Sounds great," said Tritt, who all of a sudden really wanted a drink.

"Do you like brownies?" said Marty.

"I do like brownies," said Gov. Tritt.

# 60

Meghan was now looking in the rearview more than she was looking ahead. Seth was still behind her in the Escalade, and behind him, a few blocks back, was the Miami Police cruiser. The officer was clearly following them; she was going through red lights to keep up. But so far she was keeping her distance and hadn't activated her lights or siren. Meghan wondered why that was.

She checked the cross street as she went through an intersection: Fifteenth. Ahead was the I-395 overpass. She was entering downtown Miami, which meant she was getting close to Brickell Avenue, at the end of which lay the bridge back to Key Biscayne. She made up her mind: Even if the officer tried to stop her, she would keep going, try to make it to the hotel. Or, if it came to that, she'd try to stop the police car, run interference, so Seth could go ahead with the Haitians. She was already in deep shit, she figured; a little deeper wouldn't make much difference.

She shot between the two big swoopy buildings that made up the downtown performing-arts center. Biscayne Boulevard split apart here, the southbound and northbound lanes separated by a wide median. She zoomed under I-395; a few seconds later the American Airlines Arena loomed on her left. She glanced in the rearview; Seth was still right with her, the Miami Police cruiser well back. She looked forward.

"Oh shit," she said.

About a hundred yards ahead, south of the Third Street intersection, were four Miami Police cars, lights flashing, completely blocking the southbound lanes of Biscayne Boulevard. Now Meghan knew why the cruiser following her hadn't tried to stop her. She took her foot off the gas, looking around frantically. Her first thought was to hang a right on Third Street, but as she got closer she saw it was blocked by a long double line of cars waiting for a light. This left one option.

"Shit," said Meghan, hanging a squealing left onto Third directly against one-way traffic. Honking cars swerved out of her way as she barreled across the northbound lanes of Biscayne Boulevard and into the big semicircular front driveway of Bayside Marketplace. Behind her, she heard more horns, then the unmistakable *bang-bang-bang* of vehicles colliding in chain reaction. Meghan screeched the cruiser to a stop and looked back. The Escalade was still right behind her. Beyond it, the intersection of Biscayne and Third was a chaotic scene of automotive carnage. Meghan stomped on the accelerator again, her plan now being to go out the other end of the Bayside driveway and escape northbound on Biscayne, but flashing lights in that direction told her she'd be driving right into another roadblock.

"Shitshit*shit*," she said and opened the cruiser door. From Biscayne Boulevard came the sounds of shouting and sirens. Many sirens.

She ran back to the Escalade. Seth had the window open.

"This is bad," he said. "This is really, really bad."

"I *know* that," said Meghan. "You think I don't know that? We need to get out of here *right now*." She opened the rear door, gestured to Laurette. "Come on!"

"Come on *where*?" said Seth.

"In there," said Meghan, pointing toward the Bayside complex. "I'm thinking we go out the other side, maybe get a taxi or something."

Cyndi and Seth got out of the Escalade, then helped Laurette and her children get out. Cyndi was closing the back door when she noticed something on the seat.

"Seth," she said, reaching for it.

"What?"

Cyndi handed him the red velvet ring box.

"Ohmigod," he said, taking it. "I almost forgot about this."

"Will you guys hurry *up*?" said Meghan. She herded the group onto a sidewalk leading into the complex. Seth and Cyndi got on either side of Laurette, helping her along. Meghan, behind them, glanced back toward Biscayne Boulevard. The sirens were louder, but at the moment she saw no police officers.

She did, however, see Trevor.

He had sat up and was pressing his face against the rear window of the police cruiser. He was looking at her.

"*Shit*," she said. "You guys go ahead. Hurry!"

As Seth and Cyndi helped Laurette and her children along the sidewalk, Meghan ran back to the cruiser and opened the rear door. Trevor had bled all over the backseat. She could see the oozing wound on his right thigh, surrounded by dark matted fur.

"You poor thing," said Meghan, softly. "I am so sorry about this. But they'll fix you up. You'll be OK, OK?"

Trevor just looked at her and blinked. She leaned forward quickly and kissed him on his left cheek pad, then turned and started running down the sidewalk after the others. She came to a clot of cruisers, recognizable by their blinding white sneakers, stoplight red sunburns and spherical shapes. As she sprinted past, one of them screamed.

Meghan looked back, stopped and for what felt like the five hundredth time in the past half hour said, "Oh shit."

Trevor, on one leg and two arms, was following her.

"Where the fuck are they?" said Castronovo.

He had pulled the Navigator to the curb on the southbound side of Biscayne Boulevard, which was now blocked in both directions by police cruisers and the wreckage of what looked like at least a dozen crashed civilian vehicles. A crowd was gathering, consisting of onlookers and police swarming from their cruisers.

"There," said Brewer, pointing to the left. Castronovo looked and saw Seth and Cyndi, supporting the Haitian woman, walking quickly into the Bayside complex. Trotting up behind them was Meghan. Just behind her, limping but covering ground, was Trevor.

In two seconds Castronovo and Brewer were out of the car, trotting toward Bayside.

"OK," said Brewer. "First priority, we get the Haitians out of here. That's what Mike told us to do. And we stay away from the cops."

"What about Meghan and Seth?" said Castronovo.

"Like I said before, they're on their own."

"And you still don't want to call Mike."

"Do *you* want to try to explain this to Mike?" said Brewer.

"No," said Castronovo.

"So we get the Haitians and get the fuck out of here," said Brewer as they reached the Bayside walkway. "And we definitely kill the monkey."

Even by Miami standards, this was a weird group making its way through the Bayside crowd. In front were Seth and Cyndi, holding tight to Laurette and her baby, with Stephane right behind. A few steps back were Meghan and Trevor, who was dripping blood but gamely keeping up, his eyes focused always on Meghan. The cruisers stopped and stared, not sure whether they were seeing some kind of performance or actual reality. They all had their phones out, taking video. Whatever this was, it was definitely YouTube quality.

They had reached a crowded plaza. Directly ahead was a marina, and on either side were buildings full of stores and restaurants.

"Where's the taxis?" said Seth.

Cyndi looked around. "I think that way," she said, pointing along the water to the left. "Maybe we could get one up on the port road."

They angled left across the plaza. With each step the crowd around them grew thicker; they were drawing a lot of attention. A man asked Meghan if he could take a picture with her monkey. Meghan said it was an orangutan, and no. From the distance behind them came the sound of sirens, more and more. Seth glanced back across the plaza, looking for pursuing police.

Instead he saw Castronovo and Brewer. They had just reached the edge of the plaza and were scanning the crowd, Brewer's face blood-smeared. Seth quickly turned away.

"We have a problem," he said.

"What?" said Meghan.

"Your dad's thugs are back there."

"Shit," said Meghan.

"Keep moving," said Seth. "They haven't seen us yet."

"I see them," said Castronovo, pointing. "Over by the water. Big crowd around them."

"Out of the way, asshole," said Brewer, shoving a cruise passenger aside.

Seth looked back. "They saw us," he said. "They're coming. Excuse me! Let us through, please!" He and Cyndi tried to push forward, but the crowd was becoming impenetrable, penning them to the railing that separated the plaza from the walkway along the marina's edge.

"Cyndi!" called a raspy voice.

Cyndi looked over the railing. "Duane!" she called back.

He was standing, with Blossom draped over his shoulders, at his usual post at the end of the *Barco Loco* gangplank. "What're you doing here?" he called.

"We're trying to get out of this crowd!"

"Lemme give you a hand." Duane trotted up some steps through an opening in the railing, then shouldered his way through the crowd, which parted readily for the large bald man with the large white snake. Reaching Cyndi and the others, he said, "What's going . . . Whoa! Is that *Trevor*? How in the fuck did—"

"It's really complicated," said Cyndi.

Seth was looking over the crowd. Castronovo and Brewer were bulling their way through the cruise passengers, getting steadily closer. "Listen," he said, "we need to get out of here *now*."

"You can get on that boat," said Duane, pointing to the *Barco Loco*. "Lay low in there."

Seth, Meghan and Cyndi looked at each other, then around at the still-growing crowd. There was no way they were going to be able to escape through that mob.

"OK," said Seth.

"This way," said Duane. He led them along the railing, Cyndi and Seth doing their best to shield Laurette and her children from the crowd. He descended the stairs to the *Barco Loco*.

"Bobby!" shouted Duane. "We got guests!"

Bobby Stern, a tall, thin man who cultivated a black piratical beard, appeared on the pirate ship deck, holding a glass of tequila. His eyes swept the boarding party, stopping on Trevor.

"Is that a gorilla?" he said.

"No," said Duane. "Orangutan."

"Ah," said Stern. He raised his glass. "Welcome aboard."

Seth put his arm around Laurette and started walking her toward the gangplank. She balked, staring at the boat. Stephane clung to her, looking terrified.

"They're afraid of the boat," said Seth.

"It's OK," Cyndi said to Laurette. Carefully, she took the baby from Laurette's arms.

"Yeah," said Seth, "it's OK." He took Laurette's hand in his, looked in her eyes. "I know you had a bad experience, but you have to trust us, all right?"

Laurette clearly didn't understand a word he was saying. But this time when he started toward the gangplank, she and Stephane went with him. Cyndi followed, carrying the baby. Behind them, Meghan was trying to coax the weakening Trevor onto the gangplank.

"What happened to his leg?" said Duane.

"He got shot," said Meghan.

Duane was incensed. "Who the fuck would do that?"

"Two assholes."

From the plaza came the sound of commotion. Duane and Meghan looked up and saw Castronovo, then Brewer, barge through the crowd and reach the railing.

"*Those* two assholes," said Meghan.

Brewer spotted them, pointed. He and Castronovo started shoving people aside, heading for the stairs.

"Come *on*," said Meghan, pulling Trevor by the hand onto the gangplank. "Can we start the boat? We need to get away from here *right now*."

Duane looked up at Bobby Stern, still holding his glass of tequila, observing the drama from the bridge of the *Barco Loco*.

"Bobby," called Duane.

"Yo."

"You up for a getaway cruise? We got some orangutan shooters looking to board us."

Bobby raised the glass to his mouth, downed the contents in one swallow, smacked his lips, then declared, "Nothing I hate more than an orangutan shooter." He reached down, hit the ignition. The *Barco Loco* diesel rumbled to life. "Pull in the gangplank and cast her off!"

"Aye, aye!" shouted Duane, scrambling aboard with Blossom.

Exactly twenty-three seconds later, the *Barco Loco* was pulling away from the dock. Exactly eight seconds after that, Castronovo and Brewer reached the water's edge. Duane, standing on the deck next to a propane cannon, smiled across the widening gap between dock and boat at the two fury-reddened faces. He waved and said, "Ahoy, cocksuckers!"

"Now what?" said Castronovo.

"After I kill the monkey," said Brewer, "I'm going to kill that guy *and* his snake."

## 63

**Blaze Gear couldn't** get the *Titanic* out of her mind. Specifically, she was thinking about the part in the movie *after* the ship hits the iceberg, but *before* the passengers realize they are in deadly peril. For a while, everything seems perfectly normal: the lights stay on, the band keeps playing, the waiters keep serving drinks . . .

And yet they are doomed. They just don't know it yet.

This was what Blaze Gear was thinking about as she frowned at her iPad. On the surface, things seemed to be going fine. All the really important timeline items—the bride's hair, the bride's makeup, the bride's manicure/pedicure touch-up—were proceeding on schedule and without incident. The governor had arrived. The floral installations had been installed, the gazebo decorated, the chairs arranged precisely on the lawn. The tables were set for the dinner, each fork, knife and spoon, each glass and plate, each place card perfectly aligned.

But beneath the veneer of perfection and order, some things were amiss. The groom, for example, was missing. Tina had been unable to reach him; Tracee and Traci had both been dispatched to find him and both had failed. The groomsmen were insisting that Seth had simply gone for a walk, and Blaze, whose most important job was to keep the bride calm, had assured Tina that this was so. Blaze hoped it was so.

Like it or not, a truly successful heterosexual wedding required a groom.

Also missing was the maid of honor. This was not potentially as big an issue as the lack of a groom, but it was troubling. Also troubling was the fact that the father of the bride apparently had greeted the governor of the state of Florida wearing a flamingo costume. Blaze could not think of a good explanation for this. It did not seem at all like the Mike Clark she knew. Maybe it was a rich-person joke, or some kind of Episcopalian thing.

She hoped the flamingo suit would soon disappear. She also hoped, fervently, that the groom and maid of honor would soon reappear.

Meanwhile she would do everything in her power to keep things sailing smoothly forward. But even as she ticked off, right on schedule, the next item on her iPad timeline—the bride's mother's hair—she could not escape the stomach-clenching feeling that somewhere, beyond her sight or control, the Clark–Weinstein wedding was taking on water.

## 64

**Fifty feet from** where the *Barco Loco* had just left the dock a larger boat, the *Bay Wanderer*, was preparing to cast off. The *Bay Wanderer* was a sightseeing boat that took passengers on a ninety-minute tour around Biscayne Bay, during which, it was promised, they would see the lavish waterfront homes, or former homes, of rich and famous people, including Al Capone, Gloria Estefan and Vanilla Ice.

Yolanda Berkowitz stood at the entrance to the *Bay Wanderer*, collecting tickets from boarding passengers, telling them they could either go forward to the downstairs lounge or upstairs to the open-air deck. Yolanda would also serve as the tour guide for the cruise, pointing out the sights over the PA system, making the same jokes she'd made a thousand times ("Coming up," she'd say as the boat approached a ridiculously huge mansion, "is my boyfriend's house"). Yolanda was in a good mood. The weather was nice and the boat was almost sold out, which meant the crew would probably split a decent haul from the tip jar.

The *Bay Wanderer* captain, Joe Sarmiento, blasted the horn twice: *Time to go.* The dock men were untying the lines, and Yolanda was closing the gate, when Castronovo and Brewer trotted up. She didn't like the looks of them, especially Brewer, who still had blood oozing from his nose wounds.

"I'm sorry," she said, "you'll have to catch the next boat."

"We're with the police," said Castronovo, yanking the gate open and stepping aboard, followed by Brewer, who shut the gate behind him.

"What do you mean *with* the police?" said Yolanda.

"This is an emergency," said Castronovo. "You need to cooperate, you understand?" He held open his coat, showing her his gun. "I said, you understand?"

Yolanda nodded.

The dock men had finished casting off. The *Bay Wanderer* started moving.

"Take us to whoever's driving this thing," said Brewer.

## 65

The *Barco Loco* had left the marina and was going under the overpass to the Port of Miami. Cyndi and Meghan, down on the main deck in front of the bridge, had found a roll of paper towels and some duct tape, which they were using to jury-rig a diaper for the baby and a bandage for Trevor's leg. They'd also found a bag of potato chips for Stephane, who had never eaten potato chips in his life and thought they were the most wonderful food ever.

On the bridge, Seth stood with Bobby Stern and Duane, both of whom held a glass of tequila. Seth was looking back toward the Bayside Marketplace plaza, now a confused, swarming mass of people, some of them police officers. He didn't see either Castronovo or Brewer. He hoped they'd given up.

"So," said Bobby as they cleared the overpass, "what exactly is the plan?"

Duane looked at Seth. "Aren't you supposed to be getting married?"

Seth touched his pocket, felt the ring box. "I am," he said. "Today. Very soon, actually."

"Congratulations," said Bobby. He nodded toward the deck. "I assume one of these lovely ladies is the bride?"

Seth shook his head. "Nope," he said.

"Really," said Bobby.

"It's complicated," said Seth.

Bobby nodded. "So I probably shouldn't even ask about the orangutan."

"I appreciate it," said Seth. "Listen, I know this is a huge favor to ask, but do you think you could sail us to the Ritz-Carlton?"

"On Key Biscayne?"

"Yes."

"I can't put you ashore," Bobby said. "That's a beach, shallow water. But I can get you close and you could take the dinghy in."

"Seriously?" said Seth. "That would be great."

"My pleasure," said Bobby. "Any man fleeing from the police with three women, two children and an orangutan is a friend of mine."

Seth looked at his watch. "How long do you think it'll take us to get there?"

Bobby frowned. "This ain't exactly a speedy craft. Let's see . . . up Government Cut, out around Fisher, Virginia Key . . . Say twenty minutes, give or take."

"OK, great," said Seth. "I'm going to go make a call." He headed forward, toward the steps down to the main deck.

Bobby and Duane watched him go. Bobby raised his glass. "To the groom," he said.

"To the groom," said Duane.

They drank to that.

"Better him than us," said Bobby.

They also drank to that.

## 66

Marty, summoned by a call from Kevin and Big Steve,
entered the Groom Posse suite in a mellow mood. He had just left the
Corliss suite, where Wendell, sitting next to a half-depleted platter of
brownies, was introducing Florida Gov. Derek Tritt to the many subtle
complexities of World of Warcraft.

The mood was a good deal more tense in the Groom Posse suite.
Kevin was pacing; Big Steve was sitting on the sofa, hunched forward,
staring at the TV screen, which showed a furrow-browed Lisbeth Renaldo next to a headline that said GANG GOES APE AT BAYSIDE.

"What's up?" said Marty.

"Quiet," said Big Steve, pointing at the screen.

". . . chase ended in this multiple-car wreck on Biscayne Boulevard
outside of Bayside Marketplace," Renaldo was saying. The screen
showed a street strewn with dented and smashed cars at various
angles, dazed drivers wandering among them. "Police say that sixteen
cars were involved, but it appears that nobody was seriously hurt. In
the confusion, the suspects abandoned their vehicles and fled on foot
into the crowded shopping complex—with the orangutan."

"Orangutan?" said Marty.

"Shh," said Big Steve.

"Police are questioning witnesses," said Renaldo, "but Action 5
News has learned that there are reports the gang may have fled by

boat. We have also just received this video, taken by a tourist at Bay-side, showing members of the so-called Ape Gang making their way through the crowd."

On the screen now was a shaky video, evidently taken from some-where inside a crowd of gawkers. At first it was mainly the backs of heads. A voice could be heard shouting, "Excuse me! Let us through, please!"

And then there was Seth. He was on-screen for two seconds, his arm around Laurette. This was followed by a flash of Meghan's face, then Trevor's.

Renaldo said, "Police are asking anyone who has—"

Big Steve muted the sound. The room was silent.

"Holy mother of fuck," said Marty.

"I know, right?" said Kevin.

"What is he *doing*?" said Marty. "With an *orangutan*?"

"He says it's complicated," said Big Steve.

"You talked to him?"

"He called a little while ago. He wanted to make sure we were in the room. Said he's bringing some people here."

"What people?"

"He says that's also complicated."

"Does he know he's supposed to be getting married? Like, *soon*?"

"I assume so," said Big Steve. "Tina's looking for him. She's been calling here."

"Oh Jesus," said Marty. "What'd you tell her?"

"I said he went for a walk," said Kevin.

"He *went for a walk*?"

Kevin shrugged. "Best I could do. Short notice."

Marty slumped onto the sofa. "This is very, very, very bad," he said. "If he fucks up this wedding, Tina will kill him. She will remove his balls with barbecue tongs."

Kevin and Big Steve nodded, knowing that this was hyperbole, but only mild hyperbole.

"Maybe he'll get here in time," said Big Steve. He looked at his watch. "There's still a little time."

"Except he's probably going to get arrested," said Kevin, nodding toward the TV. "He's on there every thirty seconds. He's like the fucking GEICO gecko."

"He's gonna need a lawyer," said Marty. Kevin and Big Steve looked at him.

"What?" said Marty.

"Marty," said Kevin, "don't screw this up worse than it already is."

"What are you talking—"

The phone rang. Big Steve grabbed it. "Hello? Jesus, Seth! What the—OK, OK. Yeah, he's here. Hold on." He handed the phone to Marty.

"Seth?" said Marty. "What the . . . OK. Yeah. OK, go ahead."

For the next several minutes, Marty listened in silence, except for emitting the occasional "Oh Jesus." Finally, he said, "Are you sure? I mean, couldn't they just . . . OK. OK. When?" Marty looked at his watch. "OK, we'll be there. OK. Bye."

Marty hung up. "Jesus," he said.

"What?" said both Kevin and Big Steve.

"He's bringing the Haitians."

"What Haitians?"

"The ones he had in his room. Remember? He told us?"

Blank stares.

"OK, he had these Haitians in his room, which he found in the ocean. He was hiding them from the police while this guy tried to find their sister. But then Mike Clark's security guys grabbed them."

"Why'd they do that?" said Kevin.

"Apparently Mike didn't want them around because they might interfere with the wedding. So he had his guys, like, kidnap them. So Seth and Cyndi and Meghan went after them and they got the Haitians back, but there was some shooting . . ."

"*Some shooting?*" said Kevin.

"That's what he said, some shooting, and now the cops are after them for various things they think they did even though, according to Seth, they didn't really do any of them, including, supposedly, a robbery."

"A *robbery*?" said Kevin.

"What about the orangutan?" said Big Steve.

"He didn't really explain the orangutan," said Marty. "But here's the thing. He wants to bring the Haitians back here, hide them in this room. He doesn't want them to get into any trouble."

"Why's he so concerned about them?" said Kevin.

"He didn't go into it. He just said it's very important. So he wants us to go out and meet them. They're all coming here, to the hotel—by boat."

"Where, exactly?" said Big Steve. "Out there on the beach?"

"Yeah. The beach."

Kevin went to the balcony window, looked out. "There's a bunch of boats out there right now," he said.

Marty went over and looked. "Those aren't them," he said.

"How do you know?"

"Because," said Marty, "Seth says they're on a pirate ship."

# 67

"You see that boat?" said Brewer. "The pirate boat?"

From the bridge of the *Bay Wanderer*, Castronovo was pointing at the *Barco Loco*, a quarter mile ahead, turning right into Government Cut.

"I see it," said Joe Sarmiento, at the wheel.

"We want you to catch that boat."

"That's not the route we take," said Joe. "We're supposed to follow a specific—"

"We don't give a rat's ass what route you're supposed to take," said Brewer. "The men on that boat have committed robbery and kidnapping. There are innocent victims aboard that boat. This is a police emergency, and you need to cooperate with us."

"Can I at least radio the base, let them know—"

"No," said Brewer, stepping close. "You're not going to radio anybody. You're going to do exactly what we say. You catch that boat, understand?"

"OK," said Joe. He glanced at Yolanda Berkowitz and shrugged. *Hey, they have guns.*

Yolanda, her face reddening, faced Brewer. "Those are innocent people down there," she said. She pointed down toward the observation deck, behind and below the bridge enclosure, where rows of cruisers sat expectantly in the sun. "They paid for a tour. They have nothing to do with this. You can't just—"

"They'll be fine," said Brewer. "Everyone will be fine, long as you cooperate. We just need to catch that boat, that's all. Then we're out of your life."

Yolanda reached for the door handle. Castronovo grabbed her arm and said, "Where are you going?"

"I'm the tour guide," she said. "I'm supposed to give the tour. I stand out there by the microphone."

"Right there," said Castronovo, pointing to a microphone mounted on the wall next to Sarmiento. "Use that one."

Yolanda looked at Joe, who shrugged again. She turned the knob to PA, unhooked the microphone, held it to her mouth, pressed the key. "Ladies and gentlemen," she said, "welcome aboard the *Bay Wanderer*. Today we have a very special tour in store for you."

Ahead, the *Barco Loco* had completed its turn into Government Cut and was disappearing behind the massive stern of a cruise ship.

Brewer nudged Joe. "Speed it up," he said.

Joe pushed the throttles forward.

# 68

The phone rang just as the Groom Posse was headed out the door to meet the pirate boat. The Groom Posse almost didn't answer, but decided it might be important. Marty trotted over and grabbed the phone.

"Hello? Oh, *hey*, Tina!" He gave Kevin and Big Steve an *Oh shit* look. "Yes, I do know where he is. I just talked to him. He's on his way here right now and . . . Oh. So you saw the TV news."

"Oh shit," said Kevin.

"Listen, Tina," said Marty, "I can explain this. Seth had these Haitian people he res— OK, so you know about that. Well, anyway, apparently those two big dudes who work for your dad— OK, you know about that, too. Right. Right. I'm sure they were, but Seth was concerned so he went to, um, get them back and apparently there were some, um *problems* tha— Right, I understand, and I'm sure Seth totally agrees— Right, no, I know you do— Of course, it's your wedding day, and I'm sure Seth totally— OK. Right. No, he shouldn't, and I'm sure he wou— Right. Right. Of course. But anyway, the important thing is, he's on his way here right now and he should be here any minute. He just called. Wha— Well, yes, they're still with him, but he's— Tina? Tina?" Marty looked at Kevin and Big Steve. "She hung up. She is *really* pissed."

"So what do we do?" said Big Steve.

"We're the Groom Posse," said Marty. "We got the groom's back."

"What the hell does *that* mean?" said Kevin.

"I don't know yet," said Marty. "Let's go."

# 69

Tina stared at the phone for several seconds. Gathered in a semicircle in front of her were her mother, Blaze Gear, Tracee and Traci. Behind them the TV was showing, yet again, the Bayside Marketplace video of Seth struggling through the crowd, his arm around Laurette.

"I do *not* fucking believe this," said Tina. She looked up. "He's bringing them back here."

"So that's good!" said Blaze, always thinking timeline. "If he gets here in the next half hour, we're—"

"It's *not* good," said Tina. "He still has those people with him! It's like he doesn't care about me at all! About his *own goddamn wedding.* All he cares about is those people who shouldn't even *be* here."

Marcia put her hand on her daughter's shoulder. "Look, Tina, once he gets here I'm sure everything will be OK."

"Except the police are after him."

"Daddy can take care of that, honey. We can make this all work."

Tina looked at her mother for a few seconds, then nodded. "Yes we can," she said. "We can make this work." She picked up her cell phone, hit the speed dial. She waited, tapping her fingers impatiently, but not in such a way as to jeopardize her manicure.

"Hello, Daddy?" she said. "Your guys screwed up. Time for Plan B."

## 70

The *Barco Loco* had reached the ocean, having motored past the line of cruise ships at the Port of Miami and passed though the jetties at the end of Government Cut. Bobby Stern spun the wheel right, aiming the ship toward Virginia Key and, just beyond, Key Biscayne. As the boat turned, Bobby glanced to the right and frowned. "That's weird," he said.

"What?" said Duane.

Bobby pointed astern. "The *Bay Wanderer,*" he said. "That's a tour boat. They don't come this way."

Duane looked. The *Bay Wanderer* was nearing the end of the jetties. "Maybe it's a special charter."

"Maybe," said Bobby.

"On your left," Yolanda was saying into the microphone, "is Miami's famous South Beach, which is . . . famous for its many celebrities." Yolanda was winging it; this was uncharted tour-boat territory. A few of the passengers were looking toward her curiously, but most appeared to be oblivious to the *Bay Wanderer*'s deviation from course.

They reached the end of the jetties. Sarmiento turned right, aiming at the *Barco Loco*.

Brewer nudged Joe Sarmiento again. "Faster," he said.

Reluctantly, Joe pushed the throttles all the way forward. The boat surged ahead, now yawing in the ocean swells. Behind the bridge, a few passengers were starting to look concerned.

"Say something," Castronovo ordered Yolanda.

Yolanda keyed the microphone. "Coming up on our right, ladies and gentlemen, is Key Biscayne, which is the home of many, um, residents. To your left is, more or less, Europe."

They were gaining rapidly on the *Barco Loco*.

"What am I supposed to do when we catch him?" said Joe.

"You're going to pull up next to him," said Brewer. "And I'm going to get on board and take some people off."

"What if he doesn't want to stop?"

"He'll stop," said Brewer.

"What the hell is he doing?" said Bobby.

"Looks to me like he's chasing after us," said Duane.

The *Bay Wanderer* was now less than a hundred feet behind them and closing fast.

"It definitely does," said Bobby.

"Hey, Seth!" Duane called down to the deck.

Seth looked back, saw Duane beckoning him to the bridge. He trotted back and up the steps.

"What?" said Seth, coming up the ladderway.

Duane pointed back at the *Bay Wanderer*.

"We think he's chasing us."

Seth shaded his eyes, squinted at the fast-approaching tour boat. He focused on the figures on the bridge.

"Shit," he said. "That's them. That's the guys who are after us."

"They hijacked a tour boat?" said Bobby.

"These are not good guys," said Seth. "Can we go any faster?"

"Not really," said Bobby. "I got her pretty much maxed out."

"How far to the Ritz?"

"Not far. Five minutes?"

"He's gonna catch us before then," said Duane. Indeed, the *Bay Wanderer* was pulling up along the left side of the *Barco Loco*.

"YOU THERE, PIRATE SHIP!" the voice of Castronovo boomed from the *Bay Wanderer* PA speakers. "STOP RIGHT NOW!"

From the bridge, Bobby flipped the *Bay Wanderer* the bird.

"Get closer," said Brewer.

"If I get too much closer," said Joe, "we're gonna hit him."

"I don't give a shit," said Brewer. "Get closer."

Sarmiento eased the wheel to the right. The gap between the *Bay Wanderer* and the *Barco Loco* began to narrow.

Behind the bridge, on the observation deck, the passengers were watching the chase with varying emotions, some concerned that something was wrong, others convinced they were witnessing a performance, a fake sea battle between the tour boat and the pirate ship. Many were using their cell phones to shoot video.

The two ships were very close now. Castronovo turned to Brewer. "Now what?" he said.

"Just keep us close," said Brewer. He opened the bridge door and stepped out, drawing his gun.

"What's he gonna do?" said Duane. "Ram us?"

The *Bay Wanderer* was now dead even with the *Barco Loco*, about ten yards away and getting closer. As Bobby, Duane and Seth watched, Brewer appeared on the exterior walkway alongside the *Bay Wanderer*'s bridge.

"Shit," said Bobby. "He's got a gun." He turned to Seth. "Would he actually shoot us?"

"That guy," said Seth, "he might."

As he spoke, Brewer raised the gun, not aiming it, but showing it to Bobby. With his other hand he drew his finger across his throat, signaling *Cut the engine*.

"Thoughts, gentlemen?" said Bobby.

"Fuck that asshole," said Duane.

"Roger," said Bobby, spinning the wheel hard right.

"He's turning away," said Castronovo. "Stay with him."

Joe spun the wheel.

"He's coming," said Bobby. He kept turning hard right, turning the *Barco Loco* a full 360 degrees, putting it back on its original course. The *Bay Wanderer* executed essentially the same maneuver but made a wider turn, in the process falling behind again. But it was soon closing the gap.

"This ain't gonna work for long," said Bobby.

"How far to the Ritz now?" said Seth.

Bobby glanced at the Key Biscayne shoreline. "Not far," he said. "But we can't outrun them."

The *Bay Wanderer* was pulling up on the left again. Brewer was now aiming his gun at the *Barco Loco*. There was a pop and a piece of wood molding on the bridge splintered. Brewer made the *Cut the engine* sign again.

Bobby again spun the wheel. "OK," he said. "So he definitely will shoot."

Both boats were turning now, making another pair of circles, the *Bay Wanderer* close after the *Barco Loco*.

"We can't keep this up forever," said Bobby.

"You got any weapons on board?" said Duane.

"No guns, no. We got the propane cannons, but all they do is make noise."

"He doesn't know that," said Duane. "Maybe we can use them to scare him off."

Bobby frowned. "Actually," he said, "maybe we can do better than that."

Castronovo stepped out of the *Bay Wanderer*'s bridge onto the walkway, next to Brewer. "We need to wrap this up," he said. "The passengers are going to start wondering what the fuck is going on."

"Just get me close again," said Brewer, staring at the *Barco Loco*.

"I don't know, man," said Castronovo. "I think we're pushing this."

"We're covered," Brewer said. He nodded toward the *Barco Loco*. "Those are suspects wanted by the police. We're ex-cops. We commandeered this boat to apprehend the wanted suspects. Doing our civic duty. That's our story."

"Yeah, but I don't think Mike's gonna want—"

"Mike wants the Haitians gone," snapped Brewer. "That was our job, and we fucked it up, and if they show up back at the hotel on a fucking pirate boat, we're going to look like idiots. I don't want to look like an idiot. Do *you* want to look like an idiot?" He turned his oozing face toward Castronovo, who almost flinched at the fury he saw in his partner's eyes.

"This is really about the monkey, isn't it?" said Castronovo. "You want to kill the monkey."

Brewer looked back toward the *Barco Loco*. "Just get me close," he said.

"You guys ready down there?" called Bobby.

"Almost," shouted Duane.

"Hurry up," said Bobby. To his left, the *Bay Wanderer* was once again pulling even. Brewer, on the walkway, raised his gun, this time very clearly aiming at Bobby. And this time, instead of responding with the finger, Bobby raised both hands in a surrender gesture. Brewer signaled *Cut the engine.* Bobby reached down and backed the throttles down to idle. The *Barco Loco* slowed, then stopped, wallowing in the swells. The *Bay Wanderer* eased closer, the two ships' hulls nearly touching. Brewer, keeping his gun aimed at Bobby, looked down onto the *Barco Loco's* main deck but saw nobody.

"Where are they?" Brewer called to Bobby.

"Below," said Bobby.

"I'm getting on your boat," said Brewer.

"What do you want?"

"I just told you, asshole. I'm getting on your boat."

Bobby shrugged. "Over there," he said, pointing forward to the gangplank opening in the *Barco Loco's* main-deck railing.

Keeping an eye, and his gun, on Bobby, Brewer sidestepped along the walkway toward the opening. Reaching it, he heaved a leg over the *Bay Wanderer's* railing, preparing to board the pirate ship.

"Now," said Bobby.

*BOOM!* went the propane cannon four feet from where Brewer was climbing over the rail.

Ordinarily the cannon barrel was empty, shooting only hot air. This time it contained roughly a pound of frozen chicken nuggets, which Seth had brought up from the refrigerator in the *Barco Loco* galley and which Duane had loaded into the cannon from the back. Propelled by the exploding propane, the frozen nuggets left the cannon barrel at a velocity of around three hundred feet per second. They struck Brewer in the stomach, chest and groin, knocking him back off the rail and onto the walkway of the *Bay Wanderer*. His gun flew out of his hand, bounced and clattered on the deck, then went overboard.

Before it splashed into the ocean, Bobby shoved the *Barco Loco* throttles full forward. He waved jauntily to the passengers on the *Bay Wanderer*, who waved back and applauded the pirate ship's captain, convinced now that they were watching a performance.

As the *Barco Loco* pulled away, Castronovo burst out from the bridge door and ran to Brewer, who lay on his back, moaning.

"You OK?" said Castronovo.

"No!" said Brewer. "They *shot* me!"

"Lemme look," said Castronovo, kneeling and lifting Brewer's polo shirt. Brewer's belly was covered with dozens of red welts interspersed with a few bleeding cuts inflicted by nugget shrapnel.

"You'll live," said Castronovo.

"I'm gonna kill those assholes," said Brewer.

"No you're not," said Castronovo. "We're going to go back to shore and try to get out of this mess. And we're going to pray that Mike doesn't fire us."

He stood up and looked at the receding bulk of the *Barco Loco* motoring on toward the Ritz, now visible in the distance. Duane and Seth had rejoined Bobby on the bridge. Seth looked back, saw Castronovo watching, smiled broadly and waved.

Castronovo, a professional, resisted the urge to shoot him.

# 71

It was a measure of the clout that Mike Clark possessed at the federal level that less than fifteen minutes after he made a phone call, four armed agents from Immigration and Customs Enforcement arrived at the Ritz. They drove a black ICE sedan and white van, both of which they left out front, instructing the hotel staff that these vehicles were not to be moved.

Their arrival was noted with interest by a valet named Philippe Jeunet. As soon as the agents entered the hotel, Philippe had his cell phone out, dialing his fellow Haitian and Ritz employee, groundskeeper Carl Juste.

## 72

"He wasn't kidding," said Marty. "It's a pirate ship."

The Groom Posse stood on the beach in front of the Ritz, watching, along with a few dozen beachgoers, as the *Barco Loco* drifted to a stop and dropped anchor about seventy-five yards offshore. Figures were moving around on the deck. The Groom Posse recognized Seth, then Duane, with Blossom on his shoulders.

"How'd he end up with the snake guy?" said Kevin.

"How'd he end up on a pirate ship?" responded Marty. "With an orangutan?"

"Good point," said Kevin.

"How're they gonna get to the beach?" said Big Steve.

"Dinghy, looks like," said Marty. The shipboard figures were lowering a pontoon boat from davits mounted on the stern of the *Barco Loco*.

Marty felt a tap on his shoulder, turned and saw Carl, in his grounds-keeper's uniform.

"You're with the wedding, right?" he said. "I saw you yesterday. You're Seth's friend?"

"I'm his best man," said Marty. "Why?"

"Because I need to find him. I tried to call his room but there is no answer. This is very important."

"What is it?"

Carl hesitated.

"If it's about the Haitians he was hiding in his room," said Marty, "we know about that."

"All right," said Carl. "There are some ICE agents here at the hotel."

"ICE?"

"Immigration. Somebody must have reported Laurette."

"Jesus," said Marty.

"So I am trying to tell Seth this, because they must not—"

"They're not in his room," said Marty.

"Where are they?"

Marty pointed. "On the pirate ship."

"On the ship? Why?"

"Long story. Some guys took them out of the hotel. Seth went after them and now he's bringing them back to the hotel." As he spoke, the figures on the pirate ship got the pontoon boat into the water.

"But they cannot come here," said Carl. "Not now."

Marty looked at Kevin and Big Steve. "Does Seth have his phone?"

"I don't think so," said Kevin. "Wait, that girl he's with does. I got her number." He dug into his pocket, pulled out the paper he'd written Cyndi's number on, handed it to Marty.

"Steve, give me your phone," said Marty. He grabbed it and dialed.

Cyndi was on the main deck of the *Barco Loco*, holding Laurette's baby. Laurette had her arm around Stephane, the two of them looking toward the beach, which is where they clearly would have preferred to be. Meghan was sitting cross-legged on the floor, gently stroking Trevor's fur. Trevor was lying quite still, as he had been since the wild boat ride had started.

Cyndi's phone rang. She shifted the baby and pulled the phone from her purse. "Hello? Who?" She waved the phone at Seth, who was standing by the rail, helping Bobby and Duane with the pontoon boat. "Seth! It's Marty!"

Seth trotted over, grabbed the phone. "Hello?" He looked at the beach, waved. "I see you. Listen, I'm bring— Oh. Oh no. Shit— Well, we can't stay out here all day— OK, OK, stay there. I'm gonna come in and try to straighten this out— No, I understand, they'll stay out here. Is Carl there with you? Put him on, OK? . . . Hey Carl— Right, I understand. Listen, can you explain this to Laurette? She has to be wondering what the hell is going on. Tell her that as soon as we can, we'll get her back on land, OK? I don't think she likes the boat— Right. OK, here she is."

Seth handed the phone to Laurette, who began an animated conversation with Carl.

Duane and Bobby drifted over. "What's going on?" said Duane.

"We have a problem," said Seth. "There's federal immigration guys in the hotel. Carl thinks they're looking for Laurette."

"How did that happen?" said Cyndi.

"Somebody must've reported them."

Meghan started to say something, stopped.

"So we have a problem," continued Seth. "We can't take Laurette and the kids in there right now."

"We can't sit out here forever," said Meghan.

"I know," said Seth. "I'm hoping the immigration guys don't find anything and leave. I'm going to take the dinghy in, see what I can find out. Also I need to talk to Tina, explain what's going on."

Meghan again almost said something but didn't.

Laurette finished her conversation and handed the phone back to Seth.

"Carl?" he said. "Right. Right. Of course. OK, tell Marty I'm heading in now. Bye." He handed the phone to Cyndi, then knelt in front of Laurette. He took her hand, looked into her eyes.

"I know you don't understand what I'm saying," he said. "And I know you're scared and you want to get off the boat. I'm really, really sorry about what you've been through today. But I promise you it will work out. We won't let them take you. OK?"

Laurette squeezed his hand and said, *"Mêci."*

*"Mêci,"* said Seth. He stood, turned to Bobby and Duane. "OK, I'm going in. I'll be back. Will you guys be OK out here?"

"We'll be fine," said Bobby.

"Plenty of tequila," said Duane.

## 73

"Here he comes," said Big Steve.

The pontoon boat was pulling away from the *Barco Loco*, Seth holding the outboard tiller. In a few minutes, he was riding a wave onto the sand and jumping out into the surf, the Groom Posse helping him drag the boat up the beach, out of reach of the waves. Seth started walking briskly toward the hotel, Kevin and Marty flanking him, Big Steve a step behind.

"What's the plan?" said Marty.

"Right now," said Seth, "I need to see Tina."

"She's seriously pissed," said Kevin.

"I know," said Seth. "I don't blame her." He looked at his watch. "But I still think this can all work out."

"What about the Haitian woman?" said Marty.

"I'm hoping you guys can help with that. Keep an eye out for the immigration agents, and as soon as they leave, Laurette and the kids can come in."

"And then what?" said Marty.

Seth glanced at him. "What do you mean?"

"I mean, they're still here illegally. They can still be picked up and sent back to Haiti."

"I'm hoping they can stay here until tomorrow, and her sister will show up and take her somewhere safe."

"That's it? That's your plan? Hoping?"

"You have a better one?"

"Not at the moment. But maybe I can devise a legal strategy."

Seth stopped, faced Marty. "No offense, Marty, but this situation is already fucked up enough."

"So you're saying you have no faith in my legal abilities."

"None whatsoever."

"Fair enough."

They were walking again, reaching the hotel.

"I think that's them," said Kevin, pointing.

Through the bank of windows along the rear wall of the Ritz they could see the four uniformed immigration agents gathered in the lobby. They were talking to a fifth figure.

"Is that a *flamingo*?" said Seth.

"That's Mike Clark," said Marty.

Seth stared at the flamingo. "You're shitting me."

"Don't worry. He gets to take it off for the wedding."

"What?" said Seth.

"They're moving," said Kevin.

Seth and Marty looked through the window. The agents were breaking up their gathering, heading in different directions.

"OK," said Seth, "you guys keep an eye on them. I'm going to go see Tina." He glanced at his watch again. "We can still make this all work." He opened the hotel door and was gone.

"Sure we can," said Marty.

# 74

"Uh-oh," said Bobby.

"What?" said Duane.

"Chopper," said Bobby, pointing north.

It was hugging the shoreline. The black-and-white fuselage said POLICE and, below that, MIAMI-DADE.

"Maybe he's not looking for us," said Duane.

"That'd be good."

As the chopper neared the Ritz-Carlton, it banked left and curved out over the water. It stopped directly over the *Barco Loco*, hovering.

"I guess he's looking for us," said Duane.

## 75

Seth rang the door to Tina's suite, waited.

The door opened: It was Marcia Clark. She was dressed for the wedding. Her hair appeared to be even more perfect than usual.

"Hey, Marcia," said Seth.

Marcia scanned Seth with icy blue eyes, starting with his unbrushed hair, moving down to his unshaven face, then his sweat-stained shirt, then his seawater-soaked pants, then his bare feet. Her gaze traveled back up to his face, her expression that of a woman who has discovered a pubic hair in her yogurt.

"I know I'm kind of a mess," he said. "But it's been—"

"Tina," Marcia called over her shoulder. "He's here." Marcia exited the suite, taking care not to get close to Seth, and walked away down the hall.

Seth stepped inside, closed the door. "Tina?" he said.

No answer.

"Tina?" He walked through the foyer, saw her standing at the far end of the suite by the balcony door, facing away from him. She was wearing her $137,000 wedding dress made of eco-sustainable fibers.

"Teen?" he said.

She turned around, and he inhaled sharply. Tina was the most beautiful woman he had ever seen, and right now she looked more beautiful than he had ever seen her. She also looked, he thought, remarkably calm.

"Teen," he said, stepping forward, opening his arms.

She raised her manicured hands, palms out.

"Right," he said, stopping.

"Did you know," she said, "that you're on the TV news?"

"Tina, I am really, really sorry."

"Sorry that you're on the news?"

"Well, yeah, that, and everything else."

"What else?"

"That I got into this whole mess."

"On our wedding day."

"Yes."

"On our *wedding day*, Seth." Tina's calm was beginning to leave her.

"I know, I know. I totally fucked up."

"How could you do this? *How?*"

"Teen, listen, please. Part of it was getting wasted on South Beach. That was just stupid. I have no excuse for that, losing the ring—"

"You *lost the ring?*"

"No, no, I got it back. I have it right here." Seth patted his pocket. "But please listen, Teen. The other part, the part about Laurette, that's different."

"Yesterday, after the rehearsal, you promised me—you *promised* me—that you would make them leave."

"I know. And I tried to. But I couldn't. I just couldn't kick them out."

Tina sighed. "You're a nice guy, Seth. But you let people take advantage of you."

"They're not taking advantage of—"

"Yes they *are*, Seth. They're *using* you."

"Teen, they're not using me. They don't even speak English. They're lost and helpless and scared to death. And then your father's two thugs grabbed them, taking them God knows where. I couldn't let that happen, Teen. It was just wrong."

Tina was silent for a few seconds. Then she said, "They were taking them to the immigration authorities."

"What?"

"Castronovo and Brewer were taking the Haitians to the federal immigration authorities."

"How do you know that?"

"Because that's what my father told them to do."

Seth was staring at her. "So you knew about this."

"Yes."

"And the immigration agents in the hotel right now, you know about them?"

"My father called them when we found out you were bringing the Haitians back to the hotel."

"*When we found out* meaning when you found out and told your father."

"Yes."

"I see," said Seth.

"No, you *don't* see. Here's what you think, Seth. You think you're being a selfless hero, I'm being a rich spoiled bitch who only cares about her wedding and doesn't give a shit about the poor Haitians."

"No I don't—"

"Yes, that's *exactly* what you think, Seth. And it's *bullshit*. Let me ask you, have you ever, in your entire life, done anything—one single fucking thing—to bring about immigration reform?"

"No."

"No. You've been busy. Well, guess what, Seth? While you've been tweeting about douche, I *have* worked for immigration reform. I've signed petitions, written letters, gone to rallies. I know more about immigration reform than you ever will, Seth. And I know you don't bring about immigration reform by breaking the law and fleeing from the police with a fucking orangutan."

"Listen, Tina, I—"

"No, *you* listen. Those people knowingly broke the law, coming here. They might have gotten away with it, but now, thanks to you and your bimbo friend and your orangutan, they're famous. So no matter what you do or I do or my father does, they're going to wind up in federal custody, and they'll probably have to go back to Haiti, where they'll be no worse off than they were. But the point is, whatever's going to happen to them is out of your hands, and it's out of my hands. Do you understand that?"

Seth was quiet for a few seconds, then said, "Yes."

"Good. So now you have a decision to make: Do you want to keep playing hero? Or do you want to marry me? Because you can't do both."

"You still want to marry me?"

"Yes. This is an aberration, this hero thing. It's not you, Seth. I know that. But it has to end now. I want those people—the Haitians, the bimbo, all of them—out of this hotel. Now. I want them all gone."

"Actually, they're not in the hotel," said Seth. He went to the balcony door, pointed out toward the *Barco Loco*. He'd been hearing the helicopter noise, and saw now that it was a police helicopter, hovering over the pirate ship.

"A pirate ship?" said Tina. "Seriously?"

"Meghan's on there," said Seth.

Tina sighed and shook her head. "Why am I not surprised? Daddy can get her off."

"I'll go get her," said Seth. "I need to at least explain what's happening to—"

"*No,*" snapped Tina. "You stay away from the boat. If you go out there, you'll be caught up in that whole mess again."

"Teen, I already *am* caught up in it."

"No you're not. Not anymore. It's over. You want to marry me, you stay away from that boat. Daddy will handle the boat. That's no longer your concern. You go get ready for the wedding. For *our* wedding."

"You really still want to marry me."

"I want to marry the guy I've been with for the past two years. The guy I planned this wedding with. That's who you are, Seth. That's the guy I want."

Seth nodded. "OK," he said.

"Good. Now go get ready. And get your guys ready. Blaze is freaking out."

Seth turned, started toward the door, stopped, turned back.

"What?" said Tina.

"I love you, Teen," said Seth.

Tina smiled, a breathtakingly beautiful smile.

"I know you do," she said.

Seth turned and left.

## 76

The wedding went surprisingly smoothly, considering everything that led up to it.

Like most grooms, Seth was nervous, but he managed to remain outwardly composed. He was glad to have Marty next to him, and Kevin and Big Steve close by. He believed he was doing the right thing.

Even so, when Seth was asked The Question—*Do you take this woman to be your lawful wedded wife?*—another question popped up in his mind: *What the hell am I doing?*

Seth hesitated then, and everyone saw it. For a few seconds, nobody breathed.

Then Seth cleared his throat and said, "I do."

A modest cheer arose from the spectators. Marty punched Seth in the arm, which was inappropriate but welcome.

The bride was just as nervous, maybe even more so. She, too, had last-second doubts. But when her time came to answer The Question, she, too, said she would.

She said it in Creole, after Carl translated The Question for her.

"You may now kiss the bride," said Bobby Stern, who, as a result of his efforts to supplement his meager income as a party-boat captain, was a notary public in the state of Florida, as well as a Realtor and certified Pilates instructor.

"Maybe just a hug," said Seth. He leaned over and embraced his new bride, Laurette Aubin—now formally, if temporarily, Laurette Aubin Weinstein. She smiled shyly and hugged him back. Meghan and Cyndi, the co–maids of honor, hugged each other, sniffing with happiness.

At that moment the *Barco Loco*'s aft starboard cannon fired, in part to celebrate the shipboard marriage, and in part to send a high-speed cluster of frozen nuggets flying in the general direction of one of the various motorboats operated by agents of various local, state and federal law enforcement agencies that had been circling the pirate boat, looking for a chance to board.

"That's almost it on the ammo," called Duane, who'd been manning the cannons. "I can't hold 'em off much longer."

"That's OK," said Marty. "Let 'em board. We might as well start the process."

"You really think this is going to work?" said Seth.

"The truth? I have no idea."

"That's encouraging."

"Hey, I'm a lawyer, not a fortune-teller."

"You're not a lawyer."

"Don't tell them that," said Marty, as the first police boat arrived.

The plan had been Marty's, hatched while Seth was talking to Tina. Marty, waiting in the lobby, had done some Googling on his phone, then made a call. When Seth emerged from the elevator, Marty hurried over, excited.

"I think I figured out a way to keep her here legally," he said.

"Tell me fast," said Seth, heading for the rear door.

They crossed the back lawn, Seth striding, Marty trotting next to him, talking fast, Kevin and Big Steve right behind.

Seth interrupted Marty in his second sentence. "That won't work," he said. "You need a marriage license, and Florida has a three-day waiting period."

"*Unless,*" said Marty, "you get a hardship waiver from a judge."

"How the hell are we going to do that?"

"We get the governor to help us."

Seth stopped in the middle of the lawn, turned to Marty. "Are you high?"

"Yes," said Marty, "but so is the governor."

It took two more minutes for Marty to convince Seth he was serious, and another two to explain the plan, which in its original form had Big Steve in the role of groom.

"Why me?" said Big Steve.

"Because you're not married," said Marty.

"You're not married, either."

"But I'm acting as counsel here," said Marty. "It would be a conflict of interest."

"I'll be the groom," said Seth.

"You can't be the groom," said Marty. "You're getting married to Tina."

"No I'm not."

The Groom Posse gaped.

"Holy shit," said Big Steve.

"Did Tina call it off?" said Kevin.

"No," said Seth. "Tina still wants to get married."

"*You're* calling it off?" said Marty.

"I guess I am."

"But *why?*" said Marty. "Seth, this is *Tina Clark*. She wants to *marry* you."

Seth shook his head. "She thinks she does. But I don't think I'm the guy she thinks I am. Anymore, anyway."

"Whatever *that* means," said Kevin.

"You sure about this?" said Marty.

"Absolutely," said Seth.

"OK, then," said Marty. "You're our groom."

"Whew," said Big Steve.

They caught up with Carl Juste at the beach. The five of them shoved the pontoon boat into the water, piled in and motored out to the *Barco Loco*, reaching it just before the first Miami-Dade Marine Patrol boat arrived on the scene. While Duane, manning the cannons, fended off the police, Marty explained the plan to Carl, who explained it to Laurette, who readily agreed. Bobby was happy to perform the ceremony, although he wondered if there wasn't supposed to be some kind of paperwork. Marty assured him it was in the works.

Bobby, aware of the circling lawmen, kept the ceremony brief. "Dearly beloved," he began because he had heard these words in TV weddings. "We are gathered here together . . ." He paused then, because that was all he could remember from TV. He racked his brain, trying to think of other wedding-related quotations. All he could come up with was part of a verse from the Dixie Cups song "Chapel of Love."

"'Today's the day / We'll say I do,'" he said. "'And we'll never be lonely anymore.'"

Bobby then asked the groom and the bride The Question. They answered in the affirmative and hugged.

Then Duane fired off the last of the chicken nuggets.

Then everybody, including Trevor, was arrested.

## 77

Tracee, or possibly Traci, burst into the bridal suite breathless. She had just returned from the lobby, where she had been dispatched by Blaze Gear in response to disturbing reports being broadcast on Action 5 News.

Traci (or Tracee) brought bad news: It was all true. The police had just paraded Seth and Meghan through the hotel in handcuffs, along with various other unsavory characters and animals.

"I do *not* fucking believe this," said Mike Clark, who fortunately, in light of the gravity of the situation, had a short while earlier been given permission by Wendell to change out of the flamingo costume. Mike kicked a coffee table hard, knocking over an elaborate complimentary display of pastries that had been sent to the bridal suite by the hotel management, although nobody had touched them because they contained carbs.

Marcia Clark shot Mike a disgusted look. She rose and went to Tina, holding out her arms, prepared to hug and comfort her daughter regardless of the damage this might do to their hair and makeup.

Tina held up a hand, stopping her mother. She kept the hand raised, standing statue-still, not even appearing to breathe. Thirty seconds passed in agonizing silence, everyone watching Tina, waiting, uncertain.

Finally Blaze Gear, the professional, took charge. She walked over to Tina and, in her most soothing yet authoritative voice, said, "Listen, Tina, I know this is not what we planned. But these things happen. We can still make this work. They'll post bail. We may lose an hour or two, but with some adjustments to the timeline we can still have your dream wedding come true."

Tina, coming out of her trance, lowered her hand, turned her head slowly and looked at Blaze, almost as if seeing her for the first time.

Blaze smiled a reassuring smile.

Tina, in a fluid motion, snatched the iPad from Blaze's hands, turned and flung it cleanly through the open balcony window.

"Or, not," said Blaze.

## 78

Sid sat in the lobby, watching the passing scene. He was waiting for Rose, who had parked him in a chair while she went to the front desk to complain that their room key was not working. By questioning Rose patiently, the clerk was able to determine that she had been attempting to open the door with her ATM card.

Her problem solved, Rose returned to collect Sid.

"I just saw Seth," he said.

"Seth? Where?"

"Here. They just took him out of the hotel."

"Who took him?"

"The police," said Sid.

"The *police* took Seth out?"

"Just now. With the orangutan from the TV. And a man with a big snake."

Rose looked around the lobby, then back down at Sid.

"That's it," she said, "no more brownies."

She helped him to his feet and they started toward the elevators. En route they crossed paths with a short, stocky man who had just arrived at the hotel in a Lincoln Town Car. The man wore a sharp fedora and was clad in black, dressed warmly for South Florida. He went up to the front desk.

"May I help you?" said a clerk, the same one who had just solved Rose's room-key problem.

"Yes," said the man. "Could you please ring the room of Wendell Corliss." He spoke with an Irish accent.

"Certainly," said the clerk, picking up the phone. "May I ask your name, please?"

"Tell him it's Van Morrison."

# EPILOGUE

Everybody got into trouble, but nobody went to jail.

Seth and Cyndi faced serious charges for their alleged assault-and-robbery spree. But as far as investigators could determine, the assaults and the robbery were actually committed by Trevor. So Seth and Cyndi were able to plea-bargain down to relatively minor charges, which, in time and with good behavior, would be expunged from their records.

Meghan also faced serious charges in connection with the assault on Officer Delgado and the theft of his police cruiser. But Meghan had a team of very expensive lawyers hired by her well-connected father, plus the fanatical support of the animal-rights community. Her legal defense—that she was emotionally distraught over the shooting of Trevor and had taken the cruiser in a desperate effort to save the helpless animal from being killed in cold blood—was supported by the drugstore parking lot surveillance video. Ultimately, Meghan, too, was allowed to plead to minor charges.

Brewer and Castronovo, also represented by Mike Clark–hired lawyers, successfully avoided prosecution by claiming that they had simply been trying, as former police officers, to apprehend what they believed to be dangerous wanted criminals. It helped that the owners of the *Bay Wanderer* refused to press hijacking charges against the Tinker Bells after discovering that their passengers that day had been thrilled by the gun battle with the pirate ship, which they believed had been staged for their entertainment. This battle soon became a regular and hugely popular part of the tour, with Yolanda Berkowitz acting as narrator.

Bobby Stern's defense was the converse of that employed by Castronovo and Brewer: He argued that he had been protecting himself and his ship from what he believed to be a pair of homicidal, gunwielding lunatics. This argument had the advantage of being at least partially true. In the end Bobby was found to have committed a variety of relatively minor maritime infractions. He had his captain's license suspended for six months, during which he became a certified CrossFit instructor.

Prosecutors wanted to prosecute *somebody* for shooting chicken nuggets from the *Barco Loco* at law enforcement vessels, but in the end they could not prove who did it. So Marty, Kevin, Big Steve, Carl and Duane—especially Duane—all got off uncharged.

Trevor also escaped prosecution, via the legal loophole of not being human. His crime spree turned him into something of a folk hero; he became a huge attraction once his leg healed and he returned to Primate Encounter, where he was given a larger, nicer cage. He had no desire to leave again. He had seen the outside world, and did not care for it.

From time to time, Meghan visited Trevor. She was close by, having enrolled in the University of Miami, where she was taking courses that she hoped would one day lead to veterinary school. Trevor was always happy to see her and let her know, in every way he could, that he still wanted to mate with her. Meghan chose to keep their relationship strictly platonic, although when the trainers weren't looking she slipped him Cheez-Its.

Officer Chris Delgado recovered fully from his injuries and was granted early retirement with full benefits. He moved to North Carolina and never returned to Miami, even to visit.

Banzan Dazu spent several weeks in the hospital recovering from a freak head injury he suffered on the day of the wedding. He was chatting up a young bikini-clad woman on the rear lawn of the Ritz, suggesting that she might benefit from an Ayurvedic massage technique that he, Banzan Dazu, would be more than happy to demonstrate to her in the tranquility of his room, when he was struck in the temple by an iPad that had apparently been thrown out of an upper-floor hotel window. The cause of the flying iPad was never determined, but the Clark family generously covered all of Dazu's medical expenses.

Seth and Laurette's marriage was viewed skeptically by immigration authorities. Among other things, Laurette lacked the required documentation; in fact, she had no documentation at all. On the other hand, the couple was able to produce a hardship waiver signed by a Florida judge, as well as a letter handwritten by the governor himself on Ritz-Carlton stationery stating that his office considered the marriage to be legal in the state of Florida.

A Miami immigration lawyer took Laurette's case *pro bono*, and it soon became clear that the legal proceedings would be dragging on for a while, during which Laurette and her children would not be going anywhere. They moved into an apartment with Laurette's sister, who had been able to work out her own immigration issues. With Carl's help, Laurette got a job as a maid at the Ritz-Carlton. Stephane was enrolled in public school and became fluent in English in approximately twenty minutes. He got good grades and became a huge fan of the Miami Heat.

Because of his ongoing involvement in various legal matters, Seth had to remain in South Florida. This meant he lost his job as a member of the Washington PR firm's Social Media Mobilization Team, not that he was sorry about that.

Seth was offered a job by Marty, who himself had been hired by Wendell Corliss as director of Special Acquisitions for the Transglobal Financial Capital Funding Group. In this capacity Marty bought pretty much any company that caught his fancy, including, at one point, a mobile ferret-grooming franchise business. At first Marty lost money, but once he got the hang of it, he lost even more money. This was fine with Wendell, who viewed the Special Acquisitions department purely as entertainment.

Marty offered Seth a good salary to come help him lose Wendell's money, but Seth decided he'd rather not work for a friend, especially a friend who was more or less insane. He took a job at Costco and enrolled in night classes at the Florida International University law school. He planned to specialize in immigration law.

Seth visited Laurette regularly, bringing her money when he had some, and always bringing gifts for the kids—usually Costco merchandise, as he got a discount.

Three months after the wedding, Seth drove to Washington to pick up his stuff, which Tina had put into storage. He asked her, via text, if he could see her; she texted back that she'd rather he didn't come to her place, but she'd meet him at a non-Starbucks coffee shop.

She kept him waiting forty-five minutes. She walked in looking, if anything, more spectacular than ever. She ordered a latte and sat down.

Seth started by trying to say how sorry he was; she cut him off, saying she didn't want to talk about it. He asked how she was doing; she said things were great. No, things were *fabulous*. Professionally, she was doing some very important work with some major international NGOs. Seth said that was great, although he didn't know what an NGO was. Tina said that things were also going very well for her personally. She mentioned the name of a lawyer she'd just had a fabulous dinner with; Seth was pretty sure it was the one who looked like Jude Law.

Seth asked how her parents were doing, and Tina said they were also great. Her father had been admitted into some kind of exclusive organization and was thrilled about it. (Mike had, in fact, been accepted into the Group of Six, although his happiness would be short-lived; he was soon to learn that the main topic of conversation among members of the Group of Six was the rumored existence of an even *more* exclusive organization, the Group of Four.)

After ten awkward minutes, during which Tina didn't ask Seth anything about anything, she said she had to go. As she stood, Seth pulled the ring box from his pocket and tried to give it to her. She said she didn't want it. Seth said he couldn't keep it, and noted that it had cost a lot of money. Tina said he probably needed the money a lot more than she did. That was the last thing she ever said to him. She never touched her latte.

**Six months after** the wedding, Seth and Cyndi moved into an apartment together. Two months after that, they arranged to have dinner with Laurette, picking her up after her shift at the Ritz, and picking up Carl as well to serve as an interpreter. They went to Stan's Transglobal Pizza of Key Biscayne. There, over a large pepperoni pie, Seth and Cyndi told Laurette, hesitantly, that they were thinking about getting married and asked if it would be OK with her—since she appeared to be no longer in any danger of deportation—if Seth and she got a divorce.

When Carl finished translating the question, Laurette started laughing; Carl did, too. Seth and Cyndi asked what was so funny. Carl tried to answer, but he and Laurette were laughing too hard, the two of them holding on to each other to keep from falling over. Eventually Carl got the answer out: Laurette had been planning to ask Seth for a divorce, as she and Carl wanted to get married.

"Ohhhh," said Cyndi and Seth.

**They had a** double wedding on the gazebo at the end of the back lawn of the Ritz-Carlton. They kept it very small. Cyndi didn't even invite her immediate family, noting that because she was Cuban her immediate family would be somewhere around two hundred people.

Marty was Seth's best man; Meghan was Cyndi's maid of honor. Carl's best man was his cousin and Laurette's maid of honor was her sister. The ceremony was performed by Bobby Stern. The other guests were the ones who'd been there when it counted: Big Steve, Kevin, Duane and Blossom, and Wesley and LaDawne, who held Laurette's baby, and who took the occasion to point out, not in a quiet voice, that she and Wesley had been engaged for *six years* without getting married once, while in the past year alone some of these people had gotten married *twice*.

Seth gave Cyndi a ring he bought with the employee discount from the Costco jewelry department. Carl gave Laurette a ring that Seth had given to them as a wedding present; it was the same ring Tina had refused to take back. Seth had told Laurette and Carl how valuable it was, so their plan was to use it just for the wedding ceremony, then sell it and buy a less expensive ring, plus a house.

After the ceremony they had a picnic reception on the beach, catered by the Majestic Transglobal Rooster. They drank beer and laughed and told stories and sang and danced in the sand.

As dusk crept over the ocean, Seth saw Laurette standing alone, looking out toward the place where he'd rescued her. She turned, saw him watching her, and smiled.

"Thank you," she said.

"*Mêci*," he answered.

Then night fell, and Laurette and Carl took their sleepy children home. One by one, the other guests also left, except for Duane, who passed out on the beach with Blossom coiled on his chest.

Finally there was nobody left awake but Seth and Cyndi, sitting close together on the sand, the two of them watching the full moon rise, big and bright, making the restless dark ocean shimmer and shine.

# ACKNOWLEDGMENTS

Thanks to my wonderful friends and semi-relatives Ron and Sonia Ungerman, who helped me figure out the plot for this book on a sailboat in the British Virgin Islands, even though by the next morning we'd forgotten everything.

Thanks to Judi Smith, for always knowing what I'm supposed to do next.

Thanks to Neil Nyren for being the calmest editor alive, and to Ivan Held and Susan Petersen Kennedy for their unflagging support, not to mention always paying for lunch.

Thanks to Michael Barson and Katie McKee for making book tours feel almost like some sick, twisted kind of fun.

Thanks to Amy Berkower and the folks at Writers House for their diligence and guidance, and above all for attaching those little stickers that show where I'm supposed to sign.

Thanks to my friend and bandmate Ridley Pearson, for all the gimlets.

Finally, thanks to the people of the truly insane city of Miami, for making this job easy. Without you, this book wouldn't exist; any errors in it are strictly your fault.